HUSH

HUSH

BOOK TWO *of the* DRAGON APOCALYPSE

JAMES MAXEY

SOLARIS

First published 2012 by Solaris
an imprint of Rebellion Publishing Ltd,
Riverside House, Osney Mead,
Oxford, OX2 0ES, UK

www.solarisbooks.com

ISBN: 978 1 78108 016 0

10 9 8 7 6 5 4 3 2 1

A CIP catalogue record for this book is available from the
British Library.

Designed & typeset by Rebellion Publishing

Printed in the UK by CPI Group (UK) Ltd, Croydon, CR0 4YY

For Dona and Jesse,
explorers of abstract realms.

CHAPTER ONE

A DANGEROUS SPLINTER

A PRINCESS, A shape-shifter, and a ghost walked into a bar.

The room fell silent as all eyes turned toward the princess. The bar was the *Black Swan*, the most prestigious saloon in the boat city of Commonground. While the house wasn't as packed as it would be come midnight, there were scores of hardcore gamblers crowded around the poker tables. Ordinarily, you could march a two-headed tiger through the joint and the players wouldn't glance up from their cards. They made an exception for the princess, known in these parts as Infidel, who was much more dangerous than a tiger, no matter how many heads it might have.

Infidel was an imposing figure as she stood in the doorway with the evening sun providing a backdrop. The first thing anyone would notice about her was that she wore her three decades well, with sculpted curves, generous platinum curls, and enigmatic gray eyes. The money-hungry men in the room wouldn't linger long on her face, however. She was dressed in the priceless Immaculate Attire, crafted for Queen Alabaster Brightmoon nearly three centuries before. Formed from the hide of the last unicorn, the legendary armor was milky white and trimmed with silver. The enchanted leather clung to Infidel's body like a second skin. Slung over her shoulder was another famed artifact of the Silver Isles, the Gloryhammer, glowing with a pale white light.

Despite her impressive armaments, it was Infidel's reputation that brought the room to a standstill. On her first night in this bar, ten years ago, she'd ripped the arm off a bruiser twice her size. The whole town soon learned that the young woman possessed magical strength and skin so tough that swords couldn't scratch her. Of course, even as her fame grew, her beauty tempted many a fool to a place an unwelcome hand upon her. Commonground possesses an unusually high population of one-armed sailors.

I say this as the biggest fool of all. My name is Abstemious Merchant, though everyone in Commonground called me Stagger. For ten years, I was Infidel's constant companion, moon-eyed in my adoration, but far too cowardly to confess my love. Yet fate can be kind to fools and cowards. Beneath Infidel's white leather gauntlet, on her left hand, she wears a ring of woven gray hair. This is my hair. I wear a matching small braid of platinum-hued locks. These serve as our wedding bands, since at the time of our betrothal there were no jewelers handy.

Fate's kindness, you see, is balanced by a wicked sense of humor. In this unfolding joke, I'm the ghost. In death, as in life, I follow her everywhere.

As a phantom, I'm unseen and unheard. If I could have spoken to Infidel, I would have advised her to wear a cloak and cowl into this place, despite the tropical heat outside. Wearing the Immaculate Attire in this city of thieves was the equivalent of walking through a lion's den wearing a suit sewn from steaks. Worse, someone in this town might be smart enough to ask why she was bothering to wear armor at all. She'd recently lost her magical strength and invulnerability. If word spread, her former enemies would turn out in droves. Plus, as her husband, I wasn't thrilled with the way the skintight armor accented her breathtaking assets. For supposedly Immaculate Attire, the outfit certainly lent itself to dirty thoughts.

Infidel's silver-trimmed boots clicked on the polished oak floor as she walked across the room. Ordinarily stone-faced poker players openly gawked and drooled, though I tried to assure myself they were hungering for the Gloryhammer in all its refulgent splendor. Glorystones are fragments of the sun. They're rarer than diamonds and twice as hard. The Gloryhammer is literally priceless; all the gold in the world couldn't buy it. The Tower clan, a family of famous knights, had passed down the weapon for generations. Alas, the last surviving man of the line had recently been reduced to soot. Infidel now owned the hammer, under the legal precedent of finders, keepers.

Infidel didn't look back at the gawking crowd as she arrived at the bar. Battle Ox was bartending. Battle was a half-seed, meaning his mother had visited a blood house to imbue her yet-to-be conceived child with animalistic traits. If the magic was done properly, a half-seed ox child would be big, strong, and tenacious. Do the magic wrong, and you get Battle Ox – a full blown minotaur with horns wider than his considerably broad shoulders.

In the more civilized parts of the world, an infant born with a bovine face would have been put to death as a horrid abomination against nature. In Commonground, Battle's visage seldom merited a second glance. Despite the name inflicted by the pun-happy denizens of Commonground, Battle was a rather gentle vegetarian. While he would willingly eject a rowdy patron if the need arose, his true calling in life was drawing beers with perfect heads of foam. My mouth watered at the smell of the amber fluid.

Battle nodded at my wife. "A lot of people here won't be happy to see you back" he said, in his gruff, bass voice. "Odds were running ten-to-one that Greatshadow would fry you."

Infidel leaned on the bar. "How did anyone know we were going to slay the dragon? The mission was a secret."

Battle shrugged as he picked up a glass and a towel. "The Black Swan started taking bets on the outcome of your dragon-hunt the second you left town. The volcano's been belching lava for the last week, so we figured Greatshadow is still alive."

"Well, maybe he is and maybe he isn't," she said. "The Black Swan will get the full details. Tell her I need to see her. Now."

Battle put down the glass he was cleaning. "You ever learn the word 'please'?"

"Don't mess with me. I've got one hour to get back to the *Freewind* and don't have time to waste. I've got something the Black Swan needs to see immediately."

Battle shook his furry head. "No can do. She's already in a meeting. Going to be a lot longer than an hour."

Infidel unclasped the top three buttons of her leather armor and peeled it back, showing the top of her cleavage. Battle's eyes bulged.

"You see this?" Infidel pointed to a black speck the size of an apple seed that nestled in the ampleness of her décolletage.

"Uh...," said Battle, his mouth hanging open.

"This is Menagerie. What's left of him."

Remember the shape-shifter who came into the bar with us? Menagerie used to be the most feared mercenary in Commonground. A blood-magician of unparalleled skill, Menagerie could turn into any of the scores of animals that used to decorate his tattooed flesh. Menagerie had barely survived our dragon hunt. Since shape-shifting into tick form, he'd yet to change back into a man. A telepath of our acquaintance informed us that Menagerie had been so traumatized by his brush with death that his mind was shattered.

Battle couldn't know any of this, of course, but Infidel didn't have to produce any further explanations. Men are willing to believe almost anything while they're looking at a woman's breasts.

"I'm the only one that can hear him since he's latched onto me," she said, while his eyes were fixed on her. "The Black Swan has a potion that will change him back to human, and he has to drink it within the next five minutes or he'll die. Do you want to tell the Black Swan she's lost her most valuable employee because you were too timid to interrupt a meeting?"

Battle frowned. No, no he did not want this, was what I was seeing in his eyes. But he also looked as if he had his doubts.

Infidel wasn't particularly gifted at lying. If Battle asked any follow-up questions, Infidel would probably be in trouble.

Fortunately, Battle was too cleavage-addled to notice any holes in her story. He grunted, "Wait here," then went through the curtain covering the doorway behind the beer kegs, leaving Infidel alone. At least, as alone as a woman can be, with a brain-damaged shape-shifter sipping her blood and her disembodied husband hovering close behind.

Infidel turned around, leaning back against the bar.

Every eye in the house was staring at her.

The *Black Swan* may have the classiest joint in Commonground, but it was still a den where desperate men gathered to try to make an easy fortune. Their already questionable judgment was numbed further by generous tankards of booze. Ordinarily, order was maintained by the Swan's infamous hired muscle, the Three Goons. Even when the Goons weren't present, their reputation kept most people in line.

Of course, aside from Menagerie, the Goons were now dead. If the patrons knew about the dragon hunt, did they also know that the bar's most feared enforcers weren't coming back?

Infidel reached over her shoulder and grabbed the Gloryhammer. Instantly, its enchantment kicked in. Her skin glowed faintly as she rose off the floor ever so subtly. In addition to granting her flight, the hammer also enhanced her strength. The boost was nothing like her former arm-ripping power, but anyone looking at her had to be sizing up their odds of getting their skulls smashed.

The odds were too high even for this room full of hardened gamblers. One by one, all eyes looked back at the cards in their hands. The roulette wheel was spun again, dice were jiggled in cups, and in less than a minute the saloon had resumed its normal routine. Infidel slowly drifted back down to the floor.

Then Hookhand and his Machete Quartet walked in from the street. If I had a heartbeat, it would have skipped. I had history with Hookhand. When I was alive, my primary revenue came from locating ruins in the jungle and salvaging lost treasures. Hookhand used to make his living by having an uncanny knack for showing up just as I was climbing out of some god-forsaken tomb with a sack full of artifacts, which I would trade in exchange for not being nailed to a tree and flayed. This arrangement lasted for years, until Infidel started adventuring with me. In the intervening decade, there've been about seventeen different members of the Machete Quartet. Infidel normally doesn't let them suffer for too long. Hookhand hasn't been as lucky. When he first came to Commonground, he was known as Fairchild the Nimble. Now, he's got one eye, his nose is squashed against his cheek, and he walks with a prominent limp. He's got maybe six teeth left, and, of course, where he once had a right hand, he now has a hook, a big nasty one, the sort you might use to gaff a large fish.

Despite a decade of serving as Infidel's punching bag, Hookhand was a feared figure in the city. His gang was made up of street urchins he recruited just after they hit puberty, when they're strong and agile enough to swing a machete like it's a dagger, but too young to have any fear of life and limb. Once they join the quartet they become Kid White, Kid Blue, Kid Green, and Kid Black, based on the color bandana they wear. Hookhand doesn't like to waste a lot of time memorizing names.

In theory, the black bandana is worn by the gang member with the most seniority, but I didn't recognize this kid at all. If I'd seen him before, I would have remembered; the boy was obviously a half-seed, part hound-dog by the look of him. He had an ugly pair of canine teeth, but any air of menace was diluted by his floppy ears.

"Well, well," said Hookhand as he spied Infidel. "If it ain't ol' Ripper herself. I see you killed the knight. Quite a prize, that hammer. Quite a prize indeed."

Infidel nodded. She leaned forward, resting her hand on the shaft of the Gloryhammer like it was a cane. She said,

"Surprised to see you back in town. I thought you were up on the mountain, robbing pygmies."

"The volcano's been spitting lava ever since we saw you and your friends fly out. Looks like you made the dragon mad. I made the executive decision to place some distance between us and the caldera." Hookhand looked around the room. "Where are your friends?"

"Who are you talking about?" Infidel asked. "I don't have time for coyness."

"Zetetic the Deceiver. He was right by your side, carrying a baby dragon."

"Your eye's playing tricks on you." Infidel shook her head. "Never met the guy."

"Zetetic has a large red 'D' tattooed in the middle of his forehead. He's easy to recognize, even two hundred feet in the air."

"Your depth perception isn't what it used to be," said Infidel.

"True enough." Hookhand slowly limped toward her. His gang spread out to the far ends of the bar. There was no way that Infidel could keep all four of them in her field of vision. There was a time that wouldn't have mattered; a machete would have bounced off her invulnerable hide. While the Immaculate Attire protected her body, at some point in the convoluted chain of ownership from Queen Alabaster Brightmoon to Infidel, the helmet had disappeared. Infidel's head and neck were completely vulnerable. But Hookhand couldn't know this, could he?

Hookhand stopped about eight feet away. Infidel didn't look perturbed. Was this just for appearances, or was she really that confident?

"I want Zetetic," said Hookhand.

"You want to turn him in for the price on his head? Old news. He's working for the Church of the Book now. They don't want him dead any more."

"I thought you didn't know him," said Hookhand.

"I don't," said Infidel. "But you know I bounty hunt. I stay informed."

Zetetic had split company with Infidel shortly after getting back to Commonground. He'd promised Brokenwing, the only other survivor of our ill-fated dragon hunt, a visit with a former teacher who was the world's foremost authority on dragon anatomy. Since Brokenwing was a rather badly mangled young dragon, they'd departed on their quest with understandable alacrity.

"If you like to stay informed, here are a few facts for you," said Hookhand. "We saw eight people go into the Shattered Palace. You were part of a dragon hunt organized by Lord Tower and Father Ver."

Infidel laughed. "Father Ver's a truthspeaker and Lord Tower's the most respected knight of the church. I, as my nickname implies, am a notorious infidel. A knight and a priest wouldn't be caught dead in my company."

"I think getting caught dead is precisely what happened," said Hookhand. "You were disguised as some kind of mechanical woman to fool them. It doesn't take a genius to figure out what happened. You and Zetetic betrayed the others. You're carrying Tower's hammer and dressed in armor that used to be worn by Ivory Blade. I didn't see Blade go into the Shattered Palace, but I'm guessing I'd find his corpse if I went poking around."

Blade had died a good week before we reached the dragon's lair. But, although his conclusions were off, Hookhand had some surprisingly good intelligence. How did he know so much?

I studied his thugs closer. In addition to Kid Black being part blood-hound, Kid Green had distinctly hawkish features, including freakishly alert eyes and feathery sideburns. Kid Blue's overly long arms clued me in that he had some monkey blood. Kid White had some jaguar in him, judging from his cat-eyes and the mottled patches in his close-cropped hair. A hound, a hawk, a monkey, and a jaguar would make damn good spies out in the jungle. Kid Black, the dog-boy, and Kid White, the half-jaguar, had reached the opposite ends of the bar, machetes drawn. There was no way Infidel could watch both of them at once.

Infidel retained her cool as she pressed a gauntleted fist into her palm and cracked her knuckles. The sound echoed around the room. Half the gamblers abandoned their chips and headed for the door. Infidel's brawls were hard on bystanders.

Infidel took the hammer in both hands, and once more her skin went luminous. She said, "Lord Tower could fly. He had impenetrable armor made of solid prayer. If you take your accusations seriously, you might tell these children to get where I can see them. If I could kill someone like Tower, what makes you think these kids stand a chance?"

"Tower wouldn't fight dirty," said Hookhand, snapping his fingers. The Machete Quartet lunged, but Infidel had anticipated the signal. The hammer flared to solar brightness as she shot up ten feet, snapping to a halt inches beneath a broad ceiling beam. Most of the machete blows hit her boots, leaving little more than scuff marks that were swiftly erased by the armor's magic. Kid Blue, the monkey boy, dropped his machete and hooked his long, skinny fingers into the heel of her right boot. He used his momentum to swing his legs up, grabbing her belt with his toes, then flipped up to grab the shaft of the hammer with both hands. Kicking into her chest, he grunted as he tried to pull the weapon from her grasp. The speed and power of the assault caught Infidel off guard and she lost her grip with her left hand, though her right hand held on.

The monkey child placed a foot on Infidel's face as he struggled to twist the hammer away. Infidel responded by opening her mouth and sinking her pearly whites deep into Kid Blue's heel. A shudder ran along my intangible spine. Biting the bare foot of someone who'd been walking around the docks of Commonground was the most reckless thing I'd ever seen Infidel do, and I'd watched her dive headfirst into the jaws of a dragon. But the tactic worked. Kid Blue shrieked as he let go of the hammer, dropping back down to the floor, where he landed on his outstretched hands and somersaulted back to his feet. Nimble little devil.

The jaguar kid was no slouch either. With Kid Blue clear, Kid White sprang, flat-footed, from the floor to the bar, to the shelf of liquors behind it, then shot toward Infidel like an arrow, with a savage swing of his machete. The chiming of the booze bottles as he kicked off caused Infidel to look over her shoulder, and she spun in time to block the machete blow with the Gloryhammer. She jerked her knee up to connect solidly with the kid's chin. The half-seed was stunned and fell hard, landing spine-first on the back of a wooden chair, his body folding backward at an acute angle that made me wince.

Infidel pointed the hammer toward Hookhand. Her eyes were narrow slits of murder as she shot toward him. But in her rage she either didn't notice or didn't care that a slender tube of bamboo had appeared in his hand. He drew breath as he raised it to his lips. He blew so hard I thought his eye was going to pop out of his skull. A cloud of red powder caught Infidel right in the face as Hookhand dove to the side. Infidel gasped as she hit the cloud, then grunted as she slammed into the floor. Her armored shoulder took the brunt of the blow, but the impact was enough to topple chairs around the room. She bounced across the oak planks, losing her grip on the hammer. Her eyes were scrunched tightly together as she slid to a halt on her back.

As a ghost, my senses are muted, but even my nostrils burned from the cayenne cloud that hung in the air. Infidel's face was blood-red with the pepper. She tried to breathe, but her throat closed after the barest gasp. Even when she'd had impenetrable skin, she couldn't have shrugged off an attack like this.

Kid Blue, the monkey child, sprang across the room and landed on Infidel's right hand, pinning it. Kids Black and Green followed suit, pinning her left arm and both legs, respectively. If she'd still been super-strong, she could have flicked them off like fleas. Now, her limbs trembled, but her weak spasms couldn't shake them.

The Gloryhammer hung in mid-air, where it had come to rest after bouncing off the floor. Hookhand snatched it with his good hand. His eye went wide as the hammer's power filled him. He tilted back his head and laughed. "At last! At last!"

His feet left the floor as he moved toward Infidel. "I've watched a lot of machetes bounce off that pretty head of yours," he said. "I've long dreamed of seeing your brains splattered across these planks. Considerate of you to deliver the perfect tool to get the job done."

Hookhand continued to drift toward her, approaching at a speed fairly described as lackadaisical. Was he trying to prolong the moment? Was flight with the hammer harder than Infidel made it look? Or was Hookhand still afraid of her?

"Hold her tight, boys," he said, pausing a few arm-lengths away.

"She's weak as a kitten, boss," said Kid Black, the dog-boy who trapped her left arm beneath his knee, as he ran his hairy knuckles through her hair. She twisted her head away from his fingers, unable to open her eyes. She'd started breathing again, rapid shallow spasms that had to be filling her lungs with fire. Sweat poured from her brow and bright red snot ran from both nostrils; I couldn't tell if it was blood or cayenne. Any normal person would have been moved to either pity or revulsion by the sight, but Kid Black was staring at her with barely disguised lust. "Such pretty hair. So soft. So pretty, pretty soft."

"She won't be soft when she catches her breath," said Hookhand.

"She's weak now," said Kid Black, stroking her chin, then tracing his fingers down the ivory arc of her throat. The top buttons of her armor were still undone. "Weak and helpless."

"Just like a dog," snickered Kid Blue, the half-monkey. "Always looking for something to hump."

"I thought he was always looking for something to eat," said Kid Green, the falcon-child.

"She could be both," said Kid Black, folding the top of the leather breast plate down to reveal her pale cleavage. He lowered his long narrow face to her throat and licked at her sweat.

I screamed in my rage, my impotence to alter things in the living world stabbing at me like a knife.

Hookhand held back, his eye a little glassy as he watched Kid Black run his hairy hand along the top of Infidel's cleavage. Infidel's face was already scrunched up as much as humanly possible, and pinned as she was I couldn't tell if she was even aware of this assault.

"Wake up!" I screamed, my ghost voice hauntingly silent in the room. "Wake up! Wake up! Wake up!"

"Ow," said Kid Black, yanking his hand away.

"What?" asked Kid Green.

"Something bit me."

"Wake... up..." My voice trailed off as I saw that the tick on Infidel's breast had vanished.

Kid Black put the edge of his hand into his mouth to gnaw at the tiny parasite digging into him.

Then his head came apart.

Menagerie could change shape faster than the eye could follow. His powers flowed from blood magic; his human form had been covered scalp to toe in tattoos inked with the blood of the animals they represented. He'd been able to switch between these forms instantly, and even vast differences in sizes hadn't been a barrier to his magic. He'd been able to change from mouse to elephant as swiftly as he could between lion and tiger. I'd never before pondered what would happen if he'd entered a person's mouth the size of a tick, then turned into a full-sized blood-hound. As it happened, Menagerie's expanding body proved powerful enough to rip Kid Black's skull open from the inside out.

Kid Black flopped backward, his lower jaw missing, his upper jaw cracked open in such a way that I could see his brains. As his body hit the floor, his ghost was knocked loose. His spirit rose above his corporeal form, looking bewildered. Since dying, I've had the ability to see ghosts as they depart the mortal world, and occasionally to converse with them. I felt like saying something particularly nasty to this spirit. I know the dog-boy was poor street trash, a freak, never standing a chance at a normal life, but any pity I might have been able to summon had vanished the instant he started pawing my wife. Unable to summon sufficiently nasty curses from my normally abundant lexicon, I lifted my middle finger to his spirit as it flickered and faded.

The hound dog that had sprung fully formed from Kid Black's mouth growled as he faced Hookhand. Hookhand shook off his confusion about what he'd witnessed with remarkable speed, and swung the hammer overhead, aiming for the dog's skull. The hound lunged forward, sinking his teeth into Hookhand's groin as the hammer splintered the floorboards.

Infidel's eyes jerked open, bloodshot and brimming with tears. Her blurry gaze fixed on Kid Blue, who was pinning down her right forearm with both his hands. The monkey child had his eyes on Hookhand, probably wondering where he was going to swing the hammer next, and failed to notice Infidel's left hand was now free.

Infidel reached for the scabbard on her hip. A moment later, a dagger was hilt deep in the center of the monkey-child's chest. He looked at her with sad eyes as he toppled over. His spirit stuck around no longer than the dog-boy's.

Infidel sat up, fixing her gaze on Kid Green, the half-seed falcon pinning her legs. Sweat from her brow washed a fresh flood of cayenne into her eyes and once more her lids scrunched shut as she gasped in pain. Kid Green leapt up, bringing his machete overhead two-handed, preparing to cleave her skull in half.

Hookhand continued swinging the Gloryhammer wildly. A sledgehammer is a remarkably inappropriate instrument for removing a dog from one's crotch. It is, however, a surprisingly effective tool for bashing in the head of your own henchman, if you're not careful. The hammer connected with the falcon child's skull with a sound a watermelon might make after it was thrown off a roof. Kid Green's machete flew into the air as he fell, lifeless.

I watched with a sick feeling in the pit of my stomach as the tumbling machete fell toward Infidel's blinded face. Then a huge, three-fingered hand flashed through the air and snatched the machete in mid-flight. It was Battle Ox. He turned with a snort toward Hookhand, who was floating now, using the power of the hammer as poorly as it could possibly be used, smashing furniture right and left with his all-powerful weapon as the hound dog between his legs twisted out of the path of every blow.

With a swift, precise chop of the machete, Battle lopped off Hookhand's remaining hand at the wrist. The hammer spun up to the chandelier, smashing the crystal, but Battle Ox's thick hide protected him from the rain of shards.

Hookhand wasn't so lucky. A finger-length dart of glass sank into his remaining eye. He fell to the ground, crying in pain, until Battle brought his whimpering to an end. Hookhand's ghost bubbled up from his corpse. Usually, spirits resembled the bodies that housed them, but Hookhand's spirit was small and gnarled, a scarred, broken thing that stank of rot and despair. His pathetic yellow eyes fixed on me as his toothless mouth voiced my name. I lunged toward him and he shot downward, percolating through cracks in the floorboard, dragged to whatever hell awaited. The hound dog sensed that his opponent was no longer a threat and released his jaws. He loped back over toward Infidel.

Battle ran back to the bar and snatched up a bottle of whiskey. He pulled off the stopper as he approached Infidel. The hound leapt into his path, hackles raised, snarling.

"This is the only thing that's going to wash off that pepper," said Battle. "Water will make it burn worse."

"He's right," I said to Menagerie.

The hound went silent as I spoke, then stepped aside.

"Hold still," said Battle as he knelt, taking Infidel's chin in his massive hand. "This is going to feel worse for a minute, but it might save your eyes."

Infidel seemed to understand, growing calm as Battle tilted the bottle over her face, letting it come in a deluge that washed away most of the cayenne. He motioned for one of the bar maids to bring him a second bottle. The light in the room was dizzying as the Gloryhammer bounced around in the rafters, casting stark shadows. Battle's eyes narrowed as he studied Infidel's face. Infidel had a splinter of wood jammed into her cheek from her impact with the floor. A half dozen other small cuts speckled her face from where fragments of chandelier had hit her.

He washed away the remaining pepper with most of the second bottle. A barmaid handed him a dishtowel, and he used it to wipe Infidel's face. She sat up and grabbed the towel, taking control of cleaning the last of the cayenne from the creases around her eyes. She let out a long sigh as she forced her eyes open and looked down into the towel, flecked with blood.

A few seconds of silence passed as she pulled the splinter from her cheek. It was, by any objective standard, a trivial wound. But I could tell from Infidel's eyes that she understood that this splinter might be the most dangerous injury she'd ever received. Her secret was revealed. Given the speed rumors spread through the city, it was only a matter of hours before everyone learned she'd lost her powers.

"I thought you couldn't be cut," Battle said.

"You've seen me bleed before," Infidel whispered, her voice weak from pain. "That assassin with the shadow blade. The right magic can break my skin."

"The floor ain't magic," he said. Battle put the whiskey bottle into her hands and helped her to her feet. A bare inch of fluid sloshed in the bottle. "Drink the rest of it."

"Can't," she said. "I might be pregnant. Maybe it's an old wives tale that whiskey will hurt the baby, but I'm not taking any chances."

"Damn!" said Battle, shaking his horns. "She did it to me again!"

"What?"

"The Black Swan. She bet me you'd have a baby this year. I mean, Stagger's dead. If he was still around, maybe, but I just can't believe it otherwise. Who – ?"

"Stagger's the father," said Infidel as she managed to stand on her own. Her eyes were bloodshot, but worked well enough that she spotted the Gloryhammer bouncing around in the rafters.

"Help me grab that," she said to Battle. "The Black Swan's probably going to bill me for the damned chandelier. Better stop that thing before it floats behind the bar and takes out the inventory."

"Right," said Battle, grabbing her by the hips and lifting her overhead. She stretched her fingers as far as she could, barely touching the shaft of the hammer, yet the barest touch was all she needed to regain control. It slid fully into her grasp and she floated to the floor.

The hound dog came up to her and sat before her, its tongue hanging out.

"Whose dog?" she asked.

"Um, ain't that Menagerie?" Battle asked. "I saw him leap out of what was left of Kid Black's skull."

Infidel looked down at her chest, running her fingers along the red bump where the tick had once rested.

"Menagerie?" she asked the dog.

The dog said nothing. Menagerie had always been able to talk before, no matter what shape he'd worn.

"Menagerie?" I said. The dog tilted its head in my general direction, but said nothing. There was intelligence in his eyes, but dog-level intelligence, none of the tactical genius that normally burned there.

"We'd better get him to the Black Swan, fast," said Battle Ox. "She's working on the potion now."

"Riiiight," said Infidel, sounding confused. "Right, the potion."

She placed the whiskey on the bar as she followed Battle. I wasn't surprised she'd refused the drink. She hadn't drank much before. It's not so tough to give up something that you never enjoyed in the first place. But, I wondered, when Hookhand first showed up... were Infidel's taunts meant to scare him off? Or was she trying to provoke him? This was her first fight since losing her powers. Had she chosen an opponent she'd routinely beaten in the past to test her new combat style with the hammer and armor? Imagining Infidel going the next nine months without a brawl was a lot tougher than imagining her going nine months without a drink. Once word got out that she was vulnerable, was there any place in the world she'd be safe?

CHAPTER TWO
OBSERVER OF DOOM

INFIDEL LIMPED AS she followed Battle Ox down the hall to the Black Swan's chamber. She was favoring the leg that had taken the bulk of the machete blows. The Immaculate Attire couldn't be cut, but that didn't mean she couldn't be hurt. A machete might not be able to break her skin, but it was still like being whacked with an iron bar. It couldn't feel good.

The last time I'd seen the Black Swan, she'd been nothing more than a skeleton. This hadn't slowed the old witch down much. Her spirit continued to animate her bones, though without a throat she'd been reduced to 'speaking' by pointing to letters on a board. The Black Swan claimed that death was too trivial an obstacle to stand in the way of her great mission. She says she's a time traveler, using her knowledge to accumulate wealth and power today so that she can prevent a 'dragon apocalypse' that she's lived through in the future.

I'm not sure I believe her. The Black Swan has a propensity for using manipulation and outright lies to gain the upper hand. But she'd also told us that Infidel would soon be pregnant, which seemed impossible at the time, since I was dead and Infidel wasn't open-minded to new suitors. What we could never have imagined was that Infidel's quest to kill Greatshadow would take her bodily into the spirit world, where we'd been able to reunite as the world's most star-crossed lovers. It was certainly plausible that Infidel was pregnant now, since in the ghost realms my spirit had been as functional as my old material body. On the other hand, when we left the spirit world together, Infidel had physically returned to the land of the breathing, while I'd faded back into ghosthood. If we'd conceived a daughter, as the Black Swan prophesied, would the unusual circumstances of her conception affect her?

Menagerie followed closely behind Infidel, looking and acting like an ordinary bloodhound, sniffing the floor as he walked. Shaking off his tick form hadn't repaired his mind. Was there any flicker of his humanity left? His loyalty toward Infidel was a hopeful sign. During the dragon hunt, Menagerie and Infidel had formed a friendship. Perhaps the dog retained some human memories.

Battle pushed open the polished mahogany door to the Black Swan's chamber. He motioned Infidel inside, but didn't follow us. The room had changed dramatically in the last two weeks. Then, the walls had been covered with tapestries and filled with antique bedroom furnishings. The place had reeked of potpourri, a concentrated floral miasma that hadn't quite masked the undercurrent of rot that hung in the air.

Now, the walls had been stripped down to the bare wood, and every last stick of furniture had been removed. Freed of its clutter, the Black Swan's chamber proved surprisingly spacious. My old sail boat could probably have fit in the space. At first glance, it looked as if someone might be testing that theory, since there was a white canvas sail covering the floor.

In the center of this canvas was a small cloaked figure kneeling before an iron sculpture. The sculpture drew my eye first. It was a shapely woman, slightly larger than life. It was cast iron, black as soot, highly articulated, so that there was a separate plate for each rib of the torso. Both arms were finished, ending in delicately formed hands sporting long, slender fingers, though the sharpened steel nails provided a detail of menace to a work of art that would otherwise have been noteworthy for its beauty. The face was mostly done, with separate plates for each cheek and a small nose that sat above intricately jointed steel lips. The eyes were closed, and I noted the fine detail of the wire eyelashes. The top of the head wasn't finished, and as

I drifted around I noticed that the back of the head was open. Sitting in the cavity of the dark steel was a stark white skull.

I looked down at the cloaked figure, whose hands were busy working on the right ankle. The left leg was finished, a sleek curvy gam that would have been the pride of any bride when her groom had hitched up her hem to remove her garter. A row of rivets ran up the back of each leg like the seam of a stocking. As I drifted lower to admire the workmanship, I must confess that my eyes lingered a moment on the heart-shaped buttocks, so smoothly finished and perfectly formed that they looked soft, despite being formed of iron. The illusion of softness vanished instantly, however, when one reached the unfinished right leg, which was nothing more than a jointed steel rod jutting from the hollow of the hip to the recognizably human foot. Floating lower to better observe the sculptress (for, despite the cloak, it was apparent that the artist was female, given the slenderness of her form and her delicate fingers), I saw that she had no tools. Instead, she was shaping hard ingots of raw pig iron with her hands as if it was mere clay. Her fingers moved in a dizzying dance as they twisted and kneaded the metal, forming and fastening ankles to a feminine metal foot that sported razor toenails.

The sculptress completed the ankle by scraping away a bit of the iron rod of the leg and exposing a patch of pure bone. The lower half of the rod, apparently, enclosed a skeletal tibia and fibula. The Black Swan's leg bones, no doubt. The sculptress spun delicate silver wires to link the bone to the ankles, which sat like bracelets upon the foot.

"Wiggle your foot," the sculptress said, looking up.

The Black Swan lifted her skeletal right leg and twisted her foot from side to side. She wiggled her toes in an eerie approximation of life, though with the plates of the various pieces sliding silently across one another, her toes reminded me more of hard-shelled beetles than human flesh.

"Excellent," the sculptress said, guiding the Black Swan's foot back to the floor.

With her head tilted up, I could see the artist's face. Her most striking features were her eyes, a shocking emerald hue that was almost certainly the result of magical manipulation. Yet if she'd manipulated her eyes for aesthetic reasons, it made little sense that the rest of her features were so much less... felicitous. Her age was difficult to judge; the right half of her face could have belonged to a teenage girl, but the left half of her face was slack and wrinkled, the flesh a pale gray next to the rosy hue of her other cheek. Though her cloak concealed much of her scalp, she appeared to be completely bald, her head speckled by large dark warts.

The sculptress rose, stretching her back. The sleeves of her robe slipped down, revealing that her left arm and hand were supported by an iron brace. She glanced back at Infidel. "I'll step outside so the two of you may talk."

The Black Swan's iron eyelids clicked open, revealing empty bone sockets. There was a sucking sound within her chest, like a bellows drawing in air, followed by reedy musical notes, something like an accordion. The sculpted jaws jerked open and snapped shut as the overlapping plates of the steel lips sliced up the notes pouring from the mouth. The resulting sound was almost, but not quite, completely inhuman. And yet, however inferior the construct's vocal apparatus might have been to a living human throat, I found, with grudging admiration, that I could understand individual words. "Stay and work, Sorrow. The princess and I have nothing to hide."

Infidel frowned. She, of course, had many things to hide, including the fact that she was a princess. But she shrugged and said, "I can't stay to chat. I need the money you owe me for the dragon skull."

"You traded those funds to Menagerie," said the Black Swan. "You used them to purchase the silence of the Three Goons when you infiltrated Lord Tower's party in a disguise Menagerie helped to design."

"Fine," said Infidel. She nodded toward the dog. "This is

Menagerie. Give him all the money he's owed. Since he's a bit impaired in the hand department for the time being, I'll carry it."

"This isn't Menagerie," said the Black Swan, turning her vacant gaze upon the hound. "This is merely a physical echo of his blood magic, a spell lingering on after the death of the spellcaster. Soon enough its magic will burn out and this soulless thing will vanish."

"Or you could help him," said Infidel. "He's worked for you for years. Use your magic to restore his memories."

"It isn't a question of memories. It's a question of soul. There's no spirit within this creature. It looks like a dog, but it isn't truly alive. Any funds due Menagerie will be sent to his family. As for this sad little pseudo-dog, I recommend you kill it swiftly and put an end to its miserable half-life. I owe it nothing."

"How about Aurora? Do you owe her anything?"

"She collected the last of her wages when she left my employment."

"I'm not talking about wages. I'm talking about the fact that she was your loyal companion. She's dead now, killed by Greatshadow. I'm in possession of the Jagged Heart, the sacred relic she died to defend. Stagger made a promise to return it to her homeland. I intend to keep this promise. I'm hoping you'll help."

The Black Swan shook her iron head in a smooth, mechanical motion. "Stagger could make no such promise. He's dead. You killed him."

"You of all people should know that being dead isn't the same as being done. Stagger's ghost has been following me. He's with us right now, I think. We were reunited in the spirit world." She rubbed her ring finger where the band of hair I'd woven for her sat. When we'd returned to the land of the living and my physical form faded back to nothingness, the ring of hair had remained intact. Why this should be, I don't know.

Perhaps there's genuine magic in a wedding vow after all. "We were married there."

"Now you're merely a widow." The Black Swan sounded mocking, with her squeaking, artificial voice. "And you're pregnant, as I foretold."

"On the assumption that I'm pregnant, I need to return the Jagged Heart as quickly as possible. I'd rather not be adventuring in some faraway land when I start dealing with morning sickness. But that doesn't kick in for about a month, right?"

"I'm uncertain. I myself was childless," the Black Swan said.

"A month. Six weeks," said the sculptress as she fastened the plates of the calf to the shin plate. "Not that I've had personal experience."

The Black Swan's empty orbs gazed toward the Gloryhammer. "My dear, I can't help but notice you're in possession of a magic artifact known to grant its owner the power of flight. Why do you need my help? You can simply fly to Aurora's home in Qikiqtabruk."

Infidel shook her head. "Flying isn't as easy as it looks. If I go too fast, I can't breathe. Even flying slow wears me out. Flying for an hour is like hanging from a branch for an hour. I'd rather not have my arms give out when I'm over the middle of the ocean. I need a ship, a very fast ship, if I'm going to complete this mission. As luck would have it, the *Freewind* is in port."

"The *Freewind?*" The Black Swan tilted her head and gave what might have been a look of skepticism, though her empty eye-sockets made it difficult to interpret her expression. "You can't seriously intend to seek passage aboard what's currently the most wanted pirate ship on the seas. Every navy on the planet is hunting the Romers."

"And no navy can catch them," said Infidel. "The *Freewind* is the fastest ship in the Shining Lands. And we both know that the charge of piracy is bogus. Gale Romer is an honest woman who's been branded a pirate because of her opposition to slavery."

"She's scuttled entire ships and stolen their cargo."

"She's raided slave ships and released men from their chains," said Infidel, crossing her arms. "The fact that she's an outlaw is an indictment of the law, not of her."

The Black Swan nodded slowly. "Captain Romer's moral code isn't truly the issue. Whether the charges against her are just or unjust, you place yourself in great danger by seeking passage on her vessel."

Infidel shrugged. "I'm a wanted criminal in the same kingdoms hunting her. It's not like I'm safe anywhere outside of Commonground. I'll take my chances with Captain Romer. She tells me the *Freewind* was chartered weeks ago by a single passenger; she's not at liberty to tell me whom. But her employer didn't show up to depart this morning at the prearranged time. If they don't show up by sundown, the contract is broken. She says that if I'm there with money in hand when the sun sets, she'll let me hire the ship."

"Very well. While I question your wisdom, I must admit that the *Freewind's* reputation for speed is unmatched. Perhaps, in your shoes, I would make a similar choice. Since the Gloryhammer is of no use to you as transportation, I'll give you the money you need in exchange."

Infidel laughed. "I'm in a hurry, but I'm not an idiot."

"What else do you have to offer me?"

"Information. You must be dying to know what happened with Greatshadow."

"I know the dragon is alive. You failed in your mission to kill him, placing the world in great peril when he seeks revenge."

"That's nowhere near accurate. I'll give you the complete story for the money."

"My dear, I employee the most gifted diviners from the furthest reaches of the known world. I personally have lived though the events of this day a dozen times in my efforts to avert the impending apocalypse. I know all I need to know of your dragon hunt."

Infidel crossed her arms. "You didn't know Stagger is still around."

"What does it matter if his spirit lingers? He's hardly the only ghost in this port. What's more, he can't endure for long if he has no anchor to the material world."

"I'm his anchor."

"This isn't accurate. The bone-handled knife was his anchor, but you lost this in the ghost lands."

Infidel furrowed her brow. Zetetic and Relic were the only other entities to know that my soul had become trapped in the dragon bone in the handle of my grandfather's hunting knife. Technically, we hadn't lost the knife. It was tucked into the belt of the pants I was wearing when we came back to the material world. It stayed in the ghost realms with me. The pants, too. I can take the knife out and hold it, despite the fact it's as much a phantom as I am now. What good an intangible knife does me I can't say. If I had some intangible toast perhaps I could butter it, assuming I had some intangible butter.

But I digress. The Black Swan continued scolding Infidel. "You also lost the battle against Greatshadow in the spirit realm. Lord Tower dealt Greatshadow's physical body a mortal blow with the Gloryhammer; Aurora slew the beast with the Jagged Heart, but was killed by the creature's death throes. Father Ver's mission was to kill Greatshadow's spirit before the beast could grow a new body. But he died, so the mission fell to you. And Greatshadow banished you back to the material world before you could strike the final blow. Have I missed any significant detail?"

A few. Greatshadow hadn't banished Infidel; he'd opened a portal for her after she spared his life in exchange for a promise not to seek revenge. Infidel had convinced the beast that the element of flame was well served by mankind. We cut down forests and hollow entire mountains of coal to feed

Greatshadow's appetites. Were he to wipe us out, he'd be one hungry dragon. We left the spirit world with Greatshadow feeling a grudging appreciation of mankind rather than a deep bloodlust for revenge. We count that as a win.

Infidel had a few bits of information the Black Swan hadn't hinted at. She knew that Relic had turned out to be Greatshadow's own child, an infant dragon named Brokenwing with genius-level intelligence and an excess of ambition. And, she knew that Zetetic, the Deceiver, had also survived, and where he was heading next. Would she try to barter this information?

Infidel pressed her lips tightly together. With what looked like great reluctance, she said, "Fine. You've forced my hand. I do have one thing left to trade. Stagger's boat is stuffed with old books, maps, and notes detailing his explorations. Plenty of treasure seekers would pay through the nose for these documents. I'll trade you the entire collection for the *Freewind's* fee."

The Black Swan shook her head. "You can't seriously believe that a heap of mildewed notes scribbled by a notorious drunkard are worth anything."

"We both know they're worth a great deal. Stagger recovered hundreds of artifacts from the ruins of the Vanished Kingdom. He left behind hundreds more, too big to carry. He documented his explorations carefully, just like his grandfather."

The sculptress looked up. "This Stagger... is he the grandson of Judicious Merchant?"

My grandfather was famous throughout the scholarly world for his masterwork, *The Vanished Kingdom*. The legend surrounding him and the book had only grown larger when he disappeared four decades ago, swallowed by the jungle-draped ruins he'd spent his life exploring. We'd recently discovered Judicious was still alive, living in a treetop village with the Jawa Fruit tribe. Just shy of a century old, my grandfather spends his retirement lounging naked in the sun, attended by his countless pygmy offspring.

Infidel studied the sculptress for a second, her eyes lingering on the woman's withered face, before she answered, "Yes. Stagger was an explorer like Judicious."

The Black Swan released a single, high-pitched accordion note. It took me a second to recognize the squeak was intended as a scoffing laugh. "Judicious Merchant was a gentleman scholar who braved the dangers of this island to expand human knowledge. Stagger was a wastrel who exploited his grandfather's research to loot ancient treasures to slake his thirst for whiskey."

"Don't hold back, Swan," I said. "Say what you really thought of me." She'd been much more diplomatic when she'd haggled for some of the junk I looted. I mean artifacts I looted. I mean artifacts I rescued from their forgotten tombs and brought back so they could be properly appreciated.

"I want those papers," said the sculptress. "I'll pay for your use of the *Freewind*. I'm the mystery client who failed to show up. This project has taken longer than I'd anticipated. I fear I've lost track of time."

"Indeed," said the Black Swan. "I hope you don't plan to pass on the expense of your additional hours to me. I'm not to blame for your poor time management."

"I certainly believe you *are* to blame," said the cloaked woman. "You made me rework your breasts eleven times!"

"I remain unsatisfied," the Black Swan grumbled. "They don't look natural."

Given that they were cast iron, it was impossible to dispute this. On the other hand, I thought they looked like a reasonable approximation of boobs, about the size of grapefruits, nicely proportioned to her chest, with decorative floral rivets for nipples. Still, no matter how well sculpted in size or shape, they lacked a certain quality – Pillowiness? Bounce-factor? Jigglability? – that hampered their ability to stir lust.

The sculptress sighed and rubbed her eyes. She turned from the Black Swan and approached Infidel, extending her hand. "We've not been introduced. I'm Sorrow Stern."

"My friends call me Infidel," said Infidel, with a handshake. Menagerie raised his left paw.

"How cute," said Sorrow, shaking the paw. "You've trained your dog well."

"I can't take credit. I can't even call him my dog. No matter what this old witch says, Menagerie's a person. Somehow, I've got to help him remember this."

"Hmm," said Sorrow, taking the dog's head between her hands and staring into his dark eyes. "The Black Swan is right. I sense only magic animating this creature, not a human soul."

"Menagerie once told me he felt like his soul had been long ago devoured by all the animals that lived inside him. I'd be happy at this point if we can change him back into his human form. I think if he could see his human self in a mirror, it might jog his memory."

"I'm afraid I can't help. I've yet to master the art of sculpting living flesh."

"Wouldn't that be easier than sculpting solid iron?" said Infidel.

"To the contrary," said Sorrow. "You're familiar with the teachings of the Church of the Book? The foundational belief that all of reality is formed of four base elements, matter, spirit, truth and lies?"

"I just spent a few weeks in the company of a Truthspeaker and a Deceiver. I've heard the subject debated, yes."

"I'm a materialist," said Sorrow. "By manipulating the proportions of truth and falsehood in certain matter, I'm able to shape it to my will. Iron is simple, being almost completely devoid of spirit. It possesses no internal conception of itself to resist alteration."

"I'm sure this is a fascinating subject," Infidel said, "But sundown is, like, ten minutes away. Let's talk about our deal."

"Of course. As I said, I'm the client who reserved the use of the *Freewind,* paying for passage both to and from the island with the advance given me by the Black Swan. There's no need for money to exchange hands. I'll simply write a letter informing Captain Romer that you're representing my interests and taking command of the charter. Supply her with whatever destination you wish. I'll be remaining on the Isle of Fire for some time, if Stagger's papers are as extensive as you say."

"You won't be disappointed."

"I'm sure I won't be," said Sorrow. She walked back to the Black Swan and knelt. On the floor beside the ingot of pig iron lay a notebook covered with elaborate sketches of the iron woman that now stood in a semi-finished state before us. She turned to a fresh page and, using a razor freshly minted from the raw iron, cut free a sheet of white parchment. She then ground the razor to dust between her fingers, allowing the black iron to sprinkle on the page. With a fingernail, she twirled the ebony filings around, lining them into looping letters. I admired the crispness of her handwriting, and felt a stirring of familiarity as I watched the care with which she crossed her T's and dotted her I's. While the shape of her letters were softer and more rounded than my own handwriting, I recognized the same underlying rigidity that had been drilled into my penmanship by the monks at the orphanage in which I was raised. The whole authority of the Church of the Book rested upon the sacredness of the written word. Learning to write correctly was as important as learning to pray. Sorrow's handwriting would have delighted any monk. Booze, a lack of piety, and general laziness had rendered my own once neat calligraphy somewhat less pleasing to the eye.

She finished the letter in moments, rolled it up, and sealed it with a band of iron foil. She handed it to Infidel. "I should finish my work this evening. I'll meet you at Stagger's boat in the morning so I can take possession of his papers."

"Agreed," said Infidel.

Infidel departed, limping on the leg that had taken the machete blow. I was nervous about her passing through town noticeably wounded, with visible cuts on her face. This isn't a good town to show weakness. But, once she was outside, she'd no doubt use the Gloryhammer to fly to the *Freewind*. Not exactly stealthy, but the skies of Commonground were a lot safer than the gangplanks.

Since I knew where to find Infidel, I lingered behind. I had a hunch I wanted to follow up on. I moved my face before the Black Swan's vacant eyes.

"You can see me," I said.

Then, slowly, the hollow sockets began to fill with translucent fog, knitting itself into ghostly orbs, which burned with a soft glow. The fog flowed over the iron cheeks and lips, growing denser, until I found myself staring at the face of a young woman rather than the mechanical mockery of one. The woman had thick black eyebrows and an angular nose a bit too large for her face. The iron lips didn't move; the bellows stayed silent. Yet, as the woman's ghost lips parted, a voice in my mind said, "I'm... aware of you."

"I thought you might be. Your barbs seemed a little gratuitous if you didn't think I was around to suffer. Why didn't you tell Infidel I was here?"

"I don't wish to encourage her memory of you. The sooner she forgets you, the sooner she'll be free to master her own destiny."

"She's free now."

"No. She's undertaking a dangerous quest to fulfill a promise *you* made. It's an unnecessary risk, and a pointless distraction."

"Distraction from what?"

"The dragon apocalypse! Have you failed to pay attention at all?"

"Greatshadow isn't angry at humanity. Infidel showed him mercy when he was at his weakest. He's promised not to seek revenge."

"And yet, again and again, I've lived through the day in which the primal dragons rise against humanity. I'll never be able to erase the memory of blizzards blasting even the southernmost islands, the sea rising to swallow whole cities, and mountains crumbling like sand castles as the earth shakes off mankind like an annoying flea."

"Tragic. But why must Infidel be the one who stops this?"

The Black Swan sighed. "Infidel's former power was derived from dragon blood flowing through her veins. She alone possessed the sheer physical might to perform the heroic undertakings required to spare mankind. Behind the scenes, I arranged that she would come to Commonground so that I might oversee her training. But instead of becoming a focused, highly skilled warrior under my command, she met you and was seduced by your slovenly ways. Now, she's an undisciplined brawler, although, stripped of her powers, she'll not remain one for long. Unfortunately, in the timelines where I had you killed, Infidel is corrupted by her rage and assassinated by the Church of the Book long before her powers mature to the point that she can slay Greatshadow."

"Well, she has no powers now," I said. "You'll need some new pawn for your game."

"True. Which is why I'm placing my hope in Sorrow." She motioned to the sculptress still shaping her thighs. "Unlike Infidel, her talents are meshed with a driving ambition and a grand vision. As Princess Innocent Brightmoon, Infidel's childhood was too sheltered and pampered to allow her to grow into a serious adult. Sorrow has been tempered by tragedy from an early age. She has a heart full of hatred and bitterness that spurs her ever onward toward her goals of revenge."

"She seems nice enough."

"I assure you, *nice* is a word seldom used to describe Sorrow. And, unlike Infidel, she loathes men; foolish love will never distract her from her greater destiny."

I shrugged. "What you do with this woman is of no concern to me. I want you to leave Infidel alone. If you don't...." I let the thought trail off. I felt like I should be inserting a threat, but couldn't really think of one.

"Are you attempting to be menacing?" she asked.

"Maybe."

"You're failing at it. I've nothing to fear from you. You shall not linger in this world for much longer."

"You've managed to stick around a long time. Why can't I?"

"I never surrendered my hold on my bones," she said. "I renew my energies by bathing my skeleton in blood. You performed a similar trick with your knife. But now that you've foolishly removed it from the mortal world, you're fated to fade away. All actions require energy, even the actions of a spirit. Currently, you're empowered by the dragon blood that the bone-handled knife drank in Greatshadow's realm. That magic may sustain you for some time. But, with no further source of blood, your energies will fade. One day you won't even have the power to remember your name. Soon after, you'll vanish from this world forever."

I ground my ghost teeth. Could I believe her? Where was the profit in lying to me? On the other hand, what was the profit in telling me the truth? "My actual bones aren't all that far from here. What if Sorrow builds me a new body like yours?"

"I think cast iron breasts would look even more ridiculous on you than they do on me."

"You know what I mean."

"Abandon hope, Stagger. Though I despised you in life, I'm not so hard-hearted I take pleasure as you suffer in death. You love Infidel, but her love for you will only lead her to a tragic end. In the most probable future, Infidel will die on her journey to Qikiqtabruk. Your daughter will never be born. Do you wish to linger as an impotent observer to the doom of those you hold dearest? Move on, poor ghost, to the great unknown."

"I can't help but get the feeling you're manipulating me," I said. "You're taunting me so I'll do something. But what? Just tell me what you want. Maybe if you'd tried that with Infidel, she would have become the savior you wanted her to be. By trying to treat her like a puppet, you've gotten her strings all tangled."

"There is nothing more I need from you, Stagger. Return to your bones."

"You're not getting rid of me that easily."

She raised her ghostly hand and waved me away.

Suddenly, I was on a sandy bluff, overlooking the sea. This was where Infidel had buried my body. The sun was low against the water, almost gone. My grave of white sand had been somewhat flattened by wind and rain, but there was a man-sized bulge in the earth that hinted that bones lay beneath.

"Maybe you *can* get rid of me that easily," I said, scratching my ghost scalp. What now? Was Infidel really in danger? Or was the Black Swan trying to trick me into stopping her mission? If so, how? What could I do?

Impotent observer of doom. That didn't sound pleasant at all. But as long as that little band of hair was on Infidel's hand, there was at least some small part of me left in the world. Blood wasn't the only source of magic. I was determined to hold on powered by nothing but love.

CHAPTER THREE
SERIOUS, HARD-WORKING PEOPLE

THE SUN WAS below the horizon but the sky remained luminous, casting eerie shadows across the hill that held my grave. In the dimming light I stared at the ground, imagining my body six feet below. Not even a month had gone by. How much of me was recognizable underneath this mound of sand? I'd done a lot of digging around the island. Some places in the deep jungle, the soil was so dank and worm-ridden that a corpse would disappear inside a week. Here, on a windswept hilltop, in salty sand, baked daily beneath a tropical sun... perhaps my corpse had mummified. Certainly my bones were intact. Probably my teeth and nails and hair. The colorful shroud Infidel had fashioned from a stolen pygmy blanket might still be recognizable.

Why I found it comforting to think that I might be slowly turning into jerky instead of jelly, I can't say. I suppose that as long as I have bones, I have hope. I've heard that on the island of Podredumbre, the natives dig up the skeletons of their ancestors on the winter solstice and bring them back into their homes for a feast in their honor. Perhaps one day that ritual would catch on here. In fact, winter solstice was only a few days away, though in the eternal summer of the Isle of Fire I doubt many of the residents of Commonground would even notice.

There was a moment of morbid curiosity where I contemplated thrusting my head underground. I'd discovered while exploring the pygmy tunnels as a ghost that, in pitch darkness, I could see the faint aura given off by all material objects. Given that mirrors weren't any use to me now, it might be interesting to see my face once more.

Instead, I clenched my fists of fog and turned away, floating upward. Some things are best left unseen. Above me, the boldest stars were starting to glow in the darkening sky. I drifted on the sultry wind that flowed down from the jungle slopes, the moist air redolent with a thousand species of orchids. I rose nearly a mile before I spotted Commonground, roughly twenty miles away. Even at this distance, the city was aglow with the lanterns of countless ships. The beaches around the bay blazed with funeral pyres. It had been weeks since Greatshadow attacked the city, but new corpses washed ashore with each tide.

I set off for Commonground at a leisurely pace, lost in thought, wondering if Infidel had done the right thing by sparing the dragon. I was shaken from my reverie by a faint high-pitched wail. I scanned the horizon. Was it some sort of bird? It sounded almost human, and it was definitely getting louder.

Then I spotted what looked like a man flashing toward me against the darkening sky. At first glance, it looked like Battle Ox, tumbling head over heels through the firmament. But the flying figure hurtled closer, and I made out a heavyset man dressed in a bearskin vest and wearing a horned helmet. His thick sinewy hands were clamped tightly to a two-handed axe. As he tumbled past, I saw that his beard was flecked with vomit, and he shrieked at a much higher pitch than one would expect from such a bruiser. In his wake, he left a strong odor of piss. I had the distinct impression that his flight was neither voluntary nor welcome.

I could have given chase, but I was more interested in who had launched the man into the atmosphere rather than where he was going to fall back to earth. Ordinarily, if there were bodies flying this sort of distance, Infidel was involved.

Though Commonground was thick with ships, it didn't take long to spot the *Freewind*. The vessel was a long, square-rigged clipper with three masts, with a distinctive burgundy hull. I've heard that the boards were soaked in red wine before it was assembled. This isn't a standard building practice among the Wanderers, and I have no idea what advantage it might have given the ship, but I must admit it helps the boat stand out in a crowded harbor.

To my utter lack of surprise, the *Freewind* was under attack. While Commonground was a sanctuary city among the Wanderers, meaning that even the *Freewind* wouldn't be molested while at port, the attackers plainly weren't from around here and probably didn't understand the rules. Two long ships with figureheads carved to look like angry dragons had pinned the *Freewind* against the docks, rendering the ship's legendary speed moot. The attacking boats had hulls wrapped in what looked to be oily hides. At least a hundred burly men wearing bearskin vests and horned helmets swarmed from the boats, running along boarding planks or climbing the numerous grappling ropes that now draped the *Freewind*. They were roaring deafening battle cries at a much more dignified and manly pitch than the shrieker who'd passed me seconds before. While I didn't understand the language, the raiders matched the description of a race of warriors from lands north of the Silver Isles who called themselves Skellings. The only thing I really knew about them was that they were supposedly cannibals. Since their homeland was two-thousand miles away, it was doubtful they'd come this far looking for dinner.

At first glance, it looked as if the Skellings were launching their assault on an empty ship, which had to make it all the more embarrassing for them that they were failing to get on board. Those climbing up ropes had the bad luck of having the knots slip free from their grappling hooks inches before they reached the railing. Those attempting to run up gangplanks were suddenly snatched from their feet by hurricane-force winds on a bay that was otherwise calm. The waters around the ships grew crowded with flailing bodies.

One of the grapplers, however, had managed to leap for the railing as his rope broke, and I watched as he climbed aboard the all but empty deck. Suddenly, a child dropped out of the rigging, hands first, grabbing the warrior by his horned helmet. The Skelling staggered around, cursing, as the slender figure maintained a perfectly balanced handstand. As I drew closer, I saw that the mysterious gymnast was a girl, perhaps ten years old, with a very stern grimace on her face. Curly black locks spilled out from a wine-red beret that marked her as a member of the crew. Her agility at riding her unwilling mount was all the more remarkable for the fact that she was wearing a belt studded with lead sinkers that had to weigh at least fifty pounds.

After balancing on the Skelling for a few seconds, she dismounted with a somersault. The second her fingers left the helmet, the confused warrior shot into the air as if he'd been launched from a catapult. He vanished into the night so swiftly that he was gone from sight before the girl's feet even touched the deck. She bounced as if she had springs in her toes, with her hands stretched overhead. As if by magic, a rope swung toward her. She grabbed hold as it lifted her once more into the rigging.

Perhaps the phrase 'as if by magic' is a bit too coy, since I knew damn well that every member of the Romer family that owned the *Freewind* had been given magical powers as a gift for rescuing the mer-king's daughter. Though I normally avoided sea-travel, Infidel had done a stint aboard the *Freewind* not long ago as a sword-for-hire during the so-called Pirate Wars. The Romers were serious, hard-working people who neither drank, gambled, nor trafficked in stolen merchandise, which meant I didn't know them personally. Luckily, thanks to Infidel's tales, it wasn't hard to piece together who was who.

The girl had to be Poppy, the youngest Romer. The mermen had given her one of the stranger magical abilities I knew of. Basically, anything she pressed down on would spring into the air with a hundred times the force she'd applied to it.

From what Infidel had told me, Poppy was ten years old, and something of a tomboy.

The ropes were being cooperative with Poppy and uncooperative with the Skellings thanks, no doubt, to another family member – Rigger. He was only seventeen, and purportedly something of a worrywart. I'd likely find him at the wheel. I flew to the back of the boat and found what had to be him, along with two other family members. All had the same kinky black hair and red berets, along with sharp noses and blue eyes. Rigger had a narrow face adorned by an unflattering scraggle of a beard. With his slender limbs, he looked like a puppet, with a score of thick ropes wrapped around his arms and legs. He was drenched with sweat, his teeth clenched, as he drew upon his mer-gift, which was the ability to manipulate ropes with his mind. Ordinarily a ship the size of the *Freewind* would have required a crew of at least twenty, but Infidel told me that Rigger was capable of sailing the boat alone.

He wasn't alone in defending the boat, however. Standing beside him was a young woman holding a long spyglass pressed to her right eye. She was a bit younger than Rigger, perhaps fifteen, and was staring into the glass with the same sweating intensity Rigger showed in manipulating the ropes. Perhaps the fact that she had the cover over the lens explained her effort. But even with the cap she was seeing something, since she shouted out, "Another grappling hook starboard! Three men on the rope!"

Rigger nodded. "Anyone else? Should I drop them?"

"Wait... there's a fourth climber getting on... now!" She looked pleased as the screams of men falling into the water reached the wheel. It was a reliable guess that this young woman was Sage, the clairvoyant of the Romer clan.

"The attacks are slowing down," shouted the third person at the wheel, an older woman with streaks of gray in her dark hair, her skin tanned and deeply lined by a life at sea. This was Gale Romer, matriarch captain of the *Freewind*, and the reason that the Skellings kept getting gusted off their gangplanks. Gale had the power to control winds even before her encounter with the mer-king, which helped explained the *Freewind's* reputation for speed. She looked at Sage and cried, "Give me a count of the dead!"

"Thirty-seven," said Sage. "Mako and Jetsam are making short work of them."

"How's Infidel doing against those ice-serpents?"

"Hard to say," Sage answered. "The Gloryhammer is so bright I can't see through the glare."

"What's that about Infidel?" I asked, forgetting I couldn't be heard.

Fortunately, I wasn't kept in suspense long. The hatch to the cargo hold was wide open and suddenly a bright beam of light shot up from the guts of the ship as if the sun had just risen inside.

With a *whoosh*, Infidel flew from the hatch. She was completely enwrapped by what I can only describe as a python covered in thick silver fur. Three or four pythons, in fact, although it was difficult to tell where one snake ended and another began. Infidel had only one arm free of the tangle, but she had a death grip on the Gloryhammer as she rocketed into the sky, then dove, heading for the shore. I gave chase, unable to tell if she was in control of her flight or not. She flew directly for a large bonfire. In a flurry of sparks and flames, she dropped feet first into a pygmy funeral pyre, shielding her face by pressing it into the crook of her elbow. She stood there for only a second, protected by her armor as the serpents screamed. Their squealing voices were disturbingly similar to those of human babies as their oily fur ignited. Infidel leapt from the thick of the flames. The writhing serpents slipped from her torso to bunch around her legs. She rubbed her eyes and coughed for a few seconds, then spat out a gob of spit that looked blood-red, though that might have been due to the firelight. Without waiting to catch her breath, she shot off like a comet. The burning serpents couldn't hold their grip against the acceleration and fell, crying as they tumbled.

In the blink of an eye, Infidel was back at the *Freewind*, barreling through a line of a dozen burly warriors who were struggling against the wind up a gangplank, tossing them like tenpins. The water below was thick with bodies. A boy maybe sixteen years old was running atop the waves, jumping and skipping over the reaching arms of drowning Skellings. He wore no armor and was armed with only a slender rapier, but his skill with it was, literally, eye-popping. This had to be Jetsam. He had the power to run on water as if it was solid earth, and from his relatively solid footing he was moving among the struggling barbarians and driving the tip of his blade into their brains. I'd seen my share of eye-gouging in Commonground, so I wasn't too horrified by Jetsam's battle tactics, but I was slightly put off by the fact that as he danced around the waves he was *singing*, a rollicking sea shanty I'd heard a time or two sung drunkenly in bars:

And all my enemies,
Will sleep beneath the seas
Around me waves turn red
As they sink down to their bed

While it was good to see a young man enjoying his work, I couldn't help but think his light-hearted manner wouldn't contribute to a long lifespan. Almost as quickly as I'd had that thought, a Skelling reached up from bobbing in the waves behind Jetsam to try to grab the young Romer by his leg.

I shouted out a warning, despite the futility. Then, with the Skelling's fingers mere inches from Jetsam's ankle, the sea boiled and a dark shape burst into the air. Before I could even understand what was happening, the Skelling's hand was gone and all that was left was a bloody stump. Meanwhile, the shark that had bitten it off continued to fly skyward. Only, it wasn't a shark. It was Mako, at nineteen, the eldest of the Romer children still calling the ship home. He was a large man in what looked like black cotton pajamas plastered to his skin. He was heavily muscled, with an angular face and a mouth twice as wide as it should be. His hair was long and perfectly straight, clinging to his muscular neck like a coat of black ink. From sheer momentum he'd thrown himself ten feet into the air. He twisted to face Jetsam as he fell back toward the water. "Be more careful!" he growled.

As the water swallowed his brother, Jetsam called out, "I saw him, Mako! I was about to take him by surprise!"

Mako's head thrust back to the surface. "This isn't play-fighting," he growled. "These fools want to kill you!"

"They can't touch me," said Jetsam. "I saw him coming, I swear. I've killed twice as many of these guys as you have tonight."

"This isn't a game. We aren't keeping score," Mako grumbled as he sank back beneath the bloodied water once more.

"I bet we would be if you were winning," said Jetsam.

Meanwhile, one of the Skelling dragonships had been completely capsized, thanks to Infidel's aggressive hammer work. She, too, looked like she was enjoying herself. As the stricken ship sank lower into the water, she eyed the remaining vessel. She started toward it, until a blond-haired man with no shirt popped up on the deck and held his right arm overhead with his thumb pointed upward.

"I've got their boss!" the man shouted toward the *Freewind*.

Gale appeared at the railing of the boat in seconds. "Good job!"

She gazed out over the water. Only a few stragglers remained. One by one, they vanished beneath the waves, as Mako's shadow flitted beneath the surface. Given that a crew of a half dozen teenagers had finished off a hundred heavily armed warriors without suffering a scratch, I could see how Jetsam might have developed his streak of cockiness.

Gale cast her gaze toward Infidel. "Friends of yours?"

"I've never seen them before in my life!" Infidel said. "I thought they were after you!"

"They're Skellings!" the shirtless blond man called out. "They conduct random raids for a living."

"I figured they were after the bounty on our heads," said Jetsam.

"A reasonable theory," said Gale. "*If* they weren't so far from their homeland."

"Luckily, I've got their warlord tied up," said Shirtless.

"How do you know he's their warlord?" Infidel asked, drifting nearer.

"I think it will be pretty obvious when you see him."

It bugged me that I didn't know who this blond guy was. Gale obviously knew him. He looked to be in his mid-twenties, and he might have been the first man in Commonground I'd ever seen without a single visible scar. His body was flawless, his muscles perfectly symmetrical beneath taut tan skin. He had a square jaw and sharp cheekbones and teeth so white it hurt to look at them. I instantly felt a gut dislike of the man, despite no longer having a gut.

His white cotton britches were practically painted onto his skin, and it was difficult not to notice an unusually large bulge along his inner thigh. Infidel stared at him, her mouth slightly agape. My gut dislike hardened to outright hatred.

Gale grabbed hold of a rope and swung out to the Skelling's boat. I drifted overhead and saw a large warrior hogtied on the deck. I had to admit that the mystery man was good at spotting warlords. His captive was completely bald and his face was riddled with scars. Around his neck he wore a chain of what, at first glance, might have been dried fruit, but on second glance were mummified human ears. His bear skin vest sported gold buttons, and he had gold earrings as well. His gray beard and mustache were braided together and reached down to his belly button. His horned helmet was trimmed with gold, almost enough to call it a crown. He glared at his captors with utter hatred.

"Good work, Brand," said Gale, stepping forward and

kissing the shirtless guy on the cheek. Gale was old enough to be the man's mother; indeed, Mako and Brand looked about the same age.

Brand flashed his brilliant teeth in a broad smile. "I couldn't have done it without your tactical brilliance, my captain."

Gale blushed as he batted his eyelashes at her.

Infidel cleared her throat as she floated to the deck. "I don't think we've met."

"Infidel," said Gale. "This is Brand. Brand, Infidel."

"You must be new," said Infidel, stretching out her white leather gauntlet for a handshake.

Brand grasped the hand by the fingers and bent to kiss it. "I was hired on the journey here," he said. "It's my pleasure to meet you."

"Brand is my new dryman," said Gale.

"What happened to Boggy?" asked Infidel.

"Tiger shark got him when he was taking a swim," said Gale.

"Guess he should have stayed dry," said Infidel.

Brand didn't look like a dryman. Most members of the profession were older gentlemen noted for their soberness, with a reputation for stinginess rather than charm. Wanderers were a sea-faring race who'd long ago made a pact with Abyss, the primal dragon of the sea. As long as a Wanderer never set foot on land, Abyss promised that he would never drown in sea-water. Most Wanderers lived their lives completely aboard ship. They would band their boats together in remote harbors like Commonground to form impromptu cities where they socialized with one another. And so, to conduct business with the rest of the land-bound world, most Wanderer ships hired drymen. Somehow, as I watched Gale eye her employee with a look of school-girl giddiness, I got the impression that Brand had been hired for talents other than his skill at haggling for supplies.

"Is everything okay now?" a girl's voice called out from the other ship.

I looked back and saw a hound dog with two paws balanced on the rails of the *Freewind*. Menagerie? He could talk again? Why did he sound like a girl?

Then, an actual girl walked up behind the dog. She had kinky hair like the other Romers, but red instead of black. I guessed her to be about thirteen years old. She looked worried as she gazed out over the corpse-filled water. "Did you get them all?"

This had to be Cinnamon. Infidel had said that Cinnamon was the most timid of the Romers. Perhaps it was because she had the least useful magical ability. I was told that she had the power to control other people's sense of taste. She'd probably been hiding below deck. The others probably didn't want her underfoot in battle.

"I kept your dog safe like you asked, Infidel," she called out.

"Appreciate it," Infidel said, with a salute.

Gale, meanwhile, had knelt before the captive warlord. She grabbed him by the beard and turned his face toward her.

"Why did you attack us?" she asked.

He responded by hocking up a gob and spitting in Gale's face.

The stink was powerful enough to wrinkle my nose in the spirit realm.

"Oh, lord," gagged Infidel, covering her mouth.

Gale calmly wiped her cheek.

Brand stepped toward the far end of the boat. "How can anyone's breath smell so bad?"

Gale shrugged. "The main meat in a Skelling's diet is rotten fish soaked in lye. It has a distinctive aroma."

"I'd heard they were cannibals," said Brand.

"Don't believe everything you hear," said Gale. "The Skellings come from an island where nothing grows but grass and thistles. They don't have a lot of dietary options."

"I'd eat thistles before I'd eat rotten fish," said Brand.

"They eat thistles for breakfast," said Gale. "But I think we're getting sidetracked."

She turned her attention back to the warlord.

"Mako," she said, picking up his horned helmet from the deck.

Mako had slipped aboard when I wasn't looking. He stepped forward and took the helmet. He opened his jaws far wider than any man should be able to, revealing saw-rows of teeth, and without bothering to say grace bit into the helmet and devoured it in a half-dozen bites, horns and all. He spat out the golden bits into his palm. "No sense in wasting these."

The warlord's eyes grew rather large.

Gale tried her question again, this time slipping into a language I didn't understand. "Jabber jabber," she asked.

"Jabber *jabber*," the man growled in response. "Jabber jabber *jabber!*"

They went on like this for five minutes. The warlord's answers kept getting shorter and shorter. Gale paused for a moment and had Mako chew up the warlord's battle ax. The man looked distraught. I got the impression the weapon might have been a family heirloom.

The questioning resumed. Finally, the man answered with what turned into a monologue of utter gibberish that ran on for ten minutes.

Gale nodded, then stood from her squatting position, stretching her hands overhead to work the kinks from her back.

"What'd he say?" asked Infidel.

"It's a little convoluted," said Gale. "Apparently, they came here to set up an ambush. He says there's a two-hundred-year-old witch named Purity who has enslaved all their women and turned them into a brain-washed army. She's got a grudge against Ivory Blade, since he stole some kind of sacred harpoon, and she's heading to Commonground to capture him. They want to find him first to use as bait to get their women back. When they got into port, they saw Ivory Blade fly onto my boat. They sent the ice-serpents in to take him by surprise, then decided to raid the boat when they realized there were only a handful of men on board."

"Ah," said Infidel. "They must have mistaken me for Blade since I'm wearing his armor. And the harpoon this witch is after must be the Jagged Heart."

"So you know more about this than you've let on," said Gale.

"And yet I really don't," said Infidel. "Here's everything I know. Aurora told me that the harpoon was carved from the shattered remains of Hush's broken heart. Hush became the primal dragon of cold after her heart splintered into a thousand pieces when she was jilted by Glorious, the sun-dragon. The ice-ogres used the largest fragment of the heart as the tip of a harpoon that Aurora said was used to hunt ghost whales."

"Whales have ghosts?" asked Brand.

Infidel didn't answer him. She said, "Aurora said the harpoon had been stolen by raiders, but she didn't really describe them. Maybe it was this witch who took it. All I know is, Lord Tower had possession of the harpoon during our dragon hunt. It was the only weapon capable of killing Greatshadow."

"Wouldn't a harpoon tipped with ice melt once it got near a dragon made of fire?" asked Gale.

"Nope," said Infidel. "I'm not an authority on the pecking order of primal dragons, but apparently cold trumps fire when it comes to elemental forces. Aurora said that cold was the eternal backdrop of all creation, while heat and flame were merely flickering aberrations."

Gale sighed. "You're leaving out one little detail, aren't you?"

"What?"

"You now have the Jagged Heart. You're wearing Blade's armor and using Tower's hammer. I assume you stole the harpoon as well."

"I most certainly did not steal it. Aurora was the high priestess of the ice-ogres. She died recovering the harpoon, which was the most sacred relic of her people. I've made a promise to see that it gets returned to her homeland."

"When you said you wanted to book passage to Qikiqtabruk you didn't mention that you'd be transporting a treasure being hunted by an ancient witch. You're placing my family in danger by bringing it aboard."

"I swear I didn't know there was a witch looking for the harpoon," said Infidel. "But, look, does it really matter what kind of cargo I'm bringing aboard? Everyone here is being hunted by the Church of the Book, the Storm Guard, and the slaving Wanderers. What's one more enemy?"

"If you're my passenger, I have an obligation to defend you. I can't do that if you're keeping secrets."

"I don't need defending," said Infidel.

"Don't you?" Gale asked. "I've been too polite to mention it, but your face is covered with cuts and bruises. When you were last aboard my ship, swords bounced off your skin, and you didn't bother with armor."

Infidel crossed her arms. "You Wanderers make a big deal out of privacy. I'll ask you to respect mine."

"Don't speak to me of respect. You're asking me to risk my family. It's easy to forget this here in the tropics, but the northern kingdoms are in the thick of winter. The coast of Qikiqtabruk is completely ice-locked. There will be no safe harbor."

"Aw, Ma, don't be like that," said Jetsam, who was no longer standing on the waves but was instead doing a breaststroke in the air above his mother. I'd forgotten that in addition to being able to walk on water, Jetsam could swim in air. "If we make another boring run between the Isle of Apes and Raitingu I'll go crazy. Let's go to Qikiqtabruk and fight some witches."

Mako stretched his lanky arms overhead to snatch his brother by the belt. He yanked Jetsam back down to the deck and said, "Speak to Mother like that again and I'll break your jaw."

"No jawbreaking, please!" said Infidel, looking embarrassed to be in the middle of a family dispute. "Look, the whole reason I'm hiring the *Freewind* is that I don't want to fight anybody. I want to get up north as quickly as humanly possible, hand the harpoon to the first ice-ogre we meet, then get the hell out of there. If I liked cold weather even a little bit, I wouldn't live on the Isle of Fire."

"So what's your hurry?" asked Gale. "I'd be more open-minded about this mission if you were waiting until summer. The north sea isn't nearly as treacherous then."

Infidel bit her lower lip. She stared at Gale for several long seconds. Finally, she took a deep breath and said, "If you must know, I'm pregnant. I think. I want to get this over with as quickly as possible before my health won't permit it."

Gale chuckled, then dismissed Infidel's concerns with a wave of her hand. "You'll not be so fragile as you imagine. I first sailed the Sea of Wine when I was six months pregnant with Levi. You'll be fine if you wait until summer."

"Or," said Brand, stepping forward, "Or, we can accept the mission now, but for an extra fee."

"You've already admitted that Sorrow paid a large fee for you to carry her to any destination she wanted. Just because I'm choosing the destination doesn't mean you can change the price," said Infidel.

"We negotiated that price without full disclosure of the value of the cargo," said Brand. "Due to the need for additional security, our standard fee must be doubled."

Gale didn't look upset that Brand was launching into a negotiation to sail to a place that she'd just said was too dangerous to sail to. Wanderers are notorious hagglers; Gale was no doubt voicing protests as a basis for negotiating a higher fee. Brand was now doing the job he was paid to do by double-teaming Infidel.

Infidel smirked. "Double is outrageous. I'll offer a five percent bonus if, but only if, we get attacked by... what was the witch's name again?"

"Purity," said Gale.

"Right. If Purity attacks, and if I can't handle things myself, you get a bonus. These Skellings took us by surprise, but out on open water, I could have sunk both vessels before they even got near."

Gale shook her head. "Five percent isn't a serious offer.

Forty percent is the lowest I can go. The safety of my family is paramount. I'll not risk their lives for petty sums."

"And the fee should be paid whether or not we see combat," said Brand. "Sage is capable of spotting enemies long before they spot us, giving us an edge on evasion. This is a valuable service. We shouldn't be penalized for being good at our jobs."

"If she's so good, why didn't you see these Skellings coming?"

Gale frowned. "She took note of them. It's my own fault for not believing they would attack in Commonground. Here, all Wanderers are sworn to come to the defense of other Wanderers."

"And yet they didn't," said Infidel.

Gale gave a weary sigh. "These damn slave wars are ripping the very foundations of Wanderer society to shreds. I've blood relatives on at least a dozen ships in this port. That none would come to our aid is a heavy burden. And further proof that defending you against attacks will be a burden that falls completely on my immediate family. A twenty-five percent bonus paid up front would be the absolute bare-bones sum I could consider fair."

Before Infidel could make a counteroffer, I was distracted. Something was crawling on my right hand. The sensation of being touched was unnerving after my weeks of intangibility. I stretched out my arm and spied a large silver mosquito perched upon my knuckles. I froze, paralyzed by the strangeness of the moment. I was no entomologist, but could any bug be agile enough to alight upon something with no more substance than a cloud? The sensation had to be an illusion. He must be flying in the spot my hand occupied, and it was only my imagination that I could feel him.

It was a fine theory and I might have convinced myself if the creature's wings had been moving.

Shaking off my paralysis, I brought my hand closer to my eyes. The mosquito wasn't a living insect, but instead a finely constructed bit of jewelry, with a body of silver and legs of jointed copper wire. Its delicate wings were formed from gold leaf so thin it was translucent. The mosquito had glass eyes that served as tiny mirrors, reflecting my ghostly visage as we stared at one another.

"I... I've seen you before," I whispered.

To my utter astonishment, my phantom breath fogged the delicate wings.

The mosquito didn't react.

I swallowed hard.

After I'd died, when Infidel had first returned to town, she'd fought an undead giant. The unliving thing had been sewn together out of a two or more corpses, a patchwork monstrosity with inhuman strength in its misshapen limbs. The giant had given Infidel quite a beating, but she'd eventually pounded it to pulp, using its own torn-off arm as a club. When she'd dismantled the torso, she'd found a small cage, and within that cage was a glowing mosquito. This one lacked the inner radiance, but how could it not be the same creature? How many magical mosquitoes were there flying around in this town?

"Wh... what are you?" I asked. I felt certain that some higher intelligence was gazing at me through those glass eyes.

The thing answered me by doing a little dance back and forth. A tongue like a tiny corkscrew worked itself out of the construct's mouth. I shook my hand to throw the thing off, but too late. The mosquito sank the corkscrew into my skin, and all my frantic hand waving failed to loosen it. I watched as a bead of ruby ichor rose around the tiny hole augered in my wraithful flesh. I reached out with my other hand to tear the insect loose.

Before my fingers could close upon it, the mosquito placed its mouth against the small pearl of blood that sat upon my knuckle. Nearly microscopic jaws snapped open, and a glass pipette thrust down into my ghost blood, drawing the bead up into its belly.

The jaws clicked shut. The noise was too faint to truly hear, but in my imagination it echoed like the lonely clang of dungeon doors.

I recovered my wits sufficiently to flick it with my fingers. The blow tore the insect from my skin. As it tumbled, the tiny mosquito spread its wings and took flight. I was none the worse for wear, save for a small smear of blood where the creature had feasted. I watched it buzz a drunken path across the deck, unseen by the assembled Romers. I cast one last glance at Infidel. Though my instincts were to stay at her side, I threw myself into the air, narrowing my eyes to concentrate on my ever-accelerating target. I didn't know why it wanted my blood or where it was going. Despite my normally inquisitive nature, I honestly didn't want to learn. I had to stop this thing.

CHAPTER FOUR

AN EXCEPTIONALLY UGLY BIRD

THE MOSQUITO DOVE over the edge of the railing. I gave chase as it flitted above the stinking tide. The bay of Commonground emits an open-sewer aura under the best of conditions, but since the tsunami churned up the muck it's been especially gag-inducing. The mosquito was barely a foot above the water, darting around pilings and between boats and their anchor chains with an agility that would have shaken me if I'd been a bat or a bird. I ghosted through these obstacles as if they weren't even there.

The fact that this mystery bug had touched me meant that I could touch it back. I gave it a good swat with my right hand. It darted to avoid the blow, but the tip of my middle finger managed to clip its wing, sending it into a tail spin as it neared the hull of a boat. To my chagrin, it passed straight through the tar-impregnated wood without leaving a scratch.

I flew into the ship's hold, spotting the mosquito easily in the pitch black interior, despite the jumbled maze of barrels and crates. The thing was glowing with an internal magic that my phantom eyes could easily track. At any rate, even if I hadn't been able to see it, I could have followed the high-pitched buzz of the mosquito's golden wings.

The mosquito zipped out of the hold, then shot strait up, disappearing though the pier above. I emerged onto a boardwalk crowded with bodies. Now that night had fallen, the denizens of the city were out in force. Cutthroats and whores stumbled groggily along the pier, searching for breakfast at a time when law-abiding men sought out supper. The area was crowded with ramshackle shacks slapped together by river pygmies, who cooked plantains, turtle eggs, and crabs on charcoal grills stoked to ruby heat. Dark amber rum with a whisper of coffee was the beverage of choice for this clientele, and I felt a pang of longing as I caught a whiff of the much cherished elixir.

I lingered for a fraction of a second, distracted by the aroma, and spotted faces of former friends among the crowd. Ol' Scummy Stone was sitting on a bench, drinking from a silver flask he'd won from me in a game of darts. Scummy was in his sixties and had survived for decades in this rough-and-tumble town using the same strategy I'd employed, which was to be obsequious enough that no one had reason to kill you, but not so pathetic that you aroused actual hatred. Further down the planks I saw Rose Thirteen; by this point she'd had twenty husbands, but her name had gotten locked down after she botched the job of poisoning husband thirteen and had to finish him off with a hatchet in the door of the Drunken Monkey Saloon. Her hair was streaked with gray now, but she still had the same lushness of figure that had caught so many men in her orbit. Despite her propensity toward murder, she was welcome company on a night of drinking, since she knew more dirty jokes than a sailor. She was also Commonground's only competent seamstress – she'd mended the pants I'd died in.

If the mosquito had meant to distract me by tracing a path through places and faces familiar to me, I'm vexed to confess that it succeeded. It had put a hundred feet between us as I paused to reminisce. I caught one last glimpse of the tiny beast as it zipped into Big Blue's Bug and Bun Barn at the end of the pier. I flew after it, but the second I entered the restaurant I lost focus. My mouth watered as I caught sight of plates full of yeasty fried dough stuffed with bananas and lemon spiders. Unfortunately, for a ghost, concentration equals movement. For the briefest second, the mosquito vanished from my mind and I found myself stalled in the middle of the bug barn, stirred to hunger.

It took only an instant to shake off my reverie and zoom out the back wall, but it was too late. I couldn't spot the mosquito amid the chaos of lights and bodies, nor hear its faint buzz beneath all the laughter and shouts. Outwitted by an insect!

The creature had been heading due east when it first took flight. There wasn't much left in that direction. Once, Bigsby's fish house had been the central feature of that area, but the tidal wave had left nothing but slanted timbers thrusting up from the water. I wondered if Bigsby would rebuild, assuming he was even alive. Between the volcano erupting, the tidal wave, and the avatars of Greatshadow burning everything in sight, the population of Commonground wasn't what it used to be.

Flying over the barren water, I noticed a dim glow on the shore no more than a mile distant. This was no funeral pyre or bonfire; I guessed it to be the faint, flickering light of numerous candles.

Which, indeed, it was. There were hundreds of slender tapers thrust into a circle of raked beach sand, forming a spiral pattern. I flew higher to better perceive the design and found myself mesmerized by the snail-shell shape, unable to turn away.

Within the center of the whirl of light was a familiar figure. Sorrow Stern knelt on the beach, laying gnarled bits of driftwood together into a shape that bore a vague resemblance to a man. Its legs were splintery remnants of a mast split by lightning. Its arms were thick branches of dark teak, the fine grain looking almost like muscle beneath a thin coat of damp sand. For a head it possessed a large coconut still in its husk, given a jagged mouth by a machete chop and what could pass as eyes formed by two oval pecan shells. The twin iron nails that held the false eyes to the surface glinted like irises in the candlelight. To the sides of the head were curled tamarind seed pods that served as makeshift ears.

For the first time I saw Sorrow free of her hood. She'd stripped off her cloak and wore a bright red dress that left her shoulders bare. It looked more appropriate for a ballroom than a beach.

She was smaller without the cloak, with a figure best described as girlish, but I found her age a mystery. The left half of her body was withered, the limbs supported by iron braces, but her right half looked young and strong. Her head was shaved, adding years to her appearance. Her scalp was dotted with dark studs, some of which flashed as they caught the candlelight. I found myself drawn in along the spiral, fascinated by the bumps on her head. They looked, for all the world, like the blunt heads of nails. There were half a dozen, one gold, another silver, another rusted iron, one green copper, one that might have been glass, and the last with the appearance of polished wood.

She stood, lifting her hand straight up as if she were reaching for me as I hovered overhead. I heard a buzz and the silver mosquito flashed toward her fingers, alighting gently on her outstretched palm. She knelt once more, opening the barrel chest of the driftwood man she'd built, revealing a small cage of golden wire. She opened a tiny door and the mosquito crawled inside.

"Wandering spirit, thou shalt roam no more," said Sorrow, her voice deeper than what should have come from her slender throat. "By thy blood I bind thee to this body of wood. Thy soul shall be its soul."

She shut the door to the cage.

Long ago, before arriving in Commonground, I worked on a fishing vessel in the Green Straights, where swordfish are caught with hooks of tempered steel fed out on long weighted lines. I'd had the misfortune of running one of those hooks through my hand, the point slipping between the bones of my little finger and ring finger, just beneath my knuckles. I'd been beaten by professionals, during my years at the monastery, but nothing quite prepared me for the pain as the weighted line played out and snatched me overboard.

That same pain now seized me in every pore. I felt invisible hooks slip into my mouth, scraping across tooth and tongue and bone. Hooks pierced my eyes and ears, slid into my neck bones, tangled in every rib. I thrashed against the unseen barbs that tormented me, beating the night air with my ghost limbs, to no avail. Fine silver threads appeared all around me, connecting my wraith-form to the driftwood man. With a sound like fingernails dragged along guitar strings, the lines all went taut and reeled me in.

For a moment, everything went black.

When I opened my eyes again the world was painted in shades of amber. My limbs felt numb and heavy. I could barely turn my head... and yet, to my surprise, I did have a head to turn. I was a physical being once more, my body cold and stiff, but undeniably present. I raised an arm that felt weighted with iron and brought it to my face. With my monochromatic vision, I could make out the gnarled remnants of the base of a mangrove tree, with five finger-length roots jutting out. Such was the resemblance of the root to a hand that I imagined I could close the fingers into a fist, and as I thought it, it happened. I felt the friction of finger against finger, felt the damp grit that coated the limb grinding into wooden flesh.

Sorrow loomed above me. Unlike the rest of my monochrome world, she looked crafted from a rainbow, a being of pure energy swirling within the translucent flesh of a woman. Her voice was thunderous in my seed-pod ears:

"Ghost, you are bound to this body of wood. It was alive once, but devoid of spirit, as you were alive once, but are devoid of body. I give you dominion over this form for a time, 'til decay and entropy reduce this shell to dust, and the last spark of your animating spirit fades from this domain. Until you meet this final death, you are my property, and shall obey my commands."

I attempted to offer my opinion of her demands in the form of a string of artfully delivered curse words. No sound emerged from my coconut lips. Despite having a mouth, I discovered I had no tongue. I sat up, feeling clumsy and disoriented. My eyes had difficulty keeping the world on the level as I swayed first to the left, then the right. I had only a muted sense of proprioception. I stretched out my driftwood arms, fingers splayed, to steady myself on the sand.

It felt, I must confess, a good bit like being drunk. Had I really spent fortunes in pursuit of this sensation when I was alive? *This* had been my preferred state of existence, listing through the world like a ship with a damaged keel?

Perhaps I'd paid freely for this sensation in life, but in death I'd grown used to sobriety, and wanted it back. Still seated, I scraped out letters on the sand using my gnarled fingers.

P-L-E-A-S

I don't know what she thought I was about to ask, but Sorrow dropped to her knees before my wooden body and placed her lips upon the jagged gash of my new mouth. She sucked in air from my coconut and I felt dizzier than ever.

She broke off the kiss and stood, turning her back to me. Of course, since she appeared to me as nothing but numinous energy, I could see through her clothes, her skin, her ribs and lungs, all the way through to the other side, where her hands were busily knitting something dark and cold. It took me a second to understand it was a little doll made of twigs and grass. She brought it to her lips and breathed into it.

My own body suddenly felt warm.

She stood the tiny doll in the palm of her hand and said, "Rise."

I rose, feeling as if unseen hands had taken me by the arms to help me stand. The world was askew, with my head lopsided upon my shoulders, until she adjusted the head of the miniature and my own skull rolled to right the world. I glanced down at the letters I'd written; they seemed very far away. My new body was a good foot taller than my old one. Sorrow looked tiny as I loomed over her. But despite our different statures, there was no question that she was the dominant entity in our new partnership.

"Those letters," she said, glancing at the sand. "Erase them."

I wanted with all my soul to disobey, but instead my left foot dragged across the letters, blotting out my pitiful attempt at communication.

"You remember how to write," she said, softly. "Perhaps you have other memories from your former life. I have no power to force you to forget them. But forget them you must, or your days will be agony."

I slowly shook my head. I could still say, "No," at least.

"Whoever you were, that person is dead," she said, sounding defiant. "You had your chance at life, and you had your chance to move on to the abstract realms when you passed away. It's your fault you've lingered and become fuel for my creation. I'm not to blame for the fate that has befallen you. I'm simply a weaver, a materialist who is able to sculpt lifeless matter into useful forms. Your soul no longer served a purpose; its energy was wasted on aimless wandering. I've done you no harm, ghost. Indeed, I've given you a gift; a few final days of purpose."

I again shook my head, "No." The grinding sound of my coconut skull swiveling on my wooden shoulders was unnerving.

She didn't look directly at my face as she said, "You have no choice. In the morning, I shall take possession of a large quantity of manuscripts. I don't trust the scoundrels of this port sufficiently to hire assistants to help move them. You'll serve as my porter, as well as my bodyguard. Just as wood is tougher than muscle, so too are you stronger than a man, and impervious to pain. You will make a formidable warrior if needed. Fortunately, I'm not one who behaves recklessly. With luck you'll never need to expend your energy in battle."

She walked off beyond the edge of my vision. I couldn't turn my head sufficiently to follow her. She returned a few minutes later with a bundle of clothing. "Get dressed. You won't pass for human, but in Commonground that's not such a rarity. In this garb, you'll draw less attention."

The paralysis that inflicted me vanished and I was able to take the clothes she offered. Unfortunately, my freedom of movement was decidedly limited. Any of the ordinary actions one might take while dressing seemed permissible, but when I wanted to wheel around and dash for the forest, my body proved deaf to my commands.

The clothing was surprisingly fresh and clean. Given my resemblance to a scarecrow, I'd expected nothing more than rags, but there was little evidence that these clothes had ever been worn before. Perhaps she was as adept at knitting cloth as she was at molding steel or shaping wood. The pants were heavy wool; they no doubt would have been hot and scratchy if I'd still had skin. The shirt was even rougher; fabrics aren't my specialty, but I believe it was woven from jute, more suited for burlap bags than clothing, though given the splintery nature of my new joints, perhaps the thick fabric was a good match. Heavy cloth gloves and sturdy leather boots hid my plainly inhuman extremities. The final touch was to cover my coconut skull with a tri-corn hat, matched with a large bandana hiding most of my face and neck. I imagined I looked a bit like a bandit in the get-up.

"You're rather dashing, with that crimson bandana," Sorrow said, adjusting the way it rested on my cheeks, if a coconut had cheeks. I found myself curious about what other colors I might be wearing. With my amber vision, I'd thought all my clothing was shades of brown, but for all I knew she might have dressed me to rival a peacock.

"Follow," she said, and I followed.

WE PASSED THE night in one of the luxury suites aboard the *Black Swan*. I'd been in similar suites before. During the times in my life when I was blessed with money, I saw little reason to hoard it. "Seize the day!" was my motto, though in practice this usually meant "grab the bottle!" The old *Black Swan* had been destroyed when Greatshadow attacked Commonground, and this new room was so clean and polished that the light of a single bedside lamp hurt my new eyes. Sorrow hadn't bothered to give my coconut face a nose, but when she hung her cloak in the closet, the scent of fresh pine was powerful enough I could taste it in my false mouth despite my lack of a tongue. Formerly, the rooms I'd stayed in had sported artwork in which scantily clad pagan goddesses had been a popular theme. Now, the paintings on the wall were all landscapes in muted colors. I suppose it was more tasteful, but I also thought it was a little dull.

Sorrow placed me in the corner of the room and told me to sit. She returned to the door and sealed it shut by molding the frame to the wood of the door itself. She stripped down unselfconsciously before me, changing into a simple cotton nightgown. Again, I noted the health of the right half of her body, and the dark veins, wrinkles, and amber blotches of her left side. "You may not move tonight unless danger arises while I'm sleeping, in which case you are free to defend me. Remain alert; your senses may be dulled by your new encasement, but you have far less to distract you than you did in life. You have no need for sleep or food or water now; focus your attention on any noises from the hall."

She climbed into the bed of silk and was asleep in moments, the covers pulled almost to her chin despite the tropical heat. Her bed was surrounded by a veil of mosquito netting, but I could see her easily enough, even in the darkness. Like Infidel, she proved to be a restless sleeper. All through the night, she tossed and mumbled.

I wondered how she had come to be named Sorrow. It seemed off-key for a nickname, since it was neither cruel nor funny, and it didn't strike me as the sort of name a person would willingly choose for herself. But it made little sense as a given name, either. What mother would wish such a label upon her daughter?

* * *

Sorrow rose before dawn, lingering a while before a mirror as she ran her fingers around the dark, inflamed flesh surrounding one of the nails driven into her scalp. This was the nail that looked like it was carved from mahogany. To judge by her wincing, the wound felt as painful as it looked. She applied a bit of pressure and a bead of thick amber puss bubbled up. She wiped it away with a cotton ball soaked in alcohol, as a deep frown once more lined her face. She worked the last of the puss from the wound, and took a moment to drag her fingers around her scalp. Even in the dim candlelight, I could see a haze of stubble had arisen during the night. It seemed her baldness was the product of a razor.

An hour later we were back outside, amidst a cacophony of hammers and saws. Commonground was busily being rebuilt by the river pygmies, and the docks by the Wanderers, both of whom relied on the town as an economic hub.

I followed Sorrow to the shore and recognized the path she was walking toward a tangle of dense trees. Sitting in the upper branches of one particularly robust mangrove was what was left of a sailboat. The ground beneath the boat had been picked clean by river-pygmy scavengers, but despite the relative ease of climbing the gnarled and knotty trees, it looked as if the boat was unmolested. Even out of water, everyone would have recognized this as my boat. In life, I was hardly a fearsome enough figure to discourage looters. Infidel, however, had a reputation as someone who didn't trifle with thieves. She'd lived here a few days following Greatshadow's attack, and had made it her home since returning from the hunt. Until word got out that she'd lost her powers, the place was safe.

"Climb," said Sorrow, as she hopped upon my back. Her arms wrapped around my neck in a way that would have choked me if I'd needed to breathe. I barely felt her weight upon me. Nor, I should note, did I much feel my own weight. The soggy driftwood had dried a good bit during the night and my limbs felt stronger and steadier than they had before. In one of the few civil conversations I'd ever had with Hookhand, he told me that when he'd first put on his hook, it had been a lifeless weight strapped to the stump of his arm, but over time he felt as if the ghost of his hand had flowed into it, and that, impossible as it seemed, he'd been able to feel things with the cold iron.

While there was no mistaking my new body's crude sense of touch for the nuance of actual flesh, I found that there was some truth to Hookhand's story. My phantom fingers had flowed into the roots beneath my gloves, and I could sense the pressure as I grasped the branches, and feel the spiky bark digging into my wooden palms. My sense of hearing had improved during the night, and though I was hampered by my single-hued vision, my ability to focus was improving.

I climbed over the railing of my boat. The vessel had been in poor repair for years, but a few weeks in the branches had warped and twisted the deck into a surface where not a single plank could be described as flat. It looked as if the whole thing could fall apart in a good stiff wind, though that was currently being tested, as the omnipresent sea breeze kept the whole structure swaying. Sorrow dropped from my back and called out, "Hello?"

There was no answer. She looked around, then crouched to enter what remained of the cabin. I knelt to watch. I was never fastidious in my housekeeping, but the place was a disaster even by my slovenly standards. The boat had obviously flipped end over end when the tidal wave carried it here. Everything had been drenched as well, and what books I could see were coated with mold. My heart ached as I contemplated the ruined pages. Despite my early years in the monastery orphanage where I was taught to read and write, I've always considered myself an autodidact. I've stuffed my skull with information both trivial and profound without the guidance of any teachers other than these books. I mourned their death as much as I would have mourned the passing of a human friend.

I couldn't blame Infidel for the poor state of my belongings. Even if she had emptied out the cabin and tried to salvage the books, the truth was most had mildewed long ago, as I tended to keep my reading material in tottering stacks by my bedside rather than safely arranged in glass cases. Perhaps it was the combination of my lax housekeeping and the tidal wave destruction that had led Infidel to simply ignore this mess. She slept in a hammock she'd strung in the branches above the deck, with a patch of sail stretched overhead serving as a roof.

Sorrow sighed. She grumbled, as much to the wind as to me, "My grandmother used to say one should never buy a pig in a poke. I'd imagined the grandson of Judicious Merchant would have taken better care of his writings."

I silently chuckled inside my driftwood cage, delighted at her consternation. For while I'd been a lackluster guardian of my reading materials, I was far more diligent with my own writing. Somewhere under all the clutter and debris was my grandfather's sea chest. It was tightly constructed from high quality cedar and utterly air tight. All my important papers were probably safe inside, but she had no way of knowing this. It was her own fault for not carving me a tongue, or even allowing me to write in the sand.

Sorrow cast her gaze upwards, shielding her eyes with her hand. Infidel was coming near, the Gloryhammer glowing like a second sun. A darker shape followed closely behind, flapping awkward, ungainly wings. Some sort of injured pelican?

Infidel covered the half mile that separated us in mere seconds, wisely choosing to land on a thick limb beside the boat rather than on the deck itself. She nodded in greeting toward Sorrow, then looked at me. "Who's this?"

"A little extra muscle," said Sorrow. "I haven't bothered to name him yet. I guess I'll call him Drifter."

"You can't just ask him his name?"

"He's the strong silent type. Very, very silent."

By now, the flapping shape that had followed Infidel caught

up, lighting on the branch beside her. It was a creature I'd never seen before, with the body, legs, and ears of a hound-dog, but with wings, big webbed claws and a long, ungainly beak like a pelican. The overall appearance was comical, but also unnerving, for the creature's form was ever shifting, with the margin around his neck and chest where feathers transitioned into fur ebbing and flowing in slow, rippling waves.

"That's your, uh, man-dog?" asked Sorrow. "The shape-shifter? Menagerie?"

"Yeah," said Infidel. "This morning I found him on deck chewing on a freshly killed pelican. His face was coated with the blood. I was going to leave him at the ship, but when I jumped into the air to fly here, he turned into this and gave chase."

"Maybe the pelican blood gave him a new form?" Sorrow said.

"Maybe. But he also sucked my blood when he was a tick, so why didn't he change back into a human?"

"I'm not an authority on blood magic," said Sorrow. "But, I can see the auras of living things, and this creature has not even the faintest hint of a human aura. It doesn't possess the spiritual template to change into a man."

"Whatever," Infidel said. "Humans are vastly overrated in my book. I hope Menagerie gets better, but for now you have to admit it's kind of cool that I have a flying dog."

Sorrow shrugged and looked back into the cabin. "That's a very positive attitude. It would be equally accurate to say that you merely have the affection of an exceptionally ugly bird."

"There's no need to be nasty," said Infidel.

"Is there not?" said Sorrow. "I entered into this deal foolishly, I admit. The citizens of Commonground aren't famous for their honesty. There was something about your aura that led me to trust you. Most dishonest people have feeble and dirty auras. Yours was bright and clear; I thought that in this city of sin, I'd somehow stumbled upon a true innocent. Yet, rather than finding the organized collection of books and maps I thought I was purchasing, I find only rotting litter."

Infidel stepped gingerly onto the deck. "I didn't cheat you," she said, ducking into the cabin, motioning for Sorrow to follow.

Sorrow glanced at me and said, "Don't move," then followed.

Menagerie lingered behind, perched on the branch, staring at me, his head tilted.

Though I couldn't move my physical form, I tried to speak. A ghost voice tore from my ghost throat and echoed in my ghost ears, though the morning air was silent save for the chirping of birds and the distant stir of the waves.

"Menagerie!" I called to the dog-bird. "Can you hear me? Can you hear me?"

The dog furrowed his brow as it loped onto the deck. Its head became almost fully hound as it took the time to sniff me, then flowed back toward pelican as it sat on its haunches and looked up at my face.

"Can you hear me? Say something," I said.

He didn't say anything.

"Speak!" I said.

Nothing.

"Roll over!" I said, feeling bad that I was treating a man who had once been a brilliant mercenary as if he had only the intelligence to do canine tricks.

He kept staring. Did he not hear me? Did his dog form not understand that command? What other commands could I try? I couldn't tell him to heel or fetch since I was immobile. Telling him to sit was pointless since he was already sitting.

"Shake?" I said, rather tentatively since I couldn't move my arms.

Menagerie raised his right front leg with its webbed bird's foot. With his hound dog eyes, he looked positively heartbroken when I left him hanging.

CHAPTER FIVE

SORROW WOULD SOON KNOW MY NAME

"By the sacred quill," gasped Infidel as she dragged my sea-chest out onto the deck. The thing was five feet long, three feet tall and wide, solidly constructed and stuffed to the brim. I'm surprised she could move it without her old powers. She collapsed against the railing and wiped her brow. "That wasn't fun."

"I'm learning not to believe everything I hear in Commonground," Sorrow said as she, too, emerged from the cabin.

"Look, don't get distracted by all the ruined books," said Infidel. "The real treasure's in this box."

"I was referring to the stories I'd heard of your strength," said Sorrow. "I'd been told you were as strong as a score of men, but even one man could have gotten that sea-chest out of the cabin with less effort. I'd also heard that swords bounced off your skin, but your face certainly doesn't lend much credence to that claim."

"Oh," said Infidel, sliding her fingers along the thin brown scabs that lay upon her cheeks. "My powers, uh, only kick in when I'm fighting. I don't waste magic on moving furniture."

"I see," said Sorrow, kneeling in front of the chest. She contemplated the big brass lock on the front. "Do you have the key?"

"Sorry," Infidel said, shaking her head. She grabbed the Gloryhammer. "Stand back and I'll knock the lock off."

"That won't be needed. If you're willing to damage the lock to open the chest, there's no need for me to respect its integrity."

She grasped the padlock, squishing it between her fingers like a ball of clay. She twisted the metal and tugged it away from the chest, stretching it like taffy until it snapped.

"Looks like you've got some inhuman strength of your own there," said Infidel.

"Nonsense," said Sorrow. "My strength is unremarkable. As a materialist, I comprehend ordinary matter in a way that your untrained eyes cannot. You believe the illusion that the material world is made of solid objects. I can see through this illusion."

"You sound like Zetetic," said Infidel. "In Greatshadow's lair, we encountered a room carved from false matter. It had no fixed form or color. He said this was the original state of all matter."

"I sound nothing like Zetetic," said Sorrow. "Though I never met the man, Deceivers believe all of reality to be a shared fiction, lacking objective truth. I don't dispute the reality of the material world; indeed, I study it and understand it. The key concept is that the things we think of as solid objects are composed of much tinier particles. If you could shrink to the size of a flea, the smooth surface of this lock would be revealed as a rugged landscape of boulders. Shrink to the size of a dust mote, and you would find that the boulders are built of individual grains. If you could become so small as to be invisible, you would find that these grains cling to one another like damp sand. Even a child on the beach can sculpt and mold damp sand using only their bare hands."

"But that lock wasn't made of sand," said Infidel.

Sorrow shrugged. "My analogy is difficult for the uninitiated to follow. The true nature of matter is so counterintuitive that our language lacks words to accurately describe it." She pulled her cloak back, revealing the scalp full of nails. "Even I couldn't learn the truth through mere language. I had to have reality driven into my brain directly. Every nail in my skull is made from a pure material form. These have been placed in contact with the portion of my mind that perceives the corresponding substance. The copper nail gives me command over copper, which was the primary component of this brass lock."

Infidel grimaced when she saw Sorrow's scalp. I was a little queasy myself, since the wooden nail that had been infected this morning was now even worse. Dark veins ran from the wound, which was now an ugly bruise, almost black, fading to lighter hues of amber at the edges.

"Most metals are simple," said Sorrow. "In their natural state they hold a faint echo of the primal spirit of Krag, the dragon of earth, but this spirit is driven out in the smelting process. Thus, they have no will to resist my magic. I recently expanded my repertoire to include wood. It's been a thousand years since Verdant, the primal dragon of the forest, last spread his spirit into trees, but even so, as once-living material, wood possesses a cellular memory that can fight my manipulations. It's exhausting in both body and spirit to make use of it. However, it's worth the price I pay, since wood can be imbued with a persistent animating spirit, unlike iron or copper."

Infidel's brow wrinkled. "I'm not sure I'm following you. Are you saying *anyone* could bang a nail into her head and gain your powers?"

"With the right nail, in exactly the right place, to precisely the right depth," she said. "But not anyone. Only women are able to master the art. Feminine prowess in magic is a threat to the male assumption of superiority. Thus, the patriarchal powers-that-be label me a witch and a heretic. So be it. I wear their slurs as a badge of honor."

Infidel grinned. "I know where you're coming from. I hated it at first when people called me 'Infidel.' Now I've come to like it. I guess it was your enemies who named you Sorrow?"

As she spoke, Infidel repeatedly scratched the scabs on her face. It was almost impossible to look at Sorrow's scalp, with its festering wound and stubbled hair, and not feel itchy. If my own hands hadn't been paralyzed, I would have been scratching my coconut dome.

Sorrow frowned. "I thought it was impolite in Commonground to inquire about the pasts of others."

Infidel shrugged. "Yeah, it is. But I'm curious. From your accent, you must be from the Silver Isles. Most girls there get named something churchy, like Faith, Hope, or Innocent. Sorrow isn't a name I've heard before."

"My father was especially, as you say, 'churchy.'" Sorrow looked down at the mass of copper in her hands. She'd wadded it up into a tight ball. "Have you heard of Judge Adamant Stern?"

Infidel raised an eyebrow. "The commander of the Judgment Fleet? The guy who hanged his own mother?"

Sorrow nodded. "You know of him."

"Who doesn't?"

"Indeed. His story is well known. As his daughter, I have witnessed the aspects of his personality that brought him infamy first hand. An accusation was made that his mother was a weaver... a witch. He had her head shaved, but found no nails. He did, however, find scars. My grandmother claimed these were childhood cuts and scrapes, but the letter of the law was that if her head were not free of blemish, she was to be hanged. I was nine years old at the time. My grandmother was everything to me. My mother had died giving birth to me... This is why my father named me Sorrow."

"Harsh," said Infidel.

"He never once showed me kindness. He barely spoke to me, allowing my grandmother to raise me as if I were her own daughter. After he hanged her, he left me in the care of the family maid to raise me as he pursued his career upon the seas. What he didn't know was that our maid was truly a weaver. She gave me my first nail, of silver. Not long after, she was discovered. She was tortured to death and confessed to converting me to the dark arts. But this I learned second-hand, since I was on a boat to the Isle of Grass by the time her head was being shaved by my father."

"The Isle of Grass? The *Freewind* was attacked by Skelling's earlier tonight."

"This far south?"

"Yeah. About a hundred of them. They used furry white pythons for attack dogs."

"Snow-wyrms. Despite their reptilian characteristics, they're actually a relative of otters. But why would they venture so far from home?"

"They said some witch named Purity had kidnapped their women and they'd come here to find her."

Sorrow's mouth fell open. Then her eyes narrowed as she said, skeptically, "So you know of my past. I would prefer you confront me directly with your questions rather than take such an oblique approach to your queries."

"What the hell are you talking about?" asked Infidel. "Wait? Are you Purity?"

"Don't be stupid." Sorrow rolled her eyes. "Purity was a weaver of great renown. It's said that her magic kept her alive for two hundred years."

"Hmm," said Infidel, studying Sorrow closely. "Your age *is* kind of hard to pin down."

Sorrow frowned. "If you must know, I'm only twenty-two. The left half of my body withered when I unsuccessfully tried to master bone-weaving. Unfortunately, I mistakenly inserted the bone into the portion of my brain meant to command wood. I've paid a terrible price for this failure."

"Tough break," said Infidel. "So, you're not a two-hundred-year-old witch. But from your reaction to her name, I'm guessing you know her."

"No," said Sorrow. "I know only her legend. She was originally a maiden dwelling on the north shore of the Silver Isle, until she was kidnapped by Skellings. She was brutally raped during her time in captivity, but eventually a drunken Skelling carelessly placed his sword by her bed as he prepared to abuse her. She killed him and a dozen other men on her escape. She nearly died upon the high seas in an open boat she'd stolen, until she was rescued by a mysterious old woman with strange powers. This was the legendary witch Avaris; she took Purity under her wing and taught her all the arts of weaving. Purity returned to the northlands with her newfound powers, intending to exact revenge upon the entire race."

"Avaris? I've heard that name before. The Black Swan supposedly learned to travel through time with her help."

"Yes," said Sorrow. "Time-weaving is one of the abstract arts, the highest class of witchcraft. I manipulate material objects, but dream of one day expanding my powers to the manipulation of abstract forces. Avaris is the only witch to have mastered all the material and abstract realms. If I could speak with her for even five minutes, I'm certain the knowledge I could gain would transform me."

Infidel nodded. "So, when you went to the Isle of Grass, you were looking for Purity. And, if you could, you'd like to learn a few things from Avaris?"

"I sense a hint of disapproval in your tone."

"History is a subject that bores me, but even I've heard stories about Avaris. She's one of the most evil women who ever lived. She used to eat children!"

"History is written by victors," said Sorrow. "Once, the weavers were a force to be reckoned with, willful women with powers rivaling those of gods. The men of this world could not tolerate the threat to their sovereignty, and used the Church of the Book to turn the world against the weavers and hunt them down. Unfortunately, men possess a greater stomach for bloodshed and brutality than most women. They ended the era of weavers through a campaign of violence. They now ensure the subservience of women through a phallocentric mythology that treats us as inferior beings."

Infidel cracked her knuckles. "I like to think I'm doing my small part to help women get back into the bloodshed and brutality business."

"I'm not content with playing a small part," Sorrow said, clenching her fists. "The world I was born into is fundamentally corrupt. The grand crimes committed against humanity are so audacious that all notions of right and wrong are upended. The rich and the powerful build their civilization upon the backs of the weak, justifying their cruelty and theft with a fictional moral code supposedly enshrined in a book that no man has read."

Infidel nodded. "Sister, you don't have to preach to me that civilization is screwed up. That's why I do everything I can to avoid it."

"I'm not content to run. I'm going to tear it all down." There was a hard determination to Sorrow's voice I found chilling. "I'm going to destroy the Church of the Book, topple the kingdoms of men, and establish a new golden age."

Infidel stared blankly at Sorrow for half a minute, uncertain what to say. Finally, she cleared her throat. "It's good to have goals."

"Yes," said Sorrow. "But I need more than goals. I need power, and I need allies. If you're truly aware of the unjust nature of the world, and even half-deserving of your legend as warrior, why not join me in my battle?"

"Because it's a stupid battle," said Infidel.

"How can you be so blind?" asked Sorrow.

Infidel crossed her arms. "I think you're the one who might be missing her own contradictions. You think you're wise enough and smart enough to remake the world? Don't you see that anyone arrogant enough to think that is likely going to wind up making things worse?"

"I would rather try to remake the world and fail than hide in this remote backwater and avoid the struggle for justice."

"If you think I avoid struggles on the Isle of Fire, you've got a lot to learn."

"You fight pointless battles against freaks and scoundrels. It's hardly a worthy struggle."

"There's a difference between battles and struggles," said Infidel. "Fighting is easy for me. My struggle has been to learn to love and trust after being raised in a life where these words had been stripped of meaning. My struggle now is to rise above a life where my main pursuit has been to amuse myself, and remake myself into a mother who can raise a child. I've lived most of my life stuck with the same attitudes and emotions I had when I was fifteen. My struggle is simply to grow up."

"Wouldn't you rather raise your child in a world more just than this one?"

Infidel shrugged. "This world isn't so bad. Stagger used to take me up into the jungle, where we'd explore vine-draped ruins and eat fruit fresh straight from the tree. We'd make our beds under stars so bright and crisp it looked like the sky was full of glorystones. Civilization might have its problems, but the world... the world's all right."

"What a waste of your talents," Sorrow said.

"It sounds like you've got more powerful allies in mind anyway. What about Purity? Did you find her when you visited the Isle of Grass? Was she able to help you?"

"No," said Sorrow, sounding bitter. "I found only Purity's grave. The tales of an ageless witch who tormented the northern land proved only a myth."

"Those Skellings were pretty insistent that someone was stealing their women." Infidel stood up. The hammer glowed as she rose slowly into the air. She drifted over to the long beam of what had once been the mast of my sail boat, now straddling the branches of three different trees. I noticed for the first time the long, skinny roll of canvas lashed to the mast. Odd. I hadn't had sails rigged on the boat since I owned it.

She untied the rope and the canvas dropped into her hands. I noticed that the white cloth sparkled like it was coated with diamond dust... or frost. She unrolled the canvas above the deck and the Jagged Heart dropped, tip first, into the wood.

The harpoon stood there like a second mast, carved from a spiraling narwhale horn.

"Purity is supposedly stealing their women to build an army to look for this," said Infidel. "It's the Jagged Heart. Belonged to a friend of mine named Aurora. The Church of the Book stole it. I've made an oath to take it back."

"The ice ogres may not give you a warm reception," said Sorrow.

"I'm armed with a big hammer made of solid sunlight," said Infidel. "They won't give me any guff."

"I admire your confidence," said Sorrow. "But the northern realms are dangerous. Your quest may not be as simple as you think."

"I think it's a more realistic goal than wiping out the church and overthrowing all the kingdoms of the world."

Sorrow sighed, then turned back to my sea-chest and finally opened it. I could taste the clean odor of cedar in the roof of my mouth as she gingerly lifted the lid.

The contents were mostly intact. From my limited view, it looked as if a bottle of squid ink had broken as the boat had tumbled, but the damage was mostly to the items packed on the right side of the chest, where I'd kept blank parchment and writing material. Three quarters of the chest looked untouched by the spill, and this was where I'd stored a life's worth of maps and notes. Two life's worth, since at least half the material had been drafted by my grandfather, Judicious Merchant. Waves of nostalgia washed over me as Sorrow began to gingerly lift papers from the chest. Her eyes were wide with excitement.

"Marvelous," she whispered, as she unrolled a master map of the island. "Well worth my investment, if it leads me to my quarry."

"You know, I've been almost every place Stagger's been," said Infidel. "You might save some time if you just asked me for the location of whatever it is you're looking for."

"Perhaps. But you're unfamiliar with the witch nails in my scalp. You've never seen them before."

"So?"

"So I'm looking for more of them. And somewhere on this island, I believe I shall find the grave of Avaris."

"She'd dead? I thought she was still out there handing out magic powers to mean girls like Purity and the Black Swan."

"Those leads have proven elusive," said Sorrow. "The Black Swan denies any connection to Avaris. But there is another oral tradition that says Avaris once had a palace here on the Isle of Fire, where she commanded an army of witches, until they were wiped out by the Church of the Book. According to legend, this island is home to a vast graveyard of weavers. My study of witch nails is hampered by the fact that there are so few weavers left. Much of the knowledge I seek has been lost. My hope is that I will discover nails in the skulls of old weavers that will provide a template for me to take my studies further."

"Hmm," said Infidel. "Can't say I've heard about a witch's graveyard."

Sorrow flipped through the notebook in her hand. "Did Stagger have any sort of indexing, or organizational system?"

"Sure. If he thought it was important, he put it in the sea chest."

"This might take a while," Sorrow grumbled, as she looked at the reams of parchment.

"This might be a waste of time," said Infidel. "Stagger used to give me long, drunken lectures on pretty much every scrap of stone or bone we yanked out of the ground. He never said a thing about Avaris."

"He was older than you, correct? He'd explored the island before you met him."

"Yeah, but you didn't know him. Stagger was... uh... what's the word I want?"

"Loquacious," I offered, from my ghost cage.

"Chatty. Get a few pints in him and he wouldn't shut up.

I've heard about every damn rock he ever turned over in this jungle." She sighed, placing her arms across her chest in a way that looked almost like she was trying to hug herself. "By the sacred quill, he used to bore me, but it was worth sitting through an hour of meandering drudgery for the five minutes of brilliant wit that would suddenly spill from him. He'd make me laugh 'til my face hurt." She shook her head. "Now, I even miss the boring lectures."

"I wish I could have met him," said Sorrow. "I've heard he was the best authority on the secrets of this island."

Again, I appreciated the irony that Sorrow had stripped herself of the chance to have what she really wanted, which was a conversation with me. Of course, I would have disappointed her. I'd never found the legendary witch's graveyard. I took a little delight in knowing that the woman who'd imprisoned me had wasted her money buying my papers. There was nothing in those notes or maps that would direct her to Avaris.

Which isn't to say I didn't have some idea of where to look. I do know my history, after all. Supplement this with a little legend and rumor, and I knew where I'd start looking, based on three pieces of evidence.

Item One: The weavers had reached the peak of their collective powers five hundred years ago, during the rein of King Glorified Brightmoon. Ol' Glory, as he was called, vowed to wipe out all the witches in his kingdom, and commissioned a blacksmith to craft a weapon up to the job... the Gloryhammer. He entrusted the weapon to one of his best knights, Stark Tower, ancestor of Infidel's former fiancé. As impressive as the Gloryhammer might be, Stark actually took his duties so seriously that the had an even more dangerous weapon commissioned, an ebony sword called the Witchbreaker. This blade was said to be forged from iron stolen from the gates of hell. Anyone killed by the blade was instantly banished to the pits.

As you might guess from someone who felt the need for such a weapon, Stark took a no-nonsense approach to his job, and eventually people started calling *him* Witchbreaker instead of the sword. According to legend, he killed over ten thousand witches. He was allowed to keep any valuables his victims might have had, and if they had children, he had the legal authority to sell them into slavery. The Tower clan remains obscenely wealthy to this day.

Like any rich person, Stark liked to travel in comfort. When Avaris fled more civilized climes to set up shop on the Isle of Fire, it's said that Stark gave chase in nine ships filled with servants and building supplies and erected a castle for the duration of his stay.

Item two: The bay of Commonground is the only place on the island with a safe harbor for cargo ships carrying enough swag to equip a castle. Odds are excellent he would have built his home near the bay.

Item three: There are, in fact, several big stone ruins a few miles upriver from the bay that are sometimes called "the Knight's Castle." They're so close to Commonground, they're the first place every amateur treasure hunter strikes out for. I've done some poking around, but didn't waste much time because my grandfather's notes indicated he'd explored the place and found nothing. He also recognized, architecturally, that the walls were the work of middle period stone masons from the Silver Isle, not remnants of the Vanished Kingdom. He'd moved on to more fruitful targets deep in the jungle. But about a half mile away from the Knight's Castle there are some earthen pits grandfather noted as possible burial sites. He never made any notes about digging them up. I did a few test digs, but they didn't strike me as particularly promising. There were no headstones. The fate of Stark Tower is unknown; there's at least six different legends of how, where, and when he died. But if he'd been buried at these mounds, he almost certainly would have had a stone monument. I'd assumed the unmarked graves had been for his servants and slaves. But what if it had been where he'd buried his prey?

I strained to move my wooden limbs. Not long ago, this would have been exactly the moment in my thought process where I charged into the jungle with a shovel, a dozen flasks of rum, and my invulnerable best friend. I sighed heavily, then rattled the invisible bars of my ghost cage and shouted out a common four letter word for 'excrement.'

This triggered Menagerie, who'd been perched on the rudder. He hopped over to me and raised his left paw toward my gloved hand.

"I didn't say 'shake,'" I grumbled.

Infidel had turned her head when Menagerie went into motion. Sorrow, too, glanced up from the pile of papers she had spread out before her.

"Looks like your dog wants to practice his tricks. Though why he's trying to shake hands with my golem I have no clue."

"Twenty-four hours ago, whatever brains Menagerie had left had were squeezed into a tiny bug," said Infidel. "Cut him some slack."

Sorrow shrugged and looked to the sky. "No point in trying to make sense of this here."

"Golem?" said Infidel.

"Hmm?" asked Sorrow.

"You said Drifter is a golem?"

"Yes," Sorrow said.

"I took apart one of those a couple of weeks ago. It was made mostly of bone; Relic called it Patch. But, I had the impression he'd stolen Patch rather than making him. Was he your work?"

"If only," Sorrow said, shading her head. "My attempts at bone-weaving were where all my troubles began."

"I think your troubles might have started when you hammered nails into your skull in order to get back at your father," said Infidel. "But who am I to judge?"

Sorrow frowned deeply. "The avenues of the Silver City are lined with statues of men like the Witchbreaker, whom they praise for his wisdom and courage because it would be unseemly to openly recognize his true accomplishments, the mass slaughter of women who dared dream of a better world. I would gladly drive a hundred nails in my head – a thousand – for the power to set things right."

"You've got a ways to go," said Infidel. She looked like she was counting the studs; I had as well. Sorrow had six.

Sorrow closed the lid of the sea chest. She looped a finger-thick strand of copper trough the clasp and closed it into a solid ring.

"You see only the physical nails," said Sorrow. "Each weaver must master seven physical elements. Iron, copper, and glass are the simplest arts. Gold and silver are also highly valued, as mastery of these materials provides a life of comfort. There are very few fragments of glorystone large enough to craft a nail from, but a weaver who did so would be welcomed in the court of any earthly king. There are over twenty potential materials to master, but it was my intention to round out my five minerals with two spiritual transitions – wood and bone."

Her voice grew quieter. "Since the church has been ruthless in its suppression, I had no one to guide me on my sixth nail, one of bone. I later discovered that the codex I'd stolen to guide me had been deliberately sabotaged by the church. The irony, of course, is that if I had mastered bone-weaving, I could cure my physical ailments. I'd be healthy again, free of this half-crippled body."

"Can't you get another bone nail?"

"Yes. But I dare not move forward without the guidance of a more experienced weaver."

Sorrow turned to me and said, "Carry this chest to the *Freewind*."

"Why the *Freewind*?" asked Infidel.

"I've footed the bill for its services. I need a quiet place to rest and study Stagger's notes at my leisure. The master cabin isn't luxurious, but it will serve my purposes."

"You said I could have the ship! I've already got my stuff in the master cabin."

"I said you could direct the captain to sail you wherever you wished. You may still do so. I'm only using the master cabin as an isolated and safe place to study. I can return to the Isle of Fire once I've read these notes."

"Where am I supposed to bunk?"

"Where did you bunk when you were a mercenary during the Pirate Wars?"

"They'd set up bunks in the hold. But I wasn't pregnant then."

"I'm sure you'll find someplace comfortable to sleep," Sorrow said, with a dismissive wave of her hand.

By now, I'd picked up the sea chest. I'd never been able to lift it when it was full, but my wooden body flicked it from the deck as if it weighed no more than a pillow. I balanced it on my shoulder as I headed over the rail. The drunken feeling of the previous night was almost gone. The women's voices above me grew fainter as I climbed down the tree. Infidel sounded determined to keep possession of the cabin.

Eventually I couldn't hear their voices at all. Perhaps I was too far down the beach. Or perhaps Sorrow had won the argument. I knew she wouldn't back down; it was obvious to me that she was heading north in hopes of learning more about the mystery witch the Skellings were after. Infidel could be pretty stubborn, but she was debating a woman who practiced self-inflicted brain damage as a hobby. You can't win against crazy.

Two seconds later, Infidel flashed overhead, the Gloryhammer blazing before her, the Jagged Heart leaving a light trail of snowflakes in her wake. Menagerie flapped past a moment later, so close I could probably have jumped up and grabbed his tail.

I had nothing to lose. I shouted out, "Heel!"

Menagerie spun in mid-air, tracing a long, gliding arc back to me. He landed on the black sand I trudged across and fell into a loping pace beside me. With all four paws on the ground, his bird-like elements slipped into his larger mass and he was almost full dog again, save for a few stray feathers in his fur.

"Good boy!" I shouted.

He looked at me as if awaiting another command. I've always been indifferent to dogs. On this island, I'm more used to eating them than befriending them. But this dog had a bright look in its eyes. I liked him. I'd never cared much for Menagerie as a man. He was too cold and, well, mercenary, which was a shame, since I know that Menagerie was an avid reader, and under different circumstances we could have perhaps discussed books.

Suddenly I wondered if I was in the presence of a dog who might remember the alphabet.

"Make an 's'!" I said, in that high-pitched, overly enthusiastic tone one uses when talking with dogs. "Make an 's' in the sand, boy!"

Menagerie ran a little ways ahead, paused as if sniffing the ground, then pushed out a serpentine squiggle. If I'd had freedom to do anything other than carry the sea-chest, I would have jumped and clicked my heels. Unfortunately, I didn't even have the power to sway from my direct path toward the dock, so I stepped in the newly drawn letter. I couldn't even look back to see how much survived.

"Good dog!" I cried. "Now a 't'!" He did so. "An 'a'!" Unfortunately, I was walking fast enough that I couldn't see all the letters before I marched past them. I did see that the 'r'" at the end of my name looked almost like an 'n.'"

So my name was on the beach. Infidel was probably already back at the *Freewind*. Would Sorrow walk this way? Would she notice the letters? Would she think twice?

Despite my growing sense of futility, I called out five more letters before we reached the gangplank that led from the beach up onto the pier.

I turned at a ninety degree angle to ascend, and with what I hope was force of will but what might simply have been my body shifting to balance on the rickety boards, I glanced back down the beach. M-E-L-O-G – R-E-G-G-A-T-S, it read, upside down, or at least something to that effect.

Sorrow was nowhere to be seen.

But as I turned my gaze back to the docks, I held out the briefest glimmer of hope that Sorrow would soon know my name.

Which sounds a little ominous, now that I think of it.

CHAPTER SIX

STAGGERMANCY

IF THE RESIDENTS of Commonground were fazed by a driftwood man walking among them, they managed to hide their astonishment behind masks of utter indifference. Of course, many of these masks of indifference were on men who owned actual masks, robbers and highwaymen who eyed the sea-chest on my shoulders and pondered what it might contain. Fortunately, I was protected both by broad daylight and broad shoulders. My barrel-chested form no doubt discouraged the more cowardly thieves. The fact that I was accompanied by the world's ugliest dog may also have helped keep eyes from dwelling in my direction too long. I could hear Menagerie following at my heels, his webbed claws clicking as he loped along.

As I approached the far end of the pier, I spotted the *Freewind*. Brand was standing alone on the deck, looking around furtively, as if making certain no one was watching him. Seeing no eyes upon him (I was still some distance away), he waved toward some barrels on the dock. "Hurry," he called out, in a voice that was half shout, half whisper. A cloaked figure broke from behind the barrels and scurried up the gangplank to the ship. From the person's height, I assumed this was a pygmy, but the fine silk cloak might also have concealed a child or perhaps a petite woman. The cloak certainly looked like it belonged in a woman's wardrobe, embroidered with lacy floral designs.

Brand guided the short woman toward the hold, looking over his shoulder to see if they'd been spotted. He didn't see anyone looking at him, but I did. The *Freewind*, like many ships, sported a figurehead carved to look like a shapely woman. And I swear that it wasn't a trick of the light when the figurehead twisted from her bolted-on position beneath the bowsprit and peered out across the deck, her eyes narrowed as she watched Brand and his guest.

By the time I reached the gangplank myself, Brand and his visitor had disappeared. The figurehead slipped back into her rightful position. I trudged onto a deserted ship. The command that had allowed me the freedom to walk here wore off as I reached the middle of the deck. I stood there still as a statue. Menagerie came around and sat before me, looking up as if he expected a new command.

There was a noise off to my left. Menagerie turned his head as I strained my peripheral vision to see Brand climbing the stairs from the cargo hold. He appeared lost in thought, a bit worried. He again looked around to make sure the deck was empty. When he spotted me, his eyes bulged.

Five seconds of comic discombobulation followed as he jumped backward at least a full yard while reaching for his sword. He whipped the blade free from its scabbard in what would have been a jaw-dropping display of reflexes if he hadn't then dropped the weapon when he stumbled on a thick coil of rope and failed to keep his feet under him. He tumbled backward, but used his momentum to keep rolling so that he was carried back onto his feet. The sword had fallen across the coiled rope, and with a fluid motion he stomped the tip of his blade with the toe of his boot, causing the hilt to fly up to his waiting hand. He pointed the blade at me and shouted, "Halt!"

Of course, I was already halted.

This sank in a few seconds later, as Brand tightened the grip on his weapon and demanded, "Who are you?"

Who am I? I wanted to shout. *Who am I? I'm Abstemious Merchant, known throughout this bobbing metropolis as Stagger, grandson of Judicious Merchant, husband of Infidel, slayer of dragons! I'm an explorer of lost worlds, a scholar with a Brobdingnagian lexicon, and a connoisseur of fine spirits to boot. That's who the hell I am!*

Unfortunately, lacking a tongue, I could only glare at him with my pecan peepers.

"Could you at least growl at this guy for me?" I asked Menagerie.

Menagerie wasn't looking at me. Instead, his eyes were turned skyward. Long shadows rapidly stretched out before us.

Infidel shouted from about the level of the mast, "You can put the sword away, Brand. The big guy's coming with us."

Infidel landed on the deck with a solid thump. The harpoon was attached to her back with rope, jutting up from between her shoulder blades like a flagpole. She had three bright red skewers of grilled meat in her left hand. She tore off a chunk and tossed it to Menagerie, who caught it in mid-air and swallowed it with a single gulp.

She studied the dog intently for half a minute as he stared at her, his eyes begging for more. She sighed. "Dang. I thought he might turn into a monkey. At least part of one."

She tossed Menagerie another chunk, then tore into a skewer herself.

"Where is everybody?" she asked, her mouth full.

"Gale took her family over to the *Aggressive* to meet with Captain Dare. He's traveled the northern realms and can provide advice on navigating the coast of Qikiqtabruk in the dead of winter."

"I thought that Sage handled all the navigation," said Infidel, with oily chili sauce glistening on her lips like blood.

"Sage's powers work best if she knows what she's looking for. A map can save her hours of blind searching."

Infidel took a swig from the silver flask of coconut milk tucked in her waistband. "Sorrow said she's also been up north, so maybe she can help guide us as well."

"Ah. Then Sorrow does exist," said Brand. "On the voyage here, she shut herself into the stateroom the second she came aboard and took all her meals there. I never caught even a glimpse of her. Poppy says she's an aged crone with one dead eye and an iron claw in place of a hand."

"That's about right," said Infidel. "Except she just looks old; she's actually about your age. A shame, given your taste in older women."

Brand grinned. "Experienced women, you mean. Skinny little naïfs whose greatest challenge in life has been to decide what color ribbons to put in their hair bore me. Even if they're halfway competent in bed, their post-coital conversations are unfailingly vapid."

"Careful," she said. "I used to be one of those skinny little naïfs."

"I don't believe you," said Brand. "I've heard that you single-handedly took out one of Greatshadow's avatars by jumping down his throat and punching his brains out from the inside. I'm guessing that in the sack you must be equally bold."

Infidel's cheeks flushed. "I, uh... hmm. If you know about the dragons, you also know I can crush men's skulls like eggshells?"

"There are such rumors."

"Well, skulls aren't my favorite part of a man's anatomy to crush," she said.

Brand laughed, but it sounded forced to me.

At this point, I heard Sorrow's limping gait on the gangplank. With the iron brace on her leg, she was anything but stealthy.

"Now you get to finally meet her," said Infidel pointing toward the approaching witch with her last monkey skewer.

Though my back was to her, I could feel Sorrow growing closer.

Infidel said, "Brand, this is Sorrow. Sorrow –"

Sorrow raised her hand to cut Infidel off. "I know who he is. He's the captain's gigolo."

Both Infidel and Brand looked taken aback by her directness. Sensing she'd broken some unwritten social code, Sorrow tried to explain herself. "I'm sorry if I come across as brusque. I've many things on my mind at the moment. I don't have time for pleasantries."

"I'm guessing you're not interested in post-coital conversation either?" asked Infidel.

Sorrow furrowed her brow. "Are you... propositioning me?"

"By the Divine Author, no!" Infidel laughed. "You're not my type."

"So what is your type?" asked Brand.

Infidel sighed. "Tall, dark, and deceased." She tried to grin as she said it, but didn't quite succeed.

"I'll be in my cabin. Tell Captain Romer to see me there for her orders." Sorrow didn't look at me as she said, "Follow."

I followed. In desperation I called back to Menagerie, "Do something!"

But Menagerie didn't even turn his head. He was focused on the third skewer of monkey.

We went below deck, into the voluminous hold. The *Freewind* was small for a clipper, just under two hundred feet long, but the hold seemed especially large because it was especially empty. Most ships that had been in port more than a week would already be filled with cargo. I could only deduce that the bounty placed upon the *Freewind* was bad for business. What reputable merchant would place his cargo on a ship that the world's most powerful navies had sworn to sink?

Toward the rear of the boat, beneath the poop-deck, was a walled-off section divided by a narrow corridor. I followed Sorrow down this passageway. On each side were cabins filled with bunks. At the end of the hall was an oak door with brass hinges. It opened to reveal a small but tidy room, nearly thirty feet across but only about eight feet deep. I had to crouch to navigate beneath the broad ceiling beams. Sunlight spilled through portholes upon a bed large enough for two, a sturdy looking desk with an oil lantern hanging above it, and a table in the far corner with a large pitcher, a wash basin, and a chamber pot beneath it. The room was spotless, and smelled of furniture polish and fresh linens.

"Place your sea-chest by the desk," said Sorrow as she closed the door.

I did so.

"Go beside the table and fold yourself as small as you can manage. I've no need of you for now."

I sat by the table, folding my legs up along my barrel chest and hugged them with my driftwood arms. I found my obedience distasteful and humiliating. I hadn't enjoyed being manipulated by Truthspeakers as a child; I certainly didn't find the experience any more pleasing as an adult.

Yet, in my misery, there were two tiny flickers of hope.

Flicker one: For better or worse, I was still near Infidel. If Sorrow had decided to remain on the Isle of Fire while my wife sailed north, I would have been inconsolable. Flicker two: She'd said, *your sea-chest*. Had she meant only, "the sea-chest that you carry?" Or had she seen my message on the beach and now knew my true identity?

I waited. My world narrowed to the slight band of gleaming wood floor directly before me. With my head folded down, the rest of the room was blocked by the brim of my hat. I listened. Sorrow busied herself with settling into the room and sorting through the contents of the sea chest. After a time, Captain Romer visited the cabin.

"I understand you wished to see me, madam?" said Gale.

"I want you to tell me everything you can about the Skellings who attacked you," said Sorrow.

Sorrow listened intently, but I couldn't make out any details that Captain Romer added to the story that Infidel hadn't also covered. True, Infidel hadn't mentioned the sea-worthiness of the hide boats, and Gale went on about their construction at length, but I sensed that this wasn't information of interest to Sorrow.

The only follow-up questions Sorrow asked were about the witch.

"And the Skellings said that this witch was searching for the *Freewind?*"

"Not precisely. She's hunting for a magical artifact."

"Do you think there's a chance this ship will come under assault by her forces?" Sorrow asked.

"She might try," said Gale. "But on the high seas we can evade her. If you're truly concerned about avoiding her, I do have... options. May we speak in the fullest confidence?"

"Of course."

"When you hire the *Freewind*, you hire the fastest ship available for travel by sail. But, for an additional fee, there may be shortcuts that would trim our travel time and make us utterly untraceable."

"I know of these so-called *shortcuts*," said Sorrow. "I'd rather take my chances with an elderly witch than risk my sanity in the abstract realms."

"Of course, madam. Quite wise of you."

I was a little taken aback by the way that Gale was taking such a subservient role with Sorrow. Wanderers are known for their independence and freedom-loving nature. It seemed odd that the captain of a ship should be so obsequious. On the other hand, the one thing that Wanderers loved as much as freedom was money. Sorrow was no-doubt well compensated for building the Black Swan a new body.

If the rest of the world was no longer eager to hire the *Freewind*, I suppose I couldn't begrudge Captain Romer for bending over backward to make her remaining customers happy, but at the same time it didn't sit well with me. I've never treated a person differently based on the size of their purse. It mattered nothing to me if you were rag-picker or royalty. If you could tell a good joke and were generous enough to laugh at my attempts at wit, you were fit company to share a pint.

Perhaps it comes from having been raised by monks. Their vow of poverty took hold in me, even if their vows of faith, abstinence and chastity did not.

Sorrow concluded the conversation by giving orders about her meals. Captain Romer acknowledged them and left the cabin, thanking Sorrow for her business. Just as I learned a little bit about the captain by overhearing their conversation, I also think I learned a few things about Sorrow. It was easy to believe she'd been the daughter of a wealthy and powerful judge. I'm guessing she'd had a whole complement of cooks, maids, and butlers growing up. Perhaps she'd never been trained to be nice to the hired help.

Above me, I could hear Gale shouting out commands and Rigger responding. I was near the porthole. Perhaps due to my stillness, my wooden ears caught a whispered conversation that ensued as the sails rattled and flapped up the masts.

"I don't like setting sail with an empty hold." It was Mako's deep voice. "You shouldn't have been so dismissive of Captain Dare's offer."

Gale's answer was much more difficult to hear. "It's not enough that Levi betrayed us? Now you question my judgment?"

"I'm not Levi," said Mako. "I'm just saying –"

"I know what you're saying. But Dare's splitting hairs. He won't take a cargo of slaves, but he'll gladly fill his hold with the shoddy food stocks the slavers purchase in order to feed their human chattel. We've sacrificed too much to engage in such compromises."

"By your logic, any cargo in the world is unacceptable," Mako said. "Most of the iron ore and the coal used to smelt it comes from mines worked by slaves. Are we never again to accept a load that includes steel? Every golden moon in the Shining Land is stamped with the image of a sovereign who supports the slave trade. Are we to refuse these coins for our future wages and be paid only through barter?"

Gale answered, but her words were lost as the ship groaned. The sails had caught the wind and the ship began to gently roll as she headed from the harbor. I wished I'd been above to see our departure. Clippers sport more sails than any other ship, making an impressive sight when all their canvas is unfurled. Also, I welcome all opportunities to expand my vocabulary, and the sailors I've known over the years have filled my head with terms like *spankers, flying jibs* and *mizzen topgallants*. I'd enjoy the opportunity to finally make sense of all the terms and figure out which of the thirty-plus sails was which.

Of course, from the sound of things above, I doubt that any of the Romers would have found the time to explain their jargon. A clipper this size normally set to sea with a minimum crew of twenty, and the Romers numbered seven – eight, if you counted Brand. Even with their magical talents, I imagine they had no time for a lubber like me to be wandering around the deck.

Further shouts drifted through the porthole, enough to catch Sorrow's attention. She went to the small window near me and peered out.

"That didn't take long," she mumbled.

From the shouts above, I gathered that the *Freewind* had been ambushed the second it sailed from the harbor onto the open ocean. Out here, the rules that made Commonground a sanctuary no longer applied. I wanted to ask questions about the nature of the assault, the number of ships, how close they were, etc. At the very least, I would have liked to stand and look out the porthole. It was not to be. Instead, all I know is that the winds grew ever stronger. The sunlight through the portal brightened, and above the splashing of waves I heard a thunderous crack, like lightning splitting a tree trunk.

Sorrow chuckled. "Infidel's not half bad with that hammer."

There were further cracks. Finally, Sorrow turned away with a shrug. "That's that," she mumbled. The shouts from above had a decidedly celebratory tone. I had the feeling we weren't being chased any more.

Sorrow settled at her desk. She opened a page of a fresh notebook and a new bottle of ink. As I tuned out the noise above deck, I heard the faint scratching rhythm of her quill racing across paper, trapping thoughts into words.

Lulled by this familiar noise, I dropped into memory. Since

becoming a ghost, I'd not slept or dreamed. I never grew weary. I had no eyelids to close if I wished to sleep. But now, my wooden body felt, well, wooden. Heavy. It possessed a gravity that weighed down my thoughts. I was lulled by the sound of waves washing against the hull as we swayed across the sea. The muffled shouts of Romers in the rigging sunk into my seedpod ears, sounding not of this moment, but of some long distant past. Murmurs layered beneath whispers lay beneath the pulse of water, like a heartbeat, my heartbeat, so familiar after such a long absence.

Thus, for the first time in death, I found myself perched upon the precipice of sleep...

...then, slowly, I drifted free. My ghost fingers slipped loose of my knot-root hands as if they were oversized gloves. My legs twitched and came loose of their wooden counterparts and it felt good to wiggle my toes freely once more. I craned my neck, pulling free of my coconut mask. I was loose! I rose, my spirit spilling from the boundaries of its wooden cage.

Then I stopped short.

Silver wires still jutted from my phantom flesh.

I grabbed them and tried to yank them free.

Something yanked back, hard and fast, and I was pulled into the wood, into the barrel chest, shrinking ever smaller until I was tiny enough to be fit into the golden cage, then smaller still as I passed into the belly of the silver mosquito.

Though I must have been no larger than a flea to fit in such a compact space, I felt whole. And, indeed, I still looked whole; the curved silver surface of the interior of the mosquito's belly reflected me perfectly. I looked just as I had when Infidel and I escaped the spirit realm after confronting Greatshadow. I was wearing the black boots and pants Zetetic had conjured for me, as well as the ridiculous red velvet cape, though it was now mostly in tatters. I was bare-chested; in the spirit world, I'd given my shirt to Infidel to replace her own shredded clothing.

I touched a jagged hole in my belly. This was my fatal wound, inflicted by my own knife.

And of course there was the knife.

I reached under the cape to my hip where the bone-handled knife was slipped into my belt. The knife was plain looking, simple, but elegant in its match of form and function. It had been my grandfather's hunting knife; the blade was eight inches long and sturdy, with a pattern in the metal almost like fingerprints, where the steel had been folded in on itself a dozen times as a skilled blacksmith had worked in carbon to temper the edge. The hilt was a single length of yellowed bone; only after death had I learned this was dragon bone. The natural magical resonance of such beasts had trapped my soul within the weapon.

I was a ghost imprisoned in the belly of a jeweled mosquito. But how many ghosts had knives?

I rushed the wall, stabbing the silver. I laughed as my blade sank through the foil skin. Cutting through the mosquito's metallic hide was no more difficult than cutting through the hide of a wild boar, something well within the scope of the blade's intended purpose. In moments, I'd cut a flap in the side of the artificial insect. The mosquito didn't protest as I pushed my arm through, followed by my head and shoulders. In another moment, with quite a bit of kicking and struggle, I'd worked myself loose of my silver prison.

But not quite free. I remained locked inside the golden cage. Worse, silver wires still hooked into my flesh. Tentatively, I grabbed the wire hooked into my left thigh. I took the knife and sliced the wire in twain.

Then screamed.

Then screamed some more.

It was the worst agony imaginable. It was as if a knife had been stabbed all the way into my thigh bone and was now twisting, digging at the marrow. I gritted my teeth to resist the pain, and tried to breathe deep breaths. In desperation, I retrieved the loose wire from the gilded floor and placed it back in contact with the length of silver line hanging from my leg. The metal ends flowed together. Instantly, the acute pain turned to welcome numbness.

I limped to the cage wall and slid down, my back to the bars as I struggled to catch my breath, until I remembered that I didn't need to breathe. I was acting purely on instinct. Calmness settled over me. I looked out beyond my gilded cage, to the barrel chest in which this strange artificial heart was suspended.

Hmmm.

It struck me as curious that, having bound my spirit to this mosquito, she'd then sealed the mosquito inside a cage. I walked back toward the insect. In relative size, it loomed over me like an elephant. Viewed at this scale, the craftmanship was even more remarkable. I could now see the tiny bolts that fastened the leg joints, and the tightly coiled iron springs, far finer than a human hair, that powered the gold foil wings. The faceted eyes were made of glass lenses flickering with rainbows as I walked around them, gathering up the silver lines in my hand.

Sorrow's powers were over gold, silver, iron, copper, glass, and wood. There was gold on the bars, the mosquito was largely silver, with iron springs and copper wings and glass eyes. The wood was the larger form, the golem itself.

What did it all mean?

This may seem like a curious statement from a ghost, but I really have never thought much about the supernatural. Yes, my life was awash in magic. My best friend could jump over buildings, I'd been raised in a religion where I regularly witnessed men editing reality with their words, and I hung out on a daily basis with shape-shifters and ogres. I had no propensity toward skepticism, but I also never bothered to try to learn any magical arts. None even intrigued me. The art of truthspeaking I found morally reprehensible; the art of deceiving was difficult to unravel from the art of driving yourself insane; blood magic was an excellent avenue for contracting hideous parasitic diseases; and elemental magic was a good way to draw the unwelcome attention of dragons. I followed few rules in my unruly life, but "don't annoy dragons" was one I faithfully obeyed.

Zetetic had told Aurora he'd become a deceiver after studying forty different types of magic and finding all of them to be valid, even if the underlying premises contradicted each other. Aurora had protested that they couldn't all be true. Her fundamental assumptions about the structure of the universe were completely contrary to the fundamental assumptions of Father Ver, for instance. She'd said that some things must be false if other things were true, and asserted that it couldn't be both night and day at the same time.

"Unless the world is a sphere," Zetetic had answered.

He'd also said, "All truth is local."

I think Zetetic's point was that magic works because people believe it works. Magic flows from human faith. Maybe I wasn't well educated in existing systems of magic, but if all magical systems were just the product of the mind, could I create new one? It wasn't as if I was completely ignorant of magical thinking. I'd spent years of my life with my nose wedged between the pages of books. I'd learned a lot of symbolism in my studies. Did my current prison have some symbolic significance?

The mosquito was obvious. It's a widespread belief that blood contains the soul. Ordinary mosquitoes drink blood, so spiritual mosquitoes drink spirit blood. As for the cage, well, a cage is a cage. It holds creatures against their will.

What about the materials? Gold was easy. It symbolized perfection and wealth, but also greed. Was I trapped by a golden cage because I was greedy? At first I shrugged off the notion. Money never meant a damn thing to me. But were there other aspects of greed I was overlooking? Certainly, booze had been a weakness in life. I'd been more than willing to steal it, and when I wasn't stealing it directly, I was stealing other people's possessions and selling them to keep the precious elixirs flowing.

Of course, before I could ever escape my golden cage, I had the more immediate problem of losing these silver wires running through me. Silver commonly symbolized purity and innocence, but also sagacity and lies. Old men with silver hair are respected for their wisdom; smooth liars are said to have a silver tongue. The children of wealthy men are said to be born with silver spoons in their mouths.

It's impossible to think of wealthy men and not think of King Brightmoon, ruler of the Silver Isles. If he wasn't the wealthiest man alive, he was certainly in the top five. The moon is often associated with silver. The most common coin in the world was a small disk of silver ringed with gold, minted by the king's treasury, and commonly called a moon. Infidel, King Brightmoon's daughter, was named Innocent, and she has silver hair. I respect her for her purity and innocence, despite knowing that the woman I've grown to love is merely the adult mask of a damaged child.

Could the silver somehow represent her? Was I trapped here by my love for Infidel?

It seemed at once self-evidently true and also obviously false. I had no evidence the silver mosquito had been designed to capture me; I had the impression it had been looking for any old ghost it might find. I was probably over-thinking this.

But could over-thinking lead me toward a magical art?

All the magicians I'd ever known had spent their whole lives in the study of a single concept, elevating it in importance above all else. I've witnessed some pretty amazing results; Ivory Blade, for instance, and his somnomancy, rending the veil between the dream realms and our own to give life to nightmares. It was a little late for me to start studying dreams, or to seriously puzzle out the aspects of the various elements that bound me like some amateur alchemist. But I'd spent my whole damn life trying to understand myself.

If all truth was local, could I somehow understand myself so fully that I could alter my local truths and be free?

I chuckled ruefully.

"Great," I said, my voice tiny in the vastness of the wooden barrel. "I'm placing my hope in Staggermancy."

CHAPTER SEVEN

SEA OF WINE

"WAKE!" COMMANDED SORROW.

I lifted my coconut head, feeling groggy. Had I been sleeping? Had my shrinking to explore the silver mosquito and golden cage been only a dream? The room was now dark. How long had I been out?

"Rise," said Sorrow, just as the ship shuddered strongly enough to throw her from her feet, slamming her into the oak door. The room had seemed immaculate before, but the impact was enough to raise dust hidden in the crooks and crevasses of the wooden beams and planks. Sorrow coughed, raising her hand to cover her mouth. "We're under attack!"

I stood, trying to make sense of the noises coming from every direction. The whole Romer family was shouting at once. A dog was baying as if there was a full moon. The timbers of the ship groaned and popped. Above all this, I could hear a woman's voice shouting. It wasn't Captain Romer; whoever it was had a thick accent I couldn't quite place. The only words I was certain she'd shouted: "...Ivory Blade!"

Sorrow braced herself against the door as she climbed back to her feet. "You're not to try to communicate with anyone. You're forbidden to write! Beyond these restrictions, take whatever actions are needed to defend this ship, its crew and its passengers!"

I nodded, acknowledging the command. I glanced toward the desk and the overturned bottle of ink. I clenched and unclenched my fingers. To be expressly forbidden to write must be the ultimate tonic for writer's block. If a quill had been thrust into my hand at that moment, I could have written volumes.

Sorrow threw herself onto the desk, stretching across it to reach her bed, tossing aside a pillow. She drew a yard long shaft of pitch black iron from between the mattress and the wall.

"If we face who I believe we face, a sword will prove mightier than a pen. Fight with all the savagery you can muster. Infidel's life may be at stake."

She handed me the iron shaft and I saw that it was indeed a sword, no doubt forged by her own fingers and drawn to a razor-sharp double-edge.

"Make haste!" she cried.

I threw open the door and lumbered into the narrow hall. All the cabins were open and the Romer girls were sitting in their bunks, looking only half awake. The last door in the hall jerked open, revealing Captain Romer's quarters. Gale leapt into the hall, her tangled, sweaty hair fastened behind her neck with a scarlet ribbon. In the shadows of her cabin, I could see Brand's blond hair bobbing as he struggled to pull on his boots.

Gale hadn't bothered with boots; she was barefoot in her cotton britches, and her billowy blouse was only tied together across her breasts. The captain bounded up the stairs to the deck in two leaps, drawing her cutlass. I gave chase, though my bulky form slowed me in the tight hall. I nearly fell as the ship lurched once more. The timbers didn't so much groan now as scream.

I emerged behind Captain Romer, who'd skidded to a stop on a deck slick with frost. It was night, as I'd guessed. Every lantern that hung in the rigging had gone dark, their flames extinguished beneath ice at least an inch thick coating everything in sight. Of course, "in sight" was somewhat limited by the pale fog that hung in the air, narrowing the world to a circle about twenty feet around me. The only light came from Captain Romer's cutlass, which gave off an eerie phosphorescent glow.

Before us, on their knees, were the frozen bodies of Jetsam, Mako, and Rigger, Gale's three sons, their faces locked in silent screams beneath a sheen of ice. I'd seen this magic before.

Aurora had frozen more than her share of unruly patrons at the Black Swan, and the magic seldom proved fatal. Victims of this spell were simply shocked into unconsciousness by the sudden blast of cold, then held upright by their rigid ice exoskeletons. As long as they were freed before they suffocated, the three Romers would likely survive.

I could no longer hear Menagerie howling. I spotted a lump curled on the deck behind Mako's bulky form that might have been a frozen dog, though it was difficult to tell given the fog, the dim lighting, and the limits of my monochrome vision.

We were surrounded by at least two dozen women. At first they appeared to be frozen just as the Romer boys were, since they were coated in ice. But, at a second glance, I saw that the ice was instead shaped into armor and swords. They were plainly conscious, staring at us with narrowed eyes, their breath coming out in gusts of fog. Their lips and cheeks were very dark; beneath their semi-transparent armor, none of them were clothed. It struck me as a rather uncomfortable way to go into battle. Not that they were going into battle just yet; they were merely standing, ice blades at the ready, as if waiting for a command.

"Captain Romer, I presume?" said a woman's voice from just beyond the fog.

"What have you done to my sons?" Gale demanded.

"They are not yet dead," the voice answered. Slowly, from the fog directly before us, a trio of figures emerged. In the center was a woman also in ice armor, but unlike the others, her ice was pale white rather than clear, concealing her body. She wore a cloak of white fox pelts, and carried a sword made of jagged, bubble-filled ice in the shape of a crescent moon. I'd seen this particular ice before; it was the same substance that tipped the Jagged Heart.

Flanking the woman were two creatures like nothing I'd ever seen. My years of association with Menagerie had given me a decent knowledge of scores of beasts from lands I couldn't dream of. Somewhere in his travels he'd encountered rhinos and cobras and wolverines, or at least gotten hold of their blood. But given Menagerie's fondness for big, toothy predators, I can't believe he wouldn't have added the monsters before me to his arsenal if he knew about them. They looked like a cross between a gorilla and a grizzly bear, walking upright, with snow-white pelts, long arms ending in dagger-claws, and gaping jaws filled with fangs.

I was vaguely aware of the Romer sisters climbing the stairs behind me. Sage was clever enough to bring a lantern with her, which greatly improved the lighting, though not my sense of dread. The pale light made the riggings look ghostly.

Infidel hadn't put in an appearance yet. Had something happened to her? Or was she just taking her time getting dressed?

Captain Romer studied the woman in the white fox cloak. "Who are you? You obviously want something from us. State your demands."

"I'm known as Purity," the woman answered. "I've come for Ivory Blade."

Captain Romer frowned. "Ivory Blade isn't on this ship. He hasn't been a passenger of mine in three years, in fact."

"There's no time for your lies," said Purity. "Blade stole the Jagged Heart from us only months ago. He shielded himself from my seers with his somnomancy, but in his hunt for Greatshadow he's let down his guard. My most trusted seer has fixed her sightless gaze upon his armor, which is aboard this very ship. I've no quarrel with you or your family, Captain Romer. Give us Blade and we shall let you live. Defy us, and I shall command the ice sheet that has locked your ship within its unbreakable grasp to crush the hull of the *Freewind*. You're three hundred miles from the nearest shore, a long way for even a Wanderer to swim. Not that you'll have a chance to try. Long before your ship is torn apart my yetis and ice-maidens will finish off everyone aboard. Are you so loyal to Blade that you'd sacrifice your family?"

Captain Romer's face was completely neutral. She couldn't turn over Blade if she wanted to. But she also knew that the Jagged Heart was down below, wrapped inside a sail, and this was what Purity was looking for. The only reason to find Blade was to find the harpoon.

"Thank you for your offer," said Captain Romer. "You've made what I'm sure you feel is a fair bargain, trading my family and ship for a notorious spy who is doubtless guilty of the theft you're charging him with. I see only three small obstacles to making a deal with you."

"And these are?" asked Purity.

"First, Ivory Blade isn't aboard this ship. Second, were he aboard, it's against my code to traffic in human lives. And, third, you're mistaken in thinking the *Freewind* is trapped by ice."

Purity chuckled. "I understand your confusion. These are the tropics, after all. But the Ice-Moon Blade is a conduit for the elemental power of Hush. I could freeze a thousand earthly seas with its frigid touch."

"No doubt," said Captain Romer. "But the *Freewind* is known as the fastest ship upon the waves for a reason."

"What does your speed matter now?" asked Purity. "You've been taken by surprise. Don't you understand? Your ship is already icebound. The sea has been frozen for half a mile in every direction."

"No," said Captain Romer, kneeling. The ice sizzled as her sword of phosphors touched it, boiling away a saucer-sized hole to reveal the wooden deck. She placed her bare hand upon the burgundy wood. "You see, there is no ice upon the Sea of Wine."

And suddenly the sky was a violent amber-red, streaked with clouds, like a sunset seeping from every point on the horizon. The fog was gone and the chilly air banished by a blast furnace of hot, humid air. The ship rolled as it rose upon a wave and the sails above us snapped in the sudden breeze, cracking the ice that coated them. All around us the sea was full of blood-dark swells topped with amber foam; the scent of wine filled my mouth, stirring old thirsts.

"We sail an abstract realm where Hush does not dwell," said Captain Romer, her eyes locked upon Purity. "Here is my bargain: Free my sons and surrender, and I shall put you ashore upon a deserted isle when we return to the material world. Defy me, and I'll have you keelhauled in the Sea of Wine. Whatever hell you may believe in, this fate shall prove a hundred times worse."

"Hush," said Purity, which at first I took for a command, but then understood to be an invocation. The crescent-sword glowed like the moon and the temperature dropped noticeably as a beam of pale light flashed toward the captain. She jumped straight up, grabbing the riggings, sending a shower of melting ice down upon me as she flipped her legs up from the path of the ray. Instantly, my world dimmed as a thick sheet of ice formed on my body. I'm certain, had I been human, the shock of the cold would have incapacitated me. Instead, I simply punched myself in the face with a fist of roots and knocked the ice free.

The Romer girls joined their mother in the riggings as the ice-armored women lurched forward like zombies. It looked like the time for chatting was over and the time for hitting things had begun.

I've never been a brawler; usually, when a fight breaks out, I either hide behind Infidel or run for the nearest exit. But, after who-knows-how-long of being trapped in this wooden body, I welcomed the opportunity to let out some frustrations. I was conflicted, however; I've enough chivalry in me to feel bad about hitting a woman, even though Purity was obviously the leader of the opposition. Fortunately, I was spared from my squeamishness by being pounced upon by one of the yetis. My barrel ribs cracked as he knocked me to the deck. His slathering jaws rushed toward my face, but I shoved my left arm between his teeth before his jaws could fully close. I felt pressure, but no pain. More importantly, though this beast likely outweighed me by half a ton, I was strong enough to push him back. Remembering that I had a sword in my free hand, I stabbed the beast in the side of its skull. To my shock, the iron blade punched straight through the monster's temple and came out the other side. Its eyes rolled up in its head as it collapsed upon me.

Despite my strength, I had little leverage to push the beast off, and as imposing as the yeti looked, its shaggy hair proved to be as soft as lamb's wool, and it apparently survived the artic cold by being built largely of blubber. On top of this, the deck was coated with ice, which completely robbed me of traction. At least half a minute passed as I fought to rid myself of the dead weight. When my head was at last free, I was confronted by a horrible sight. Every last Romer daughter was frozen in the rigging, completely immobile. The second yeti had leapt into the rigging and was giving chase to Gale, who retreated ever higher, toward the crow's-nest.

All around, the ice-armored women were watching the battle above. Purity appeared displeased by their lack of initiative. "Mindless fools!" she shouted. "Don't just stand there! Go below! Bring me Ivory Blade!"

The woman nearest the hatch turned just in time to find a knife flying from below deck. The blade came to a sudden halt between her eyes. As she fell backward, Brand jumped onto the deck, a leather belt holding a dozen throwing knives slung over his shoulder. He ducked and rolled with impressive speed as Purity shot a freezing moonbeam in his direction, popped up to his feet six inches clear of the ray, and let loose with a carefully aimed blade, a thin one, almost a dart. The slender knife hit the gauntlet of ice Purity wore on her sword hand and slipped between the joints at her knuckles. She sucked in air as the Ice-Moon blade slipped from her grasp.

"Protect me!" she shouted, as the women lunged to form a human wall between her and Brand. The others closed in on

Brand, looking cautious, unsure who he'd next target with the blades he held in each hand.

Then, from the hatch, came the last person on earth I expected to see. When the mane of silver-blonde hair first thrust above the deck, I thought Infidel had at last joined the fight. Instead, a dwarf waddled onto the deck, dressed in a wig and a feminine cape, wearing dark lipstick and heavy rouge. The dwarf wore plate armor, polished to a mirror gleam, the breastplate fashioned to resemble actual breasts. Under the bizarre female attire, I recognized my old friend Bigsby, the fishmonger. He was armed with a mace, also polished to a silvery finish, which he brandished as he stepped between Brand and the advancing warriors.

"Back!" he shouted, in a falsetto pitch. "Lay down your arms or face the wrath of Princess Innocent Brightmoon, daughter of King Valiant Brightmoon, champion of the faithful!"

"You tell 'em, Sis," said Brand.

A yeti hit the deck inches before Bigsby, knocking him off his feet, and a moment later, Captain Romer dropped onto the beast's chest, driving her phosphor blade deep into his gut. The beast yowled in pain, but wasn't dead. He snatched the captain by the nape of her neck and flung her skyward, on an arc that carried her out over the waves of wine. Brand again proved to have reflexes like a cat, as he grabbed a coil of rope and tossed it on a path that would intercept Gale. The rope went abruptly taut just after she fell out of sight.

Before Brand could reel the captain in, both he and Bigsby suddenly went rigid as a sheet of ice coated them. Purity was now holding the crescent blade in her left hand, which, in hindsight, was pretty much exactly what I would have done if I'd been her. I finally managed to kick myself free of the dead yeti and rose to my feet. I was the sole defender left standing.

And then there was light. The sky that had once been sunsets in all directions suddenly had a single sun as Infidel shot up from the hold, racing high above the crow's-nest to survey the scene.

"Am I too late for the festivities?" she shouted down. "This damn armor has, like, two hundred buckles."

"Ivory Blade!" Purity shouted, raising her weapon overhead. "You've taken what's rightfully mine!"

The enchanted blade glowed. I sensed she was about to fire a freeze ray at Infidel, who had never mastered ducking. So I grabbed Bigsby by his frozen arm and threw him. He caught Purity dead in the chest and she went down hard.

The yeti Gale had stabbed was back on his feet, bleeding profusely. He turned to me with baleful eyes. I glanced down at his brother, who still had my sword jutting from his temple. Before I could bend to grab the blade, the yeti lunged toward me, jaws open wide, claws outstretched.

With a flash of light and a loud *WHAP!* the yeti vanished. Infidel was standing in front of me and the yeti was a diminishing speck hurtling out over the waves. The ice-maiden minions raised their hands to shield their eyes from the luminance of the Gloryhammer, which left them completely vulnerable as Infidel danced forward and began launching them over the sides of the boat one by one. A few landed near the ship. As they sunk beneath the waves, I swear they were laughing. It was a sound I knew well, the sound of my own laughter when I was completely sotted and everything tragic in the world was rendered comic.

I had no time to ponder the effects of the enchanted sea. Purity was rising again, sword in hand once more. Having run out of dwarves to fling, I decided it was time to put aside my aversion to punching a woman. I charged across the deck, slush splashing beneath my oversized boots. The ice coating was melting in the warm air of the Sea of Wine; indeed, Mako was now almost free of ice, and I was certain I heard him groan as he fell to his knees. Bigsby had all his ice knocked off of him by the impact, and he was dragging himself toward his platinum wig. Not having retrieved my sword, I balled my gloved root into the tightest fist I could manage and let loose with a savage right hook, clocking Purity in the jaw. Her ice helmet proved sturdy, and didn't dent or crack from the impact. I'm certain I would have killed her otherwise. As it was, her eyes lost focus, the Ice-Moon Blade slipped from her hand, and she went down, limp.

I rubbed my knuckles, not because my hand hurt, but because I'd watched Infidel do the same gesture a thousand times and it seemed perfectly natural. I heard movement nearby and spun around. There was an ice-maiden charging toward me, sword brandished high overhead. I caught her in the gut with a solid kick that shattered her armor, and she folded to her knees, vomiting on my boots.

I felt sick to my own stomach, despite, technically, not having one.

I glanced around the deck. All the intruders were down; Infidel and I were the only people left standing. Cinnamon, up in the riggings, began to slip from her frozen perch and Infidel flashed toward her, catching her just as she fell. In seconds, Infidel had peeled the remaining frozen Romers from the ropes and brought them to the deck. By now the ice that remained in the sails and riggings had turned into a rain. Water ran off the frozen figures on the deck in great rivulets. The air echoed with people sucking in gasps of air as the ice covering their faces fell away.

I wanted to run to Infidel and hug her, to let her know I was still with her, but this lay beyond the scope of the freedom Sorrow had granted me. Fortunately, I was free to help protect the crew, so I knelt beside Mako and brushed off his remaining ice. He shivered uncontrollably, but seemed okay. I moved on to Brand. I freed his face in short order, and he sucked in air through chattering teeth.

"Everyone on this deck will survive," a female voice said behind me. "You must save my daughter."

I turned around. The nude woman who served as the figurehead for the ship had somehow crawled up from beneath the bowsprit to stand before me. Although *stand* may not have been the right word, since she didn't have feet. She was a ghostly form, floating, looking almost solid enough to touch from her breasts up, but with the rest of her composed of mist so fine it would likely have been invisible if the bright glow of the Gloryhammer hadn't made it shimmer.

"That horrible woman below told you not to talk," the figurehead said. "But you're not the only ghost upon this ship. I'm Jasmine Romer, Gale's mother, and the first captain of the *Freewind*. My spirit is now locked within these timbers. Unlike you, I've chosen my fate."

I was frustrated that I couldn't ask for further details. Not that there was time for palaver.

"My daughter drowns within the Sea of Wine. You're her only hope. The inebriating spirits cannot harm your wooden form. Save her!"

I loped to the railing where Gale had gone over. The rope was now completely limp. I looked down. It's uncanny how, in large quantities, wine can look just like blood.

"Where's your boss?" Infidel asked me as she helped Sage back to her feet. Sage was only fifteen, and had looked small when I saw her next to Rigger, but she was a good three inches taller than Infidel.

I wish I could have at least shrugged to answer Infidel's question. Sorrow hadn't cared enough about the outcome of the fight to help defend the ship in person.

I bent over the railing, listening. I could hear laughter, a drunken, high pitched guffawing. I scanned the waves and spotted Captain Romer far out in front of the ship, not where I'd expected her to be at all.

"I'm bringing the ship back around!" Jasmine called out to me. "Prepare to jump!"

Gale's drunken laughter grew louder as we lurched across the waves. I pulled up the slack rope that trailed in the water and wrapped the end around my wrist. As I did so, the captain's laughter suddenly died off. I looked down and saw only a single hand, stained amber, as it sank beneath the waves.

I leapt, leaving my tri-corn hat hanging in the air. I wondered if my wooden body floated. It was called 'driftwood' for a reason. Luckily, I didn't need to test my seaworthiness for long. I practically landed on top of Captain Romer, her body limp as I wrapped my free arm around her. The line around my wrist snapped taut, and I wondered just how much force it would take to tear my arm free of my torso. Fortunately, Sorrow's handiwork proved suited to the task. My arm held, even when my body slammed into the hull of the ship.

I was beneath the surface. Captain Romer's head bent backward as I gazed down upon her, her jaws slack, small bubbles rising from her lips. I'd heard that Wanderers had a pact with Abyss, the primal dragon of the sea, that guaranteed they would never die from drowning, but his pact apparently didn't extend to – how had Sorrow worded it? – the *abstract* realms.

Far below, I saw a light; I think it was Gale's phosphorescent sword tumbling ever deeper, growing fainter. For the most fleeting instant, I swear the sword came to rest upon something pitch black, undulating, serpentine, and vast. A sea monster? Whatever it was, the sword slid from its back and vanished into darkness. Whatever I'd glimpsed was free to move about without my ability to track it.

It was well past time to leave. Though it was utterly graceless, I placed Romer's limp belly against by crotch and wrapped my legs as tightly as possible around her hips. With both hands free, I dragged myself up the rope, in yard-long lunges. In a few seconds, I was above the surface. Instinctively, I tried to breathe. Captain Romer displayed no such instinct. As I made my way slowly to the deck, she didn't cough, or even twitch.

By the time I reached the rail, a half-dozen arms reached over to grab at us. Mako and Brand both looked fully recovered from their ordeal, and as they lugged me over, Sage and

Jetsam grabbed their mother and pried her free of my leg-lock. Menagerie was back on his feet, or paws at least, and Bigsby had recovered both his wits and his wig, and was currently tying Purity's arms behind her back. Infidel, I saw, had taken possession of the fallen Ice-Moon Blade. Her enchanted armory was growing rather impressive.

I found my way back to my feet and looked around for my hat. I spotted it near the bow. I reached it, but before I could bend over, the ghost of Jasmine Romer once more materialized and lifted the hat from the deck, offering it to me.

"Well done," she said.

I wanted to shake my head, but couldn't. I could make no attempt at communication due to Sorrow's command, but I was certain that Gale was dead.

"You're troubled, young spirit," she said, her voice growing soft. "You spotted it, didn't you?"

It? Was she talking about the sea monster?

"The beast that tracks us is Rott," she said with a sigh. "The dragon of entropy and decay. He passes freely between the material world and the abstract realms. He is the only truly universal elemental force."

If I'd been able to speak, I would have asked if there were a dragon of taxes. But, considering that her daughter was dead, I was grateful that my lack of voice spared her from my tasteless humor.

"Do not think that, by surviving the death of your body, you've cheated Rott for long. There is no true immortality. Things fall apart, even things that are only the memory of things. In the end, entropy will devour us all. We risk destruction any time we traverse this realm. But, for now, you've brought my daughter another day, at least."

As she said this, I heard coughing behind me. Captain Romer was flat on her back, her arms flailing limply as she spat up wine. Mako and Rigger flanked her, and Jetsam was at her feet. Suddenly, her eyes snapped open and she let loose a high-pitched shriek that devolved into laughter as she kicked Jetsam hard in the chest and let loose with twin uppercuts that caught Mako and Rigger beneath their chins. She sprang up as they went down. Her motions were exaggerated and woozy, but she landed on her feet and managed to snatch up a belaying pin from the pin rail. She brandished the improvised club as she shrieked, "I'll kill the lot of you!"

She let loose a fierce growl to give weight to her threat, but mid-way through her her growl changed into giggling.

"I'm on it!" shouted Infidel, flying across the deck in a single hop to land in front of the drunken captain. She said firmly, "Put the club down! You know who I am, right?"

"Infidel," Gale laughed, before unleashing a haymaker punch with the belaying pin. Infidel blocked the blow with the shaft of her hammer. Gale attempted a kick, but Infidel dodged by jumping a yard into the air and hanging there.

Suddenly a gust of wind howled across the deck, catching Infidel and throwing her back. She tried to spin in the air to take control of her flight, but succeeded only in turning her face toward the foremast as she raced toward it. With a sound like a butcher's mallet pounding a slab of tough meat, Infidel slammed into the wood. The Gloryhammer was left floating in the air as she dropped to the deck, blood pouring from her temple.

CHAPTER EIGHT

INADEQUATE VESSELS

FOR THIRTY SECONDS, pandemonium reigned. Mako and Jetsam tackled their mother as she cursed, giggled, and got in a couple of good licks with the belaying pin before being dragged down by their weight. A dozen ropes snaked toward her to snare her thrashing legs, until violent winds pushed them back. Cinnamon rushed forward, dodging her mother's kicks, crouching to place her hand on the bare skin of her mother's midriff. Gale's drunken giggles cut off in mid-breath, replaced by gagging. Her limbs went limp as all color drained from her face. Jetsam released his mother's arm and leapt skyward, kicking to gain altitude as she began to projectile vomit the wine she'd swallowed. Now too sick to command winds, Gale was quickly wrapped by Rigger's ropes. Even after she'd emptied her stomach, Gale continued to spit, trying to rid her mouth of whatever foul flavor Cinnamon had inflicted upon her.

Meanwhile, Bigsby jogged across the deck, holding his wig on with one hand, as he stretched his other hand toward the Gloryhammer, which hovered in mid-air six feet directly above Infidel's fallen form. "I claim the holy power that is my birthright!" he cried as he used Infidel's butt as a trampoline to leap for the hammer. Bigsby's jump was a good six inches short of his target. Please note that I do not, in anyway, place the blame on the springiness of my wife's derriere, which I assure you is more than adequate. He landed on the deck, hard, his plate armor clanging, and was pushed to his belly by a snarling dog with wings. Menagerie had finally recovered from his chill.

I moved toward Infidel, who lay limp and unconscious on

the deck. I wanted to kneel and investigate her injuries, but this simple act lay outside the range of freedom that Sorrow had granted me. I couldn't even motion for one of the Romers to come to her aid.

To add further to the distractions that kept Infidel from getting help, one of the ice-maidens recovered her wits and leapt to her feet just then, grabbing Sage from behind. Sage looked curiously unworried as the ice-maiden pressed a sword against her throat and shouted, "Jabber jabber jabber!" This might have been a threat in her native tongue, but on this boat all it meant was, "I'm an idiot! Kill me!" Her request was carried out a heartbeat later by Brand, who sank one of his throwing knives deep into the orbit of her left eye.

Rigger neutralized the threat of further ice-maidens waking by having every rope in sight come to life and bind their hands and feet. His brow was furrowed in concentration, his lips pressed tightly together. Despite the heat and humidity of the Sea of Wine, his lips were nearly blue, and his limbs were visibly shaking beneath his black uniform, soaked with icy water.

Sage shouted, "Poppy! Go get Rigger a blanket before he freezes to death!" She ran to Rigger's side. "We have to get him out of these freezing clothes."

"We're all drenched," said Poppy, who was also shivering. "Why aren't you telling him to get me a blanket?"

"If Rigger gets sick, the *Freewind's* all but crippled," said Sage. "The rest of us are expendable."

"No one's expendable," Mako said. He'd already pulled off his soaked shirt and boots, and his muscular body had shaken off the effects of the cold. "Bring blankets for everyone, Poppy."

Meanwhile, Jetsam had also gotten over his chill, perhaps because of the exertion of swimming through the air around the now limp sails. He dove down from near the tip of the mainmast to land beside Bigsby. He dropped to his knees and grabbed the fallen dwarf by his cheeks.

"Who are you?" he demanded as he drew his dagger.

"Whoa, whoa, whoa," Brand shouted, holding up his hands. "It's okay. She's with me!"

"Only if she's a stowaway," Jetsam said, shaking his head. "We officially have two passengers aboard, and she's not one of them. And why are we saying *she*? She's plainly a *he*!" He snatched Bigsby's platinum locks and shook them before the dwarf's face.

"I am too a she!" Bigsby screamed, grabbing Jetsam's sinewy wrist and twisting to no avail. "I'm Princess Innocent Brightmoon!"

"It's true," said Brand. "She's my sister. I'm Prince Steadfast Brightmoon!"

"You're both mad," said Jetsam, rubbing Bigsby's makeup off with his sleeve.

Now it was Mako's turn to join in the confrontation. He grabbed Brand by the throat and pushed him against the mast. I noticed for the first time that Mako's fingers were webbed. He pushed his toothy face inches from Brand's pale blue eyes and snarled, "You're no prince! You're nothing but carnival trash! Your looks and charm may have reduced my mother's wisdom to that of a teenage girl –"

"Hey!" shouted Sage. Poppy had returned with a heavy wool blanket, which Sage draped over Rigger's skinny shoulders.

Mako continued: "I took care to learn everything there was to know about you once you became our dryman. Before you turned up in Commonground, you traveled the Silver Isles as a member of the Slinger Carnival. You were the show's knife thrower."

Sage glanced at the dead ice-maiden who'd tried to take her hostage. "You've got to admit he's good at it."

"Not so good that he could survive on the income from his act. My sources say his true gifts lay as a pick-pocket."

Brand gave a surprisingly natural-looking smile for a man on the verge of having his windpipe crushed. "You only know I'm a pick-pocket because it was part of my act. I would always return what I stole. I'm no thief, and I'm not 'trash' simply because I traveled with a carnival. I joined them because I was searching for my long lost sister who had been magically transformed into a dwarf. Dwarves frequently seek employment with carnival freak shows. It seemed like a good place to look."

"I'll admit I've heard stranger stories," Jetsam said, spitting on his captive's face as he wiped away the last of the rouge and mascara. "But this can't be the lost princess. This is Bigsby, the Fishmonger! I recognize him now that he's not painted like a tart. He's lived in Commonground since before I was born!"

"No!" Bigsby sobbed. "I've always been Princess Innocent! I only appear to be an old, ugly dwarf due to a witch's curse!"

There was a loud sigh from the hatch. Sorrow's head was just above deck. "Witches get blamed for everything," she grumbled. She climbed the rest of the way up the stairs and looked around. Her brow furrowed at the sight of all the semi-nude women bound on the deck. "The missing Skelling women, I presume?" She nudged a yeti with her boot. "That pelt should bring a nice price."

"We've captured their leader, no thanks to you," said Mako, taking his eyes off Brand, but not his grip. "What was so important you couldn't help save the ship?"

"Excuse me?" Sorrow said. "It wasn't my job to fight them. You're getting paid to protect your passengers. I thought you Wanderers understood contracts."

"If these ice-maidens had killed us all, I'm sure that you could have waved the contract in their faces and made them understand the error of their ways," Mako said.

"But they didn't kill you all, or any of you, as far as I can tell. Anyway, your charge that I did nothing is baseless. Perhaps you failed to notice the seven-foot-tall wooden golem who fought by your side?" She knelt and yanked my sword from the yeti's skull. "Catch," she said as she tossed me the blade, and I caught.

She looked around at the sky.

"And would someone care to explain why we're no longer in the material world?"

"No," said Mako. Then, with his meaty hand still clamped on Brand's throat, he turned to Rigger and Sage. "We're trapped here until Mother recovers. The two of you keep your eyes peeled for any trouble. We've sent many an enemy to the Sea of Wine, and I'd hate for them to show up now."

"If they do show up, there's nothing we can do," said Rigger, shaking his head sadly. "Without Mother, there's no wind."

"If there's no wind, no ghost ships can come hunting us," said Sage, trying to sound positive.

"They could have row-boats," said Jetsam.

"I'm taking mother to her cabin," said Mako. "We can do nothing but wait for her to sober up." He turned toward Jetsam, and Cinnamon who stood nearby. "Take Brand and the dwarf below and place them in manacles. Ordinarily I'd keelhaul a stowaway, but the dwarf is plainly insane. I'm not going to punish a man for losing his mind."

He tightened his grip on Brand's throat as he brought his face close and smiled. It was a smile from a nightmare, saw-toothed and twice as wide as it should have been. "As for you, I haven't figured out your game. I should just rip out your throat for helping conceal a stowaway."

"Ma will tan your hide if you kill her dryman without asking permission," Jetsam said as he guided the dwarf toward the hatch. "Remember how mad she got at Levi?"

"I'm not afraid of Ma," Mako said. "But I'll wait until she sobers up before deciding this scoundrel's fate."

He stepped back as Cinnamon moved forward and took Brand by the hand. Brand's mouth suddenly puckered.

"You'll go below and play nice or my sister will put a taste in your mouth that will have you cutting out your own tongue. Understood?"

Brand nodded.

Satisfied that Brand was neutralized, Mako walked toward

Purity, unconscious on the deck where Bigsby had hogtied her. "Rigger, since she's bound, use your power to guide her down to my cabin. Once Ma's tucked in, I'll see to it that this witch is stripped of her armor and properly disarmed."

"You'll do no such thing," said Sorrow.

Mako raised his eyebrows. "With my mother incapacitated, I'm captain. The safety of this ship is my responsibility."

"That is not in dispute, but I don't care for your tone. I fear that you mean to abuse this woman in her helpless state."

Mako's face twisted into a snarl. "Choose your words with care. I've won't stand here and take your baseless slander."

"And I'll not stand by as a defenseless woman is strip-searched by a lone man, no matter what his reputation."

"I can help," said Sage. "Though I assure you she'd suffer no abuse if Mako were alone."

Sorrow nodded. "This is acceptable. But search her and bind her properly so that she doesn't lose any limbs to gangrene. Gag her so that she may not speak. Don't interrogate her until I can properly construct iron bands of negation to baffle any delayed magic she might seek to trigger with her words."

"Good call," said Sage. "There's something strange about her. Her internal light is all indigo."

"You can see auras?" Sorrow asked, sounding surprised.

"I see lots of stuff," said Sage, shrugging.

"How long will it take you to construct these bands?" grumbled Mako.

"As long as needed," said Sorrow, now kneeling next to Infidel. "It's not something that should be rushed. Something that must be rushed, however, is treatment of this woman's injuries. This wound on her temple will require stitches." She looked up at me. "Drifter, take her to my quarters. Bring the hammer. Its light will prove useful."

As the various Romers vanished down the stairs with their captives, I grabbed the Gloryhammer in my gloved hand. Not having any convenient place to carry it, I improvised and shoved it down the back of my shirt. I knelt and scooped Infidel into my arms. I lifted her as a groom lifts a bride across a threshold, although whatever romance the moment may have held was negated by the two inch gash on the side of Infidel's head that gushed blood with every heartbeat. Praying that Sorrow could mend Infidel's wound, I stepped onto the staircase and descended once more into the dark hold.

SORROW'S LIPS WERE pressed tightly together as I arranged Infidel on the bed. Sorrow removed her cape and hung it on the back of the door, then pulled the front of my shirt open. The Gloryhammer along my spine was powerful enough to push beams of sunlight through the gaps in the barrel staves that formed my chest. The gore on Infidel's brow glistened with the illumination.

"Who knew you'd make such a convenient lantern?" Sorrow asked as she slid a towel under Infidel's head. She went to the table in the corner and washed her hands in the basin. She then brought over the pitcher of water and a second towel and began to clean Infidel's wound.

"As you may suspect, I've some experience tending to scalp injuries," she said. "They always look worse than they are."

It took only a moment to dab away the blood. Sorrow then produced a razor and scraped away a few fine hairs that extended down from Infidel's scalp. She swabbed the area with clear fluid from a small bottle – vodka, from the smell of it. Infidel's face clenched, despite her unconscious state.

"This wound isn't so bad," said Sorrow. "But I must work fast. She may wake soon. Move one step to your left."

I did, as Sorrow turned Infidel's head so that the light fell directly on the gaping flesh. I wondered for a moment if I was seeing bone beneath the gash, but it was all just amber on amber to my wooden eyes. Sorrow produced a silver needle that looked too large for the task at hand. I expected her to thread the needle, but instead the metal came to life, wriggling like a serpent, stretching and tapering until it was as thin as a hair before plunging into Infidel's flesh. The silver filament rose and fell, rose and fell, moving through the torn skin as if it had a will of its own. In less time than it's taken me to tell it, it reached the end of the wound and tugged itself tight. Sorrow dabbed her handiwork with a fresh corner of the towel and wiped away what blood had bubbled up during the procedure. Now that the skin was clean, no further blood seeped through. Infidel's wound was neatly stitched together, the silver thread so fine as to almost be invisible.

Finished with her work, Sorrow turned back the bed's linens and commanded me to place Infidel beneath them. With her injury turned away from me, my wife looked as if she was merely sleeping.

Going once more to the basin, Sorrow washed her hands. Without looking at me, she said, "You're forbidden to injure me or in any way seek to take revenge. Should anyone attempt to harm me, even Infidel, you're obligated to defend me."

I nodded.

Drying her hands, she crossed back to the desk. She lifted one of my notebooks, my favorite one, actually. I used a lot of different materials for writing. Parchment, made of old animal hide, is fine to write on, but the pages are thick, so you don't get many pages in a book. There's also papyrus. It's the cheapest writing surface available, just flattened reed mats woven together by river pygmies. It's a pain to write on and it falls apart with use, but you can buy more than you can carry for the cost of a pint of ale. And then there's paper; the Church of the Book manufactures this sacred material at a remote nunnery on the Isle of Apes. Supposedly it's made of ground-up trees boiled in nun's urine impregnated with spices. This seems an unlikely recipe, though Wanderers who trade with the island tell me that the fumes from the nunnery make their eyes sting five miles out to sea, so who knows?

Paper is smooth, white as cotton, and thin enough that a book barely an inch thick can have a hundred flexible, yet durable pages. Its main drawback is that it's expensive as hell. The only reason I own so many notebooks made from paper is that most knights and priests of the Church of the Book own them. A steady stream of these people have flowed to Commonground over the years to kill the woman I love. They'd failed their quests, but succeeded in supplying me with good writing material.

The notebook on the desk had belonged to a church assassin who called himself Penumbra. He'd attacked Infidel with shadow swords, blades that could hurt her even when she was invulnerable. So it had been a particular pleasure to loot his backpack and find this notebook. It was sturdy, bound in black leather, yet compact, just five inches across and seven inches tall. It had fit nicely in my jacket pocket, and except for ten pages of coded notes at the front that I'd never figured out, the rest of it was blank. When I'd gotten it, I'd been so enamored that I vowed I would write something special within its pages, an epic poem, perhaps, or my own authoritative history of the Vanished Kingdom that would replace my grandfather's famous book as the epitome of scholarship.

Seven years later, no pen of mine had ever marked the notebook, though Sorrow had now filled another ten pages with her looping, elegant script. Turning beyond the last page she'd written anything on, Sorrow cut a blank sheet loose with the razor she'd used to shave Infidel's temple. She folded the paper into a long, tapered wedge, flattening it out, then turned toward me. It looked a bit like an origami snake that had been stepped on. She stood on tip-toes to place the paper sculpture between my gaping coconut jaws, then used silver thread to sew it into place, or so I assume. I couldn't see what she was doing, obviously, but the sound of a silver needle punching through paper and coconut husk has a rather distinctive rasp within the confines of a hollow skull.

When she was done, she stepped back and said, "You may now speak."

"Really?" I asked. If I'd had eyebrows, they would have shot up. I *could* speak! Sort of. "Is that me?" I said, cringing at hearing the words. "I sound... funny."

"Don't be ungrateful," said Sorrow. "You're making words without lungs, throat, palette, teeth, or lips. You have only a paper tongue that vibrates to approximate the noises you would have made in life. You should be amazed at the cleverness of my craftsmanship, not critical."

"I sound like a squirrel playing a kazoo," I protested, though no tone of protest came through. I could neither shout nor whisper; all the sounds coming from my paper tongue were of roughly the same volume, which wasn't terribly loud. On the other hand, if anyone had come aboard the *Black Swan* with a squirrel that played a kazoo, I would have paid money to see it. Perhaps Sorrow was right; the fact that I could make recognizable words at all was a thing worthy of note. When had I become so jaded?

"I saw the letters on the beach. You're Stagger. These are your notes."

"Yes," I said, then nodded toward the bed. "And this is my wife. Will she be okay? Why hasn't she woke up?"

"Infidel was sound asleep when the ice-maidens attacked; I could hear her snoring in the cabin next door. Her body was already primed for slumber. It's too soon to worry."

"It's never too soon to worry," I said. "And It's not just her I'm concerned about. According to the Black Swan, she's pregnant with my daughter."

"The Black Swan is a manipulator of the highest order," said Sorrow. "I would place no faith in what she says unless there's a written contract involved, and then you should read every last word of the fine print."

"Now that you know who I am, will you set me free?"

"You're valuable to me," said Sorrow. "I invested a

tremendous amount of time and effort in creating a soul-catcher. I'm not prepared to throw that away. Besides, you were an unbound spirit when I found you. It was only a matter of time before you faded away to nothingness. You can last much longer now that you're embodied again."

"You said I would burn out."

"It's true. Your life energy isn't infinite. But this was true before you were captured as well. For now, it is to the benefit of both of us that you occupy this form."

I wasn't certain of this. I'd enjoyed my freedom as a ghost, the ability to flit around as I pleased, my thoughts instantly translating into movement. On the other hand, this new body did have a tongue. I desperately wanted to talk to Infidel.

"Fine," I said, crossing my arms. "Having a body again, even this clunky wooden one, isn't completely unwelcome. But from now on, I'm not your slave to boss around. I'll work with you as an equal partner."

She snorted. "You're in no way my equal, ghost. *You* are the echo of a drunken tomb-looter whose life's work amounts to a few hundred pages of barely legible notes. *I* am a master of fundamental materials, driven to remake the world. A century from now, you will be completely forgotten, while I will be remembered as the woman who freed humankind from the authoritarian clutches of a wicked church and ushered in a new age of enlightenment and equality."

I laughed, or tried to. My paper tongue turned it more into the sound of sneezing.

"Are you amused?" asked Sorrow.

"For someone smart, you're remarkably ignorant of the word 'hubris.'"

"This would apply to me only if I felt confidence in excess of my capacity," said Sorrow. "I assure you, I never fail at my goals."

"You have a self-inflicted hole in your head that's killing you," I said.

She frowned. She looked ready to change the subject. Glancing back at the maps spread on the desk, she asked, "Do you know where to find the Witch's Graveyard?"

"Maybe," I said. "There are folk legends and intriguing place names that provide clues. I can't make any guarantees, but give me half a day and a pick-axe once we're back in Commonground and I can probably root out the truth."

"You can draw me a map?" she said.

"Already drawn," I said, motioning toward the desk.

"Show me. You're free to move as you wish, though I do not release you from the command to save me from harm."

I walked to the pile of documents and pulled the corner of a sheet of parchment jutting out from beneath the stack. It had a purple ring on it from where I'd sat a bottle of wine while discussing the map with a potential buyer at the Black Swan. I tapped a roughly sketched rectangle next to the ring. "This place is called the Knight's Castle. It's a complex of stonework a few miles upriver from the bay. It's been picked over pretty thoroughly, but there is one noteworthy feature, several hundred yards off the main complex. It's overgrown with trees, but when I surveyed the land here" – I took a quill from the ink bottle and drew an X at the western edge of the castle – "there are several acres marked by evenly-spaced, rectangular depressions. No headstones, but even without them, it looks exactly like a graveyard where all the coffins have disintegrated, letting the soil collapse down into the graves."

My 'X' looked a little barren. So I drew a circle around it, then jotted 'Witch Graveyard' above it. Those words looked lonely, so I wrote beneath them, 'Treasure!'

"The embellishment isn't necessary," said Sorrow.

"Sorry," I said. "Old habit. In the dry spells between finding actual relics, I supplemented my income by selling maps to treasure hunters from the Silver Isles. I saw a steady stream of barbers, barristers and haberdashers who'd run away from their boring lives and demanding wives to get rich quick by looting the Vanished Kingdom. Nearly all my customers got themselves killed during their first week in the jungle, so repeat business was lousy."

"Couldn't the hollow depressions be evidence the graves have been dug up?"

"There would be mounds next to the depressions. This is just gut instinct, but I don't think anyone's dug there because the area's kind of boring. Every year or two somebody stumbles over a vine-covered temple housing idols with jade eyes and golden earrings. The folks who built the Vanished Kingdom weren't noted for doing things small or subtle. Treasure hunters would rather hack away vines from a hundred mounds of boulders hoping to find an old temple than take a shovel to unmarked graves where everything has probably rotted."

"The nails I'm seeking wouldn't rot," said Sorrow.

"Why not? Bone rots. Wood rots. Iron rusts. I guess the gold and glass might survive a long time underground."

Sorrow gave my arguments a dismissive wave.

"You know little of the higher arts of weaving."

"I know damn little of the lower arts, for that matter. Considering that the church has pretty much wiped out your kind, I think I can be forgiven a little ignorance."

"While I've perfected the manipulation of the material world, within limits, there is self-evidently more to the known world than matter. This ship currently sails in one of the abstract realms."

"I know a little bit about abstract realms," I said. "They're like dream worlds, only shared. They form the foundation of somnomancy."

"I would dispute this," said Sorrow. "Somnomancy isn't a distinct magical art in my opinion. It's more akin to the reality manipulation of the deceivers, only the somnomancer is being lied to by his unconscious mind. The abstract realms, on the other hand, are real, unless you believe we are dreaming now."

"Do you have any convincing evidence that we're not?"

"Don't try to play games with me. I've no patience for such things. My body weakens with the passage of each day; each heartbeat is like a grain of sand through an hourglass. I'm keenly aware that death waits for me if I don't reverse the damage to my body."

"And your plan to save yourself is... abstract nails?"

"Avaris is said to have possessed a nail of time. Imagine the power to being able to sculpt and mold seconds and moments to your will! I thought the Black Swan possessed it, but her skull was unblemished."

"What would such a nail look like? How would you even hammer it in?"

Sorrow sighed. "Sensible questions. I don't know. I'm hoping to gather clues from context when I finally discover the skull of an ancient witch."

"If I weren't a walking, talking pile of driftwood, I might be inclined to call you crazy."

"I'm not crazy," said Sorrow, clenching her right fist. "I'm mad. Mad at my father, mad at the church and the damned Divine Author. I'm mad because I see the world as it truly is, not as the veil of convenient and comforting illusions everyone else embraces. I'm mad to be facing this fight alone."

I shrugged. "You could try being nicer to people. Commonground is full of people who have grudges against the church. Hell, a lot of people probably have grudges against your father personally. You could probably make some allies if you weren't so, uh... um... intense."

"You were about to say 'bitchy.'"

"Maybe."

"My father is blunt, demanding and stubborn. People call him a great leader. Yet when I display these same qualities, I'm dismissed as a bitch."

"Please note that I did avoid the word," said Stagger. "Twenty years ago, the execration would have crossed my tongue with barely a thought. But I've heard Infidel called a bitch a thousand times, when her greatest sin has been that she is insufficiently fearful of men who enjoy being feared. If you must fuss at me, please focus on things I actually say."

"My apologies," said Sorrow. To my surprise, she sounded sincere. "Perhaps I'm overly defensive. I've survived as long as I have by being suspicious of everyone."

I sighed, though my paper tongue turned the sound into the buzz of fly wings. "I'm really not your enemy. I couldn't care less if you wish to wage war against the church. I live in Commonground because it's one of the few places on earth where the church has no power. Hell, that's pretty much why everyone who isn't a Wanderer or a pygmy comes to Commonground. A lot of them would probably cheer you on."

Sorrow's shoulders sagged as she shook her head. "In some circumstances, the enemy of an enemy can be a friend; for me, the enemies of my enemies almost always prove to be unreliable scoundrels who view me as an easy victim."

Part of me wanted to pat her on the back and say, "There, there." She sounded lonely and worn out, and I'm a man with an excess of empathy. On the other hand, given that she had enslaved me and showed no inclination toward releasing me, my empathy could only go so far.

She rubbed her eyes. "I need to sleep. It will be hours before Captain Romer has recovered from her excursion into the Sea of Wine. I'm interested in learning how we got here. I assume Mako knows more than he's telling."

"I have a few insights. I saw Captain Romer lean down, touch the bare wood of the deck, and announce we were sailing the Sea of Wine. I also know from talking to Wanderers in the past that the Sea of Wine is sort of a gateway to their afterlife. If she dies, do you think we'll be trapped here?"

"She won't die," said Sorrow. "And don't think of our situation as trapped. We're in the safest place imaginable at the moment. We don't have to worry about assault by the

Judgment Fleet, pirates, or Skellings while we're here. We're the only living things upon these waves."

"But maybe not beneath them. I saw... something... lurking beneath the ship. A big, black serpent." I was hesitant to say all I knew. I didn't want to accidentally reveal the ghost of Jasmine Romer to Sorrow.

"Abyss, perhaps? The primal dragon of the sea has a pact to protect Wanderers."

"I don't think so. I've seen Abyss. He's more of a giant turtle. This thing was covered in big black snake scales."

"Hmm. That fits the description of Rott," said Sorrow. "It would be appropriate that the dragon of decay would dwell here. Wine is a product of rotting grapes, after all."

"That's a terrible thing to say about one of my favorite beverages."

"I appreciate wine not for its flavor but for its inspiration. Destruction is the precursor of creation. Perfectly good fruit when crushed and allowed to molder releases something new and precious. I would not be so eager to bring the kingdoms of the world to ruin if I didn't believe something far more vibrant would emerge."

"You're not going to be overthrowing anything if Rott gets a sudden whim to swallow this ship."

Sorrow shrugged. "If he does, he does. Some things are too big even for me to worry about. For now, it looks like Infidel will get to use the stateroom after all. I'll go sleep in her bunk."

"Where should I go?"

Sorrow shrugged again. "Stay by her side, if you wish. For now, I release you of all restrictions save the command to protect me."

She opened the door, took her cloak, and left.

I was alone with Infidel, who had turned onto her side and was hugging her pillow. Her sleep now looked more natural than it had when she'd first been tucked in. I had renewed hope that she would recover fully.

If I'd been a courageous man, I might have woken her.

Now that I had the freedom to speak to her, I knew that I couldn't. Between her quest and her pregnancy, she had enough worries without having to concern herself about my fate. And yet, there was still so much I wish I'd told her when I was alive.

I went to the desk, to the notebook with its neatly trimmed page cut to build my tongue. At least a hundred sheets of blank paper remained. This book had always looked so pristine and promising that any words I'd contemplated filling it with had seemed unworthy to stain its pages. Now, at last, I had a message deserving of its snow white fibers.

I took the book and the bottle of ink and crouched as I left the cabin. The Romer men were arranging their captives in the hold. Many of the ice-maidens had been taken alive, and we now had quite a cargo of prisoners.

Above deck, the sky was the same unchanging omnidirectional sunset. The waters had grown still, and the sails hung limp in the quiet air. The ice was nearly gone, leaving only a few puddles here and there.

I moved to the bow and sat cross-legged, placing the book before me. I steadied my ink and quill.

Dearest Infidel, I began. *It is a great injustice upon my part that I have spent so many years in your company, pen and paper always at hand, and somehow failed to write you a love letter. Yet fate has granted me the chance to atone for this oversight. Perhaps the Divine Author is a romantic after all.*

And so the words flowed, page after page, as I spoke of my hopes and confessed my regrets, and told her of my love. My normally opulent vocabulary faded as I wrote, as my language turned simple and sincere. Perhaps, in their simplicity, I even managed to capture some truth, though I fear that words will ever be inadequate vessels for the cargo of emotions. Yet on I wrote, undaunted, placing heart to paper in a setting that, while strange, was also familiar. In death as in life, I felt at home adrift on a Sea of Wine.

CHAPTER NINE
THE VESTIBULE OF SELF-ABNEGATION

I HAD NO way to measure the time I spent writing. My body no longer possessed the natural rhythms of weariness or hunger, and the unnatural sky gave no hint of the passage of time. I filled twenty pages with my scratchings. My wooden fingers were numb instruments, so my clumsy cursive was a mess of smears and smudges. The only saving grace was that, for the first time in memory, I was writing completely sober. My lines of script were attractively parallel, rather than undulating serpents that sometimes overlapped one another.

It's possible I could have kept writing until the book was filled. I'd moved on from singing the praises of Infidel's virtues and was now discussing the future, specifically our unborn daughter. Infidel and I were both from a culture where women were regarded as inferior and subordinate. Infidel, born a princess, had less freedom than the most humble baker or candle-stick maker in the Silver City. Men were allowed to own property; women were allowed to be property.

Commonground, for all its anarchistic freedom, was little better. While it's true that an exceptional woman like the Black Swan could become a powerful force, and strong women like Infidel and Aurora were essentially free to live as they wished, the reality was most women in Commonground survived as whores. The notable exceptions, of course, were the Wanderers. Of all the various societies throughout the long string of islands sometimes called the Shining Lands, only among the Wanderers was there a true sense of equality between the sexes. I suppose it rose both from their professed belief in individual freedom and the practical realities of their lives. They lived as close family units on boats. Even in traditional homes on land, women frequently are the true masters of a household, the ones whose decisions are treated as final by the children, while the men serve mainly as enforcers of the women's will. On land, women are mostly trapped within their own houses, kept busy raising children and cooking meals, while men are free to roam about and engage in commerce and spend their relatively plentiful free time plotting wars and forming governments. Among the Wanderers, the men are just as confined to the ships as the women, and when it's time to visit a neighbor, the whole household moves as one.

Yet I did not wish my daughter to become a Wanderer. Wanderers fancy themselves travelers and explorers, visiting a hundred ports a year, citizens of the world. In truth, they seldom stray more than a few hundred feet from their boats, and never set foot on land. Casting anchor in Commonground is a pale experience compared to exploring the jungles of the Isle of Fire. The view from a crow's-nest is not the same as the view from atop a mountain. For all their vaunted freedom, the Wanderers were curiously self-imprisoned.

I wanted my daughter to be boundless. I wanted her to stride the world with the knowledge she was equal to anyone, able to freely look into the eyes of kings or paupers, without looking down upon either. Infidel had spent much of her adult life reacting to the fears drilled into her as a child. I made my life choices haunted by the shame I'd experienced as a boy abandoned by both of his still-living parents. I look at Sorrow and I see her childhood bitterly seeping out of every pore. Could a human be raised free of fear, shame, or bitterness? Free of greed, pride, or privilege? Was I already dooming my daughter to failure by wishing such a utopian upbringing upon her?

My musings were shattered as a scream tore from the hatch.

"Hurry," a woman's voice said beside me. I looked up and

once more found myself staring at the imposing naked breasts of the ghost of Jasmine Romer. "My daughter isn't in her right mind. She'll hurt herself, or others, if you don't stop her."

I closed the book mid-sentence without waiting for the ink to dry. I stood, just as Mako leapt up the stairs onto the deck, blood streaming from his nose.

He bent backward to avoid a dagger that flew by his head, then did a handspring back to the railing before bouncing into the rigging. His mother climbed to the deck half a second later, with Sage locked in a stranglehold beneath her right arm. Gale was wearing a modest cotton nightgown, white but blood-spattered, and her hair, normally woven in a tight braid, hung loose around her face, showing the gray streaks within it. Sage was a little taller than her mother, with an athletic build, but she was either holding back out of fear of hurting her mother, or Gale simply had more experience as a brawler. No matter how Sage twisted to escape, Gale kept her forearm tight across the girl's throat. I moved toward the fight, hoping I could keep Gale from killing her daughter.

Before I reached her, Gale let go of Sage, throwing her roughly against the mast. Sage sank to the deck, looking dazed. Gale cried, "I gave life to you all, and I can take it! The next hand that touches me I'll cut off, I swear!"

Since she had no sword currently in hand, her words were probably bluff, but her half-strangled daughter and bloodied son looked hesitant to test her. I ran toward her, arms outstretched. She turned to face me. My wooden legs weren't built for stealth, but I leapt from fifteen feet away with more than enough strength to fly the distance. Her reflexes well-honed, she leapt from my path, but I clipped her legs with my outstretched arms and we both fell to the deck. My wooden fingers clamped onto her ankle. She pummeled me with her fists and scratched at my wooden face with her nails as she screamed, "It's hopeless! All hopeless! Let me die!"

I shifted my bulk to pin her legs. Tears streamed down her

cheeks as her limbs lost strength, her frantic motions devolving into spastic tremors. "By the seven stars, it's over! *All over*. Can't you see the dread doom that pursues us? Better to drown in the wine than to be chewed in the maw of such a beast!"

"What beast?" I asked, startling both her and myself with my squeaky, buzzing voice.

She sobbed. "It's no use. Oh, my vanity! I thought I could steer this ship between the teeth of destruction. I thought mine was the hand upon the wheel of destiny. But there is no wheel!" She choked as snot and mucus bubbled from her lips. "There is no wheel!"

Her face was drenched with sweat and mottled by dark red patches, as if stained by wine.

"She's completely mad," Sage said, rising on wobbly legs.

"It's delirium tremens," I said. "She's been poisoned by alcohol. She's hallucinating!"

"What can we do?"

Sadly, I knew. While I'd never been so far gone that I'd been unable to tell reality from dreams, I'd lived the last ten years of my life with a subtle tremor that seized my hands on those rare moments when I'd been completely sober. There was only one treatment.

"More wine," I said. "Or something stronger. It's her only hope."

"You want to cure her drunkenness with more drink?"

"It's the only thing that can help once you start seeing hallucinations!"

"But what if she's not hallucinating?" asked Brand, who practically made me jump out of my wooden skin as he spoke only inches from my ear. His head had popped up from the hatch leading to the hold. "Can't you smell it? The air has shifted. The wine is being replaced by vinegar."

Mako growled as he glared at Brand, "Who freed you? You were in manacles just moments ago!"

"Please," said Brand, rubbing his wrists. "If you know about my circus past, you also know I did escape work. Plus, your mother likes to, um, play games. This wasn't the first time I've worn those shackles. Once you've seen the key, picking a lock is child's play."

Mako snatched the dagger his mother had thrown at him from the mast. "You insolent bastard! I'll kill you!"

But as he raised his arm to strike, a thick rope snaked down from above and caught his wrist. "Calm yourself, Mako," shouted Rigger, who'd been watching from the poop deck this whole time. "We lost Levi because he couldn't control his temper."

"I would say that was more due to mother's temper," said Sage, brushing her hair from her eyes, stuffing the stray strands back beneath her red cap.

"You can talk about your family history some other time," said Brand, kneeling beside Gale and stroking her sweating brow. "Your mother is trapped deep in a thicket of despair. I can help her find her way back."

"She just needs wine," I said.

"There are things better than wine for curing a damaged soul," said Brand, he picked up Gale. For a woman in her forties, she looked small and girlish cradled in his muscular arms. "Leave her to me."

Mako let loose an inhuman growl as he watched Brand carry Gale toward the hold. Mako bit the rope that held his arm, but another caught him just as swiftly. He cried, "Rigger, I'm going to kick your ass once I'm done killing this fool!"

"Grow up!" Sage said, stepping directly underneath Mako. "You're always trying to solve problems by making threats."

"Because the rest of you idiots don't listen!" Mako thrashed as more ropes wrapped around him. "Have you all lost your senses? Mother's not in her right mind. She's seeing things! And you're going to let this bastard take advantage of her?"

Brand didn't react to his words as he carried Gale down the stairs.

Sage put her hands on her hips. "I haven't gone crazy, and neither has mother. She's not hallucinating. Look behind the ship!"

Rigger swung Mako back to the stern and dropped him. Mako stared at the water in silence, his lips pressed tightly together. I moved to the back to see what he was staring at. Mere feet below the water was what appeared to be an oily black stain stretching out behind the *Freewind* for a mile or more. This dark shape was serpentine, a hundred yards across at its thickest point, and here and there small islands of tar broke above the waves along what would have been the serpent's spine.

Only, as the waves continued to wash in ever-lightening shades of amber foam, the beast rose higher still and I could see I wasn't looking at the spine of an enormous serpent, but at the belly. The thing was obviously dead, but that didn't make it any less menacing. Its lifeless head was twisted sideways in the water, its toothy jaws opened in a giant V aimed straight at the *Freewind*. The gaping maw was more than wide enough to swallow the ship whole; any individual fang of the beast was as thick and long as our foremast. The waves pushed the jaws open and shut in a lazy, listless chew.

Sage pointed her spyglass at the thing, which I found odd given that the monster was pretty hard to miss with plain old eyesight. But, after a moment's study she said, "This thing is drifting faster than we are. We've only got about ten minutes before it hits."

We all glanced up at what sails were set. Every canvas hung limp. There wasn't enough of a breeze to push a feather, let alone a ship. I looked down from the sails to see the whole Romer family now above deck, along with Bigsby, once more wearing his wig. Sorrow, wrapped in her cloak, was coming up the stairs followed by Infidel, still in her armor, her bed-head hair a fright.

"Somebody want to fill me in on what's going on?" Infidel asked, sounding groggy. "The last thing I remember was trying to help Gale."

"How did mother hurt you?" Sage asked as she studied Infidel's brow. "I saw a cutlass break over your head at Half-Moon Bay without even leaving a scratch!"

Infidel sighed. "I need you to keep this a secret. Right now, I'm not invulnerable. My strength is gone, too."

"You were knocking those ice-maidens half a mile out to sea," said Jetsam, scratching his head.

"All in the hammer," said Infidel.

"You should have told us," said Mako, sounding angry. He shoved his face inches from Infidel and said, "You assured us you wouldn't need protection! We trusted you!"

"The only injury I've suffered has been because your mother fights dirty, not because of our attackers," said Infidel. "Between my armor and my hammer, I can handle myself."

"Your armor might be a little more effective if you wore a helmet," said Jetsam.

Infidel nodded. "I hate helmets. Who wants to wear a steel bucket on their head when you live in the tropics? But, yeah, maybe it's time I learned to like them."

"If we'd known you didn't have your powers, we could have taken extra steps to protect you," said Mako.

"I don't want anyone putting themselves in danger because of me."

Sorrow joined the conversation. "Aren't others in greater danger if they're depending on physical skills you no longer possess?" She punctuated her sentence by spitting. At first, I thought it was an act of contempt, but then she swatted the air before her face and said, "Excuse me, but a fly just flew into my mouth."

She hardly need have said it. Flies were everywhere now.

I buzzed in with my paper voice. "Sorrow, there's a sea serpent following the boat. It looks dead. But I think it might be –"

"Rott?" said Sorrow, half in surprise, half in excitement. She sprinted to the rail.

Jetsam was already at the back of the boat, floating in the air, kicking his legs slowly to hold his position above the rudder. He let out a long, low, whistle, which was interrupted by gagging. "By the southern stars, what a stench!"

I was about to join with the others at the back of the ship when I caught a motion from the corner of my eye. I turned and found the ghost of Jasmine Romer once more hovering above the bowsprit. She motioned me towards her, and I obeyed.

"It's a pretty big coincidence that a primal dragon would show up just at the same time we're attacked by Purity," I said.

"It is no coincidence for Rott to appear anywhere," said Jasmine. "The entropic force he represents is omnipresent."

"Maybe entropy is everywhere, but mile-long dead snakes sure aren't. Something's causing him to show up here. Is Purity summoning him?"

"That's doubtful. Rott isn't like Hush or Abyss or even Greatshadow, who all maintain their intellect and personalities. The elemental force Rott commanded long ago consumed his very sense of self. He's essentially mindless, incapable of ordered thought. Only the barest flicker of animalistic hunger compels him to manifest. Bluntly, if he's here, he's come to feast."

"If he keeps turning the Sea of Wine into vinegar, we'll be in a real pickle," I said.

Jasmine wagged a ghostly finger in my face. "Don't make light of this! Though Rott isn't conscious of his actions, he can sense that the cosmic balance is off. Lives have been lost without their life force returning to the source. He hungers for the missing energy."

"What are you saying?"

"My body died, but my soul never left the world. The same is true of you."

"And your point is?"

"When Avaris helped prepare this boat to house my soul, she took precautions to hide my spirit from Rott's notice. I suspect that Sorrow, being inexperienced in her craft, has taken no such precautions. Just as a dead body emits a stench that draws vultures, the scent of your decaying soul has drawn the ultimate scavenger. Rott will consume this ship to feed his hunger."

"Oh," I said, raising my hand and running it along the back of my coconut scalp, as if I still had hair. "That's unfortunate. Why hasn't he bothered me before now?"

"Until now, your spirit dwelled on the material realm. Your soul is just one of thousands of lost spirits existing at any time. Rott feasts in the material world at his leisure. Here on the Sea of Wine, you're his sole focus."

"Then get out of here," I said. "Shift us back to the real world. Problem solved."

"Only my daughter can trigger the magic," said Jasmine. "Complicating matters further, it's now daylight in our home seas. We can only make the transit in the dead of night."

"So... what? You expect me to jump off the ship so this thing will leave the rest of you alone?"

Jasmine said nothing as she lowered her head.

"Oh," I said.

"I can think of no other reason Rott would manifest so aggressively. He's never before molested us within this realm."

As it happened, our conversation unfolded near where I'd been writing to Infidel. I barely had to walk a yard before leaning down to lift up the book. I clumsily ripped out the half-finished letter and folded it into a thick bundle. I tugged away the bandana that hid my hideous coconut skull and tied the letter within the cloth. Flies landed on my gloved fingers as I worked.

I took one look back at Jasmine. I sighed, or tried to. "The first time I died, it was just a dumb mistake." I shook my head. "I mean, it's something you might tell a seven year old: 'Don't run with a knife in your hand!'" I stared down at the bundled letter for a long time. "I guess it's appropriate that my death was careless, given how careless I was with my life. But you know… good things came of it. I'm going to have a daughter. I want to be there to watch her grow up."

"I understand," said Jasmine.

I looked back to the stern. Infidel was floating there, next to Jetsam, her eyes fixed on the doom that drifted toward us.

Even at this distance, I could hear that Jetsam was singing again, a little barroom ditty called 'The Death Song.'

"Oh you can die from scurvy,
And you can die from plague
You can croak when a rattle snake
Bites you in the leg
You can die from shaving
From a thousand tiny cuts
Or go out in a world of pain
By a swift kick to the…"

Mako jumped up and grabbed his brother by the ankle, yanking him down.

"That's enough," he said.

Enough, I thought, though the thought had nothing to do with Jetsam's singing. Instead, the thought reflected a sense of peace that settled over me. Jasmine was asking me to die. But was this such a sacrifice considering I was already dead? I'd had my time in the world. I wanted more. But deep down, I recognized the fundamental selfishness of the desire. Who was I, among the hordes of mankind, to dare ask for more than my allotted time? I'd gotten a lifetime. Wasn't that enough?

I said to Jasmine, "You seem to know more about being dead than I do. It caught me by surprise that there was something after life. What happens once I throw myself down Rott's throat? What follows death after death?"

"I've never had the courage to find out," said Jasmine, turning her face away, hugging herself.

I slowly walked to the back of the boat. Was I doing the right thing? If my life had ever caught the attention of a biographer, it's a sure bet he could have written my story without checking a thesaurus to find a synonym for 'self-sacrifice.' Maybe I could wait a little while longer, until the dragon was actually chewing on the timbers, just to make sure what I was about to do was really necessary.

Infidel's boots were a good two feet off the deck as she studied the approaching monster. Curiously, in life, whenever I dreamed of Infidel, I nearly always dreamed we were flying. It was natural to see her in this element. And in her white armor trimmed with silver, it was a simple thing to imagine her in a wedding gown. She deserved a more regal ceremony than our shared vows in the midst of that shadowy jungle. Yet those vows had been made, and I held them to be sacred. This was my bride, she wore my ring, she carried my child, and for her I would throw myself into the teeth of any monster.

And such a monster! Rott was fully at the surface now, a bloated corpse crawling with flies, riding so high upon the waves that its dead, flapping jaws opened to reveal a cavern more than large enough to swallow the *Freewind*. The sky was no longer sunset red, but black as a million oil-black gulls, feathers falling from wings of bone, spiraled through the air in vast clouds to feast upon the corpse of their carrion master.

The Romers seemed paralyzed as they stared at the horrid thing less than a ship's length off the stern.

"The waves smell like pure vinegar now," said Cinnamon, wrinkling her nose.

"Should we... attack it? We have bows," said Mako. It was the first time I'd ever heard him sound doubtful.

"Even it wasn't already dead, that thing's the size of an island," said Rigger. "It wouldn't even notice."

"How can it notice anything? It has no eyes! Nothing but empty sockets!" said Jetsam.

"Something's drawing it to us," said Sorrow. "Something..."

She turned toward me, her eyes full of understanding.

"Is there nothing we can do to... to discourage it?" asked Mako.

Rigger shook his head. "How do you discourage the dead?"

Taking this as my motto, I embraced my final moment with gusto. I walked to Infidel, whose head was conveniently at the level of my own thanks to her defiance of gravity. I spun her and gave her a powerful hug, taking care not to crush her. I pressed my coconut jaw against her cheek and tried to whisper, "I love you no matter what," though my kazoo voice bleated the words in such a graceless tone that the Divine Author alone knows what she might have heard. Then I thrust the folded letter into her grasp, leapt to the railing, and with a roguish tip of my tri-corn hat announced, "As I stand in the vestibule of self-abnegation, I wish to say that I have no regrets. Unfortunately, that would be the foulest lie. I fiercely regret my impending absence." I fixed my pecan eyes squarely on Infidel, who looked utterly confused by the erratic behavior of Sorrow's driftwood construct. I directed my final words to her alone: "If I had a thousand lives to give, I'd give them for you. My life was nothing but an empty glass until you filled it with the wine of your company. May the Divine Author guide his sacred quill to write the happy ending you deserve."

All the Romers were staring at me with mouths agape. I gave them a crisp salute, then turned and leapt toward the decaying beast. The jaws surged forward upon the waves as if driven by hunger. The tip of one of his teeth tore through my shirt as I fell into the chasm of his mouth. As Rott's wicked fangs closed behind me, it occurred to me that my farewell speech might have been more effective if I'd remembered to mention my name.

CHAPTER TEN
BODIES IN MOTION

THE BLACK, BLOATED tongue was covered with a wriggling carpet of worms that oozed pale puss as I tried to gain my balance. The tongue was a mass of muscular knots, stiff with rigor mortis, but my boots had trouble finding traction in the slime. The rotting skin covering the dead muscle peeled away as I slipped down to my hands and knees. The brown putrescence that bubbled up and soaked into my gloves would certainly have cost me the contents of my stomach, if I'd had a stomach. I shook my hands to cleanse them, but succeeded only in splattering the awful ick across my face. I prayed to the divine author that my paper tongue was useful only for speech, and completely insensate to taste should a drop find its way past my ragged lips.

The vinegar swells pushed Rott's jaws to chewing lazily, slamming me against the boney mouth roof. Despite the unpleasantness of my surroundings, I felt strangely unthreatened. The beast was too dead to even swallow. Would I have to crawl down its gullet to meet my final end?

I was toppled by a sudden jolt. As I rolled over, I saw that the beast's snout had collided with the rudder of the *Freewind*. If I was to save the ship, it was apparently up to me to march into Rott's stomach. The dragon of entropy was also the dragon of indolence.

My gloves found purchase in the crack of a massive tooth. I pulled myself up and struggled to advance, inch by precious inch, through the cavernous mouth. In the dim shadows at the back of the gullet I saw shapes, vaguely human. I drew closer and found that the undulation of the waves had caused the beast to regurgitate the corpses of sailors. The dead men surged toward me as the body rode on a particularly energetic swell. The walking dead I could have faced bravely, but these were the half-digested dead, as listless and lifeless as their master. I let loose a buzzing scream. Even without brains to give the dead sailors purpose or muscles to drive their limbs, their advance was effective. I was knocked over by their collective weight, struggling helplessly as they dragged me down beneath their slimy, acid-dripping forms. My left leg slipped deep beneath the tongue and with a sudden jolt I was limbless from the knee down, my wooden foot sliced free by the beast's closing teeth.

I had no time to dwell upon my own dissolution, however, for behind me was a far louder crunch. I strained to look backward and found half the rudder of the *Freewind* splintered. Was my sacrifice in vain? Was the beast not to be satisfied until all the ship was in its bowels?

"I'm the one you want," I shouted, as the jaws clamped shut, plunging me into utter darkness. "I'm the lost soul you seek!"

There was a loud crash behind me. Light suddenly filled the mouth, bright as dawn. I pushed aside the liquefying décolletage of a decaying woman to see the source of the illumination. The teeth at the front of the mouth had been shattered. Standing in the gap was a goddess in pristine white armor, her hammer ablaze. She had a red bandana tied tightly over her mouth and nose to protect her from the stench as she swung her weapon in wide arcs, shattering columns of ivory thick as tree trunks to rid the beast of fangs. Yet her eyes weren't focused on the demolition. They searched the cavernous mouth, narrowing as she spotted the mound of corpses that even now dragged me down the gullet.

In a flash she reached me, planting her feet on either side of my shoulders as she pulverized the half-gelatinized bodies with roundhouse swings of the Gloryhammer.

"Infidel!" I cried, as I grabbed her pristine white boot.

"Stagger!" she answered. "Is it truly you?"

"I'm the lost soul you seek," I said, in what would have been a sob if my tongue had been up to the task. "How did you know it was me? You haven't had time to read the letter!"

"'The vestibule of self-abnegation'? Please. Why didn't you say something earlier?"

"Sorrow didn't build me with a tongue. She just gave me the power of speech a few hours ago."

Satisfied that she'd cleared away the corpses, she grabbed my outstretched hand and pulled me, freeing my lower half from beneath the rotten tongue.

"Your leg," she said, looking pale.

"It doesn't hurt," I said. "Sorrow can make another."

"Not if I kill her first," she growled. "How could she do this to you?"

"I don't believe it was personal," I said, as Infidel helped me stand.

"Why did you jump into this damn thing's mouth?" she asked.

"Rott knows I should be dead. Sacrificing myself is the ship's only hope. You have to let me finish this."

"This thing can't chew without teeth," said Infidel, swinging her hammer to pulverize the fang nearest us.

"Look at the size of the jaws!" I protested. "It can swallow the ship whole!"

"If it can catch us," said Infidel, thrusting her hammer into the gap left by the missing tooth, then shooting skyward, dragging me to freedom. We arced back over the *Freewind*, my remaining boot clipping the crows nest as she dropped toward the bow. There was a giant cleat there that held a rope as thick as a woman's arm. Infidel dropped me, then wrapped the rope over her shoulder and launched herself toward the sky once more. She grunted as the line went taut, having flown only a few feet beyond the tip of the jibboom. Her right arm, holding the Gloryhammer, was thrust straight before her. The rope was tight enough a man could have walked upon it.

With a squawking bark, Menagerie sank his teeth into the rope and began to flap his wings furiously.

The bow of the *Freewind* creaked as this single point of force created by the two aeronauts strained to move the ship through the undulating sea.

"It's as good an idea as any," shouted Jetsam, as he threw himself to hug the main mast then pushed his feet out behind him and began to vigorously kick against the air.

"That's the spirit!" shouted Mako. He turned to his siblings and shouted, "Throw anything you can overboard! Lighten the load! We'll outrun death itself!"

"You're mad!" snorted Rigger. "These three can't drag the ship no matter how hard they try. It's a simple matter of mass!"

He ducked as a barrel shot past his head, courtesy of Poppy, though I don't think she'd intentionally aimed for him.

"Given that you're floating on an enchanted ocean being pursued by a fundamental force of nature manifesting itself as an enormous snake, I admire your devotion to logic," Sorrow said to Rigger. "But if the Gloryhammer can move a person through the air, why can't it move a ship?"

But any sense of optimism that Sorrow might have been trying to build was demolished as the *Freewind* shook violently, knocking everyone off their feet. Rott's jaws had just flapped shut, trapping the entire rear of the boat.

"Rott's momentum was greater than our own," Rigger said, rising to his hands and knees. "You can't just stop a mass like that! You can't drag a ship forward on wishful thoughts!"

Despite Rigger's pessimism, the lifeless, limp jaws washed open and the *Freewind* limped forward another yard. We were moments away from doom, but moments do matter.

"Get every sail up," said Mako.

"There's no damn wind without mother!" screamed Rigger.

"He'll have a harder time washing us down his gullet if we're fully rigged," said Mako.

"Or if his jaws were frozen shut," I whispered.

"You're thinking of Purity's sword?" asked Sorrow, kneeling beside me to examine my missing leg.

"I'm thinking of the Jagged Heart!"

"Do you know how to activate its powers?" she asked, as she grabbed a belaying pin from the deck. She began to fashion a peg leg from the wood to restore my mobility.

"Not a clue. But I watched Aurora summon a wall of ice thick enough to survive a direct blast of Greatshadow's breath using the harpoon. It's worth a try."

"And if you succeed, we'll simply be staved in by an iceberg rather than chewed to bits," grumbled Rigger.

His words were almost drowned out by ropes dancing through every block and tackle on the ship, raising all the sails in great, noisy flaps. Despite his dour attitude, Rigger was doing what he could.

Sage stood nearby, watching the sails unfurl. I felt a stir of optimism as I saw her black curls flicker in a breeze. However, although the yards of canvas settled into position, they remained limp. The only breeze had been that caused by the sails unfurling.

Sage shook her head sadly as she stared into her spyglass. "Two minutes," she said to Rigger. "If I'm calculating the undulations of the body on the currents correctly, we have two minutes before we get gnawed again. We have to gain some speed!"

"We've just enough time to puff our way out of this if we all take deep breaths," said Rigger, with mock cheerfulness.

Sage chewed her fingernails as her gaze shifted from her spyglass to the sails to the bow, where Infidel and Menagerie strained against the rope. Her eyes widened as she watched Menagerie's frantic flapping. Without warning, she bolted across the deck, toward my fallen notebook and the bottle of ink that lay nearby. She didn't waste time locating a quill, but simply popped the stopper free and pressed the tip of her index finger to the bottle as she upended it. She smeared something quickly upon the page as she ran back to Rigger, still standing at the wheel.

"Wings!" she cried, holding the book open before him. "We need wings! You can make them!"

Rigger furrowed his brow as he tried to decipher his sister's strange babblings. The crude thing she'd scrawled on the page wasn't helping him understand her. I dragged myself up on my new leg, off-balance as it was a good two inches shorter than its more carefully-formed mate.

I limped toward the wheel, and saw that Sage had drawn what looked like a banana with two big ovals coming off it. Luckily, the fate of the ship didn't rest on my understanding her gist. At the instant when I was most completely baffled, Rigger's eyebrows raised up. "I've never tried anything like this!" he said, sounding excited. "It will destroy the sails and the rigging just to –"

"Try!" screamed Sage. "We don't even have a minute before it hits us again!"

Rigger let go of the wheel and threw his hands toward the mainsail, as if he were grabbing it in his mind. He gave a violent sideways tug with his hands and suddenly the ropes rigging the mainsail shattered the thick block-and-tackle housings that held them. The ropes flew in opposing directions, jerking the mainsail completely taut. With a sickening sound no sailor ever wants to hear, the mainsail began to rip, splitting right down its center.

"Rigger!" Mako shouted, dropping the barrel he was throwing overboard and running toward his brother. "Have you lost your mind?"

Rigger didn't answer. His face was contorted, turning red, his jaw clenched as if he were straining to lift an impossibly heavy weight. The ropes pulled the split mainsails toward opposite sides of the boat, the canvas taut as kites. The ropes stayed taut even as a wave rippled through them, unleashing a powerful flapping sound as Rigger threw his arms back.

The boat surged forward with enough momentum that I had to grab the wheel for balance.

The drawing suddenly made sense.

"Wings!" Sage shouted at Mako. "We've turned the mainsail into wings!"

Rigger brought his hands forward once more, the sails dancing like flags, until they caught air as Rigger spread his arms as if he were doing a breaststroke.

Behind us, the massive jaws were once more closing.

"Just one more yard!" screamed Sage

Rigger gave a third flap, then dropped to his knees. Behind us, Rott's jaws closed on empty air.

The wing-sails suddenly went limp, dropping into the water.

"I can't hold them any more," Rigger groaned as he fell on his side. "Without the aid of the pulleys, the weight is too much! I feel as if I've torn every muscle in my body."

"Cut those ropes and sails loose!" Sage shouted. "They'll cost us our speed."

Mako and Cinnamon drew swords and ran to the taut ropes hanging overboard.

"You did good, Rigger," said Sage, kneeling beside her trembling brother. "We're moving faster than we were, and bodies in motion want to stay in motion."

Indeed, we were moving forward, though barely at the speed of a good walk. Now that the ship had been given a nudge by the makeshift wings, the Gloryhammer's magic proved sufficient to maintain our momentum. Rott remained too close for comfort, and flies still covered the ship, but even without waiting for Sage's new calculations, I could see that we were putting precious inches between us and the dead thing at our tail.

"I command you to keep pulling!" a voice shouted from the front of the ship. "Know that the royal family salutes your courage!" It was Bigsby, posed heroically upon the bow, waving his fist at Infidel and Menagerie. "When I return home, my father will reward you handsomely for your heroism!"

But instead of finding encouragement in the dwarf's words, Infidel shouted back, "My damn arm's about to come out of its socket! I can't do this much longer!"

Back at the mainmast, Jetsam suddenly dropped to the deck. Dark circles of sweat stained his black shirt under the arms. "I'm spent," he whispered.

In truth, I doubted he'd added much to our speed.

Our gains were only temporary and I had the only plan that might maintain them. I headed for the hatch to retrieve the Jagged Heart. My idea was to weigh down Rott with so much ice that he couldn't move. What could it hurt to try?

But before I could go down the hatch, I was met by a woman heading up the stairs. It was Gale Romer, her hair drenched in sweat and twisted back behind her ears in a crude bun held in place by a few pins. Stray strands were plastered to her neck, which sported a half dozen bite marks. Rather than the modest nightgown she'd worn when last I saw her, she was dressed in Brand's white silk shirt, which was cinched around her waist by a braided leather whip. Her cheeks were flushed red, her lips swollen and dark.

The oversized shirt hung to the middle of her thighs and her legs were bare. For a woman almost my age, her limbs were rather shapely; I was particularly struck by the superb design of her feet and toes. The Divine Author was also an excellent architect, though it could be that my thoughts were pushed in this direction by my stumbling attempts at movement now that one of my 'feet' was no bigger around than a coat button.

Gale climbed onto deck and wasted little time accessing the situation. A strong wind filled the remaining sails and pushed us forward. "Mako, take the wheel!" she barked. "Where's Rigger? What happened to the mainsail?"

"Rigger's hurt!" shouted Sage, as she cradled her brother's head in her lap. "He pushed himself too hard and it's all my fault!"

"We're being pursued by Rott," Sorrow said to Gale. "I advise that you take us back to the material realm. Perhaps Abyss can intervene to halt his restless advance."

"And I advise you to go back to your quarters and wait," said Gale. "A full span of daylight must pass between our jumps. We can't make the journey back until nightfall."

"Six hours to go," said Brand, glancing down at a pocket watch as he emerged onto the deck. He was as sweaty as Gale, and his shirtless back was covered with scratch marks.

Suddenly, there was flapping overhead. I looked up to see Infidel and Menagerie coming toward me. "If we've got wind, I guess I'm done," she said.

Bigsby didn't approve of them quitting. He chased after them, shaking his fists, yelling, "I didn't tell you to stop!"

Gale casually stuck out a leg to trip Bigsby as he ran past. She pinned him beneath her foot as she said, "Anyone want to tell me how this dwarf got on board?"

"Ah, right," said Brand, running his hand through his hair. "You weren't really yourself when I made introductions. This is my, uh, my... sister. Princess Innocent Brightmoon."

I stopped paying attention. I'd already heard this conversation, and I happened to know that the true Princess Innocent Brightmoon was present and accounted for. Infidel landed, and I threw my arms around her. She hugged me back, though only for a brief instant. "Sorry," she said, turning her face away, her voice catching in her throat.

"Are you crying?"

"Gagging," she said. "You kind of stink. Like, seriously. Some of that dragon goo has seeped into you."

Sorrow approached. "Indeed. I saw it – and smelled it – when I examined your leg. I'll continue to repair your physical form while I can, but I fear you may not last much more than another day or two. The wood I crafted you from is rotting at an accelerating pace. I can replace bits as they fall off, but as the last fragments of the original binding decay, so too, will the enchantment fail."

"Speaking of binding..." said Infidel, dropping the shaft of the Gloryhammer into her gauntlet with a rather menacing *slap*. "What have you done to my husband, Sorrow?"

"In fairness, I didn't know he was your husband. He was merely a wandering spirit discovered at random by my soul-catcher. A lost soul was required to animate my golem. He didn't reveal his true identity until later."

"Because you wouldn't let me write!" I protested. "For that matter, you could have built me with a tongue."

"Conversations with lost souls are tedious affairs," Sorrow explained.

"Stop saying I was lost!" I said. "I was following Infidel."

"I knew it," Infidel said. "I could feel you beside me. I never had any doubt."

"The two of you should be grateful to me for making this brief reunion possible," said Sorrow, crossing her arms.

I began to peel off my clothes. They fell apart at the seams as I tugged on them. "Tossing these rags overboard will help with my general ripeness. I'll also dip back into the Sea of Wine to try to wash more of the stink off me; the wine didn't hurt me before. Maybe alcohol will slow my decay. That was my theory in life, at least."

"Cold also slows decay," said Sorrow. "We can use the Jagged Heart to chill you after you return from your bath. The cold shouldn't harm you. But let's not fool ourselves. We'll never completely remove Rott's curse. Decay was built into your body from the start." She looked down at her withered left hand. "Just like everyone else. Now that you two are reunited, I advise that you treat your remaining time together as brief."

Sorrow took one last glance at me as she turned away. Then, she whirled back around, her eyebrows raised as she examined the staves of my barrel chest. "By the thirteenth nail," she whispered, sounding dazed. But while her eyes were fixed and motionless, her hand was busily searching the folds of her cloak. She pulled out a small silver rod which melted in her grasp, flowing like mercury to coat her hand with a thin glove of precious metal. She gingerly probed my chest to wiggle free a black shard embedded in the boards. Her gauntlet instantly turned dark gray with tarnish.

"What is it?" I asked.

"A fragment of Rott's tooth," she whispered as she looked at the object, roughly the size and shape of a man's middle finger.

"Yeah. He snagged me as I first went in."

She produced a golden coin and coated the black shard with a thin layer of the precious metal. "Gold will seal it," she said. "It can withstand corruption better than any other metal."

"Funny," said Infidel. "I thought gold was the chief cause of corruption."

I almost asked what Sorrow intended to do with the shard, but decided I'd rather not know the answer.

"You should see to your bath," said Sorrow, not looking at me.

Infidel assisted as I tied a rope around myself and slipped down into the wine. The ship was now moving at a good clip through the waves. The water buffeted me, and I climbed out mere moments after I went in, lest the current tear me apart. As I inched my way back up the rope, I watched with morbid fascination as pale white worms writhed free of the wood of my limbs. The wine had left them drunk or poisoned. They fell away, vanishing into the burgundy beneath me, leaving me filled with tiny holes.

I made it back to the deck, sodden with wine.

"How do I smell now?" I asked, as the dark fluid puddled around me.

"Just like you used to," said Infidel, as she wrapped me in her embrace.

CHAPTER ELEVEN

I COULD OPEN THE DOOR

WE LAY IN the bed, my coconut skull resting on Infidel's outstretched arm. We'd been talking for hours with a lightness that might have struck others as curious given our greater circumstances. But our marriage was built first and foremost on friendship. We'd loved each other chastely for over a decade, separated by my cowardice and Infidel's former powers. When she'd been as strong as a dragon, she'd been afraid to even hug me for fear of maiming me. My new wooden carcass was equally useless for intimacy. If our relationship had been built merely on lust, it couldn't have endured the strange barriers fate had constructed between us. Fortunately, deeper bonds held us together.

So it was ironic that we were talking about falling apart.

"Fixing your leg wasn't a problem. Why can't we do that when the rest of you rots away? Can't we just keep changing parts?" she asked, tracing my seed-pod ears with her fingers.

"I don't know," I buzzed, wishing I could whisper, or convey any tone at all. "Perhaps I'll continue being a ghost. Or perhaps I'll simply fade away."

She swallowed.

I said, "When I first... died, I, uh, I had an... experience. It's tough to describe. I felt like I was part of the larger universe. I felt like my... my energy had been concentrated in my old body, and now that it had been cut loose I was... dissipating. Spreading out. Like I was everywhere at once, a tiny part of everything. It wasn't... it wasn't scary. I felt at peace. I felt connected to something bigger than myself."

"And you think that will happen again?" She stared up at the beams of the ceiling, then closed her eyes. "It doesn't sound so bad."

"No," I said. "But it doesn't sound even half as good as staying with you."

"I want you to be with me too," she said.

"But what if I can't? What if the next time I slip free from the world I don't come back?"

"Then I'll miss you and remember you," said Infidel, stoically. "We face the same future as every other marriage. The day comes when one of the spouses is no longer around. When brides and grooms say, ''Til in death we part,' they don't know if they are making a promise for fifty years or fifty seconds. We just... we just have a little more information than most people do."

This was another reason why I loved her. Underneath her swaggering bravado, beneath the mask of her daredevil grins, Infidel was a person who understood her limits. She'd always accepted there were some fights too big for her. Unlike Sorrow, she'd never decided to avenge herself against the father who'd wronged her, or declare war on the church that pursued her. She'd merely declared herself done with their madness, and carved her life anew.

Infidel nudged aside a loose barrel slat on my chest and peered into the darkness.

"So it's costing you energy to animate this body?"

"That's what Sorrow says. I don't really feel any different."

"But you could be free if you weren't trapped inside that silver bug?"

"Actually, I've been able to slip out of the mosquito. Now I'm trapped by the golden cage that forms this body's heart."

Infidel stared into the center of my chest for several long seconds.

"I could open the door," she said.

I didn't hesitate for even a second. "The best moment of my life was the moment I opened my heart to you. Do it."

For a fleeting instant, I regretted the words. We were messing with magic neither of us understood. But it was too late to protest as her slender hand slipped into my hollow chest and found the cage. I heard a tiny *click* as the door opened.

Infidel carefully withdrew her fingers. "Did that do anything? Are you free?"

I didn't answer. Though I'd heard her, once more I had shrunk down within my enchanted body, becoming a tiny homunculus standing beside the silver mosquito, staring at the open door of the cage.

I walked to the lip. Through the slats, I could see Infidel's chest pressed next to mine, her white and silver armor gleaming in the faint light cast by the Gloryhammer, which was floating the corner, draped with a sheet to soften its glow.

I stepped out of the cage.

Instantly, the silver wires that pierced my spiritual body fell free. I was once more a full-sized phantom floating above the bed. The room seemed subtly different from the one I'd been in mere seconds before. For one thing, the room now possessed color. The bruise on Infidel's brow had a blue tint rimmed by a jaundiced yellow. The quilt we lay upon was a patchwork of a dozen faded green hues. The air in the room had been mostly dead to me before, but now smelled of wine, mixed with a shore at low-tide.

My wooden body lay completely limp. Infidel shook its shoulder. "Stagger?"

"I'm okay," I said. "I'm here." Of course, she didn't hear me.

"Stagger?" she asked again, staring desperately into my pecans as tears welled in her eyes.

I flew back into the wooden body, shrinking as I approached the cage. I stepped through the open door and the silver wires snaked to life and jabbed into me once more. I turned and found the cage door remained open. Was I now able to come and go as I pleased?

For now, I was more focused on the coming than the going. I felt my life force move into every fiber of the rotting wood.

My coconut skull shifted on my shoulders as I brought my gaze to hers.

"It's okay," I said. "I'm still here."

She hugged me tightly, as her tears came in earnest.

She regained her composure a moment later. "Good," she whispered. "Good. Because... I know you can't stay forever. But... but I don't want you to go yet."

Before I could tell her I wasn't planning on going anywhere, the door to our room swung open.

"I've finished preparing the bands of negation," Sorrow said, poking her head around the door. "Do you want to take part in the questioning?"

"Don't you knock?" Infidel asked, propped up on one elbow to look over me. "What if we'd been naked?"

"He *is* naked," said Sorrow. "Just come as you are. Gale says she'll be ready in fifteen minutes."

Infidel had never taken off her armor since the fight. We hoped that the magic that kept it immaculate would protect her from any lingering death juice that might seep from my pores. When I rose from the bed, I couldn't help but notice I left behind a faint outline of sawdust. There were tiny things with tiny jaws within me, grinding me down. This is true of all men, I suppose. I remember the same feeling from ten years ago, when I'd first noticed how much hair I was leaving in my comb.

At the end of the hall, Sorrow stood in the main hold. Purity was tied to a simple wooden chair. The left side of her face was bruised where I'd clocked her. She'd been stripped of her armor and dressed in one of Gale's night gowns. Her arms were bound behind her; her feet were tied to the legs of the chair. Surrounding her were several concentric circles of iron stretching out to a full five feet around her. I saw no signs of torture, but Purity stared at the floor with an empty gaze, as if all will had drained from her.

I was curious as to what was so important that Gale wasn't here already. It seemed like a good time to test my powers now that my heart cage was open. I leaned against the wall, crossing my arms as if I was merely waiting. Satisfied that my body was propped up sufficiently, I abandoned the cage.

It worked. I flew free once more, ghosting through the wall into what I thought was Gale's room. Only instead of Gale's room, I found I was in the bunk room that Mako, Rigger, and Jetsam shared. Mako and Jetsam stood together next to their bunks, their ears pressed to the wall.

I worked where I'd gotten turned around and flashed through another wall and found Gale speaking to Brand. I'd obviously caught them in mid-conversation.

"– unforgivable," she said. Gale was dressed once more in her captain's garb. Her long heavy coat looked uncomfortable in the sweltering confines of the room, but I had to admit she was an imposing figure in her full uniform. The padding gave her broad shoulders, adorned with gleaming brass buttons. Her buccaneer boots made her feet look heavy and solid, as if nothing in the world could push her over. Her hair was pulled back into a tight knot. Her eyes were hard and emotionless. She was standing with her hands behind her back, her posture rigid and formal.

Brand was seated on a low stool before her. He hung his head, looking like a scolded puppy.

"You're fired as my dryman," said Gale, in a calm tone.

"How about as your lover?" Brand said, managing a grin.

"Love was never part of our relationship. I've physical cravings. You satisfied them adequately, and were compensated for your trouble. It won't be difficult to replace you."

He shook his head. "I don't think you mean that."

"Are you saying you're a better judge of my true feelings than I am?"

"I think I might be, yeah," he said. "I mean, I knew when you first laid eyes on me that you wanted me for more than just my skills at haggling. But I didn't enter your bed because you offered me a job. I took one look at you and knew I was in the presence of a true woman, a creature of the world. I've looked into the eyes of many a young naïf and found them to be nothing but shallow pools. Your eyes were oceans, and I've loved swimming in your depths. I've come to know your soul, Gale."

Captain Roamer sighed. "Yesterday, I might have found such flattery charming. Now, it only adds to the evidence that you're nothing but a silver-tongued scoundrel. Bringing a stowaway onto my ship? What were you thinking? I'd have tossed you into the Sea of Wine already, but I can't help but be curious as to what your game is."

"Bigsby's my brother," Brand said, shrugging his shoulders. "I couldn't just leave him."

"Don't you mean sister?" Gale said sarcastically. "I'm not ignorant of Silver Isle politics. King Brightmoon has no son named Steadfast. And Bigsby's been selling fish in Commonground for longer than Princess Innocent has been missing. If you must lie, why lie so clumsily?"

Brand sighed. "Look, if I want to lie, I swear I can come up with a more plausible yarn than this one. I can't tell you what my game is because there is no game. I've just been reacting to events that even I find difficult to believe."

Gale crossed her arms. "Go on."

"Here's the simple truth," said Brand. "Bigsby is my brother, though we've never met before two days ago. My real name is Brand Cooper. I'm the son of Perfect Cooper, founder of the Cooper Barrel Works."

Gale looked skeptical. I was a little dubious myself. Half the barrels in the Shining Lands were made by Cooper Barrel Works. Perfect Cooper was a very wealthy man.

"My father is quite old," said Brand. "Five years ago, he fell into a seizure while on the toilet. We found him barely alive. He survived, but was a changed man. He was too weak to walk for almost a year. He couldn't even talk for over a month, but when he did regain his powers of speech, oh, he told me quite the tale."

Gale tilted her head. "And now I suppose you'll tell me a tale."

"My father has worked hard to live up to his name. He's famous throughout the realms because the quality of his product is unmatched. I was raised with the same eye toward perfection. I was trained in both body and mind to be flawless. But in the grip of his malady, too weak to lift his limbs, Father confessed that he'd been a fool to demand perfection from mere human flesh. He told me of his greatest shame; almost thirty years before I'd been born, his first wife had given birth to his first son. The child had been born with stunted limbs. His wife had died during the birth, and father had ordered the midwife to smother the baby. He couldn't bear the thought of the Cooper name being attached to a dwarf.

"The midwife vowed to follow his wishes and took the child from his home. Only, she had other plans for the baby. Circuses paid good money for freaks. In the months that followed, she began to display signs of newfound wealth. Father accused her of stealing from him. She confessed to having sold the infant."

"And you think Bigsby's that child?" asked Gale.

Brand nodded. "My father kept his secret for almost two decades. He remarried twice, but lost child after child to stillbirths. I thought I was the only child to have survived. But, on what he thought might be his death bed, he told me his dark secret. He knew the name of the circus, and the date the child had been sold. He wanted me to find my missing brother and bring him home.

"Thus began my grand adventure. The circus my brother had been sold to had disbanded years before. The acts had all joined other outfits. It took me several years to follow all the leads. At first, I looked down upon the people I spoke too. I'd lived a sheltered life and been convinced of my superiority to vagabond performers. Eventually, I saw their world was far richer than the comfortable cage of my own upbringing. My father lived in luxury, but had never been happy; the performers lived with hardship, but had joyous hearts.

"I joined the circus, and after I was finally accepted by my fellow performers, I learned the truth of my brother's whereabouts.

He was called Bigsby, and he'd fled to Commonground after being accused of murder. I went to the docks to find passage to the Isle of Fire. Unfortunately, I didn't have a single coin in my pockets. I had a purse full of moons when I first left home, but as that money ran out, I discovered I could get by with charm alone. I heard rumors that your ship was in port to ferry a passenger to Commonground, but from what I knew of Wanderers, it was unlikely that mere charm would gain me passage. As fate would have it, I also heard that you needed a dryman and decided to take my chances. When we met, I knew I'd be setting sail with you. It was love at first sight."

"Or lust," said Gale, crossing her arms. "So, assuming I believe you, why does Bigsby think he's the princess? Why are you peddling this absurd lie?"

"I don't know. He suffered severe trauma when Greatshadow attacked Commonground. In his mind, the dwarf known as Bigsby is dead, and the princess has awakened to reclaim her birthright. When I called him Bigsby, he began acting crazy. I mean, crazier. Like he was going to hurt himself. He stays relatively manageable as long as I play along with his fantasy. I'm only hoping that he remembers his true identity before we return home."

"Why didn't you tell me this?"

"Events have their own momentum. You weren't aboard when I brought Bigsby back to the *Freewind*. I wasn't certain you'd welcome an unpaid passenger who was both a freak and insane. In retrospect, my hopes that he'd stay quiet and hidden until we made it back to the Silver Isles were perhaps naïve."

Gale sighed, rubbing her temples. "Perhaps. I wish you'd been honest. Things might have worked out differently. As it is... the best I can do is spare your lives. I'll put you off the ship at the next port."

"But —"

"This is mercy, Brand. It's more than I'd show anyone else in your circumstances."

"So you do still have feelings for me?" he asked.

"If I do, I assure you, they are not feelings you want me to give voice to. For now, be content that you're merely fired instead of facing sterner justice."

"I'm more than content," said Brand. "I'm joyous. I should never have accepted the job as your dryman."

Gale turned to leave. "Then we're of the same opinion."

He spoke before her hand fell on the door handle. "Only if we both agree that there was something real between us. I should never have accepted your offer of employment, since I knew when I saw you I wanted something more. The relationship of a boss to an employee is always going to be tainted by the power one holds over the other. To woo you properly, I must approach you as an equal."

"You aren't my equal," she sighed. "Despite your claims of inherited wealth, you're a penniless vagabond, while I am a ship's captain, responsible for my family and my business. Despite my ill turn of fortune from these accursed slave wars, I'm respected as an honest woman. I've fought hard to ensure that my name means something in this world. I'm not certain I believe your story, but, if it's true, you've just admitted to pissing away your father's money and amusing yourself among carnies rather that staying focused on your mission. You're irresponsible."

He shrugged, "Opposites attract."

Gale closed her eyes and took a deep breathe. "I enjoyed you, Brand. It's been ten years since Rudder passed away. Oh, there was a man."

Brand nodded, though she couldn't see it.

She continued, "I've had no time for romance since he died. I've had quite a few Wanderers court me – good men, good captains. But I'm too old to entangle my life with a man my age, with his own family and ship. I'm proud of the life I've made for myself; I've no interest in starting anew."

"You deserve to be proud," said Brand.

Gale shook her head. "I don't deserve anything. Nothing good can come of me thinking the world owes me some reward."

"The Gale Romer I know wouldn't indulge herself with pity."

Gale turned from the door to face him once more. "Pity has nothing to do with my feelings. Unlike you, I've experienced genuine love. Rudder was my life. Love wasn't merely sweet whispers or shared desire. We were bonded so strongly we felt like one being. We were two halves of the same whole. You can't know what losing him felt like."

"I don't pretend I can," said Brand. "But no matter who you were then, now, you are your own woman."

"Am I?" She crossed her arms. "My dryman at the time of Rudder's death was a man five years my senior named Hunter. We had a completely professional relationship. He would never have violated my trust. We worked together on running this ship side by side, day after day. We were the best of friends. And then... then one night, I was a little drunk on wine, and I decided we should be more than friends."

"You sound so guilty about it," said Brand. "But you were both adults. There's nothing to be ashamed of."

"In your eyes," she said. "We kept our relationship secret for a time, unsure how my children would react. But, you know I enjoy... I like...." Her voice trailed off.

"A little role-playing," said Brand.

Her cheeks flushed red. "We were in the galley. We thought all the children were above deck. Hunter had me pressed up against the pantry with my arms bound behind my back with my blouse. I was making mock protests as he explored my body. And then... and then Levi walked in."

"Your oldest son."

Gale nodded. "I... I know how it must have looked to Levi. But... he'd known Hunter for years. He should have trusted that Hunter was no rapist. Instead, he grabbed a butcher's knife from the block and plunged it into Hunter's back."

Brand rose from the stool and looked as if he were going to

hug Gale. She pressed her right hand into his chest and forced him back down.

"I lost a son that day. I was so angry with Levi that he ran off. He now serves with the Stormguard. The Stormguard! My mortal enemies!"

Brand shrugged. "But this was before the Pirate Wars started. He wasn't betraying you then."

Gale gave a small, bitter laugh. "Oh, Brand. Listen to me, still talking about Levi. He's dead to me. Dead." She gave him a stern look. "And he wasn't the point of my story at all."

"Then what was your point?" Brand asked.

"My point is that you are an attractive man who smells fantastic and happens to be a genius in the sack. I liked playing with you. But the only reason I've let you in my bed is that you aren't my equal. You're so obviously a toy. A trinket."

"A treasure?" Brand offered.

"A diversion. You're someone I could play with. Your presence might embarrass my children, but it didn't threaten them. They knew I wasn't taking you on as their new father."

"I'm not sure Mako felt that way."

"Mako's young. He's still trying to figure out how to project strength so that he can one day command his own ship. One day, he'll figure it out. Meanwhile, the rest of the Wanderer clans might hear that I was fooling around with you, but they wouldn't be gossiping about how families might get woven together and shipping interests merged. There are no political repercussions to bedding you. If you'd been my equal, Brand, I wouldn't have wanted you. I could only let you touch me because you were so inconsequential."

Brand's shoulders sagged. "You really are an expert with your tongue, aren't you?"

"You and the dwarf can bunk in the forecastle until we get back home. Keep out of my sight. The less I see you, the less I'll be inclined to change my mind about you."

"And take me back?" asked Brand.

"And keelhaul you," she said.

With this, she turned, and left her cabin.

In the hall, she met Mako, who was closing his door behind him. Mako grinned as he gave a nod of greeting. It was obvious from his satisfied expression that he'd heard every word. Gale scowled at him. If her eyes had been daggers, Mako would have bled.

CHAPTER TWELVE
SOULS SNUFFED OUT

I FLEW BACK into my wooden body as the two Romers marched into the room. Without pausing for pleasantries, Mako grabbed Purity by the hair and pulled her head back so that she faced Gale. He tugged with such force that the front two legs of the wooden chair lifted up.

Purity's eyes remained dull as she stared at Captain Romer, who stood before her with her hands clasped behind her back, in the same formal posture she'd used when addressing Brand. The room was lit by a single whale-oil lantern above Purity's head. The reflected flame danced in Gale's eyes.

"I threatened to keelhaul you in the Sea of Wine," said Gale, in a cool, firm tone. "I may yet. However, you've so far had the good luck not to inflict a single substantial injury to any member of my family. We've killed a dozen of your minions and captured the rest. Given the pathetic nature of your menace, if you cooperate and answer our questions, I'll spare your life."

Purity's unfocused eyes showed no hint of understanding.

Gale tried her speech again, switching to Skelling. The woman still didn't react.

"She has no reason to answer us," grumbled Mako as he let go of her hair. He came around and grabbed Purity by the chin and turned her gaze toward his. He pulled his lips back to reveal his toothy jaws. "She'll be more cooperative if you let me chew on her a bit. Maybe her left ear should go first?"

"Stand aside," said Sorrow, pushing Mako away. She crouched before the woman and looked deeply into her eyes.

She shook her head slowly. "Something's wrong. I've seen this look before."

"Where?" said Gale.

"Among the Skellings. I told you I've traveled to the Isle of Grass. I barely survived my visit. Among the Skellings, women are treated as little more than cattle. There are no words in their language for romantic love. Marriage is indistinguishable from a master/slave relationship. I tried to help these women escape their oppressors, but couldn't. They'd endured such abuse that many of these women have literally had their souls snuffed out. They become empty shells, alive on an animalistic level, but devoid of free will."

"The other women we've imprisoned do seem unusually passive," said Gale.

"They're despondent in defeat," said Mako. "They were active enough when they were trying to chop our heads off."

I once more leaned against the wall and leapt from my body. All living things possess an internal light that my ghostly eyes can sense, though it's often so faint that I don't notice it in good lighting. Here in the dimly-lit hold, everyone in the room possessed a spiritual aura save for our captive. Her body gave little more light than the chair she was tied to. Her aura was a faint, flickering indigo.

I flashed back into my wooden body just in time to catch it before it toppled over.

"I can verify this woman has no soul," I said.

"How can you know that?" asked Mako.

"My eyes are different from yours." I didn't want to hint to Sorrow that I could escape her cage at will.

"Soul or no soul, if she's wilful enough to attack our ship, she's wilful enough to avoid pain," said Mako, gnashing his teeth. "She *will* answer our questions."

Infidel interrupted. "Hey, what happened to her sword? I grabbed it off the deck earlier."

"We secured it while you were unconscious," said Mako.

"Bring it here," she said.

"You've no rightful claim to it," said Gale. "It was used in an unjust assault on this ship. By the code of the Wanderers, the sword is mine."

Infidel closed her eyes and sighed. "I'm not trying to take the damn sword. I've got a hunch. I'm the only person on this ship who regularly fights using a weapon crafted from the body of a primal dragon. When I use it, I feel... it's tough to describe, but it's like an energy flows into me. I can feel it all the way to my toes. And it's not just a physical thing. For lack of a better description, I feel it spiritually as well."

"What's your point?" asked Mako.

"Since the Ice-Moon Blade is part of Hush, what if it does something similar? What if... I don't know... it empowers Purity?"

Gale nodded to Mako. "It's worth a shot. Bring it."

Mako left, muttering, his eyes narrowed. He returned moments later with the blade in his hand.

"I feel nothing when I hold the blade," he said, though his breath came out in a fog.

"You have a strong soul," I said. "Maybe its effects can only be felt by the weak."

"Careful," said Sorrow, taking the blade after coating her hands with silver to insulate herself. She knelt and placed the blade on the first band of negation. Nothing happened. Methodically, she moved the blade closer. The final band was only three inches from the captured woman's foot. As the barest edge of the blade crossed this threshold, frost suddenly painted the walls of the room.

The bound woman inhaled deeply, lifting her sagging head. Her irises, dark brown moments before, were now pale blue. She chuckled softly as her eyes fixed on Infidel.

"Ivory Blade," she said, smirking. "I never doubted you were on board."

Infidel stepped closer to Gale, so that Purity could better see her.

"People call me Infidel, not Ivory. If you really want to talk to Ivory, you're going to need a necromancer."

Purity pressed her lips tightly together, looking confused and disappointed.

"Why did you want Ivory Blade?" asked Gale.

"He stole the Jagged Heart from us! We cannot rest until it is recovered."

"The Jagged Heart didn't belong to you," said Infidel. "It belonged to the ice-ogres."

"It belonged to *Hush*," said Purity. "I am her final prophet."

"Hush is a dragon, not a god," said Gale. "What use has she for prophets?"

"Hush isn't *a* god," said Purity. "She's *the* god. She's the great unifier, the secret truth beneath all of creation. She is eternal silence and eternal peace. It's my sacred duty to usher in her final reign."

"The ogres worship Hush as a goddess as well," said Infidel. "I was friends with the priestess you stole the Jagged Heart from. If you both worship the same god, why couldn't you just have asked politely to use the harpoon?"

"The ogres are unworthy, impure beings," said Purity, wrinkling her nose. "I tolerate them merely as pawns. They know nothing of Hush's true peace."

Gale shook her head. "If you value peace, why attack my ship unprovoked?"

"If you'd turned Ivory Blade over to us, no one would have been harmed."

"You do see the underlying flaw in that argument?" asked Infidel.

"I have only your word that Blade's dead," said Purity. "Assuming it's true, I would also assume that *you* are now my most likely lead to reclaiming the Jagged Heart."

Gale and Sorrow remained poker-faced. Infidel looked like she was about to say something, then didn't. She frowned slightly. If we'd been playing cards, this would be the moment I went all in.

Apparently I wasn't the only one good at reading her expressions.

"It's here?" Purity asked, as passion returned to her voice. She sat fully upright in the chair. "The Jagged Heart is aboard this ship?"

"No," said Infidel. "I don't know where it is. Blade was already dead when I took his armor."

"You're a terrible liar," said Purity.

"And you're tied to a chair while your followers are confined by manacles," said Gale. "Infidel isn't the one being questioned here. You are."

"Ask what you wish," said Purity. "Only the guilty have anything to hide."

"First, who are you really?" asked Sorrow. "Why does everyone call you Purity? Purity was an ancient witch, but I found her grave. She died ages ago."

"Ancient?" Purity chuckled. "Do I look ancient to you?"

Sorrow shook her head. "No. You're what? Thirty-five? Forty? And, if you were the real Purity, you wouldn't have needed the sword to do your ice magic. You'd have the power embedded in your skull. But I've felt your scalp. There's not a single nail in it."

The bound woman laughed.

"What so funny?" asked Sorrow.

"You and your ridiculous scalp, studded with nails. You truly believe these to be the source of your power?"

"I've empirical evidence that they work, yes."

"You know nothing of true magic," said Purity.

"Enlighten me," said Sorrow.

"True magic is passion. True magic is hatred and anger and the thirst for revenge. This is the power that binds me to this world two centuries after my first death."

Perhaps it was my imagination, but I thought Sorrow held her head a little higher upon hearing this definition of true magic.

Gale, on the other hand, looked exasperated. "Make up your mind. Are you after revenge or peace? You can't have both."

"Don't be foolish," said Purity. "Revenge fits peace like a hand fits a glove."

"If you've nothing to hide," said Sorrow, "tell us everything. If you don't use nails to gain your power, what is the source?"

"I've told you," said Purity. "Hatred binds me. When I was thirteen, Skellings attacked my village. I watched them disembowel my father while my mother was raped. My youth and beauty spared me from the worst of their violence. I was taken as a prize to be presented to the Skelling overlord. His name was Gorg. He weighed three hundred pounds and smelled of rotten teeth. I was given to him on the eve of the winter solstice; it was considered good fortune for a Skelling warlord to deflower an innocent on that night.

"He was not gentle." Purity shook her head slowly, as if trying to fight back the memory.

"I'm sorry this fate befell you," said Sorrow. "I know all too well the cruelty of men. I intend to create a world where such things happen no more."

Purity's haunted expression changed to one of amusement. She chuckled softly. "You shall fail, little witch. Are you as blind as I was? Sheltered and protected, ignorant of the truth of the world?"

"My life has been anything but sheltered."

"Then release your dreams of a just world to the winds. They are of no more value than dust. The core of life is pain and violence. You can no more strip cruelty from the heart of man than you can peel thunder from lightning. I learned this truth well on the night Gorg tore my flesh with his violent lusts. A weaker woman would have withered when faced with such a horrifying truth, to know that nothing compels the strong to have mercy upon the weak. I, on the other hand, embraced the truth. The world belongs to those strong enough to take it. I killed Gorg with his own dagger. I gouged his eyes from his fat face, then ran into the night, losing myself in the wild, frozen wastes of the Isle of Grass."

"I've experienced those wastes," said Sorrow. "You're lucky to have survived, especially during the winter solstice."

"But I didn't survive," said Purity. "I ran until I could no longer move my legs, then fell numb and senseless in the snow. My soul slipped loose of my body and I found myself alone, all alone, on an endless plain of ice. The sky above was bright with crisp stars. There was no wind. Never had I listened to such silence. I could see my lifeless body at my feet, the skin a pale blue-white. I was draped in nothing but a bearskin blanket. My naked feet and hands had turned black. Frozen blood crusted my face, though I cannot say whether this was my blood or Gorg's.

"I turned from my body and began to walk. That weak slab of meat and bone no longer felt important to me. I journeyed for a very long time. My feet left no trace upon the snow. The quiet absorbed my every thought. All the pain of life slowly faded from memory. Not just the abuse I'd suffered, but the tiny pains, the small day-to-day agonies that accompany a body, the pangs of hunger or thirst, the needle pricks of heat and cold. I was free. Truly free, in a world where all was black and white, where peace was the final solution. The one heartache I felt, the one pain, was to think that all the living world was denied such a heaven."

"No offense, but your afterlife sounds kind of boring," said Infidel. "I've been to a couple of dead lands counting the one we're in. Both had dragons, and definitely weren't dull."

"Ah," said Sorrow. "But my afterlife had a dragon as well. Whether I had walked for hours or years, I cannot guess, but as I journeyed a shape rose on the horizon. As I grew closer I found a giant mountain of ice carved into the shape of a dragon. I entered through the mouth. Within this mountain were tunnels. I explored them, drawn by a force I did not yet understand. In the center of the mountain, where a true dragon's heart would have been, I found an altar. Upon this altar was the Ice-Moon Blade. When I lifted it, my soul was pulled inside. Hush whispered to me. Then I woke.

"I was in a new body. It was springtime on the Isle of Grass, and the fields were covered in yellow flowers. In the placid meltwater of a nearby pool I saw that I was now a woman in her fifties. She was half lame and blind in her right eye as a result of beatings. I had only the faintest echo of her memories. She'd found the Ice-Moon Blade in a streambed where it had washed down from the glaciers. My spirit now filled a body whose original soul had withered long ago.

"I murdered her husband and his brothers, even her sons who treated her as no more than a slave. Eventually I was caught and killed. My soul once more retreated into the sword. What happened in the intervening gap I don't know, but a dozen years later the blade was touched by a young woman, merely fourteen, who'd suffered a miscarriage after being kicked in the belly by her father. I rode her for a long time, and killed many men as I mastered the true power of the Ice-Moon Blade. Eventually, that body fell. To this day, the Skellings call her grave my grave. Since then, nine different women have carried my soul."

"This one shall be your last," said Mako.

"Truly? Kill this body if you wish. Drag it in the Sea of Wine for all I care. My soul will always fly free and return to the blade."

Sorrow looked at me. "Looks like you aren't the only bodiless soul aboard. Maybe Rott wasn't after you. A two-hundred-year-old soul is probably a much tastier meal."

Purity shook her head. "Do you seek to intimidate me with talk of the dragon of decay? I'm the prophet of Hush. Her power is greater than that of entropy. She is timeless. She existed before all, and will endure beyond all. From eternal cold, dark and silent, the world has flickered. Now it sputters; soon it fades. The hush of an unending winter night is the only true eternity."

"The other primal dragons would argue with that," said Gale. "Certainly the sea is eternal; Abyss is more powerful than Hush."

Purity shook her head. "The sea shall freeze, go silent, and find peace. The oceans are merely restless ice; one day they will slumber."

"I wouldn't be so cavalier about Rott. Death is forever," I said, aware of the irony that I should make such an argument.

"In the cold, even death loses power. Decay ceases; entropy grinds to a halt."

"For a little while," said Infidel, raising the Gloryhammer. "But sooner or later, the sun will rise again."

"The sun?" growled Purity. "Glorious, the dragon of the sun, shall be the first to die when the Jagged Heart is in my grasp."

"What?" asked Mako, sounding amused. "You're going to go jab the sun with a harpoon?"

"Killing it forever, yes," said Purity.

Mako no longer looked amused. His brow furrowed as he looked at his mother. "That, uh, can't happen, can it?"

Infidel cleared her throat, "When I was in Greatshadow's realm, he told me that the Jagged Heart was created when Hush fell in love with Glorious and had her advances rebuffed. The bad blood goes back a long way."

"This is stupid," said Mako. "How does one harpoon the sun?"

"You can't," said Sorrow. "Not in the material world. But in the abstract realms?"

I buzzed in with my paper tongue. "Aurora told me the Jagged Heart had the power to open the door to an abstract realm. Something called the Great Sea Above. It's like heaven for ice-ogres."

"I say it can't happen," said Mako, crossing his arms.

"I dunno," said Infidel. "Greatshadow said the harpoon could have killed him. The abstract realms follow the same rules as dreams. Anything's possible."

"No," said Sorrow. "Not anything. It's not dreams that lie beneath the abstract realms; it's myth. Myths are symbolic, resonant truth. Dreams don't have to make sense. Myths must make more sense than actual reality."

"I get that dreams are kind of random," said Infidel. "But I hardly would call the myths I learned as a child sensible. I remember one where a wolf disguised himself as an old woman. Not exactly plausible."

"It's not the details that matter," said Sorrow. "It's the message. Myths are the vessels of great truths. They teach us about justice and love and courage. They help define who we are. Every culture I know of has a myth explaining the creation of the world, and foretelling its destruction. The notion that, before there was heat and light, there was cold and darkness, is a pretty common belief. Simple symmetry predicts that if cold was the beginning, it shall also be the end. Myths follow grand cycles. Everything that is created must one day be destroyed."

Mako threw up his hands, utterly frustrated. "So you're telling me it makes sense that someone can stab the sun with a long, pointy stick and kill it? You and I live in very different realities."

Sorrow nodded. "The thing about myths is they tend to overpower reality. The great truths they carry they have the power to push aside the more mundane truths of the material world."

"That's the most absurd thing I've ever heard anyone say," said Mako.

"I agree," Sorrow said, with a shrug. "That doesn't make it false. I'm a materialist. My powers come from seeing through the illusions that limit most people when they interact with the material world. Even though my mind is superbly attuned to recognize reality, I live my life in daily pursuit of things that are not real. I search for justice. I follow a code of honor. I pursue fairness and equality. But justice, honor, fairness, equality... these aren't real. They don't exist as measurable objects. If there were a scale, and on one plate there were a single grain of sand, I could not place a single crumb of honor upon the counter plate to tip it. Yet I value these things more than food, shelter, or any comfort. I've pledged my life to advance these causes. Just because something isn't real doesn't mean it isn't true."

"Truth is stark," said Purity, staring at Sorrow. "Truth is hard. And truth is all that matters."

I scratched my coconut skull. I'd heard these words before, from Father Ver. Was it pure coincidence that I'd hear them again? Or was it just evidence that when you stripped away the quibbling details of the various faiths, all fanatics essentially thought alike?

There were three loud bangs on the boards above us that caused everyone to jump.

"Ma!" Jetsam shouted, sounding as if he were kneeling on the deck directly above.

"What?" Gale shouted back.

"Sage said to let you know it was time," shouted Jetsam.

"Thank you," Gale shouted. She looked Purity in the eyes. "You're a very lucky woman. I'm eager to get back to the material world, so, as tempting as it might be, I'm not going to keelhaul you. As for your fantasies of killing the sun, I think it's best we end this now. I'm tossing both your sword and the Jagged Heart overboard before we leave the Sea of Wine. They'll be lost forever."

"No way!" said Infidel. "The Jagged Heart has to go back to Qikiqtabruk. I've made a vow!"

"On this ship, I'm the final judge and authority," said Gale. "Consider yourself released from your vow. The harpoon goes overboard."

Infidel protested, "But Aurora –"

"– wasn't insane," I said, putting my hand on Infidel's shoulder. "Do you really think if she knew what Purity planned to do with the harpoon, she'd handle things any differently?"

"Stagger!" said Infidel. "I'm doing this for you! You're the one who made the promise to Aurora!"

"She was dying." I shrugged. "Was I supposed to say no?"

"So your vow to her was only a convenient lie?"

I crossed my arms. "There's a difference between lying and changing your mind as new information becomes available."

"What of our wedding vows? Can they also be tossed aside as new information becomes available?"

"What?" I asked, feeling dizzy. How had she made the leap to this?

Captain Romer, sensibly, had no patience for our little spat.

"Mako, meet me on the deck with the harpoon."

Infidel placed herself in front of the stairs. "No one is leaving until I've had my say." The hair around her face began to flutter, as if in a strong breeze.

"We know what you have to say," said Gale. "I admire your sense of devotion, but you cannot prevail."

"Anyone who... anyone who tries... tries to get past this door... will find out... how much I... can prevail." Infidel sounded winded. She looked confused. Suddenly, the Gloryhammer slipped from her grasp and her eyes rolled up into her head. I leapt forward, catching her before she hit the floor.

"What just happened?" I asked.

"I blocked the air from flowing back into her lungs, causing her to faint," said Gale. "She'll be good as new in a minute or so."

Mako slipped past both of us and headed down the hall.

Gale turned to Sorrow. "Is the sword safe to carry?"

"For you? I don't think it's a problem. You obviously have a robust soul. I think Purity can only flow into bodies when the host's soul is weak or absent. That's why her army seems so lifeless. She gathered other women with damaged souls to use in case her current body is compromised."

"She might be able to jump into a body even if the sword doesn't touch it," I said. "The sword was knocked from her grasp by Brand earlier. It fell a few feet away but didn't break the link."

"It didn't quite touch her now," said Sorrow. "Fortunately, all her soulless spares are shackled. There's no one she can jump to, even if she can travel more than a few feet from the blade."

Purity listened to all this talk with a blank expression. If her ghost remained inside this body, she wasn't wasting any energy on manipulating the face. Sorrow retrieved the Ice-Moon Blade carefully and handed it to Gale. They both held their breath for a second, then Gale smiled. "I'm still me."

She left the hold, climbing to the deck. I followed, carrying Infidel in my arms. As we emerged into the permanent sunset, her eyes fluttered open.

"What happened?" she asked weakly.

I paused as I looked down at her face. I didn't want to lie to her. But, if I told the truth, she'd be back on her feet, fighting to stop Gale. "You fainted," I said, which was at least partly true.

"I don't remember... were we arguing?" She lifted her fingers to the knot on the side of her head and winced.

"You've just overexerted yourself," I said, sitting her down beside the door to the forecastle. Menagerie flapped over to us and sat beside her, a concerned look in his hound dog eyes.

"I had trouble breathing?" she said, half statement, half question. "I've never fainted before."

I was glad that my coconut face and paper voice lacked expression. Otherwise, she would have readily sensed how troubled I was as I said, "It was stuffy in the hold. You've not had much to eat since you got injured. You're breathing for two now. You need to take it easy. When we get back home, our first priority is going to be to find someplace where you can live in peace and quiet."

She sighed. "Peace and quiet. It's going to be..."

"Boring?" I asked.

"A nice change," she said, scratching Menagerie on the back of his neck, where fur and feathers intermingled. "I swear, I really don't wake up in the mornings thinking, 'Boy, I can't wait to fight a dragon today!'"

I laughed, or tried to. She smiled.

Then Mako came onto the deck with the Jagged Heart, still wrapped in its frost-covered sail.

Infidel's whole body went stiff as Mako met his mother at the starboard rail. "What are they – ?"

"This is for the best," I said, placing my root-hand against her shoulder, pinning her against the boards. "Aurora would understand."

"You son of a bitch," Infidel growled, as her eyes flashed to anger. She thrust her arm toward the Jagged Heart, and shouted, "Fetch!"

Menagerie shot forward like he'd been sitting on a spring just as Mako flipped the sail over the edge, letting it unfurl, sending the harpoon toward the Sea of Wine. Menagerie's ever changing form shifted, his mouth and wings growing bigger, his body smaller and more streamlined as he flapped to full speed. Gale tossed the sword overboard just as Menagerie's jaws clamped onto the shaft of the harpoon. The weight of the harpoon proved too great for his pelican wings and he dropped like a stone, vanishing from my sight over the rail as the sword, too, disappeared.

I stood, spinning from Infidel, suddenly wishing we'd made more of an effort to find out how far Purity's soul could travel from the sword. Because, whatever faint intelligence might yet linger in Menagerie, there was also the very real possibility that he was a body without a soul.

From off the starboard rail came the laughter of a woman, as the bloody sky above us began to snow.

CHAPTER THIRTEEN
LAST, BEST HOPE

WITH A FLAPPING sound like the world's largest swan taking to air, an angel rose next to the *Freewind*. I use the term *angel* only because that's what springs to mind when one is confronted with a human body held aloft on giant feathered wings. Of course, calling the body human was stretching things a bit. The thing that flew above our ship was shaped like a woman, slender and well-muscled, but the limbs and torso were covered in black and tan fur similar to a hound. The woman's hair was a mass of long platinum curls and as the breeze pushed the hair from her face I was shocked to find that her visage bore a striking resemblance to my wife. Menagerie had some of Infidel's blood in him after all.

In the creature's left hand was the Jagged Heart. In the right was the Ice-Moon Blade. The blended thing before us bent back her head and laughed as she flapped to the level of the crow's-nest.

"What a marvelous shell!" she said, growing an extra set of arms from beneath her first two as she spoke. "It's as malleable as false matter!" The black and tan fur rippled as it changed to a downy white. The enormous pelican wings were mostly white save for their black tips, but even these faded to the color of new fallen snow. Purity's pale eyes glowed red with the reflected light of the omnidirectional sunset as she stared down at Gale and Mako.

"I'm almost grateful enough for this protean gift that I'm tempted to let you live," she laughed. "Almost."

She extended the Jagged Heart toward Captain Romer. I turned, intending to grab Infidel and carry her to safety since the Gloryhammer was downstairs in the hold, but she was gone. In the passageway beneath me I heard running footsteps.

The deck above the main hold splintered as Infidel exploded into the air, flashing toward Purity faster than I could follow. She slammed the head of the Gloryhammer into the woman's jaw with a fury that made me wince. Purity's head snapped backward, tearing at the throat, nearly decapitated by the blow. Infidel's momentum carried her skyward, leaving Purity dangling in mid-air for the microseconds it would take for her wings to realize they were dead.

Only the wings kept flapping. Even as Purity's head continued to tear from its shoulders, a new head grew in its place. Menagerie had been able to change shapes too swiftly for the eye to follow. Purity had inherited his speed.

"That was unpleasant," Purity's new head grumbled as her old head dropped toward the Sea of Wine. High above, Infidel had managed to halt her upward course and was now turning back down for another pass.

If Purity had delayed even a tenth of a second, Infidel might have stopped her. As it was, the four-armed witch waved the Ice-Moon Blade toward the mainmast of the *Freewind* and suddenly there was a full scale iceberg looming above us, the mast caught within its core. Every timber shuddered as the boat began to tilt toward starboard.

Then, with Infidel barely a hundred feet away, Purity swept the Jagged Heart across the sky, cutting open a rip in reality. A black night glittering with stars showed through the gash. Purity flapped her wings to race into this new sky just as Infidel passed through the space where she'd dangled an instant before. Infidel swung her feet down, trying to slow her descent, but by her speed I guessed she was about to smash straight through the deck. Yet before she hit, every rope in sight rose to catch her, forming an impromptu net. She punched through the deck despite this, but it sounded as if she came to a crashing halt below without breaking through the hull.

Not that it much mattered.

The iceberg around the mast weighed at least as much as the ship. The *Freewind* turned completely on its side as the iceberg crashed into the waves of wine. Everyone on deck was thrown toward the sea.

The last thing I noticed, as I tumbled toward the wine, was that the flies had caught up to us once more. I hit the rail with a jolt that flipped me roots over nuts, and the world went dark. An instant later I was submerged, unable to see. Ropes tangled about me, halting my further descent. For a panicked moment I struggled, certain I would drown, before the fluid washing about within my barrel chest reminded me that I had no lungs.

Calming myself, I searched the darkness for the red glow of the endless sunset. Instead, everything was black as pitch in all directions. Then, in the distance, I saw a light flicker to life. I turned toward it, and saw that it was a lantern held by a red-haired girl who was standing on the main mast at a 90 degree angle, walking along it like a spider. Cinnamon?

I pushed my head above the surface and the puzzle pieces slipped into place. It wasn't Cinnamon who was sideways, it was the ship. The *Freewind* was on its side, the masts parallel with the water. And, judging from its grayish hue, this was indeed water. We were no longer in the Sea of Wine. Captain Romer must have triggered our journey back.

I tried to call out to Cinnamon, but my waterlogged tongue failed to produce even a squeak. Not that my ordinarily faint voice was likely to have been heard over the noise all around. It sounded as if there was a waterfall not ten feet behind me, and every timber of the ship was groaning. Add the pops and cracks coming from the sizeable iceberg that loomed in the darkness, plus the general lapping of waves, and it's a wonder that I was able to hear Mako call out, "We're taking in water! Get the main hatch closed!"

I spun around and found the source of the waterfall. The main hatch was indeed open, and given the perpendicular orientation of the deck, the bottom edge of the gaping hole was a good foot below the waves, sinking deeper by the second. Ordinarily, the double hatch doors lay flat against the deck when open, one toward starboard, one toward port. The port door was the half above water. Jetsam appeared from nowhere, swimming through the air with graceful kicks. He released the pin that secured the hatch door to the deck and darted aside as the giant door swung under its own weight to crash shut. Unfortunately, this did nothing to ease the immediate crisis; the starboard half of the hatch was the part taking on water, and the door was beneath the waves.

I let the current carry me to the edge of the hatch, catching myself before I was pulled into the hold. With my wooden fingers stiff and waterlogged, I groped for the outer edges of the door beneath me. I found them, but the wood wouldn't budge; it was no doubt secured by a pin.

Mako appeared in the water beside me, gasping for air. He'd obviously been beneath the water, trying to move the door. "I can't see the damn pin!" he shouted. "Get the lantern closer, Cinnamon!"

Cinnamon turned from studying the ice-bound upper half of the mast and ran along the thick wooden beam with confidence. A rope swung out as she jumped. She landed at a crouch on the looped rope, dangling the lantern down until the base skimmed the waves. The water glowed, pale and ghostly.

Mako sucked in air and dived. I followed, dragging myself down along the door's edge. I reached the bottom and found Mako trying to free a wooden pin that ran through a small metal ring, securing the door. It was stuck, resisting even his enviable muscles. I reached for it to give aid, but before I drew near he thrust his mouth to the metal ring and bit it in twain. I'd never seen anyone spit underwater, but he managed to do so, sending the fragmented pin and ring tumbling into the dark depths. Mako strained to move the door, which was heavy even in air. Trying to move it through water required more than strong jaws. I braced myself as best I could and got both hands underneath the edge. Slowly, the heavy wooden door began to move. Mako got beneath it, his muscles straining as he added to my efforts. In half a minute we had the hatch jutting out at a right angle to the deck, at which point it was impossible to move it further while we were in the water.

"Where's Rigger?" Mako shouted as he thrust his head up for air. He glanced at Cinnamon on her rope. "He's obviously recovered."

"Well enough," a faint voiced cried off to our left. Rigger was sitting in the doorway of the forecastle. From above, a block and tackle with a sizeable hook descended toward us. It took Mako a few seconds to secure it to the door's edge. He and I pushed from below, but Rigger and his pulleys did the real work, lifting the door until it was free of our grasp. It closed into place and Jetsam flitted around the edges, securing a further series of pins that held it shut.

"S-s-so c-cold," Cinnamon said as she wrapped her arms around herself. Everyone was breathing out great puffs of fog, and ice was starting to form on every moist surface.

"Our course was plotted for the arctic," Mako said. "Look at the stars! See how the Tallship hangs on the horizon; we're well north of the Silver Isles."

I glanced up. Unfortunately, while I was an expert at finding my way through trackless jungles, I was completely lost trying to fix my location via constellations.

"Where's Mother?" Rigger asked.

"I don't know," Mako called back. "She was near the main hatch as we were turning water. I saw her crouch to touch the deck and trigger our journey back to the real world, but lost sight of her after that."

"Find her," shouted Mako. "Our only hope of saving the ship is to get wind under the sails to push us upright."

I suspected that was a doomed mission. With the masts

dipped down into the waves, the canvas sails were spread out beneath the water, their white forms giant, ghostly jellyfish.

"I know that Poppy was in her bunk," Mako said. "Mother, Sage, Infidel, and Sorrow are unaccounted for."

"Also Brand and the princess," said Jetsam.

"And the ice-maidens!" said Cinnamon.

"Abyss take the ice-maidens," growled Mako. "Unless they've become master locksmiths, we know where they are."

The ship groaned as it sank lower in the water. The sound was both physical, caused by the stress applied to ship's beams as it sat at such an unnatural angle, and spiritual. The ship's ghost was screaming, an incoherent howl of pain that only I seemed aware of.

I tried to speak, but again found my tongue useless. My wooden body was so tangled in rope there was no chance it would sink into the deep. I abandoned it, crossing the threshold of the golden door in my chest and flying free, a phantom once more. Instantly, my ghostly senses returned and the savage chill of the night sliced through me. The Romers were dressed for a tropical climate. Freed of the sepia hues of my wooden eyes, I could see the blue cast to their lips.

The ship groaned again and with a thought I was at the figurehead, its carved features now twisted in pain.

"I c-can't hold the t-timbers together much longer," Jasmine's ghost stammered. "S-saw off the main mast if you m-must! It's our only h-hope of r-righting the ship!"

"On it," I said.

I ghosted into the ship's hold, to the captured women in their manacles, now thrown against the ship's hull as if it were a floor. It was pitch dark; I could only see them splashing around thanks to my ghostly senses, and even this was a strain. These women's souls were like ash-covered embers, nearly invisible. Fortunately, they possessed at least some will to live, as most struggled to stand. Failing to stand meant drowning; the water in the hold was now hip-deep. Those who'd been knocked unconscious by the ship's tumble were being helped by Sage and Sorrow.

Though it was entirely the wrong moment for such an experiment, I had to know. I reached my phantom fingers into the torso of the nearest woman. Would my still vital spirit fill her nearly soulless body?

Alas, whatever trick Purity used to possess others eluded me. I felt no connection with the woman's physical form. My half-formed notion to control her and tell the others to saw the main mast free was thwarted. Worse, my faint hope that I might find a new permanent body should I somehow happen upon a soulless male was dashed almost before I'd even fully conceived it.

I shrugged the failure off. There were more pressing problems. Where was Infidel?

At the thought, the braided wedding band on my hand tugged my arm out. I followed, sensing a connection to the band of hair she wore. I ghosted into the galley. Bags of flour had burst, coating everything in a pale white powder. The air smelled of vinegar, lard, and molasses. Dark gore coated the left side of Infidel's scalp; shards of glass stuck from her hair. She was stretched out on the floor, only, as I made sense of the boat's tilt, I realized she was actually standing, and that the floor was now a wall she leaned against. She stood in shin deep water, conscious, though obviously dazed. The glove of the Immaculate Attire brushed the goop from the side of her head, leaving clean skin in its wake. She wasn't bleeding; a broken jar of molasses had shattered as it bounced around the small space and was dripping down upon her. Infidel groped for the Gloryhammer beneath the wheat-frosted water, lifting it to cast light on a large splintered hole in the wall. Or rather, the ceiling, turned sideways. This was the hole she'd punched in through. She was close to the waterline, but not quite submerged; icy waves sloshed across the broken boards as the ship pitched.

She jumped back through the hole and shot into the air.

"Where's Purity?" she shouted.

"Gone!" Mako shouted back. "The ice is pulling the ship under!"

"Not if I can help it," she called out, landing near the crow's-nest, buried beneath at least thirty feet of ice. She planted her boots on the slick surface and swung the Gloryhammer overhead in a two handed grip. With a grunt, she struck, hitting the ice with such force that her feet lifted into the air. I raised my hand instinctively to protect my eyes from the flying shards, though, of course, they passed through my phantom form harmlessly. The blow sounded like lightning striking mere yards away, and the crackling that followed had the quality of an electrical storm. Deep cracks ran through the ice and also through the frozen mainmast.

The ship screamed like a woman in childbirth as the main mast splintered at its base, then snapped completely. Infidel was thrown back as the iceberg tilted, but the hammer lifted her skyward long before her boots hit the water.

The ship shuddered as it rose slightly, but failed to right itself. All of its sails were waterlogged, and the rooms beneath on the starboard side were filled with water.

A small hatch on the poop deck suddenly banged open. Captain Romer crawled out, completely drenched. My hunch is she'd been swept into the hold by the rushing water.

Gale wasted no time. She surveyed the chaos around her and began to bark commands. "Cut all the sails! They're dead weight at this point."

Mako dived into the icy ocean, snapping ropes with his teeth. Between his speed in the water and Rigger's powers, the sails wouldn't weigh us down for long.

I flashed back into my wooden body, determined to make myself useful. Unfortunately, I was still tangled in ropes. Instinctively, I reached for my bone-handled knife, but, of course, that was tucked in the belt of my ghostly form, not this clunky wooden shell. I wound up getting a free ride as the boat tilted and slowly rose. The Romer brothers had succeeded in their task.

Mere minutes after the peril had seized us, it was over. The boat was upright, or something like it: the ship listed to starboard at least twenty degrees.

"Romers!" a woman's voice called out. I looked toward the foredeck and saw Sorrow. When had she come from below? She was standing by the ship's enormous iron anchor, which had somehow managed not to slip from the deck. She placed her hand upon the painted black iron. "Gather round before you catch your death of cold!"

The iron anchor bent upward as she grabbed it in the center. She formed it into a rough tripod, and rubbed her hands along the tip of the tripod until the iron glowed a deep cherry red. She snatched her fingers back and said, "This thing's hot as a stove, so be careful."

Cinnamon and Jetsam were beside it a moment later, their hands outstretched, steam pouring off their black sleeves.

"Thank the seven stars," Cinnamon whispered through chattering teeth.

"Hooray for witchcraft!" said Jetsam, riding the warm updraft above the hot metal.

It took a few moments for the rest of the Romers to join us. Captain Romer used her control of the wind to circulate a warm dry breeze heated by the anchor. Even the captives below would get their share of life-saving warmth. The immediate danger of hypothermia was averted. Infidel was the final arrival, landing across from me on the opposite side of the anchor, her gaze not meeting mine.

"You've some nerve to return to the ship," Mako growled.

"I did just free you from a killer iceberg," said Infidel.

"If you hadn't sent your damn monster to catch the harpoon, none of this would have happened!"

"We can't know that," said Sorrow. "Given her experience

with possessions, Purity probably sensed Menagerie's soulless shell the second she came on board. She may have timed seizing his body to take advantage of the instant Mako dropped the Jagged Shard. Magical weapons sometimes act to protect their users via enchantments their owners might not even know about. It's possible if she'd attacked while Mako carried the harpoon, she would have wound up frozen, or worse."

"This is nothing but speculation," said Mako.

"Informed speculation," said Sorrow. "The Jagged Heart isn't carved from lifeless ice; it's the very heart of a primal dragon, or a fragment of it, at least. It's more magic than matter. It bonds spiritually with its owner. It's almost a parasitic relationship, as the owner provides the weapon with mobility and purpose while the weapon provides the owner with powers and defenses. It's similar to Infidel's Gloryhammer."

"The Gloryhammer doesn't defend me as much as I'd like," grumbled Infidel.

"Doesn't it?" asked Sorrow. "The bones of your arms should be shattered by the blows you deliver. The weapon should rip from your merely human grasp as it accelerates you into flight faster than an arrow leaves a bowstring. Its enchantments protect you passively; there may be other powers you could utilize if only you knew of them."

"How would I find out about them?" Infidel asked. "For instance, I can make it glow brighter or softer just by thinking, but it seems like it should also be able to put out heat, which would come in useful in times like this. But no matter how hard I try to make it hot, it stays cool to the touch."

Sorrow nodded. "That's because the sun isn't a source of heat."

Infidel furrowed her brow, confused.

"The monk Inquisitus proved three centuries ago that heat originates within the earth and light originates within the sun. The two are attracted to one another, but have independent sources."

"I can feel heat on my face when I look at the sun," said Infidel.

Sorrow shook her head. "You feel the heat attracted to the light reflecting off your face. Inquisitus proved his theory by documenting temperatures at over nine-hundred locations. His data show that the peaks of mountains are consistently cooler than the land surrounding them. If the sun were the source of heat, mountaintops should be warmer, since they're nearer. Conversely, the bottoms of mines, far removed from the sun, are intensely hot. Thus, he proved that the core of the earth is the true source of warmth."

Captain Romer interrupted. "This is all very interesting, but let's focus on our immediate problem. Putting aside the issue of who's to blame, the fact remains that we're the only people in the world aware that there's a shape-shifting ghost planning to murder the sun, armed with a weapon that makes her capable of the crime. How do we stop her?"

"This doesn't have to be our fight," said Mako. "King Brightmoon and the Church of the Book know of the harpoon's power."

"We've got the king's daughter chained to a bunk down below," said Rigger. "We can send her to ask for help."

His voice was so deadpan, I didn't recognize this as a joke until Poppy giggled.

Captain Romer sighed, rubbing her eyes. "Have we checked on the prisoners? Is everyone okay?"

"Bumps and scrapes from being tossed around," said Sage. "They're fine."

Captain Romer nodded and looked around the ship. "Unchain the prisoners," she said. "We've got an enormous amount of work to do to get this ship seaworthy again, starting with a bucket brigade to get the water out of the holds. Any prisoner willing to pitch in will be set free at the next port. Anyone not willing to help will be pointed toward the nearest island and allowed to make a swim for it."

"Even Brand and the dwarf?" Mako asked.

Captain Romer nodded.

"Maybe the dwarf really is Princess Innocent," Poppy said.

Mako rolled his eyes. "You're as crazy as she is. *He*. As crazy as he is."

"We deal with crazy every day," said Sage. "Having a long-missing princess hiding aboard our ship is almost mundane."

"It doesn't matter," Rigger said, dismissively. "With the ship crippled, it could take weeks to deliver our so-called princess to her so-called father. Meanwhile every time the sun goes down, we'll be wondering if it's coming back up again."

"Infidel can fly her," said Sage.

"Um, no," said Infidel. "I'm a wanted criminal in the Silver Isles. I'd never get near the king."

"It doesn't matter," said Gale. "The dwarf isn't the princess. Next idea?"

Infidel asked, "If we're in the arctic, how far are we from Aurora's village? The ice-ogres know more about the Jagged Heart than anyone. We can enlist their help in stopping Purity."

"We're less than three hundred miles," said Sage, looking up at the stars.

"I could reach it in four or five hours, maybe," said Infidel. "I can take Sorrow, since she speaks the lingo."

Sorrow shook her head. "I'll be needed here. Wood-weaving is one of the material arts I've mastered. If this ship can be saved, my talents will come in handy."

"There is no 'if,'" said Gale. "We will repair the *Freewind*."

"I'm not as confident," said Sorrow. "I'll do all I can to help, but look around you. Every board on this ship has been twisted. There's not a nail or joint left flush. The *Freewind* may be beyond repair."

"Go with Infidel if that's your attitude," Gale grumbled.

"I'm sorry if you're wanting me to spout optimistic affirmations," said Sorrow. "I'm simply being realistic. But if optimism is what you are looking for, have you considered that the loss of the *Freewind* might be a positive development for your family?"

Gale's brow furrowed.

"The *Freewind* stands out in any harbor thanks to its burgundy hull. If you had a new ship, it would be harder for your enemies to spot you. You could have something like a normal life once more."

Jetsam laughed. "Normal? Have you paid any attention at all since you met us?"

Infidel interrupted. "We're getting sidetracked again. Who's going with me to the ogre village?"

Sorrow nodded toward me. "Take Stagger."

"I can't talk," I said, pointing at my mouth. Then I realized I'd heard my own words, albeit faintly. The warm breeze was drying out my tongue.

I shrugged as I lowered my hand. "I don't speak the language."

"I can work around this," said Sorrow. She reached up and grabbed the right bean pod that served as my ear, popping it off. Oddly, despite its removal, the backdrop noise of wind and waves didn't lesson.

"You'll be able to hear what this ear hears, no matter how far away you are," she said, fastening the bean pod to her golden earring with a loop of silver. "And, if I listen closely, I'll be able to hear what your other ear hears due to sympathetic vibrations. I can translate for you from afar."

"I want to be a witch when I grow up," said Cinnamon.

"You're a witch now," said Jetsam.

"Can... uh, can Infidel support my weight?" I asked. Despite the drying breeze, I was waterlogged. Although it wasn't my weight I was worried about; I knew she was still mad that I'd lied to her.

Infidel nodded. "Once I'm in the air, the extra weight doesn't really matter. Guess it's one of the powers of the hammer I don't really understand." She wasn't looking directly at me. "I'll need to wait until dawn. I don't know how to navigate via stars. In daylight, if I follow the coast line, I presume I'll be able to find the village from above."

"You might be waiting a while," said Rigger. "At this time of year, this far north, night lasts a long time."

"At winter solstice, the sun doesn't rise at all," said Sorrow, her voice trailing off.

"That's only a day away," said Rigger.

"Then that's all the time we have to stop Purity," said Sorrow.

"How can you be sure?" asked Gale.

"I can't be," said Sorrow. "But Hush is at her most powerful on the winter solstice. According to ice-ogre lore, Glorious, the sun dragon, is afraid to show his face on that day after months of being beaten back by Hush. When he does emerge the next day he's helpless as a newborn babe as he rises into the Great Sea Above. He survives only because he's so feeble that Hush pities him. Then he grows stronger and stronger, until he banishes the night completely. Only, he then takes pity on Hush for the pain he causes her, and in his moment of weakness, she once more begins to build her power."

"Ogre's have stupid legends," Mako grumbled.

"Maybe. But their myths also serve as a cultural warning against feeling pity for an enemy. In any case, Purity seems devoid of that particular emotion. What better moment could there be for her to strike than the dawn following the solstice?"

"If daylight's so short, I guess there's no point in waiting," said Infidel. "That fox-cloak Purity showed up in looked pretty warm, if anyone knows where it is. I have a feeling I'll need some good insulation once I get up in the air. Also a helmet, if there's one lying around."

If I'd had eyebrows, they'd have shot up.

"What?" she asked, sensing my surprise. "You think I can't learn?"

I shook my head.

Infidel looked at Gale. "Since I don't know how long I'll be gone, I'll carry fresh food and water for a week, if you can spare it." She cast a glance toward me and managed, "I guess I should be grateful you don't need to eat."

I nodded, relieved that she was at least speaking to me again.

"I'll get the cloak," said Sage, heading for the hatch.

"I'll gather provisions," said Cinnamon.

"There's still the question of how I'm going to find this place in the dark," Infidel said.

"I can find it," I announced.

"How?" Infidel sounded skeptical.

"Living things give off an aura. A village should stand out like a torch against the backdrop of a frozen, lifeless landscape."

"Excellent," said Captain Romer. "The two of you will be our primary plan to deal with this threat. I shall explore a second option."

"Which is?"

"There are secrets we Wanderers do not share with outsiders," said Captain Romer. "Suffice it to say, there are channels of communication within the ocean that extend far beyond human senses. It's possible I can get a message to... to my eldest son, Levi."

The Romer children's eyes grew wide at this announcement.

"Don't give me that look," Gale said.

"He'll betray us to the Stormguard," said Mako.

"No he won't," said Sage. "No matter what uniform he's wearing, he's still a Romer."

Gale nodded. "More importantly, his vessel is one of the few that could reach us in time to make a difference. The fate of the world might be at stake. If I have to swallow my pride and ask Levi for help, so be it."

"I like having a second plan," said Infidel. "Anyone got a third?"

Perhaps it was just a trick of the mind, brought on by one of my ears dangling against her cheek, but it sounded as if Sorrow started to speak. But her breath caught in her throat at the last second.

"What?" I asked. "You have a plan?"

"Not a plan, no," said Sorrow. "Nothing so fully formed."

"An idea? A hunch? A gut feeling?" I prodded.

Sorrow shook her head. "It's nothing. Undertake your mission as if you're the world's last, best hope."

CHAPTER FOURTEEN

BAD BLUBBER

READYING OURSELVES FOR the journey took some time. I needed new clothes so that my inhuman body wouldn't draw unwelcome attention, but even Mako's muscular frame was no match for my own. His pants only came to mid-shin, but his boots were tall enough that it hid the difference. With a little stuffing, his boot even made my peg leg look like a foot again. His shirt wouldn't go around my barrel chest. In the end, I wore it backward. Barrel staves were exposed on my back, but this was covered by a cape we made from old sails.

Unfortunately, as soon as I was dressed, my left arm stopped working. Sorrow was summoned. She discovered the copper wire that held my shoulder joint together was corroded and brittle.

"Sea water isn't good for any metal," she said as she fashioned me a new arm from a broken chair. "Even without your exposure to Rott you'd be falling apart."

"He's been falling apart since the day I met him," said Infidel.

Which was true enough. She'd met me when I was thirty-five. I was at my physical peak, my body hardened by years of jungle explorations. Alas, the problem with being at one's peak is there's no where to go but down. In the next fifteen years, I'd lost hair, teeth, muscle... everything but weight.

Sage had produced Purity's white fox-cloak, which fit Infidel perfectly, and complemented her Immaculate Armor as if they'd been made for each other. One of the smaller Skelling helmets had been de-horned to fit beneath her hood. It was little more than a steel hat, offering no protection for her face, but it was better than nothing.

Once she had fixed my arm, Sorrow took another Skelling helmet and stretched the metal to form a full faceplate, leaving only a gap for eyes. She placed this over my coconut noggin and wired it on. Sorrow produced a small silver mirror and I had to admit I passed as a human warrior, an intimidating one at that.

"Now the ice-ogres won't rip you apart for being an abomination against nature," said Sorrow.

"They'll just rip me apart for being human," I said. "Aurora made them sound a bit... isolationist."

"Ogres aren't known for their propitious natures," said Infidel.

"Propitious?" I asked.

"It means friendly," she said.

"I know what it means," I said. "It's just that you normally eschew magniloquence."

"I'm secure enough that I don't need to flaunt my intelligence. You use big words because the monks who raised you made you feel like an idiot. You've spent the last forty years trying to prove that you're smart."

"Ouch," I said, wounded by the penetrating sharpness of her analysis. "I take it you're still mad at me?"

"I can't understand why you didn't back me up. If Gale had just left the Jagged Heart alone, everything would be okay now. Don't you trust me?"

Sorrow cleared her throat as she ran the last of the fresh copper wires through my new arm. "Perhaps this would be a conversation best carried out in private?"

Infidel pressed her lips tightly together and nodded.

Sorrow made a few adjustments on my new arm, then said, "Almost done. Pick up the sea chest so we can test your strength."

The chest was sitting on its side behind the door, where it had come to rest following the upheaval. I grabbed it with my fresh arm and manhandled it back to the foot of the bed.

"Good as new," I reported, but my words we almost drowned out by a low, slow, unearthly wail that came from the other side of the wall, where there should be only ocean.

"What in the name of the primordial paper was that?" I asked.

"Whale song," said Infidel. "I first heard them during the Pirate Wars. The Wanderers try to keep it a secret from outsiders, but they understand the various whale languages."

"Whales talk?" I asked.

"This must be the secret Captain Romer wouldn't share with us," said Sorrow. "Whale songs travel great distances. Wanderers use the whales to pass on messages, allowing ships hundreds of miles distant to communicate."

"So help could be on the way soon," I said.

"Highly unlikely," said Sorrow. "In the summer, these waters are filled with fishing boats due to the abundance of cod. But during the winter, there's little to attract ships to these latitudes. I'm doubtful there's another Wanderer within a thousand miles."

As we talked, Sorrow shoved her hand-crafted sword into my belt. "I've been doing better with my fists," I said.

"Let's hope the only tool you really need is your tongue," she said. She gave me one last inspection. "You're as good as you're going to be. Fly safely."

We went above deck. Captain Romer gave Infidel a quick guide to the northern constellations. I noticed an odd shimmering haze in the sky. I slipped from my shell and saw the haze was rainbow colored, dancing about. I'd heard legends of the northern lights, but never expected to see them. They fluttered like an ethereal curtain draping the stars.

"Beautiful," I said, the second I'd returned to my body.

"Yes, handsome?" said Infidel.

If my mouth had been mobile I'd have smiled.

* * *

THEN WE WERE aloft. The *Freewind* quickly became a mere speck amid a sea of specks. Icebergs were everywhere. I hoped the ship regained its maneuverability before it was menaced by one of these crushing behemoths.

Once the ship was out of sight, it became impossible to guess how high we were. There were no familiar features with which to orient myself. The brightness of the Gloryhammer before us washed out most of the stars.

"I'm going to step out," I said.

"What?" Infidel yelled back.

"I'm going to step out of my body. I'll be limp for a moment."

"Go," she said.

I once more leapt from the golden cage and out through the wooden staves, sailing freely into the frigid winds. It occurred to me that if Sorrow was listening to my words, it's possible she now knew I could escape from her cage. She'd been treating me rather fairly since I'd given her the map to the Knight's Castle, but would she try to cage me again? I'd deal with that if and when I saw her.

I slowed, letting Infidel pass on. As the glow of the Gloryhammer faded into the distance, I saw that the curtains of light had dimmed, leaving behind stars of stunning crispness. Until now, I'd only seen the sky through the humid, gauzy air of my island home. Here, every last trace of moisture had frozen and dropped from the sky, leaving the stars fully exposed. I felt much the awe and wonder I'd experienced when, as a teen, I'd seen my first naked woman. I was glimpsing something ordinarily hidden from the eyes of man. I sensed that if I could understand what I was gazing upon, I would find wisdom.

Of course, the main wisdom I gathered in studying the bodies of women in my youth was that any serious course of education was going to be expensive. But these stars, these stars... The Sacred Writs are full of tales of men who go into wastelands to find communion with the Divine Author. At this moment, I grasped why. The stars were so numerous that patterns emerged wherever I glanced, as if the celestial canvas was some immense manuscript that a man might one day learn to read.

No wonder the ice-ogres thought of these starry reaches as heaven.

Of course, I had resisted the call of heaven so far. I shook off my fascination and returned to the task at hand. Looking back, though it had been beyond the gaze of my wooden eyes, I could see the *Freewind* aglow like a distant star against the inky darkness of the sea. To the north and west, I could see the sea turning white in the distance. Flying higher, I saw that I was gazing at a shoreline, like the world's smoothest, widest beach, formed of sand white as pure salt. But given the chill that numbed even my ghostly bones, I soon deduced I was looking not at sandy beaches, but at the edge of a vast, unbroken ice sheet.

Infidel was flying along the edge of this ice sheet, looking like a shooting star in the distance. With a thought, I was back at her side, animating the driftwood golem once more. She sensed my return and asked, "See anything?"

"The stars are amazing once you're free of the glare of the Gloryhammer."

"Hmm," she said. "You can't see the stars right now?"

"Not much."

"I see them fine," she said. "In fact, now that I think about it, I never get blinded by the hammer's glow. It must be one of those passive powers Sorrow talked about."

"I think I know another power of the hammer," I said.

"What?"

"When you were at the Jawa Fruit village, Tower flew straight to you, and I remember him saying that he'd told the hammer to find you. So the hammer has some kind of ability to track people."

"If that's true, why didn't he find me years earlier? He's had the hammer ever since I vanished, and was obsessed with me the whole time. Why didn't he come looking for me?"

"Maybe the hammer is like a bloodhound," I speculated. "It has to have some reference point to use for tracking?"

Infidel's face went blank as I said "bloodhound."

"You're thinking of Menagerie, aren't you?"

"Yeah," she said.

We flew on through the darkness for some time before she asked, "Is this all my fault?"

"I don't see how you can be blamed for the insane plans of a two-hundred-year-old witch."

"But what if I'd killed Menagerie when the Black Swan told me to? None of this would have happened."

"The Black Swan also told you to kill Greatshadow and you didn't," I said. "I think you made the right call. I think, against all odds, you converted an enemy of mankind into a grudging ally. I heard you explain your reasons to Zetetic. The Isle of Fire should remain untamed. I can't agree more."

"Am I crazy to want to raise our daughter there?"

"No," I said. "It's dangerous, but it's the only place in the world I've ever felt that life makes sense. You saw how happy my grandfather was living with the Jawa Fruit tribe. The island can be paradise if you respect it rather than trying to tame it."

"I know," said Infidel. "I want our daughter to love exploring the jungle just as much as we did. I want her to be able to appreciate nature by getting dirt and blood under her nails as she stalks her own meal. But I don't want her growing up as some naked, unwashed savage like your grandfather. I want her to read the books that you loved. I was bored by operas and museums and cathedrals when I was a girl, but now I want her to see these things, so that she can understand the beauty that man is capable of producing. How do I do this? How do I raise a child to be both wild and refined, civilized and feral all at once?"

"You're describing yourself, you know," I said. "Half-forest-dragon, half-princess. The ultimate blend of beast and beauty. My god, I never stood a chance. You captured my heart the moment I first laid eyes on you."

"Oh, that was just lust," she said, dismissively. "I was pretty hot when I was twenty."

"You're pretty hot now," I said.

"Actually, right now I'm freezing," she said. "My nipples are hard as walnut shells."

"It's lucky you ditched that chrome-plated bra."

She laughed, but then her voice went serious. "I'm scared, Stagger."

"Of being a mother?"

"What do I know about raising a child? What do I know about anything? Other women have mothers, sisters, best friends they can talk to. People who can tell them what to expect, what to worry about and what to shrug off. I don't have any of this. I'm thirty years old and I can rattle off a list of about three hundred people who've vowed to kill me, and precisely two people I count as friends, and they're both dead!"

"Two?" I said, instantly regretting that I sounded surprised she had a second friend.

"There's also Aurora," she said. "I mean, it's dumb. A month ago she was nobody to me. But I really connected with her on the dragon hunt. She told me her secrets, I told her mine, and... I dunno. There was a bond. It was almost like I had a sister. Which is why I feel so strongly about keeping this promise."

"I understand," I said. "But she won't know if you keep the promise or not."

"How do you know? You've managed to keep tabs on me."

"I saw Aurora move on. She went to her heaven... the Great Sea Above." I glanced up. "Maybe she's up there right now, looking down, watching us streak across her sky like a comet."

"If she's watching, she knows what a mess I've made," said Infidel. "Old Infidel would have shrugged this off. New Infidel intends to clean things up."

"Your newfound devotion to cleaning will probably be a big help in motherhood."

"Let's hope so."

"As for advice on childbirth and raising kids, Gale Romer can probably give you some guidance."

"She'll charge me for it," said Infidel. "We're not really friends. I was just a mercenary she employed. I liked her as a boss, but I can't say we were close. And after all the grief I've caused her on this trip, she probably hates me."

I didn't know what to say. Infidel couldn't return to her own family for assistance. My father was a monk and would be of no use; my mother had been a whore who abandoned me at an orphanage. I wasn't her only child, but even though I have a dozen half-siblings out in the world, they're strangers to me. My grandfather would probably be willing to help, but, as noted, he's gone feral. Also, while Judicious seemed remarkably sound in body and mind, it was no trivial matter that he was a whisker away from his hundredth birthday. It was no certain thing he'd be around in nine months.

"I don't know what the future holds," I said at last. "But if my past is any guide, things always work out."

"Not always," she said.

"Often enough," I said. "My gut tells me everything will be okay. My gut tells me you'll be a great mother."

"You don't have a gut anymore," she said.

"Well, my brains tell me."

"You don't have brains either!"

"True. All that's left is my soul. And if a soul isn't the ultimate judge of the rightness of things, what is?"

"Hmm," she said, before the faintest flicker of a grin crossed her face.

We flew on in silence. I felt as if she were happy for the moment, or at least in a state of relative peace, and I worried that it would be too easy to tip her mood back into worry.

Slowly, a curious thing unfolded. The sky at our backs grew noticeably lighter.

"Everything's turning blue," said Infidel as she slowed, turning back to watch the sky.

I slipped out of my shell to verify that this was so. An eerie twilight had broken through the gloom, distinctly azure in hue. Then, with no fanfare, the bright white upper edge of the sun peeked above the southern horizon. I'd never appreciated seeing the old dragon Glorious quite so much.

I wasn't the only one happy to see the sun. The internal glow of the Gloryhammer had intensified. The weapon gave off a slight crackling sound. Infidel held the weapon toward the distant orb.

"Feel this," she said. "Put your hand on the hammer."

I placed my gloved root on the shaft, but felt nothing. "What should I be feeling?"

"The hammer is sort of humming. It's almost like the purr of a kitten when it's being held by someone it knows."

"The Glorystones fell from the sky when Glorious first merged with the sun. Maybe the hammer remembers him. They've been separated for over a day now, since the sun never appeared on the Sea of Wine."

"Maybe," Infidel said.

But if the hammer truly had a memory, it was not allowed to dwell for long on these recollections. After a leisurely stroll across the horizon where it never quite got airborne, the distant sun once more began to recede.

We turned north and flew on, the landscape beneath us aglow in the relatively bright twilight. Against this backdrop, anything dark stood out, and far ahead I spotted specks upon the ice, small as fleas. I pointed toward the dark forms with my gloved hand. Infidel nodded and altered our course to investigate. We soon came to see that our targets were moving. As we closed upon them, the specks became two large humanoid figures crouched over a gray mass on the ice. They had their backs to us; the gray smear they were hunched over proved to be a large seal they were butchering. As one of the butchers moved to the side, I spotted tusks jutting from his lower jaw. Ice-ogres!

Infidel came in low. The Gloryhammer caused long shadows to stretch before the ogres. They turned back to look at the source of the light, raising their hands to shield their eyes.

"Sorrow," I said. "Right now would be a fantastic time for you to teach me the ice-ogre word for 'hello.'"

"Awk," she responded almost instantly.

"I can manage that," I said. "Awk! Awk!"

We were several hundred yards away. Between the faintness of my squeaky voice and the rush of wind, I can't believe they heard me. Nevertheless, something triggered them to choose this exact second to abandon their kill. They ran toward a ragged-looking patch of ice. This proved to be a deep pool of slush leading to the ocean beneath, or so I deduced as they disappeared into it.

"Damn," said Infidel, landing on the ice where they'd just stood.

"Do ogres swim?" I asked.

"They're excellent swimmers," said Sorrow. "If they had time to fill their lungs they can last almost twenty minutes underwater. Their high body fat helps retain heat. They can travel miles beneath the ice; they use their tusks to bash their way up through thin spots."

"Weird," said Infidel, with her ear almost pressed to mine. "I can hear you, Sorrow. Just barely."

"It's the sympathetic vibration of the other half of the seed pod."

"Have you... have you been listening to everything we said?" Infidel asked.

"I told you before you left that I would hear what Stagger heard. But, don't worry, I haven't been paying attention to your confessions of maternal inadequacy. We've been preoccupied here by the arrival of Levi. The whales messages found their mark."

"Levi? Gale's oldest son? He showed up fast."

"It turns out he has his mother's talent for shortcuts," said

Sorrow. "Though that's not really the thing that stands out about him." I waited for a elaboration, but she had said all she had to say on the subject.

Infidel said, "I feel bad that we scared them off. They'd done a lot of work." She was looking at the seal. It was in a relatively advanced state of butchering, the skin flayed from the muscle and stretched out to create a tidy workspace. Neat slabs of meat were spread over the surrounding ice, faintly steaming as the winter air sucked out their moisture. The nutrient-rich organs, like the heart and liver, were laid out as neatly as if they were in a butcher's window. The skull had been worked free from the spine and set aside, the lidless eyes forced to watch the dismemberment of the body. Either the ogres were fast workers or we'd frightened them away from the fruits of several hours' work.

"Maybe they're heading back to the village to sound a warning," I said. "We might be close."

"Maybe," said Infidel. "But I didn't see anything like a village anywhere near."

"Hang tight," I said. "I'm going to slip beneath the ice and figure out which way they're going."

"Go," she said.

I let go of the silver threads and slipped from my shell. I willed myself down through the ice, shuddering from both the chill of my environment and the existential crises that confronted me every time I let go of the illusion of solidity and embraced the advantages of my spectral nature.

In the water, the ice overhead was a pale translucent gray-blue through which the twilight seeped. From above, the ice looked uniform, but from beneath it revealed itself to be riddled with cracks. Since we'd been flying up from the south and hadn't spotted a village, I had a hunch that the ogres were heading north. I pursued, and a moment later spotted their faint auras. I flashed toward them just as they reached a gap in the ice. With powerful kicks, they burst upward, doing what can only be described as a reverse dive. Once above, they began to run without so much as a pause to catch their breaths.

I continued to give chase, hoping they'd reach their destination soon. They didn't. I couldn't accurately tell time, but I'm certain I gave chase for at least an hour. The blue twilight that had persisted after the sunset receded once more to black. I had only starlight to see by, but it was sufficient to reveal that the frozen ice the ogres ran across was now bordered by actual land, steep cliffs a half-mile high.

At the second hour of their headlong flight through the darkness, I began to wonder if Infidel would give up on waiting for me. I should have committed to a time limit, but planning ahead wasn't something either of us was famous for. The ogres showed no signs of weariness as I floated beside them. Aurora had told me she was a runt among her kind, and assuming that these two random specimens were closer to average, she'd been right. They were each at least ten feet tall, broad-shouldered, with arms and legs packed into seal-fur tights that fit like second skins. Given the tightness of their pants, I had evidence that these were males of the species. Their faces were the same pale blue-white as Aurora's, but squarer. Their brows were dappled with hemi-circular scars that reminded me of overlapping scales. I'd seen similar scarification as decoration among river pygmies, who sometimes marked fish-scale patterns along their shoulders and spines.

Just as I'd decided to give up and return to Infidel, I saw a glow on the northern horizon, completely different in nature from the brief sunrise I'd witnessed earlier. I flitted upward and found the cliffs cut back in a sharp V shape a mile across at the open end. Within was a frozen bay, decorated by what looked like hundreds of perfect hemispheres packed closely together. My lack of perspective made them look small at first, until I saw ogres going in and out of them through sealskin curtains. Drawing closer, I saw that they were hollow domes of ice almost fifty feet across. Most were topped with dark black holes from which smoke rose; the fires within lit the structures with a dim yellow light. Black shadows moved menacingly against the backlighting. The atmosphere above the village had the distinct aroma of rotting fish and burnt bacon, a scent reminiscent of the whale oil the Wanderers burned in their lamps, but much stronger.

Having at least a minute's lead on the two startled hunters, I flitted into the nearest dome. The smell within was so foul I reached up to pinch my nostrils, forgetting the intangible nature of both fingers and nose. In the central fire pit they were burning what looked like cow patties, though of course there were no cows within a thousand miles. Perhaps they were ogre turds; at least a dozen of the beasts were packed into this dwelling. They'd shed their clothing and went about naked. The floors of the ice dome where carpeted with thick sheets of skins, and the warmth of the room was surprising; I wondered how the walls survived. A mother ogre was nursing three youngsters simultaneously; she was equipped with four working breasts. I'd never noticed this excess of mammary glands on Aurora, but Aurora had typically dressed in a manner that concealed the true contours of her body. She'd worked for the Black Swan for two years before I learned she was female.

The ogres within the dome all lifted their heads at once. The two hunters were close enough to the village that their shouts could be heard. Flitting back outside, the commotion grew; not only were the two hunters shouting as they covered the last few hundred yards toward the village, but news of their arrival was being trumpeted in deep-barreled baritones from dome to dome.

I couldn't understand a word, as my link to Sorrow was now several miles distant. Again, I never claimed that some future monument to me would be engraved, "The Man Who Thought Ahead."

The cacophony of voices reached a crescendo as the news reached the furthest edges of the village. From my aerial position I watched as the two hunters were led along what looked to be a well-trodden path to the north. I quickly spotted why. Unlike the jagged, natural-looking cliff on the southern half of the V-shaped bay, the northern cliffs had been carved into an impressive edifice. The face was sheer granite, polished smooth, and riddled with windows and balconies. Statues of ogres sat within alcoves. I was looking at either a palace or a temple, or some blend of both.

Before I could go within to investigate, a white-clad figure emerged from the torch-lit interior of the highest archway. This was an ogre even larger than the two I'd been chasing. A cheer went through the crowd that gathered beneath. They began to chant, "Tarpok! Tarpok!" I guessed it to be his name, though perhaps it was just a more formal greeting than "awk."

Tarpok stuck out a beefy arm and the crowd fell silent. He called out to the crowd with a voice powerful enough to rattle window glass and startle the horses, if the village had possessed either glass or horses. Though I didn't speak the lingo, I sensed from his tone that he'd asked a question; most likely, "What's all the racket?"

The two hunters were pushed to the front of the crowd and shouted back something. They both waved their hands as they spoke, and between their gestures and inflection my translation was, "A two-headed creature from the stars swooped down and attacked us! We abandoned our catch and ran for our lives!"

Tarpok asked a short question that made the crowd laugh. My hunch: "Maybe you chewed some bad blubber?"

The two hunters bowed, placing their hands over their hearts in the near universal gesture, "I swear it's true."

The ogre in the window responded with an appropriately solemn and studious look. I drew closer. Tarpok was a good twelve feet tall, and solid looking. I mean, none of the ogres would blow away in a stiff wind, but something about their subcutaneous fat gave most ogres a doughy look. Tarpok was chiseled. What I thought had been white clothing was in fact his bare skin, all the better to display the elaborate tapestries of tribal scars that decorated his imposing form. I also noted that he had four dark blue nipples; apparently this *was* standard ogre anatomy.

At last, having posed in dramatic contemplation for a sufficient length of time to build suspense in the crowd, the big ogre thrust out his hand in a stiff salute and screamed, "Hack hack hack hack!" or words to that effect, which, judging from the jubilation that followed must have meant, "I believe you! I will find this star-beast and kick its ass!"

A smaller ogre appeared in the shadows and handed Tarpok a large horn carved from a narwhal's tusk. He blew into the end with a long, tooth-rattling "BLAAAAAAAAT!" As the note trailed off, a dozen shooting stars streaked down from the heavens, as if they'd been shaken loose by the call.

Tarpok disappeared into the shadows. I watched the window for his reappearance, since the crowd continued gazing in that general direction. A minute later they cheered with excitement, but I didn't see him. Then I realized he was now on top of the cliff. He was wearing a black cloak I assume was whale hide, with matching pants of the same material. He had a battle-axe with a head the size of a coffee table slung over his back, and in his left hand he carried a harpoon that was more menacing than even the Jagged Heart, a twenty-foot-long shaft of iron with the tip hammered into a flesh-mangling mess of razor-sharp serrated hooks and barbs.

I had to wonder if the Immaculate Attire would stand a chance against a weapon like this. I consoled myself that Infidel could at least escape by taking to the sky. Then I saw the crowd pivot. I noticed a lot of the stars were blotted out by something big moving overhead.

Having lived by the ocean most of my life, I've seen my fair share of whales. Menagerie had one among his tattoos that I'd never actually spotted in our tropical climes, a beast that vaguely resembled a panda in its stark black and white coloring, but was even more evocative of a dragon by virtue of a dagger-toothed mouth that could open wide enough to swallow boats. He'd called the thing an orca.

He hadn't told me they could fly.

Or, perhaps they can't, and it was merely some enchantment that kept this beast in the air. Whatever the case, I watched, slack jawed, as a sixty-foot black-and-white whale sailed up to the cliff, swimming in air as if it were water. The beast cruised with its back just below the top edge of the cliff. Tarpok leapt into the air, the crowd screaming with jubilation as he landed astride the beast. The whale was rigged with an elaborate leather harness. Tarpok wrapped his fists into the lines and tugged the beast's head toward the southern horizon. The orca let loose a loud "whuff" from its blowhole and, with a flick of its tail, surged in that direction.

The crowd gave chase from below, but the whale picked up speed with every wave of its tail. Tarpok raised his harpoon above his head and shouted, "Chakaaaaa!"

"Chakaaaaa!" the crowd screamed in unison.

With Sorrow unavailable, I held out hope the word just meant, "Good-bye," and not, "Death to star-monsters!"

I'd seen enough. It was time to get back to Infidel.

CHAPTER FIFTEEN

BONES AND TEETH

As THE TRACKLESS ice flashed beneath me, I feared I would never find Infidel. Had I been limited to ordinary sight, my fears would have been well-founded. Fortunately, when I held my left hand before me, with its phantom wedding band, I could feel a pressure like the tug of a distant magnet. At last my ghost eyes spotted her by the bright aura she cast as the only living thing for miles around.

It was fortunate I could see her aura, because the Gloryhammer couldn't be seen at all. Infidel had cleared the butchered meat from the seal skin and flipped it fur side up, then stretched out on the ice with her fox-cloak curled tightly around her, forming a very tiny tent that hid both her and the hammer. My wooden body was laid out on the ice next to her, its arms folded neatly across its chest, as if it had been prepped for burial. I jumped inside. My wooden bones clattered as I sat up. She stirred, raising the lip of her hood ever so slightly. A bright beam of light shot over the bloodied ice.

"Was I snoring?" she asked, sounding drowsy, as pale fog rolled out from the gap she'd made.

"You were sleeping out here? You'll freeze to death!"

"No, no, it's pretty comfy," she said. "The fur traps my body heat really well. I just conked right out. Were you gone long?"

"A couple of hours."

"Well, I needed the nap. I feel ready for anything."

"Trust me, you aren't ready for what's coming. Let's get out of here," I said, standing, looking north. "The two hunters made it to their village and sounded an alarm. Now the village's top

JAMES MAXEY

warrior is on his way here to do battle with the monster that stole the hunters' seal."

"That's good news, isn't it?" Infidel sat up. The moisture that had been trapped by the fur instantly turned to frost on the silver trim of her armor, and left tiny glittering diamonds of ice on her eyelashes. "We want them to come to us."

"This guy is riding a flying whale and carrying a solid steel harpoon. He looks like the very definition of bad news."

Infidel furrowed her brow. "We came here looking for help against Purity. That means we need to talk to someone important. He sounds important."

"He sounds dangerous! Let's get out of here!"

"Excuse me," said Sorrow in my ear. "Did you just mention someone riding a flying whale?"

"Yeah," I said.

"That would be Tarpok," said Sorrow.

"Is that the whale or the rider?" I asked.

"The rider. The whale is Slor Tonn."

"Is this a private conversation or can I listen in?" Infidel pressed her cheek close to my ear without waiting for an answer.

"So, you've met Tarpok?" asked Sorrow.

"Not really," I said. "He didn't see me, but he's on his way here, and he looked like he was coming for blood. The whole village was shouting him on, yelling, 'Chakaa!'"

It was difficult to hear, but I think Sorrow sighed. She asked, "What did you do to get him angry?"

"Nothing!" said Infidel. "We just startled a few hunters."

"Tarpok is the village champion," said Sorrow. "He'll lose face if he doesn't return with some corpses. He's a very dangerous fighter, but his whale is even worse. When you fight them, target Slor Tonn first."

"What?" I said. "We aren't going to fight. We're going to run!"

"Or," said Infidel, "Pardon me for having a crazy idea, but can't we try to talk to him? The Divine Author knows how many miles we just flew to do that, right?"

"Tarpok is a fight-first, ask-questions-later type," said Sorrow.

"How do you know so much about him?" Infidel asked.

"I told you I'd had difficulty on my trip up north. I escaped the Skellings only to be captured by ice-ogres. Fortunately, they treated me rather well. Their priestesses somehow knew I was a virgin, and they needed my blood for some magic ritual. But the night of the ritual was months away, so during that time I was kept in the temple, well-fed and comfortable. That's when I picked up some of their language. Luckily, I never learned what ritual the priestesses needed me for. Tarpok learned I could manipulate gold and silver, so he wanted to see my talents. I was able to bribe him and gain my freedom by promising to build him an iron harpoon with magical strength and toughness."

"So the harpoon's magic?" I asked.

"No, but he doesn't know that. Most ice-ogre weapons are made of bones and rock. Show them some steel and they think it fell from the heavens. Which, actually, it did, since I pulled the iron from a meteor they kept in the temple. But, despite its heavenly origins, the harpoon doesn't have any special powers."

"So the harpoon isn't dangerous?" Infidel asked.

"It's a twenty-foot shaft of hardened steel tipped with hooked barbs sharp enough to shave with," said Sorrow. "It doesn't need to be magic."

"But you were able to bribe him," said Infidel. "He listened to reason and he kept his end of the bargain in letting you go."

"Actually, he tried to double-cross me, but one of the ogresses in the temple helped me escape to spite him. I got the feeling there was a power struggle between Tarpok and the priestesses. Tarpok's something of a bully."

"Then we'll surrender," said Infidel. "Grovel a little. Tell him we're too scared of his reputation to even think of fighting. We'll butter him up with praise, then tell him that Purity called his mother a bad name."

"Hmm," said Sorrow. "That's not a bad plan."

"Here's a better one," I said. "While Tarpok is out here looking for us, we sneak into town and find someone to talk to who isn't riding a monster that can swallow us before we say hello."

"I feel like you're not trusting me again," Infidel said, crossing her arms.

Before we could argue further, there was a faint gurgle at our feet. The hole the ogres had escaped in was frozen over now, but a few cracks in the ice suddenly began to spurt sea water. The fluid washed over the bloody ice where the seal had been butchered, sending little pink rivulets in all directions. The water froze an instant later, locking my boots in place.

Infidel tapped the ice with her hammer, freeing the soles of my boots. The glow of the hammer cast rainbows in the frosted ice beneath us. A fresh stream of water shot up through the cracks.

Infidel bent at the knees, preparing to leap as she raised her hammer and wrapped an arm around my waist. She said, "Hold –"

I think her next word was going to be "tight," but it was rendered moot as a shaft of solid steel punched through the ice beneath my feet. My right leg was instantly torn from my body, sending me spinning backward. There was a loud *CRACK*, as if lighting had struck us. The ice bulged upward as Slor Tonn punched up from the depths, throwing us both head over heels. I fell toward Tarpok, whose feet were wrapped in the leather harness as he used both hands to drive his harpoon through my barrel chest.

"We surrender!" I squeaked.

"Pamiiyok!" Sorrow screamed in my ear.

"Pamiiyok!" I tried again. I'd slid down the shaft of the harpoon far enough that I could have reached out and shaken Tarpok's hand if he'd had one to spare at the moment.

"I accept no surrender," Tarpok growled, in my own language.

He gave the harpoon a sharp jerk to the left and I was thrown back down to the barbed head with such force that my helmet fell loose. I watched it fall away into the icy hole left by Slor Tonn's arrival. As the slats of my chest fell apart, I was shaken loose of the harpoon and tumbled head first toward the water, until my left hand snagged in the whale's harness, purely by luck. My fall halted, I grabbed the straps with my right hand and held on.

I felt dizzy as Slor Tonn wheeled in the sky and the stars above us spun. An instant later the sky gave way to ice and I saw Infidel, sprawled on the snow beneath us, looking dazed, the Gloryhammer just beyond her grasp. Tarpok drew back his harpoon to hurl it, but hesitated as Infidel looked up toward him. Her cloak had fallen open, and her helmet had come off, revealing her face and hair.

"Purity?" Tarpok muttered. Then he barked, "Kisault, Slor Tonn!"

In defiance of all ordinary physics, the whale stopped instantly in mid-flight.

"Purity!" Tarpok shouted. "How did you reach this interloper before me? Why didn't you tell me of your plans? I could have killed you!"

Infidel used Tarpok's hesitation to scramble across the ice and grab the Gloryhammer. She rose on rubbery legs and snarled. "We just wanted to talk, you jerk!"

"Purity?" Tarpok asked, utterly confused.

"Rrrrraaaah!" Infidel cried, in full warrior goddess mode, as she launched herself into the sky. I lost sight of her as Slor Tonn wriggled in the sky, either to take evasive action or to meet her head on.

It proved to be the latter, as Infidel drove the Gloryhammer into the tip of the whale's nose with a wet smack. A wave rippled through the beast's blubber, snapping some of the harness rings, and it took everything I had to hold on as the whale lurched sideways. Up above, Tarpok cried, "Chakaaaa!" and thrust the harpoon with a grunt.

Seconds later, I heard Infidel shout, "Damn it!" She sounded more annoyed than hurt. For the briefest instant, she flashed through my line of sight in a rapid arc; her long white cape was snagged by the barbs of the harpoon.

Tarpok looked perturbed that his throw hadn't resulted in a direct hit.

"Nakkertok, Slor Tonn!" he shouted.

I had no time to ask for a translation as the whale spun to hang perpendicular to the ice a hundred feet below, its body rigid as a plank. Infidel floated beneath us, trying to shed her cape, but the clasp had twisted back over her shoulder.

"Chakaaa!" Tarpok shouted again, and we descended toward the ice like God's own gavel.

Infidel managed to get the Gloryhammer beneath her, so the enchanted mallet took the brunt of the impact, smashing the ice to chips an instant before her body slammed into the freezing ocean and was promptly pushed a hundred feet beneath by Slor Tonn's bulk. Whether from the impact, the shock of the cold, or the crushing effect of descending a hundred feet underwater in the span of a heartbeat, Infidel went completely limp. The Gloryhammer slipped from her fingers and began to float upward, until Tarpok used his ape-like reach to snag it. With his other hand, he brought in the harpoon, dragging Infidel's slack body toward him.

She was barely alive. In the pitch darkness beneath the ice, her aura flickered, growing dim. Her light became so faint I became aware of a second glow, no bigger than a firefly, in the lower half of her belly. Our daughter?

With each second that we lingered beneath the frozen waves, Infidel's aura guttered dimmer, like a candle surrendering to the wind.

The bubbles of gas that had been seeping from my clothes suddenly changed directions. Slor Tonn was pointed toward the surface once more. Seconds ticked by before I could see the shattered ice toward which we swam, then, with a great splash, the mighty whale burst into the air and kept swimming in the sky.

221

As we leveled off, Tarpok shoved Infidel's body under a harness line, trapping it. Water drained from her mouth and nostrils, quickly turning to ice. She coughed weakly, her eyes closed, and began to breathe shallow teaspoons of air, the faintest puffs imaginable escaping her darkening lips.

Certain that my arms were wrapped in the harnesses, I slipped from my body. I saw the golden cage now dangled by a single silver wire within what was left of my chest. If not for my shirt holding them together, all my chest staves would have fallen away. What would happen if the golden cage were to come completely loose?

I had no time to think of such things. Instead, I let my ghostly form hover next to Infidel. Her lips had turned blue. She'd been sopping wet, and now her hair and clothing had frozen solid. Tarpok had shoved the Gloryhammer beneath the harness as well. I remembered how, in her phantom form, Aurora had been able to touch the Jagged Heart to trigger its powers. Could I do the same? If I could place the hammer in Infidel's grasp, would its magical energies revive her?

My spectral fingers sank into the glowing weapon. Instantly, I regretted my action. When I'd touched the hammer previously, it had been with wooden fingers and nothing had happened. When my spectral palm passed through the surface of the weapon, I felt the precise opposite of the surge of power Infidel had described. Instead, there was a terrible suction, hungry to devour my spiritual energies. My vision blurred as I struggled to resist the weapon's pull. In my panic, I reached for Infidel's limp hand, which lay outstretched toward me. To my astonishment, my fingers felt solid as they closed around hers. With her as my anchor, I resisted the suction of the hammer and pulled myself free.

I stared at the weapon. What had just happened? It had unfolded so swiftly, I'd had no time to understand the experience. But... there was something inside the hammer, residing in the Glorystone from which it had been carved. It felt... intelligent, ancient, vast, and lonely. So lonely. Unending solitude lay at the core of this weapon, an emptiness that wanted to consume all that it touched. What did this mean? Had I somehow encountered the soul of Glorious within the Gloryhammer? Could I possibly communicate with him if this was so? I shook my head. I dare not expose myself to this terrible emptiness again.

As frightened as I was of the hammer, I was even more frightened that I could touch Infidel's hand. Only once in my phantom form had I experienced the sensation of physical contact... when I'd felt Ivory Blade's phantom blood trickling across my fingers.

Was I now feeling Infidel's soul? Had she slipped so far loose of her mortal shell that she was now in the between realm where I dwelled, halfway between life and not-life? I wrapped my arms around her, determined to hold her soul in her body. She stirred at my touch.

"So c-cold," she whispered in my ear, though her blue lips didn't move in the slightest.

"Hug me back," I whispered, tightening my grip on her. "Take my warmth."

She didn't respond. Did she hear me? Did I have any warmth to give? What could I, a ghost, offer in comfort or strength? And yet... Sorrow had treated my soul as a source of energy that her golem could tap. This energy had taken form in my ghost blood. Sorrow had taken my life force without my permission. Could I give it willingly?

With Infidel, giving was so easy.

My hand moved to the bone-handled knife in my belt. I drew the blade across the palm of my left hand. Beads of ghostly blood bubbled up. I took Infidel's hand and made a matching cut across the palm. I rolled the bone-handled knife across my palm until it was wet, then placed it in her grasp.

I wrapped my fingers over Infidel's hand, our woven wedding bands touching. Under other circumstances, this might have been a romantic gesture, even loving. But what did I truly know of romance? What did I know of marriage, beyond the exchange of rings? My own upbringing had been devoid of parents to guide me on such matters. Most married men I met in Commonground had left their wives in distant lands, and gladly so. All I knew of marriage was that it was treated by much of mankind as a burden.

I would gladly bear any burden for this woman.

A sudden warmth flushed over me as I remembered the tropical heat of our last shared night on this earth, fleeing through the jungle, pouring sweat, my heart pounding, but not with fear. There had been such excitement in the air that evening, such a grand pulse of adventure stirring our mutual blood. Had she known then how much I loved her?

Of course, I'd finally told her when we'd met again, on the volcanic slopes of Greatshadow's spirit home in the abstract realms. There we'd held each other naked in the dry, near-blistering heat, our bodies braided into a single knot. It hadn't been imagination... my life energy had flowed into her, creating a spark of new life.

I squeezed her hand with all my strength. Our ghostly bloods mingled as our grasp grew feverishly hot. I began to sweat as I felt the spiritual flame within me gush through my veins. Like water draining from a sink, my life force began to swirl out of me, passing though the enchanted knife to flow into my bride. I raised my spectral hand and saw it age rapidly, the flesh withering, flaking away as sprites of light and heat to engulf Infidel. As I watched, her cheeks once more took on color. Her breathing grew stronger and steadier.

As quickly as the sensation started, it switched off, and my spectral teeth began to chatter. All my heat had now drained away. There was no flesh or blood left of my hand, only bone.

With a gasp, Infidel opened her eyes. I could see myself reflected against her open pupils, twin black mirrors showing a human skull staring at her.

I squeezed her hand where our rings met, but my fingers found no purchase. She was now safely returned to the material world.

And I? I fell backward, drifting in the arctic air, utterly drained. I caught a glimpse of my body as I tumbled, a mere skeleton, translucent and fading in the starlight.

I'd grown too weak to hold onto this world any longer. It saddened me to know that I would never learn how Infidel's story played out, whether she'd survive to give birth to our daughter, whether she'd live a full life long after my band of hair had fallen to dust and my memory was hard to summon.

I closed my eyes, prepared to vanish.

Then, though Slor Tonn had flown on half a mile as I'd drifted, I heard a single whispered word on the wind: "Stagger?"

It was Sorrow's voice, sounding in the bean-case ear.

I opened my eyes. A single silver filament, finer than human hair, snaked through the night sky toward me. It slithered between my jaws and hooked me like a fish, reeling me back into the golden cage.

"Stagger, can you hear me?" asked Sorrow. "What's happening? Is everything okay?"

I didn't feel strong enough to move my arms, but with effort I found my paper tongue. It was frozen solid, but somehow I coaxed from it a sickly, crinkling rattle no one could ever mistake for a human voice: "Save Infidel."

Perhaps Sorrow's attunement with the magic of my wooden body allowed her to understand me, since she answered, "If she needs saving, I take it you're both still alive?"

I felt like this deserved a sarcastic response, but I couldn't find the energy.

"You know what I mean," Sorrow amended a second later, perhaps chastised by my silence.

"Slor Tonn... from below," I crinkle-croaked. "Infidel alive... barely. I'm... used up. Nothing left... but ghost bones and teeth."

"Bones and teeth are rather durable," said Sorrow, sounding clinical. "They can last centuries. Perhaps your rate of disintegration will slow now."

Her words were both a comfort and a curse. Perhaps I could linger for centuries in this condition. But did I want to? All my strength had been stripped away. I felt as if I was in the grip of the most formidable, incapacitating hangover of all time.

"In any case, just hold on," said Sorrow. "There's not much left for me to do with the *Freewind*. Even with my powers, the damage the keel has suffered is beyond repair. Levi is trying to convince Gale to abandon ship."

I wondered what this would mean for the ghost of Jasmine Romer, but had no energy to ask the question.

"I'm going to join you once I've made preparations," Sorrow said.

"How?" I asked, or tried, as my voice gave out.

"I'll be out of contact a while as I focus on... on something important," Sorrow said. "Just hold on a little longer."

I didn't have the strength to ask further questions. I could only watch helplessly as the ogre village appeared on the horizon. Given the stark sameness of the landscape, I hadn't noticed before how low Slor Tonn was now flying. With the village providing a fixed reference, I noticed that the whale was cutting a rather drunken path through the sky. How much damage had Infidel done when she'd hit him?

I had my answer a moment later, as we reached the edge of the village and Slor Tonn failed to clear one of the ice domes. It shattered beneath his belly. The mighty whale's body trembled as he gave one last push with his tail, trying to gain altitude, but he rose only a few dozen feet before his arc leveled out. He swam through the air another quarter-mile toward the cliff temple. At that point, despite Tarpok calling out commands urging him onward, the beast's body went slack. We slammed into the ice, sliding a hundred yards across the glassy surface before skidding to a halt.

We were soon surrounded by a throng of ice-ogres. Three of the crowd were ogresses dressed in long, black walrus coats, the same style that Aurora used to wear. I'd always assumed she was merely being stylish, but now I wondered if this was some sacred garb of her priesthood, since the three black-coated ogresses began to shout commands that were instantly obeyed. They also sported the same topknots of blue hair, and were somewhat shorter than the other ogres in the surrounding crowd.

Once more, I found my lack of actual vocabulary to be less of a hindrance to understanding what was being said than one might suppose. Tarpok freed Infidel from her bindings and tossed her limp form to the nearest priestess, with a gruff statement that certainly amounted to, "Here's your damn monster."

The priestess responded with a question ending in the word, "Purity?"

Tarpok shrugged. He loosened the Gloryhammer and brandished it. His next sentence was short and declarative. I'm pretty sure it translated, "I'm keeping this."

He slid down from the whale, pausing as he caught sight of my limp form tangled in the harness. "How the hell did this get here?" was the gist of his grumble as he ripped me free and tossed me across the ice.

Almost immediately, an ice-ogre ran toward me, only to be knocked aside by another who dove and slid across the ice as he scooped up my component parts in his thick arms. He stood and growled something threatening and the dozen hungry-looking ogres staring at him kept their distance. If I could have chuckled, I would have. I think they thought I was edible. Were they in for a disappointment!

The ogre who'd claimed me carried me away, walking past Slor Tonn's mouth. The whale had vomited when it landed and the ice was covered in seal parts and half-chewed cod, which other ogres were fighting over.

Slor Tonn had what I can only describe as a split lip, a yard-long gash running up from a now-toothless segment of his upper jaw, jagging like a raw-pink lightning bolt in an arc back toward his left eye. Tarpok and a priestess stood by the beast's head, their hands upon it as they whispered words of comfort to the wounded whale. I felt a sense of remorse – no one likes to see an animal suffering – mixed with a feeling of satisfaction that Infidel had at least gotten in one good lick.

As for Infidel, I caught one last glimpse as I was carried away, when I spied the priestess carrying her toward the carved cliff-side, cradling her like a baby.

Still unable to lift a limb or even move my tongue, I was helpless as my ogre captor carried me through the village back to his home. He stooped to enter the icy dome. A trio of young ogres looked up as he entered. An ogress with four flabby teats rolled over on a nest of seal skins and asked something. My captor responded by throwing me to the floor. One of my eyes popped off and skittered across the ice as my coconut skull cracked on impact.

The ogress asked something to the effect, "How am I supposed to cook that?"

The ogre seemed to reply, "Don't vex me, woman! I've done my part!"

The ogress stirred from the bed, muttering beneath her breath as she reached to grab the nutshell. She crushed it between her thick fingers, then pulled the rest of my form to her. She quickly stripped free what remained of my cloak and pants. She looked utterly crushed as she found nothing but rotting wood underneath.

If she'd bothered tearing open my chest, she would have found the precious metals inside, and maybe the male ogre could have pretended that the whole wooden body thing was just a way of hiding his real gift, a tiny golden cage with a silver mosquito. But, instead of opening my chest, she looked up at her mate and said a single word that certainly didn't sound like, "Thanks!"

The male responded with a savage growl and a sudden, backhanded slap across the ogress's cheek. He shouted at her, a rapid string of syllables I couldn't begin to pick apart. The three young ogres all huddled together at the farthest side of the room, eyes wide with terror.

The ogress ran her hand across her mouth. She paused to study the blood on her fingertips. She said something in a calm, firm tone.

The male ogre sagged, his face going slack, his arms dangling uselessly by his side. Whatever she'd said to him had taken all the fight out of him. He turned slowly and slouched away, pausing to look at his children with a mournful gaze, before stooping to crawl from the ice-hut.

Ogre-mom lifted me up, staring at my coconut face with an expression of complete disgust. Then, without further ado, she tossed my body on the dung-fire.

CHAPTER SIXTEEN
TONGUE OF FLAME

THE FIRE WAS slow to claim me. At first, I wondered if I might extinguish the flames as the ice that coated my wooden form melted, sending water gushing into the foul slurry of whale oil and dung. The water pooled into shallow circles that hissed and turned to steam.

My paper tongue loosened as the ice crystals that stiffened it melted away.

"Save me," I whispered, but my voice was too faint for the ogres to hear over the sizzle of the flames as they licked the oak staves of my chest.

"Sorrow," I cried out, praying she would hear, not knowing what she could possibly do. Alas, she didn't answer, or if she did, I failed to hear it as my seed pod ear shriveled, crackling in the heat.

I had no choice but to abandon my wooden body. But once I was rid of it, could what remained of my spirit endure? Could I ignore the subtle whisper growing ever louder in my mind to accept that I was dead, that it was time to disperse, to surrender what slight energy remained in me back to the universe?

Within my golden cage, I tried to urge my spiritual body toward the door. I failed to budge. I lacked the energy even to crawl. I could do nothing but smolder and wonder what came next.

The paper at the back of my coconut jaws crinkled and writhed as it baked in the increasing heat. Any second my tongue would burst into flames, silencing me forever. But what was left to say?

Despite the growing heat a chill ran through me as I realized there was only one name one dare not waste if gifted with a tongue of flame. A jet of smoke curled from my ragged jaws as I spoke: "Greatshadow!"

The embers that swirled above my desiccating body suddenly turned. The swirl of sparks paused for an instant into a shape resembling the head of a horse. Twin clusters of sparks on each side coalesced into eyes, studying me.

"Help me," I murmured, with my tongue now wreathed with dancing fire.

"You are familiar to me," whispered the smoke and cinders above.

"I'm the husband of Innocent Brightmoon," I said, as my tongue crumbled to ash.

The flames about me danced into a decidedly serpentine appearance. The outline of an equine head filled with more red sparks, thickening to resemble scales. Smoke knifed into the shape of fangs as the creature's mouth parted to speak. "You are Abstemious Merchant. You brought the Jagged Heart to my kingdom to kill me."

"I came to your kingdom to rescue the woman I loved," I said, though I no longer had a tongue. This didn't hinder Greatshadow's ability to hear me. "She spared your life when you were at your weakest. You owe her."

"I owe her nothing. And you, less than nothing," the dragon said.

"It's a favor I seek, not a reward. Save Infidel. At the very minimum, help me save her."

By now, the boards in my chest had dried sufficiently to catch fire with a sudden *WHOOOMPH*. Jets of flame from my shoulders reached up like a beggar's arms, pleading for Greatshadow's aid. "Infidel reminded you of how well humans have served your purposes," I said, desperate to persuade him. "We feed you daily. Even now, you devour my body. Is it too much to ask for a little help in return?"

Greatshadow said nothing.

There was a sudden pain, sharp and stabbing, where my heart used to be. The gold and silver inside me were melting.

"Please," I whispered.

Greatshadow turned his face away. "Even if I wanted to help you, what makes you believe I have the power?"

"You *are* power," I whispered. "If you cannot aid me, then all hope is lost."

Greatshadow continued to look away. With a sigh, he said, "Your faith is great. What you ask shall be given... for a price. You will give me your body in exchange."

"Anything," I sobbed.

"So be it," he said.

The swirling flames above me took on the shape of a large red claw, reaching for my chest.

About five years ago, I'd bitten into an olive and been careless of the pit. I'd cracked a molar right down the root. Infidel had volunteered to yank the tooth, using iron tongs borrowed from a blacksmith. I downed shot after shot of whiskey until her offer sounded sensible, then let her get to work.

I should have drunk a *lot* more whiskey.

This tooth extraction came to mind as the tiny speck of blood inside the mechanical mosquito within me began to boil and bubble free from its tiny cage. It was as if Greatshadow's claws had reached inside and snagged my soul, and now yanked it loose with the same bone-mangling enthusiasm that Infidel had displayed in her amateur dentistry.

Slowly the pain subsided. The ringing in my ears ceased as I stopped screaming. The stars dancing before my eyes faded one by one. I was left staring at my clenched fingers, writhing in the air before me.

I had fingers. I had arms!

I once more had lips, with which I smiled. *I was alive!*

Only, as I sat up, I understood that I'd merely returned to my previous phantom existence, with the illusion of life, at least. I glanced down at my spectral body, nothing but dry bones when last I'd gazed upon it, and found my limbs now sheathed with muscles. My legs still glowed with internal heat, faint flames shimmering as they cooled into a new sheath of skin.

I was briefly distracted from my rebirth by a whirlwind of activity around me. The ogress and her children were grabbing their belongings and tripping over themselves as they fled the hut. The raging bonfire that my wooden body had unleashed had thrown sparks onto the sealskins that lined the room. The oily hides now burned with ferocious energy. The icy chamber transformed into a furnace as the last ogre child slipped out the door.

"Abstemious Merchant," Greatshadow roared from smoke that whirled up through the small chimney hole. "This was not your true body I've devoured!"

"Not my original body, no, but I'd gotten comfortable in it, more or less," I said.

"I've breathed life once more into your spiritual body," said Greatshadow. "I demand your physical flesh in exchange."

"I promise to dig up my corpse the first chance I get, though it's probably pretty ripe by now."

"I don't want your old shell," said Greatshadow.

"What else do I have to offer?"

"Your daughter. Her form will contain enough of your physical essence to satisfy me. You must give her freely."

I raised my fist to him. "Over my dead body!"

"Don't be so ungrateful," said Greatshadow. "I've given the aid you sought. You now owe me."

"I'm not going to let you kill my daughter!"

Greatshadow chuckled. "She would be of no use to me dead."

"Then what –"

"The Isle of Fire is my domain. I require that your daughter dwell there as she is raised."

I ground my teeth together. What game was the dragon playing at? Did he know that's what Infidel and I had already wanted for our daughter?

"That's all you ask? That she grow up on the Isle of Fire?"

Greatshadow nodded.

"Have you... have you heard us speak of this?" I asked, thinking of the lanterns aboard the *Freewind*. "It's said that you watch mankind through every flame."

"Every candle, every lantern... and every dung-filled hearth in these frozen wastes. From cook-fires on the cliffs surrounding this bay, I watched as a ship from the Silver Isles arrived this summer. I've caught whispers as an alliance was formed between King Brightmoon's men, Tarpok, and Hush's chosen prophet, Purity. I was witness as the sky above the village tore open and Purity returned in her new body, carrying the Jagged Heart."

"Purity's planning to kill Glorious," I said.

Greatshadow chuckled. "Indeed. But Purity is merely a pawn in a much larger game. There are forces at work that wish to destroy all primal dragons. It is no coincidence that the plot against Glorious follows on the heels of the attempt to slay me. Nor is Glorious the only target."

"King Brightmoon and the Church of the Book are behind all of this," I said.

Greatshadow's chuckle turned into a guffaw. "The primal dragons need fear no mortal king. Were it my will, I could burn his kingdom to bare stone. The king is a mere puppet dancing on the strings of the true threat."

I held my tongue. I couldn't help but think of the Black Swan. She'd openly admitted to working behind the scenes to manipulate world events. Could she be the puppet master? As curious as I was to learn of the greater plot, I pushed aside my questions to focus on my most urgent desire.

"Infidel," I said. "You've got to help me find her. We came here to stop the plot against Glorious. I've seen you create avatars to enforce your will in Commonground. Can you create an avatar from the fuel at hand to help us fight Purity?"

"If I were to openly meddle outside my recognized domain, other dragons would take notice. For now, you alone must aid your spouse. Have faith. Infidel has proven capable of protecting the world from those who seek to alter the balance of power."

"I'll help her however I can," I said. "But –"

Before I could get out my next word, a thunderous CRACK rang out from the ice dome above me. Half a second later, the whole dome collapsed and the flames all around me were instantly snuffed. I stood amid the wreckage unharmed, my phantom body glowing faint red beneath a coat of fine ash, as if I were metal pulled fresh from a forge. This glow slowly faded, restoring my ghostly shell to its ordinary translucence. Judging from the crowd of ogres that gathered to gawk at the fallen dome, I deduced I remained invisible. None even glanced at me as I waved my hand and said, "Awk!"

My status quo as a phantom wasn't such a horrible thing. I was free to move about again, and proceeded to do so. The burnt-hair-and-dead-fish stink of burnt seal pelts was a good incentive to move on.

Goal one: Find Infidel.

I felt for the tug of her wedding band. Nothing.

I looked down at my ring finger. My braided ring was gone, consumed by the spiritual flames Greatshadow had used to restore me.

So instead I searched for the pull of the bone-handled knife, once as powerful as gravity. I couldn't sense it. Of course, when it had been in the spirit world with me, it had never felt like anything other than an ordinary knife. It had only affected me when it had been a bridge across dimensions, a gate between life and not-life. What had happened to it when I'd left it in Infidel's grasp? When her spirit had fused once more with her body, had the knife been pulled back into the material world? Or had it simply tumbled from her grasp, an immaterial thing, now lost forever on the artic wind?

I flew toward the temple. The ogres were busy chopping a trench in the ice around Slor Tonn. The whale was still alive; I could see his breath as great puffs of steam from his blow hole. His wound had been stitched up and sealed beneath a poultice of oily jelly with a vibrant green hue. The ogres jumped back as a slab of ice around Slor Tonn's head snapped loose, sending tall fountains of water jetting up through the gaps around it. The whale flopped like a fish on a bank as the water washed over it, sending further cracks through the ice. With a powerful full-body thrash, the whale pulverized the weakened ice beneath it sufficiently to open a hole. Slor Tonn slid into the frigid waters below. I wondered if he'd regain the strength to fly.

I hovered before the cliff, studying it closely. There were at least a dozen possible entrances. The lowest and largest was a cave at the level of the bay; the ice continued inside for as far as I could see. It looked big enough to sail a boat into. I floated down, and found that the entrance was partially blocked by a mound of severed ogre heads, some little more than skulls, others looking freshly frozen. Their dead eyes stared at me with looks of indignation. Far beyond them, I saw faint lights. I decided to begin my investigation here.

Within the chamber, I found a medium-sized schooner lifted from the frozen waters and supported by what can only be described as a dry dock of ice. The ship appeared to be in good condition. Closer inspection showed that the ship was the *Relentless*; having spent my adult years in conversation with sailors from around the world, I knew that this ship belonged to King Brightmoon's Judgment Fleet. The king had empowered these ships to serve as floating courts. They enforced the law at sea, with their captains serving as judge, jury, and executioner. The judge-captains kept a commission from the ships they seized to pay for their expenses; the rest was sent to the king. Even minor infractions were enough to justify seizing a ship, cargo and crew, which could only be released after payment of substantial fines.

In Commonground, it was noted that most people who functioned under a similar business model were labeled pirates and hung from gallows in civilized ports, where the judges were revered as champions of the law. Of course, a judge would face a fate far less dignified than hanging if he dared sail into Commonground. Everywhere you look in this world, there's symmetry.

I hadn't come here looking for symmetry, but for my wife. Unfortunately, I felt no connection pulling me. A score of corridors led off from this frozen underground bay. Which to follow?

As I contemplated my next move, I spotted a light from a tunnel near the *Relentless*. Shadows danced out over the frosted wooden surface of the ship, and a robed man emerged from the hall. I guessed from his drab garb that he was a friar of the Church of the Book. Unlike the monks I'd been raised among, who rarely strayed from the grounds of their cloister, friars were nomadic holy men, traveling the world. I use the term 'holy men' loosely; while they were respected members of the church, they lacked the direct connection to the One True Book demonstrated by Truthspeakers, and, unlike monks, they took no vows of meekness. Most of the assassins who'd shown up in Commonground looking for Infidel had been friars.

This friar carried a bundle wrapped in a large sealskin. He looked quite agitated. While friars did share vows of poverty with monks and priests, this one was sporting a rather eye-catching bit of wealth; a signet ring on the middle finger of his right hand was inset with a facetted glorystone, casting a light bright as a lantern.

The friar headed up a set of gangplanks to the deck of the *Relentless*. His loud footsteps on the beams caused the door of the aftcastle to be thrown open. A large man in a heavy coat stepped out and said, "Be quiet, brother. The judge is already in bed."

"Wake him at once," the friar said, shaking the bundle of skins he carried. "He must see this."

"There's nothing in those pelts that can't wait until tomorrow," said the guard.

The friar dropped to his knees and whipped the seal skin forward, unfurling it like a blanket. Within was the Immaculate Attire, from boots to collar. A lump formed in my throat.

"Blade's armor?" the guard asked, completely befuddled. "What's *he* doing back here?"

"Blade wasn't wearing it," said the friar. "It was taken off a woman. A woman with platinum hair and silver eyes."

The guard's breath caught in his throat. He whispered, "The Infidel?"

"She fought Tarpok using Lord Tower's Gloryhammer," said the friar. "She survived being crushed by Slor Tonn, though she's been injured. The ogresses are tending to her wounds."

"What?" the guard exclaimed. "If she's wounded, she should be finished off!"

"I know!" said the friar. "The ogresses say that her death would be wasteful. They say she's more valuable to them alive."

"Did you warn them of –"

"They have no respect for my words," the friar snapped. "This alliance is madness! Judge Stern must intervene!"

Judge Stern? The judge who'd hanged his own mother? Sorrow's father?

The guard shook his head, then said, "Wait here."

I was disinclined to wait. I flew down the tunnel the friar had emerged from, hoping to find Infidel. Instead, ten yards in, the tunnel forked. On a whim, I chose the right branch. It forked again. Flying back, I chose the left branch. It led to a polished dome of ice where murals of whale hunts had been painted on the walls with frozen blood. A half-dozen corridors led from here.

With a thought, I was back at the ship. My best hope at finding Infidel was that Judge Stern would demand to see her. I'd follow him, and then what? If he tried to execute Infidel, how could I stop him?

Judge Stern emerged from the aftcastle a moment later, dressed in a thick woolen nightgown. He wasn't a terribly imposing figure, of medium height and build, with a wrinkled face that sagged on his skull. His hair was thinning, but enough remained to pull back into a frazzled braid. He had bushy mutton chops and eyebrows so thick they looked like fuzzy gray caterpillars crawling on his liver-spotted brow.

"Tell me everything you know, Brother Will," said Stern.

I learned nothing new from the testimony that followed.

"What became of the Gloryhammer?" the judge asked.

"The heathen Tarpok claimed it as his prize," said Brother Will.

The judge grunted his disapproval. "A sacred relic of the church cannot remain in the hands of such a beast," he said. "We'll deal with that matter at another time. For now, we need the ogres to guide us across the Great Sea Above if we're to complete our mission."

This would have been a handy time for Brother Will to ask, "And what is our mission, exactly?" so that I could have learned what the hell they were planning. Alas, he had already been briefed.

"If the Gloryhammer and Immaculate Attire are here, then the quest to kill Greatshadow must have succeeded, since these assets were deployed there," said Judge Stern. "The guiding hand of the Divine Author has brought these items to us on the eve of our final journey."

"Or else the mission failed," said Brother Will. "Could it be that the most sacred champions of the church have been slain by the Infidel, and she's come here to stop us?"

Judge Stern scratched his stubbled chin with his neatly trimmed nails. He nodded slowly, drew a deep breath, then said, "At present, all we have is speculation. Perhaps it's a lucky thing the woman was taken alive. I'm greatly interested in hearing her testimony. Brother Will, go inform the ogresses I shall visit the prisoner as soon as I'm dressed."

"At once, sir," the friar said, before spinning around and scuttling back down the gangplank. I followed, frustrated by how slowly he walked, though in truth I suspect his pace would have winded me if I'd still been alive. After following him for five minutes, I was grateful to have a guide; the underground passageways were a labyrinth. They were also curiously empty. I had yet to spot an ogress. Instead, I spied a dozen human men in a long hall, who sat eating from bowls filled with gelatinous lumps of whitefish cooked in a thin gray broth. They were a rough-looking bunch, no doubt the sailors from the *Relentless*. They looked well fed. I thought about the ogres in the village, so hungry they'd fought over whale vomit.

At length, we reached a cavern carved from solid ice. The place was large enough you could have fit the Grand Cathedral of the Silver City inside it. Starlight filtered down from the translucent ice roof, casting ghostly shadows all about. The front and side of the room was ringed with large ice stalagmites, matched below by stalactites; the way they jagged together almost reminded me of teeth.

The undulating floor could have passed for a giant tongue. The spiritual hairs on the back of my phantom neck began to tingle.

Brother Will hurried across the cavern, toward a gap in the ice teeth that led once more into a corridor of stone. To reach this, he passed three large boats covered in hide, similar to the ones that had turned up in Commonground, albeit lacking dragon heads.

I remembered something Aurora had said in passing, back during the hunt for Greatshadow, something I'd paid little attention to at the time: "We'd sail from the dragon's jaws into the Great Sea Above."

Despite Brother Will's brisk pace, I felt I had time to check out my hunch without losing him. I tilted my head skyward and bid my spectral body to rise. I shot into the ice, then through it, rising into the starry sky above. I flashed a mile into the air at the speed of thought before looking down.

The landscape beneath me was all white on white; the starlight provided little in the way of contrasting shadows. Off to the west about a mile away, I could make out the edge of the cliff and, beyond it, the frozen bay studded with ice-houses.

Directly beneath me was nothing but snow-covered hills leading off to the west in a succession of serpentine ridges. As my eyes adjusted, the truth slowly emerged: The ridges of the hills were formed from the spine of a dragon.

I was flying directly above the motionless form of Hush. Brother Will had just walked through the cavern of her open jaws.

Perhaps I was growing jaded. Since my death, I'd witnessed four primal dragons – Abyss, Greatshadow, Rott, and now Hush. I was no longer astonished by their sheer size. It was difficult to judge Hush's true length given that she lay with her body curled, but I would roughly calculate that from snout to tail tip she was a good five miles long. But despite her glacial size, one couldn't help but notice that she was frozen stiff and had apparently not moved in a very long time. She was more landscape than lizard.

I'd been gone long enough. I dove back down, passing straight through her snout into her cavernous mouth, quickly spotting the passage Brother Will had been shuffling toward. I flew in that direction, catching up to the friar a few seconds later.

He was descending a winding stone stairwell. Frost sparkled on the walls, lit by his glorystone ring. To my surprise, the passageway came to an abrupt dead end at a wall formed of ice. He rapped the ice with his ring. The space beyond was obviously hollow.

An ogress stepped through the ice-wall, passing through its solid surface as if had been merely a sheet of flowing water. She could have been Aurora's sister for all I knew; her walrus coat, hair, and skin tone were identical, though she may have stood a few inches taller.

"What do you want?" the ogress asked gruffly.

"Judge Stern wants to interview our prisoner. Is she awake?"

"She is," said the ogress. "But she's *our* prisoner, not yours. She attacked our villagers. She was bested by our champion. Your judge has no authority over her."

"She was carrying holy relics of our church," said Brother Will.

"We've already given you the armor. If your judge wants the hammer, I suggest he argue his case with Tarpok. In any event, you have no need to speak to the prisoner."

"I beg to differ," said Brother Will. "We've every reason to think that this woman is a great enemy of our church."

"*We* are great enemies of your church," said the ogress, in an impatient tone one might use speaking to a particularly dull-witted child. "Purity is an even greater threat to all you hold dear. Your argument isn't terribly convincing."

"Listen to me!" Brother Will said, waving his finger in her face. "Your prisoner has devoured the enchanted blood of the primal dragon Verdant! It gives her strength beyond imagining. She can bend steel with her bare hands. The sharpest blades are blunted when they strike her invulnerable skin! You don't know the danger she poses!"

"You're obviously mistaken about the identity of our captive," said the ogress. "We were able to stitch her wounds with a bone needle; her skin is no tougher than any other of your race. And if she can bend steel with her bare hands, why does she struggle so helplessly when we've bound her limbs with mere leather?"

Brother Will furrowed his brow, obviously stumped by this revelation.

I saw no reason to stand in the hall and listen to these two argue. I ghosted through the ice and found myself in circular stone cell about seven feet across. Infidel was alone, leaning against the wall, her body covered by a sealskin pelt. Her bare arms lay before her, bound at the wrists by tight loops of leather. To my astonishment, she held my bone-handled hunting knife in her left hand.

The room was stuffy, even warm, despite the wall of ice that sealed the door. Only a few gaps in the stone allowed air to flow; Infidel looked dazed and drowsy, and I wondered if she was suffocating in this nearly air-tight space. On the other hand, despite the glazed look in her eyes, the color had returned to her cheeks. Save for the numerous bruises around her shoulders, and a stitched gash on her chin, she looked not too shabby for someone who'd been crushed by a whale.

She looked up as I drifted near her.

"Stagger?" she whispered.

"You can see me?" I asked, my ghost heart freezing. Was she so close to death's door?

"And hear you," she said, keeping her voice low as she glanced at the ice wall. The light from Brother Will's glorystone cast the ogress's shadow on the ice in stark outlines. Infidel winced as she rose to meet me. Beneath her seal skin, she was wrapped from armpits to upper thigh with tight white bandages. Her feet were bound together by leather loops that let her move her feet only a few inches apart. She leaned back against the wall to steady herself. Her breathing sounded shallow.

"You're not dead?" I asked.

"I'm too sore to be dead."

"Why did they let you keep my knife?" I asked. It seemed very odd to leave a prisoner with a weapon, and for the life of me I couldn't imagine how she could have hidden it.

"The ogres don't see the knife," she said. "Only I can see it and feel it; it was stuck to my hand by dried blood. But even when they stitched up my palm, it never fell from my grasp. They ran needles through it as if it wasn't even there."

"It must still be halfway between the spirit realm and the real world," I said. "Maybe it's letting you see me."

"I wish it was letting me cut these cords," she said, placing the knife in her teeth and trying to stab the leather at her wrist. The blade slid right through, like vapor.

"You're in the middle of the ice-ogress temple," I said. "You'd have a hard time getting out of here even if you weren't tied up. To make matters worse, one of the Judgment Fleet is here, the *Relentless*. Judge Stern is on his way to interrogate you to find out of you're *the* Infidel."

"Stern?" Infidel said, spitting the knife back into her palm. "Sorrow's father?"

"Maybe," I said.

"That's a pretty big coincidence, isn't it?" she asked.

"The monks used to say that what we think of as coincidences are all part of the Divine Author's master plot."

"And that plot would be?"

I shrugged. "From what I can gather, just as King Brightmoon allied himself with the Black Swan to slay Greatshadow, he must have struck a deal with either Tarpok or Purity to help kill Glorious. Judge Stern is here representing the king's interests. Maybe. There are lots of gaping holes in my information. But, we don't have time to figure things out, because Stern's coming here to see you. You need to figure out a cover story, quick, so he won't learn who you really are."

"Or I tell him who I really am," said Infidel. "Maybe I can convince him that my father will reward him handsomely for my safe return."

"Or he puts you on trial immediately for high crimes against the church and you're dead before the day's out."

As I said this, the ice door cracked, suddenly collapsing beneath its own weight. Rather than the ogress and the friar, a tall woman with four arms and a pair of wings stood in the doorway. Save for being coated with fine silver fur, her face was a perfect match with Infidel.

"I apologize for eavesdropping," Purity said, with a slight grin. "It's the hound in me, I fear; I can hear every word spoken for a hundred yards in any direction."

"You can hear me?" I asked.

"Menagerie's animal senses detect you, if faintly," Purity said. "Have you never felt as if dogs were sometimes staring at ghosts? It seems, indeed, they are."

"Can they also *feel* ghosts?" I said, leaping forward, making a fist, putting all I had into a swing at her chin. I had one shot at taking her by surprise. That shot failed, my ghostly arm wafting through her.

"It seems not, now that you're free of your driftwood shell," she said.

"How about this?" Infidel shouted, hopping forward, raising her bound fists in an uppercut punch.

Alas, Purity caught Infidel's arms with her hands and pushed her away. Infidel's back slammed into the wall. Purity was on her a half second later, grabbing her by the neck, lifting her in the air.

"I like your spirit, princess," Purity said. "I suspect your quickness to violence explains how you've managed to retain your virginity to the spinsterly age of thirty. You're exactly who I need to wake Hush. Sacrificing one of my poor ice-maidens will never do when I can have the blood of a virgin princess!"

Infidel clawed at Purity's wrist. "Your information is out of date. I'm not a virgin. I'm pregnant!"

"Pregnant by a ghost, via copulation in an abstract realm. In the material world, your physical form has never been defiled by a man!"

"Hey!" I protested. "She wasn't *defiled*, period. We're married! And wherever and however it happened, she is indeed pregnant. I saw our baby's spirit glowing in her womb. Anyway, how can you possibly know what happened with us?"

Purity drew her face close to Infidel and sniffed the perspiration that now beaded on her brow.

"An ebony bird told me," she said, staring into Infidel's eyes. "You *are* pregnant. I can smell it in your sweat."

"So you won't be sacrificing her," I said.

"So when I sacrifice her, I'll be sacrificing two virgins at once," said Purity.

"Why do you need to sacrifice anyone?" I asked. "What the hell is going on?"

"This world has seen its last sunrise," said Purity, dismissing me with a wave. "There's nothing you can do to stop me. The ogresses have gone to prepare the boats. Tarpok stands ready with the sacred harpoon. Stern even now dons his sacred garb and readies his Writ of Judgment. Leave this place, little ghost. I find your faint murmurs annoying."

"It makes no sense!" I protested. "Killing the sun is insane! What can you possibly hope to gain from such a thing?"

Purity glanced at me. "An end to ceaseless, pointless chatter, to start with. I've been to the Promised Land, little ghost. I've seen the world in its pristine state, before the sky was tainted by the sun. All the world was once in permanent winter, beneath a silent, smooth blanket of white, slumbering like an innocent child, until it was raped by noise, by heat, by light. It is time to complete the circle, and return the world to purity."

"You're out of your frozen mind," I said.

"And you're annoying me," Purity grumbled. "Go away, little ghost."

When the Black Swan had used similar words, I'd been pushed away against my will. Whatever magic she'd used, Purity hadn't mastered it. I felt no force compelling me to leave. So I wonder if she was surprised when I disappeared?

CHAPTER SEVENTEEN
THAT INFIDEL

MY FINAL TEN minutes in the material world were somewhat hurried. Of course, I was unaware that my moments left were so few. Perhaps there were things I could have done differently, though it's too late for second guessing.

With ten minutes left, I willed myself back to the deck of the *Freewind*, arriving at the speed of thought. The ship had been tidied up somewhat, but was still listing. From the bow of the ship, looking toward the stern, I couldn't help but notice that the mizzenmast and the foremast were tilting in opposite directions.

The other thing I couldn't help but notice was the giant. I blinked, certain that my phantom eyes were confused. There was a naked man at least a mile tall wading in the ocean beside the *Freewind*. The waves broke against his belly button. Above him, the darkest, most menacing storm clouds I'd ever seen churned violently, though for some reason the seas all around us were relatively calm and only the barest breeze stirred the air. Gale's handiwork, perhaps?

"Your eyes do not deceive you," said Jasmine Romer, materializing before me. "This is my eldest grandson, Levi, which is short for Leviathan. You may guess the magical gift granted him by the Mer-King."

"He gets big?"

"And stays big," said Jasmine. "Once, he was able to return to human size, but he has not done so since he fell in love with a young cloud giantess. He's thrived in his new world, and is now a commander aboard a hurricane."

This was interesting, but had nothing to do with my reason for returning to the ship. Before I could tell Jasmine about Infidel's peril, Levi bent over the *Freewind* and used fingers the size of tree trunks to gently scoop up Cinnamon, Sage, and Poppy from the deck. He lifted them toward the swirling clouds high overhead. It made me notice how quiet the ship was. Shouldn't ice-maidens still be working their bucket brigade?

"Levi feels the *Freewind* is beyond repair," Jasmine said, shaking her head sadly. "The keel has been damaged and Sorrow said she'd be unable to mend it unless the ship was in dry dock. Only Gale, Mako, and Rigger remain aboard, vowing to see the ship to port. Their stubbornness may be the death of them."

The mention of Sorrow snapped my focus back to my immediate problem: "Infidel's been captured. From what I can figure out, Purity has been allied with the ice-ogres and the Church of the Book to kill Glorious for some time now. They plan to use Infidel as a human sacrifice to wake Hush. I don't think we have much time to stop them."

"Then let's hope my grandson's aim is as good as he says it is," said Jasmine.

"I need to find Sorrow," I said. "I'm hoping she can... wait, why should we worry about Levi's aim?"

"Because an hour ago, at her request, he threw Sorrow at the ice-ogre's village."

And that's how the first minute of my last ten came to a close.

Nine minutes left: I willed myself back into the sky above the ogre temple. Sorrow was nowhere to be seen. Had she fallen short? Assuming that Leviathan's strength scaled magically, and that Sorrow had been a mere pebble in his hand, was even he big enough to fling her this far?

I glanced down at Hush's mouth atop the cliff. Should I go back and try to find Infidel? What could I do there when I did find her, other than annoy Purity? There had to be a better plan.

I looked south, back in the direction of the *Freewind*. If I went back there, could I convince Leviathan to come up here? He'd gotten to the *Freewind* quickly enough. I had some experience with hurricane-force winds; he could probably cover a hundred miles or more in an hour. But as I looked toward the horizon, I saw a bright speck against the night sky, like a shooting star with no trail, hurtling toward me.

With a thought, I flew closer. As the distance closed, I realized I was looking at a sizable bird. My sense of scale, however, was thrown off by the difficulty of judging size with only the stars as a backdrop. I drew closer still and found that I wasn't looking at a bird; I was looking at a pair of copper limbs shaped to resemble albatross wings, covered with fine glass feathers that sparkled in the starlight. Judging from the human figure at the center, the wingspan was at least sixty feet across.

At the center of the wings was a suit of jet black iron armor. Behind the helmet's gleaming glass faceplate, I caught a glimpse of a woman gazing out. Sorrow?

Who else could it be?

She sailed past, leaving only a soft tinkling sound in her wake, like wind chimes in a gentle breeze. With a quick glance at the ground flashing below, I saw she was flying at a pace that would have left Slor Tonn in the dust. Of course, 'leaving in the dust' is really only an appropriate metaphor for horseback riding; fifty years of earthbound existence had left me unprepared for good analogies in describing the speed of flight. Suffice to say, she was moving very damn fast. I gave chase, as one moment bled into the next.

With eight minutes to go, I realized I had no way of speaking with Sorrow. My wooden body was now completely gone... save for the one seed pod ear-ring that Sorrow wore. I caught up and peered through the glass visor that protected her from the wind. It was apparent she couldn't see me, and it was difficult to tell given the tightness of her iron helmet if she still wore the ear. I brushed my spectral fingers along her left cheek and found the pod. My fingers tingled as they connected with whatever faint magic remained in the dry vegetation.

I stretched next to her and placed my lips against her cheek.

"Can you hear me?" I shouted.

I heard nothing, but Sorrow jerked her head to the left.

"Stagger?" she said, though I could barely hear her above the rush of wind. "Where have you been? What's wrong with your voice?"

"Body's gone," I said, trying to keep things as simple as possible. "Purity's in the dragon's head on top of the cliff. She's captured Infidel."

Sorrow's eyes scanned the landscape. She gave a quick nod. "I see it."

I looked in the dragon's direction, surprised that Sorrow had found it so easily, and discovered that Hush's head of translucent ice was now aglow with a pale blue light. Sorrow's wings sang out like a thousand tiny bells as she tilted into a dive, heading straight for the dragon's skull.

Even with the amazing speed with which Sorrow flew, we were still so far away. Impatient, I zipped back in the cavern of Hush's jaws, with seven minutes left.

The three walrus-skin boats had been dragged into the center of the room. In one boat stood Judge Stern, Brother Will, and the bodyguard from the ship, now dressed in the Immaculate Attire. Behind them sat a crew of human oarsmen. Judge Stern held a yard-long tube of rolled-up parchment with both hands. The scroll glowed faintly in my ghostly vision. It was still sealed, but I recognized it at once as a Writ of Judgment.

These sacred documents were issued by the Voice of the Book himself; they were not issued lightly. If the Voice of the Book pronounced you guilty of a crime deserving death, and the Writ of Judgment was read in your presence by a duly appointed authority of the Church, you would die.

In the second boat stood Tarpok, holding his cast iron harpoon straight as a flagpole, his chest thrust out, looking as if he were in command of the world. The Gloryhammer hung across his back, slung on a strap of seal leather. Behind him were three ogresses – all priestesses, judging from their garb – and a dozen human sailors from Stern's boat at the oars.

In the final boat loomed Purity, in a boat manned by ice-maidens. She held the Jagged Heart, which proved to be the source of the light I'd seen outside. In the brightness of the glow, it was difficult to look at Purity directly, though I had no choice. She was holding Infidel by the throat, dangling her off the front of the boat. Infidel squirmed in her grasp, which was loose enough to allow for some cursing.

"You prehistoric witch!" Infidel shouted, vainly trying to stab Purity with the phantom blade of the bone-handled knife. "You can't be this stupid! The judge will kill you the second you've completed his dirty work! It's probably your name on the scroll!"

"The judge knows this is a one-way journey for him," said Purity. "He's willing to die for his cause. How can I not trust a man like that?"

Judge Stern frowned. "If your trust in me is so great, I wish you'd allow me to question your prisoner. I fear, if she is the Infidel, her dragon-tainted blood may ruin your sacrifice. There's no way her spiritual essence can be considered innocent."

Purity chuckled. "There's no dragon blood in this poor girl's veins. I'd be able to smell it. She may be *an* infidel, but she's not *the* Infidel."

I was hovering near the roof of the cavern. No one knew I was there. I had to get Infidel free. There was one thing I hadn't yet done as a ghost that sprang to mind, though whether from inspiration or desperation I cannot say.

With six minutes remaining, I flew down from the cavern toward Purity, waving my phantom limbs for all they were worth, thrusting my face inches before the old witch's mug. I screamed at the top of my ghost lungs, *"BOO!"*

To my utter astonishment, it worked. Purity flinched, dropping Infidel to grab the Jagged Heart with all four hands.

She looked frightened as she swung the harpoon in a clumsy arc, using it as a battle staff rather than a thrusting weapon. Given my proximity, I was nowhere near the blade. This proved fortunate, since the shaft of the harpoon impacted my ghostly ribs with a sickening thud that knocked me backward. I flitted toward the roof, clutching my chest. The pain was unbelievable. My ghostly bones had been broken. How could ephemeral mist fracture?

Despite my lack of actual lungs, I coughed violently. Dark blood sprayed from my phantom lips.

Purity composed herself as she realized the source of her ambush. She tilted her head back and laughed.

"Little ghost!" she said. "I thought you'd fled! You should use more caution. Don't you know this harpoon is used to hunt the dead?"

Actually, I did know that. Aurora had said that she used the harpoon to hunt phantom whales. Apparently, it could injure phantom men as well. I was glad I hadn't been near the pointy end.

Infidel had landed on the ice and was trying to wriggle away. Judge Stern's bodyguard had leapt from his boat and was loping toward Infidel to retrieve her. The form-fitting Immaculate Attire didn't flatter his rather large gut. Any sense of comedy I might have felt about his appearance in the armor vanished the second he drew his long sword with his eyes fixed on my wife.

"Before you kill me," I said to Purity, blinking away tears as blood dribbled down my chin, "you should know that Infidel was right. I spied on Judge Stern earlier and he has three Scrolls of Judgment; one for Glorious, one for you, and the last one for Hush!"

It was a lie, of course. At least, if it was truth, it was a truth I couldn't verify. I felt lightheaded as I wiped blood from my mouth. It glistened on my ghost fingers, red and wet and warm.

I looked down at the bone-handled knife in Infidel's hand as she made one last desperate, instinctive attempt to use the phantom blade to cut the leather that bound her legs. Blood on the knife had always pulled my ghostly form more fully into the material world. Would the blade still react to blood?

I flew down and closed my bloody fingers around the intangible steel. I shuddered as I felt it drink.

Five minutes left.

I remained a ghost. But the bone-handled knife, coated with my blood, suddenly sliced through the leather that bound Infidel's legs. The guard stood over her, sword drawn. Infidel kicked with her now-free left leg, letting loose a loud grunt as she put her full strength into the guard's right knee cap. With a popping sound, his leg bent backward. He toppled toward her, chopping his blade toward her brow.

Infidel raised her bound wrists, straining to pull her hands apart. She caught the falling blade against her leather bindings. It didn't quite cut through. She twisted her arms and yanked the sword from the guard's grasp. Bracing the sword between her knees, she slid her wrists along the sword's edge and was free.

She sprung to her feet with a back flip, sword in hand. Before anyone could react, she sprang forward and punched the tip of the blade into the back of the guard's skull, in the half-inch gap between his helmet and his collar. His flailing limbs instantly went slack. Everyone on Judge Stern's boat turned pale.

"Yeah," she said, with a glare in their direction. "*That* Infidel."

I wasn't certain she should be boasting, given that she was half-naked, bruised head to toe, and armed only with a long sword and a semi-material hunting knife, facing off against a shape-shifting witch and a half-ton ogre carrying weapons crafted from dragons. In fact, as much as I admired her swagger, I really hoped she'd find her inner Stagger and run like hell. Before I could draw a pained breath into my broken chest to offer the advice, the roof caved in.

Four minutes to go.

A chunk of ice the size of an elephant smashed into the floor between Infidel and the three boats. Something dark sat atop it, but vanished in a blizzard before my eyes could focus. Infidel reacted with surprising calmness, stepping backward to avoid the gusting snow. Some of the mariners aboard Judge Stern's boat didn't wait for the air to clear before jumping ship and making a break for it. Stern cast a wicked glance backward, the ferocity of his gaze halting the remaining mariners from abandoning their posts.

The snow cleared and revealed Sorrow crouched atop an imposing boulder of bluish ice. Her wings had either been torn away by impact, or she'd shed them to improve her freedom of movement. Her iron armor clung to her like a coat of paint. She stood, stretching her left hand. Iron razors six inches long sprang from her fingertips.

Her other gauntlet crumbled, revealing her right hand, blood-red with rust. For some reason, her naked hand was far more menacing than the clawed gauntlet.

"I come to this place intending no malice," she announced. "Purity, we're kindred spirits, aware that the world is an unjust place. We seek, in our own fashion, to better it; I would rather be your friend than your foe. But I cannot let you extinguish the sun. Renounce your plans and join me on a more constructive path. If you refuse, I give my solemn vow that I will kill everyone in this room."

"You're the crippled materialist," Purity scoffed. "The pathetic failed witch who nearly killed herself with a bone-nail. Despite the drama of your entrance, you've no power to enforce your threats."

The iron and glass helmet that covered Sorrow's features flowed backwards like mercury, revealing her face and scalp. From my hovering vantage point, I counted swiftly: One, iron. Two, copper. Three, glass. Four, gold. Five, silver. Six, wood. And seven... seven was something black as tar, something that made my eyes ache and my stomach turn.

Sorrow said, in low, firm tones, "I've carved a nail from a fragment of tooth belonging to Rott, the all-consuming. I now command the elemental force of decay. I possess the power I've long sought to remake the world. It does not suit me to have the world end just as I gain the ability to save it."

The helmet spread back over her scalp and face. She said, calmly, "I will begin killing when I count down from three. Three."

Which, as fate would have it, were the number of minutes I had left.

Purity glared at Sorrow's red right hand. I had trouble taking my eyes off it myself. We both had to be wondering what Sorrow's new powers might do to ghosts.

Sorrow had her gaze locked on Purity. From the corner of my eye, I saw Tarpok lean back in his boat, hefting his iron harpoon over his shoulder.

"Sorrow!" I wheezed, though of course no one in the room but Infidel and Purity could hear me. Infidel started running toward Tarpok, but it was too late. He hurled the massive shaft of steel, which flashed through the air between him and Sorrow.

Sorrow proved more attentive than I'd supposed. She stretched out her right hand, palm open like a shield to catch the harpoon's razor tip. The horrible weapon turned into a cloud of reddish dust, swirling to settle on the ice at Sorrow's feet.

"Two," said Sorrow, though I technically had over two and a half minutes left.

The mariners in Judge Stern's boat once more scrambled overboard. Stern spun around and barked, "Any man whose boot touches the ice shall be hanged!"

The sailors didn't even pause.

Sorrow, on the other hand, turned her head slightly.

"Father!" she called out, in astonishment.

This distraction was all that Purity needed. She lunged forward, her vast wings unfolding, as she thrust the Jagged

Heart like a pike. The tip barely touched Sorrow's frozen armor before Sorrow caught the shaft with her red right hand.

Instantly, Sorrow's armor spider-webbed with cracks. As she moved, the iron began to flake away, rendered brittle and useless by the Heart's extreme chill. The narwhal-horn shaft yellowed where Sorrow touched it, but didn't disintegrate.

The impact knocked Sorrow backward. She slipped from her icy perch. Her armor shattered into scraps of black shrapnel, skittering across the floor as she landed flat on her back. Purity came to rest on the icy boulder where Sorrow had perched a moment before.

"Foolish girl," the shapeshifter growled. "You come here and boast that you wield the power of a primal dragon? What of it? I've surrendered myself to Hush for two full centuries. I'm more than her prophet; I am her avatar! You brandish the power of decay? Cold stops decay!"

Sorrow opened her mouth and drew a breath. I knew her next word would finish her countdown.

But Sorrow wasn't my sole focus of attention. In the exact same span of seconds that Sorrow and Purity had fought, Infidel sprang into action. Tarpok had just thrown his harpoon, his right arm still outstretched. Infidel no longer had the dragon strength that had allowed her to leap rivers in a single stride, but she was a well-muscled woman in her prime who could cover the twenty-yard gap between her and Tarpok in heartbeats. Tarpok was rising, regaining his balance, when Infidel reached his boat. The upper lip of the leather vessel was eight feet off the ice, but Infidel leapt to within inches of the edge, sinking her bloodied knife into the leather, using it as a pivot point as she swung her body up. In the blink of an eye, she was over the rim, leaving the bone-knife dangling in the leather. With a snarl, she placed both hands on the hilt of her long sword, planted her feet firmly, and drove the honed steel tip with all her weight into Tarpok's belly.

The point of the blade skittered along his stomach, tearing

a gash in the sealskin coat he wore. Beneath it, pale white flesh was revealed, and a tiny line of beaded blood. Her most powerful blow had only scratched him.

Infidel had no time to prepare a second strike. Tarpok caught her by the hair and snatched her from her feet.

"I'm going to wring your scrawny neck," he grunted, as he brought her face inches from his own.

Infidel reached over his shoulder, her fingers closing around the shaft of the Gloryhammer. The weapon flared as she took command of its power. Tarpok and Infidel shot skyward with the speed of lightning, towards an intact section of the roof. Tarpok's head smashed into the ice, sending a spray of crystalline daggers flying in every direction. Infidel curled her body beneath his as they rose. On impact she drove her elbow straight into the ice-ogre's throat.

Unfortunately, the awkwardness of her position caused the Gloryhammer to tear from her grasp, and they both tumbled back to the floor. They slammed to the ice ten feet behind Sorrow just as she said, "One."

I actually had two minutes left.

Sorrow lay on the ice wearing only a modest silk slip. The braces she'd once worn were gone; her limbs looked to be in full health once again. Perhaps she now had the power to reverse entropy as well? She kept her eyes fixed on Purity as she rose.

"You were warned," the young witch said. She opened her mouth wide as her belly swelled. With a violent convulsion, she vomited, sending a jet of oily black fluid spraying toward Purity. The air instantly stank of rotten meat, a foulness that gagged even me.

The spray broke into black droplets in the air, which began to flitter and buzz. Purity was swallowed by what can only be described as a tornado of flies. The flies swelled forward from the whirlwind, engulfing the three boats. Screams filled the air as the black cloud covered everything.

Meanwhile, on the ice behind Sorrow, free from flies, Infidel had recovered half a second before Tarpok did. On her knees, she ripped the Gloryhammer free of the leather straps that held it on the ogre's back. She rose to stand above the fallen warrior.

Infidel looked rough. Her impact with the ice had torn loose the stitches on her brow, and bright red blood flowed across her cheek and down her throat. If she felt any weakness, she didn't show it. She lifted the Gloryhammer with both hands high above her head.

Tarpok, flat on his back, had by now recovered enough to recognize his danger. He swung his right arm up to protect his face.

It didn't help. Infidel swung the hammer down with such force that it snapped his forearm, driving flesh and bone down to pancake flatness as it impacted with his face right between his tusks. His head caved in, squeezing his brains out through his ears.

Infidel stumbled backward as she tried to avoid the sudden gush of blood rolling toward her feet. She looked pale and exhausted as she landed on her butt. The impact caused her to drop the hammer. She took a deep breath as she probed the bleeding wound on her brow with her fingers. She pulled away her hand, coated with her own blood.

To balance herself, she placed that hand upon the ice beneath her. The ice throughout the cavern instantly turned pink.

My final moment:

The cloud of flies turned white as the insects developed a coat of frost. They plummeted from the air, bouncing as they landed with tiny tapping sounds that built to a deafening crescendo, like a billion bits of gray hail striking a tin roof all at once. In the aftermath, Sorrow had proved unable to live up to her boast of killing everyone.

Not that she hadn't given it her all. The human sailors were dead, or nearly so. Half of them were little more than skeletons wreathed in maggots, the other half were still-living men with skins swollen to the bursting point by writhing things within them, gorging on their organs.

The only man unaffected was Judge Stern, who hugged the Writ of Judgment tightly to his breast. These documents were often protected with glyphs to ward off damage; the protections must have shielded the judge as well.

The boat of the ice-maidens was none the worse for wear. The ice-armor that coated the women had proven impervious to the flies.

The trio of ogre priestesses on the final boat were also unscathed beneath shells of ice, but the oarsmen who'd shared the boats with them had been utterly maggotized.

Standing on the boulder of ice, Purity looked down at Sorrow. The shape-shifting witch had sheathed herself with icy armor.

Sorrow took a step backward, bringing her fists up, her brow furrowed as if she was pondering how to respond to this turn of events. But if she'd not expected her attack to be thwarted, she was even more surprised when her feet slipped out from under her and she landed on the pink ice with a wet *smack*.

The dragon's frozen tongue was melting, and melting fast.

Sorrow and Infidel struggled to make it to their feet. They were both soaked by the time they stood. The cavern floor was now six inches deep with pinkish water. The cavern was filled with the aroma of spit mixed with a little blood. The fluid was now deep enough that the sealskin boats were starting to float.

With a wave of the Jagged Heart, Purity literally froze both Sorrow and Infidel in their tracks, trapping their bodies in ice.

"Hush has tasted virgin blood!" Purity shouted, looking toward the trio of ogresses. "We've only seconds before the dragon awakens and propels us into the Great Sea Above! Secure our prisoners and place them in the center boat!"

The ogresses leapt from their boat and ran to Sorrow and Infidel. One paused before Tarpok long enough to kick him in the gut, before aiding her sisters in lifting the frozen bodies and rushing back toward Purity's boat. The Gloryhammer was retrieved as well, along with the corpse of Stern's bodyguard, still spotless in the Immaculate Attire. The ogresses understood the artifacts were too valuable to simply leave behind.

The old witch looked over her shoulder. "Judge Stern, as your crew has proven inadequate to the task at hand, would you be so kind as to move to my boat?"

The judge looked dazed, but he nodded and climbed out into the knee deep water. He paused for a moment, looking down at the remains of his men, then reached into the boat to grab something I couldn't see and stick it in a pocket of his robe. The entire cavern shuddered as he sloshed toward the middle boat.

"Hurry!" Purity cried, watching events from her perch on the ice boulder. "Hush wakes!"

In response, there was a groan, soft at first, building to a deafening roar loud enough that Judge Stern covered his ears as the ogresses helped to push him into the center boat. The frozen forms of Infidel and Sorrow were tossed in like stiff baggage, coming to rest in the middle of the vessel.

The dragon's groan faded, ending with what could only be described as a sob. The noise reminded me, for all the world, like the cry of a woman who'd just been told of the death of a lover. It was the sound, on the most primal level, of a broken heart.

And then the blood came, gushing up the dragon's throat in a great carmine flood. It surged through the chamber, lifting the boats. The dragon's jaws opened to let the blood flow out toward the cliff edge in a great river ten feet deep. Purity flitted down from her icy perch as the flood engulfed it, landing in the central boat.

To the right, the boat that Tarpok commanded spun in the current, the bone-handled knife sticking from its bow.

Despite the fact that my broken ribs made me feel as if my torso was full of shattered glass, cutting me with even the feeblest of motions, I stretched my arm out as I flew toward the boat. The knife was now solidly in the material world. Was there enough of it still in the middle realm where I dwelled that I could grasp it?

I almost laughed as my fingers closed around the hilt and yanked the blade free.

The boats were racing forward now, on the river of roiling gore, with Purity standing on the bow, harpoon in hand, her eyes scanning the horizon in the direction of a sunrise which might never come.

This witch had to die.

I flew toward her with the fullest speed of my imagination.

She caught me mid-flight with the Jagged Heart, moving faster than I could follow, driving its tip into my chest beneath my left collarbone. With a push and a twist, my ghost heart was torn free from its arteries and forced down to meet my liver.

The bone-handled knife slipped from my fingers to land at the witch's feet. I opened my mouth to curse her, but only a bubble of blood escaped.

My time in the material world had come to an end.

CHAPTER EIGHTEEN

DEAD IN THE WATER

How much of what happened next is memory and how much is dream is difficult to say.

I hung upon the Jagged Heart like a pig upon a spit. Purity grimaced as my ghost blood ran down the narwhal shaft in dark red spirals, staining her hands. She tried to shake me loose, but the barbed head held me tightly. In the end, she was forced to awkwardly manipulate the harpoon close to her so that she could grab the portion of the staff that jutted from my buttocks. I hung upside down in the boat for a moment. I saw Judge Stern remove his heavy black cloak and drape it over his frozen daughter.

"You attempt to warm her in vain," one of the ogresses said with a scowl.

"I merely wish to hide the shame of her unclothed limbs," said the judge.

By then, Purity had shifted her grasp on the harpoon. She shook the shaft over the edge of the boat and I slid, face down, toward the growing river of blood. I splashed into the fluid, blinded for a moment by the opaque tide, before I floated face up to the surface. I felt no pain. I could not move, or even blink. I bobbed along in the current, utterly limp. Just as I could no longer reach for one of the oars cutting into the blood mere feet from my shoulder, my mind, too, lost its ability to hold on to reality. I felt as if fog rolled in from the edges of my memories, blotting out all that remained of my consciousness.

And yet... and yet I do have impressions of my journey into the realm beyond. Perhaps some faint spark of personality remained to bear mute witness to my fate. Or, equally plausible, I've imagined details to fill in the gaps.

Be it truth or dream, this is my recollection:

When the river of blood reached the edge of the cliff, rather than spilling over to flood the ogre village below, the river darkened and spread outward, into the air, flowing toward the stars. My corpse was carried by the current far ahead of the boat that carried Infidel. Purity stood on the bow, the harpoon held before her like a battering ram. A pale glow originated from the Jagged Heart and spread across the sky, triggering a magnificent display of the northern lights. Behind the boat, Hush stirred, her icy body rising, her coat of snow and ice falling away to reveal a crystalline dragon the size of a mountain. As she spread her snowy wings, blizzards spun from the tips, dancing outward in ever-strengthening waves. Much of the world would wake to a morning covered with snow.

The blood flood continued to rise, though at some point my perceptions flipped and instead of rising, we were falling. The stars above were now the stars below, and we fell, one and all, toward the vast black sea of night. As the waters grew closer, I could see that the stars, so small at a distance, were actually bits of ice, brilliant as diamonds. They continued to grow larger as I fell, growing from flea specks to fragments the size of fingernails, to chunks as large as my palm, to floes as big as boats, until they became small islands, hundreds of yards across. I smashed into the waters that separated these icy isles. The sea was awash with light. As I bobbed back toward the surface, I saw that the cold waters were dense with phosphorescent krill, glowing ghostly shades of green and blue. *Ghostly* was an especially apt adjective, since the krill looked like translucent wisps of light rather than beings of flesh. I understood, at last, the origins of the auroras we'd witnessed in these northern latitudes.

By pure chance, my face turned heavenward as I reached the surface. Purity's boat was nowhere in sight. Snow clouds roiled high above, filling the sky, reflecting the pale glow of the sea.

From these clouds emerged a whale. It was Slor Tonn, his head split open. I could see through his great black and white form as he tumbled through the air. He was as much a phantom now as I'd been. He splashed into the waters some distance away from me. My body was tossed by the waves created by his impact. I found myself upside down, my lifeless eyes staring into infinite blackness, my feet now above water. I could not move to right myself. I don't know how long I drifted, numb and silent.

Dead in the water.

Then, far below, a faint circle of white, like a smoke ring, growing, rising toward me.

It was Slor Tonn. His massive jaws were opened into a toothy circle. His jaws clamped down on my waist, severing my legs. The last thing I remember, or dream I remember, is the pressure of his tongue flattening me against the roof of his mouth before he swallowed.

And then there was nothing.

AND THEN THERE was something. In the dark and silent void, I heard... music. The song was faint, the far-away voices of women singing, unaccompanied by instruments. I couldn't recognize the words; the language sounded like that of ogres. It didn't matter. The music was the most beautiful thing I'd ever heard, haunting and heartbreaking yet joyful, filling me with loneliness, then promising to take that loneliness away.

My peaceful communion with this ghostly melody came to an abrupt end as I was vomited from the belly of the whale. Imagine a sound like a cat coughing up a hairball, assuming you were inside the cat, and the cat was fifty feet long. This disgusting cacophony served as my trumpet to awaken me to judgment day. I found the will to open my eyes as I was squeezed through the whale's undulating esophagus, my passage illuminated by reeking buckets of half-digested ghost krill. I exploded out upon the whale's great pink tongue, my arms flopping uselessly. My left hand snagged against the whale's saw-like teeth and was severed as I was spat out across an ice floe. The pain of losing my hand was agonizing. The pain of everything was suddenly unbearable. My chest was nearly hollow; half my guts had spilled out when Slor Tonn had snapped me off at the legs. My heart was trying to beat, but faced the difficulty of having been chopped to mincemeat by Purity's harpoon.

I squeezed my eyes tightly to hold back the gush of tears. Never had I hurt so badly, not even when I'd died the first time in the material world.

There were voices around me: ogres, judging from the deepness of the tones and the harsh, hacking syllables of their vocabulary. Not such a big surprise, I guess. The Great Sea Above was heaven for ogres.

Clenching my teeth to control the pain, I managed, through extreme force of will, to open my eyes. I was flat on my back on the ice. An ogress crouched above me. She was nude save for a necklace of whale teeth, and her pendulous breasts nearly touched my nose. She shifted, giving me a better view of her face, although I wish she hadn't. Her visage was a horrifying mass of blisters and raw flesh, black around the edges, as if she'd been burned. Above her blackened tusks, her pale blue eyes were gentle, even kind. Her hair was pulled back into a severe top-knot, the hair singed and frizzed.

Her half-charred lips were set in what can only be described as a bemused grin.

"I was there the night the fortune teller predicted the sea would swallow your bones," she said. "She forgot the bit about getting spit back out."

"Aurora?" I gasped.

"Yep," she said. "I'm guessing you're in a world of pain."

Tears streamed down my cheeks as I swallowed hard. "Unbearable."

She reached into a pouch at her side, then pushed something rubbery between my teeth. With her meaty fingers, she worked my jaws, forcing me to chew. The taste was like raw, rotten kidney mixed with licorice. I wanted to spit, but she held my lips shut. I decided to swallow. Given that my stomach had fallen out of my rib cage, it was the fastest path toward getting rid of whatever foul thing she was poisoning me with. However, as I swallowed, my pain eased. It wasn't just a numbing that came over me, but a flush of heat and energy.

"That was a slice of dried adrenal gland from a polar bear," Aurora said. "The gland sits next to the kidney, so your saliva is going to taste like urine, I'm afraid. Give it a minute to kick in and you should feel better."

I nodded. "Not even a minute. That's pretty good stuff."

Aurora shrugged. "Get used to it. Now that you're dead, you'll be eating it by the fistful. It's pretty much the only thing to soothe the pain."

"I've been dead for weeks. Until now, it hasn't really hurt," I said.

"Last I saw you, you hadn't passed on to the afterlife. You were just sort of a pathetic ghost haunting the woman you used to love."

"Still love," I said. "Nothing's pathetic about that. And last I saw you, you'd been fried by Greatshadow, and your ghost was off to the Great Sea Above to find your family."

Aurora picked me up, placing me upright on the ice. We were surrounded by a score of ogres in various states of decay. Most were short a limb or two. Some were missing heads. "I found them."

I raised my remaining hand and said, "Awk." The ogres who could manage it raised their hands to return the greeting. They were a sad-looking lot. Most were chewing on rubbery bits of bear gland like gum. Even from a distance, their breath smelled of piss.

"I thought the Great Sea Above was heaven for your people," I said. "Why is everyone in pain?"

"Heaven and hell are myths of your people. For my people, there is life, and beyond. Once you are in the Great Sea Above, you're immortal. Your body no longer ages. This also means that it no longer heals. You remain in the same state you died in, unless you suffer further injuries here, or your corpse decays or is damaged back in the material world. Ordinarily, this isn't a problem. We entomb our dead in ice, where their bodies may remain unchanged for eons. Alas, when I was driven from the temple, the conflicts that followed led some ogres to desecrate the bodies of my relatives. The call song I sing extends back thirty generations. I should be surrounded by legions; only this small band remains."

"I'm sorry," I said.

Aurora shrugged. "Eternity is too long to dwell on regrets. For now, I'm grateful for what I have. I'm among those I love. My family needs me. I have a purpose, which makes me happy. And now that my oldest friend has found me, my happiness is increased even more."

"Really?" I asked, trying not to sound shocked. "I was your oldest friend? I always thought you didn't much like me."

"You?" she chuckled. "You were likable enough, but I was speaking of Slor Tonn." She looked up. Slor Tonn floated directly above us. "I'm sorry he's passed on, but happy he found me. I'm not surprised. There was always a bond between us." She looked down at me. "On the other hand, I'm completely befuddled that you're here. Your kind normally passes on to different realms."

"I'm a bit surprised myself."

"I assume there's some logical explanation?"

I shook my head. "I don't think logic has much to do with this."

I told my story, starting with Infidel promising to return the Jagged Heart, all the way up to the point where Purity stabbed me. It took a long time, long enough that I required a second dose of bear gland, but Aurora listened patiently, as if she had nothing but time.

In the end, she nodded, contemplating what I'd told her.

"I'm probably missing some important details," I said. "I don't really know who this Tarpok character is, or why he'd ally himself with someone like Purity."

"Tarpok was my eldest brother," said Aurora. "He was the biggest, strongest, toughest ogre in the village. I was his runt sister, in a family with twenty siblings. As a hunter, Tarpok brought great prestige upon my family. Then I entered the priesthood, and eventually became high priestess. In my youth, the villagers would look upon my father and say, 'there is an ogre who deserves respect, for his semen has produced the mighty hunter Tarpok.' Once I was high priestess, the praise changed, and they said, 'this great ogre's semen has blessed our village with Aksarna the wise.' Aksarna, by the way, being my true name. As you can imagine, this hurt Tarpok's pride."

"I would think it would hurt your mother's pride, hearing your father get all the credit."

"Tarpok and I have different mothers. Father has produced twenty children, by seven different mates."

"Oh. Are ogres polygamous, or is child birth just that difficult?"

"Ogres are fiercely monogamous. Most of my father's wives were murdered by younger women wanting to catch my father's attention. Only after the old wife was out of the way would father choose a new wife."

"And he'd choose a known murderess?"

"It showed she had passion. It's considered highly flattering if a female is willing to kill to gain access to your semen."

I furrowed my brow. I tried to be open-minded about cultural differences, but this was a bit much.

"Semen is *very* important to my people," Aurora said, sounding worried I hadn't caught on. "Which added to Tarpok's shame. He was a mighty hunter, yet his first bride bore him no children. He murdered her two years later and took a second wife. She, too, bore no children. Then he married Sinnatok, a widow who had four young children, so she was certain to be fertile. This marriage, alas, produced no offspring. Whispers grew that Tarpok the mighty was really Tarpok the seedless. Women snickered as he passed. His shame was great."

"Tarpok seemed pretty popular when I saw him," I said. "Your people must have gotten over the fact he was sterile."

Aurora shook her head. "Now that I've rejoined my family, I've learned what happened in my absence. With the Jagged Heart gone, the priestesses were weakened. Tarpok announced that we were at war with the Skellings, and that he was to be our warlord. He took up residence in the temple, since it was the most defensible structure. He killed any priestess who objected, but spared the few who broke their vows of chastity in an attempt to, shall we say, sanctify his semen."

"From what I can count, there were only three who agreed."

"Three too many," Aurora grumbled. "There were twenty-five priestesses in various stages of training. All should have chosen death over defilement."

"They might not have had a choice," I said. "He's almost twice their size. You can't blame the victims of a rape."

"I can blame any priestess who has not attempted to slit his throat, or failing that, to slit her own. Can you imagine the blasphemy of what he's done? He had the entire village watch as he defiled the priestesses upon the western altar, then had them announce that, by bathing his genitals in their holy blood, he had healed his infertility. It was further proclaimed that he'd been given a divine vision that he was to build a great army to one day stand against those who had stolen the Jagged Heart. It was essential that the village produce as many offspring as quickly as possible. He announced that he was going to sleep with every ogress in the village, taking a different lover every night, so that his blessed seed might produce a new crop of warriors. This pronouncement didn't go over well, as you may imagine."

"It sounds like he went insane," I said.

Aurora nodded. "Tarpok may have been insane, but he was also unquestionably the greatest warrior in the village. The strongest men declared war on him, and it was during this war that his ancestors, and therefore my ancestors, were desecrated. The fighting lasted years, but Tarpok eventually prevailed, and built a monument from the skulls of those who'd opposed him. The remaining men of the village became rather more philosophical about Tarpok sleeping with their spouses. Some of the women resisted at first, but after a few of his early partners became pregnant, most went willingly. Tarpok was the embodiment of male power. The chance to be filled by his semen was a great temptation."

"So was he *was* cured by sleeping with the priestesses?"

Aurora shook her head. "By sleeping with every woman in the village, he could claim that any child born the following year was a product of his seed. But he didn't demand chastity on the part of his lovers; most were probably impregnated by their true husbands."

"I have a hard time thinking that a monster like that gets cheered by the crowds I saw."

"Ah, but there's one final, perverse twist. The men who challenged Tarpok were the best hunters in the village. After they died, Tarpok alone accounted for over half of the meat the village fed upon. My people are on the verge of starving, and flattering Tarpok is their best route to being fed."

"But he's the reason they're starving!"

Aurora shrugged. She said something in her native tongue.

"I'm sorry, I didn't catch that," I said.

"It's a proverb of my people. *Wisdom is the first thing devoured by an empty belly.*"

"I'm afraid your people may be even hungrier now, since Infidel caved in Tarpok's face."

"There was a time when this would have concerned me," said Aurora. "But everyone I knew will be dead soon enough."

"Because Purity's going to murder the sun?"

Aurora shook her head. "Because the lifespan of an ogre is but a single beat of a heart when measured against the expanse of forever. Being dead gives one a sense of perspective. What was the point of all the struggle? In the end, death will claim the just and the unjust. For all the harm that Tarpok did to my people, he's here now, another of the dead in the endless sea of death." She stared out over the ice floes. "As blood kin, he will be drawn to our family song. I look forward to assisting him with his pain."

"You'd soothe the pain of a villain who's done such harm?"

"I said assist, not soothe."

"Ah."

"But this will happen in its own time. Now, we have a more pressing matter." She pointed toward the horizon. "In little more than an hour, Glorious will once again rise over the edge of the sky. Purity will no doubt use this moment to strike. If we're going to stop her, we must depart at once."

"I'm very happy to hear you say this," I said. "I was worried that your newfound stoicism might keep you from taking the threat seriously."

Aurora whistled to Slor Tonn. The whale did a cartwheel, then plunged into the water nearby. "I care little about the fate of the world. But Purity was responsible for robbing me of the Jagged Heart. Even now, she defiles it with her heathen grasp. I cannot let this be."

"Purity's no pushover," I warned. "She's got all of Menagerie's shape-shifting powers, plus ice powers just like you."

"Actually, I don't have those powers any more," said Aurora, sounding apologetic. "My spiritual connection with Hush was severed when I came here."

"Oh. Then we might be in a rather lopsided fight."

"She's sailing in a walrus-skin boat," said Aurora. "We'll be riding a flying whale. This fight may be lopsided in an entirely different direction than you think."

Slor Tonn floated up beside the ice-floe and Aurora lifted me, slinging me over her shoulder. "Hold tight," she said, as I wrapped my arms around her neck. She shoved another bit of bear gland between my lips. I pushed it between my teeth and cheek and sucked on it to make it last longer. Aurora jumped onto Slor Tonn's back.

"He doesn't have his harness any more," I said. "He's as naked as we are."

"Who needs a harness?" she asked, walking toward the center of the whale, right behind his blow hole. She made a clicking noise with her tongue and the whale slapped his tail against the water, then surged skyward. Aurora crouched, keeping her center of gravity low, her arms spread for balance. I tightened my grip around her neck.

We climbed swiftly, as the dead ogres on the ice-floe began to sing their family song to call Aurora back. For a moment it seemed that the higher we climbed, the louder the voices grew, but soon their voices faded, lost to the wind. As Slor Tonn banked in response to Aurora's clucked and grunted commands, I caught a glimpse of her family on the ice below, now small as bugs.

"Aren't you afraid you won't be able to find them again?" I shouted above the rushing wind.

"I can hear my family song no matter where I travel," said Aurora.

"How about the Jagged Heart? You said you used to be able to feel its tug."

"I lost that connection, I fear," said Aurora.

"So how will we find Purity?"

"I don't think we can, unless we get exceedingly lucky. She's on a tiny boat on an infinite ocean. We'll never find where she is now, but we don't need to; we know where she's going. Fortunately, Slor Tonn can carry us to Glorious before he ever rises above the horizon."

"We're just going to fly to the sun?"

"Why not?"

"And what will we do when we reach it?"

"Talk to Glorious," said Aurora. "Ask him not to rise until we've eliminated the threat."

"Oh." I found the directness of her plan a little unsettling. "Do you really think it will be that easy?"

"I'm almost positive it won't be. But we should try a direct approach and deal with complications only if they arise."

And on we flew. Below us, the ocean spread out like a jeweler's display case, with glistening gems spilled against a backdrop of black satin. Above us was endless darkness, save a floating blue-green ball no larger than a grapefruit.

"What's that?" I asked, pointing with my stump.

"Our old world," she said. "The material world. We lived there."

"It's so small," I said.

"It's far away," she said. "Maybe a thousand miles."

"Wow," I said, surprised I could see anything at that great a distance.

Of course, I'd seen this orb before, when falling back from the realm of the dead where Greatshadow dwelled.

"I've now been in three different realms of the dead," I said.

"What of it?"

"Zetetic, the Deceiver, said that there was no objective reality. He said we were all the authors of our own worlds, and our unconscious collaboration creates what looks like solid reality, but is, in fact, nothing but a malleable fiction. What if the realms of the dead are like this? We spend all our lives imagining what the afterlife will be like, and then, when we die, that's what we get. Doesn't that mean we'd have the power to change things if we wanted to?"

"If we could change things to what we want, I wouldn't have half of my flesh burned away," said Aurora. "I'm guessing you'd still have your legs and your hand."

"But that's not the way I imagined my afterlife. I always assumed that, when I died, I'd just fade away. That's almost what happened, until my soul got sucked into the bone-handled knife."

"Look!" Aurora said, pointing into the distance. I could see nothing but ice floes and black ocean where she pointed. "A boat!"

She used her clucking, snorting commands to steer Slor Tonn back down toward the ice. I narrowed my eyes, trying to see what she'd seen. At last, I spotted it: a single walrus-skin boat, empty of passengers. A few oars lay in the bottom. I saw a rip in the bow, where Infidel had dug in with her knife.

"This was the boat Tarpok and the priestesses were in before Sorrow unleashed her plague of flies," I said.

Water sprayed over us as Slor Tonn came to rest in the dark water. Aurora leapt from the whale's back into the center of the boat. She grabbed an oar and deftly maneuvered the vessel toward the nearest bit of pack ice. Then she hopped out and dragged the boat onto the ice.

"This boat is a great treasure!" she exclaimed. "Not all of my ancestors retain the bodily integrity needed to swim. This will allow us to extend our hunting range. We should turn back and take it to my family."

"What does a boat matter if the world is on the verge of ending?"

Aurora looked up. "If the world ends, it will become even more crowded here. My family will require resources to remain comfortable."

I had to admire her pragmatism. "If this boat is here, Purity must be near."

"Perhaps. The currents that flow from the material world into the afterlife are chaotic. She could be miles away."

"Then let's stick with the plan," I said. "Let's find Glorious first."

"You weren't this impatient when you were alive," Aurora grumbled. But I'd won the argument. She left the boat on the ice floe, as she hopped once more onto Slor Tonn, and steered him toward the horizon.

"Hold tight," she said. "We won't stop again until we're within shouting distance of the sun."

CHAPTER NINETEEN

NOTHING NEW UNDER THE SUN

"There's one thing I don't understand," I said to Aurora as Slor Tonn sailed through the dark sky.

"Only *one* thing?" she asked, in mock astonishment.

"One thing immediately pertinent," I corrected. "When we were hunting Greatshadow, Father Ver sounded pretty confident that killing the dragon would have no effect upon the continued existence of fire. He said that the primal dragons were just interlopers who had merged their spirits with existing elemental forces. Killing the dragon would free the element, not destroy it. For instance, the church killed Verdant a long time ago, and trees continue to do okay."

"So you're wondering if this mission is even necessary?" Aurora asked.

"I mean, suppose Purity does kill Glorious. I'm completely at a loss to figure out if she's here to hunt his body or his spirit, but does it matter? Isn't the sun still going to be around? I hate to sound callous, but would our lives be worse in any way if she succeeds?"

Aurora sighed.

"You sound disgusted by my question."

"Not disgusted," she said. "Just a little... weary. The Church of the Book has gone out of its way to hide the true history of our world. Most of the so-called 'civilized' men I've spoken to have been brainwashed by the church's dogma, to the point that they insist their self-evident falsehoods are the only truth. For those of us privy to the actual reality, conversations about the world's origins with the church's faithful are a little tiresome."

"I'd hardly identify myself as one of the faithful."

"But you were raised by the church," she said. "You judge everything you're told by how well it meshes with the myths of your childhood."

"I also judge the myths of my childhood by how well they mesh with reality. For instance, the Church of the Book teaches that the world is precisely one thousand and eighty-two years old, that it sprang into existence fully formed the day the Divine Author finished writing the One True Book. But I earned my living exploring ruins that my grandfather calculated to be at least three thousand years old. I've gotten my own hands dirty on the roots and rocks of the Vanished Kingdom, and grandfather's math makes much more sense than the church's attempt to explain away the evidence."

"They bother to explain away the evidence?" she asked. "Most believers I speak to aren't even aware there is evidence."

"The monks said that the world looks older than a thousand years because that's the way the Divine Author wanted it to look. A creator can give his creation attributes of a past, even if it was created only moments before."

"That's stupid," said Aurora.

"Maybe. But a lot of smart people buy into it. When I was nine, I was studying literature under a monk named Brother Brown. One day we took a break from reading stories and he asked me to write one. I composed a tale about a knight named Lord Brilliant. Brother Brown kept asking me for details of my character, and my imagination was more than eager to supply them. I remember that when my story began Lord Brilliant was twenty, which seemed rather old to me at the time. I remember his hair was the color of golden wheat. He was strong enough that he could carry his horse across a dangerous bridge. His parent's names were, um... Honor and Faith, if memory serves. Oh, and his favorite food was snails in mustard sauce."

"I can't believe that would be anyone's favorite food," said Aurora.

I shrugged. "I'd heard that rich people ate such things. At the monastery we mostly ate barley and salt cod. Anyway, in my adventure, Brilliant undertook a ten-year quest to hunt down... uh... hmm."

"Hunt down what?"

"Uh... don't be offended, but he hunted down ogres. I was just a kid. I didn't know any personally at the time."

Aurora shrugged. "We tell our children that humans use ogre bones to flavor their soup. Don't worry about it."

"Anyway, my point is, my twenty-year-old knight undertook a ten-year quest. So when I was asked by Brother Brown how old he was at the end of the tale, I said he was thirty. But my teacher pointed out that I had created Lord Brilliant only that morning. He was little more than a few hours old. But, he possessed properties, such as parents, that indicated a much longer existence. Brother Brown explained that our world could also appear to be much older through the same principals. To this day, I really haven't thought of a good argument to challenge this."

Aurora shook her head. "By that logic, the world might only be a year old. Even one minute old. Nothing really existed before we started this conversation. There'd be no way of ever knowing the truth."

"Truth isn't as solid for me as it once was," I said. "The way Zetetic's magic worked... it was like he was creating new realities by the second. I saw it with my own eyes. Who am I to judge what's real and what's unreal?"

Aurora sighed. "Humans are so weak-minded. Your kind confuses philosophy for fact. How is it you came to rule most of the known world?"

"We don't make our weapons out of ice, for one thing. It gives us a little more range."

She rolled her eyes. "We're off-topic. Let's get back to Glorious. Do you ever wonder why the Vanished Kingdom is three thousand years old? Why you don't find traces of something older?"

"Sometimes. Was there a civilization before the Vanished Kingdom?"

"No," said Aurora, somewhat emphatically. "There was nothing older than three thousand years. The world existed before then, but we can never know for how long, since three thousand years ago marks the invention of time. Before then, there were no fixed days or years."

"That makes no sense whatsoever."

"It's a human failing that you wish for the world to make sense. You'd rather embrace a sensible lie than an absurd truth. Time was the invention of Glorious. It was his whole reason for merging his spirit with the sun."

"You're losing me," I said.

"Before three thousand years ago, the sun was a wild thing. It followed no set course across the sky. Sometimes it raced across the heavens, other times it loped at a leisurely pace, pausing to nap at the apex of its climb. Some days it rose in the east, other days in the west or north or south. Nor did it always journey across the vault of heaven toward the opposing horizon. Some days, it would lazily roll back down the sky to finish where it had started."

"If there were days, then there was time," I said, having instantly spotted the gaping hole in her logic.

"But now, a day is a fixed measurement. The sun passes through the sky on a schedule. Its path is so steady, we can divide days into hours, minutes and seconds, or lump them together into months or years. Has it never struck you as odd that the sky has an agenda? It's self-evident, from the regular procession of moon phases, eclipses, and other celestial phenomena, that there is some guiding intelligence imposing order upon them. Glorious is that intelligence."

"I know that in the Vanished Kingdom, Glorious was revered as a god. The ruins are rife with big disks representing the sun."

"With good reason. Glorious made civilization possible. Before he merged with the sun, agriculture couldn't take hold.

Of course, this wasn't Glorious' goal when he fixed the sun into a specific course. He had no idea he was creating the conditions needed for humans to thrive."

"Then why did he do it?"

"Who knows? Perhaps you can ask him yourself. Look ahead."

I did so, and saw what she was referring to. The black sea beneath us was lightening, taking on hues of pale blue, tinted with pastel pinks. The ice floes beneath us grew ever thinner, until at last there were no stars to be seen. We flew on, and at length the ocean grew still and took on the perfect azure of a calm tropical lagoon. Far in the distance, like a vast white pearl too dazzling to look upon directly, was the sun, floating calmly amid the blue.

Aurora raised her beefy arm to shield her eyes as we grew closer. She said, "It's funny that, in telling of the invention of time, I've so lost track of it. Here's the short answer to your original question: Glorious' body was destroyed when he merged with the sun. You know that Hush loved Glorious, and was willing to betray Greatshadow to mate with him. But Glorious spurned Hush; he was too fixed on his plan to merge his soul with the sun to waste his energies on such a thing as love. Hush, in her anger, attacked him, striking a mortal blow just as he was merging with the sun. Her blow killed his reptilian body, but this proved a boon, since it liberated the spirit of Glorious to freely merge with the sun. Hush threw herself at the sun in her rage, but succeeded only in gouging a large crater. The rubble from this blow fell to earth."

"The glorystones," I said.

"Exactly. And, as the glorystones rained down like fire, they caught Greatshadow's attention. At the time, he was merely an ordinary dragon who specialized in elemental flame magic, and he was curious about this new source of heavenly radiance. He flew to investigate, and found Hush standing over the body of Glorious. She confessed that she had offered herself to Glorious and been rejected. Greatshadow's rage at this revelation was the final push needed to fuse his soul with the elemental flames he'd mastered, marking his birth as the primal dragon of fire. As Hush realized she'd lost both Glorious and Greatshadow, her heart shattered, and the chill wind that rushed into the void pushed her across the elemental barrier to become the primal dragon of cold."

"So, if his body is already dead, all that's left of Glorious is his soul," I said.

"Yes. He is, in some ways, the most vulnerable of the primal dragons. We must warn him. If he dies, the sun will no longer be guided by his intelligence. It will once more meander through the sky unpredictably, meaning the end of world as we know it."

"Purity has a different idea. She thinks the sun will be extinguished. But it's hard to think that the Church would be going along with this plan if they thought that was right. They must think things will pretty much stay the same."

Aurora fell quiet as she thought this over. Finally, she said, "What will follow the death of Glorious is an open question. Let's hope we never learn the answer."

And on we flew.

Have you ever approached a bonfire on a dark beach? From a distance, the fire is bright white at its core, while everything around is draped in black shadows. Yet when you are directly beside the fire, the shadows don't seem as stark, and it's possible to gaze into the flames and see the individual logs burning, a hundred glowing hues of yellow and red and white mixed with streaks of dark black soot.

So it proved to be with the sun. The yellow white pearl floating half-submerged in the still blue water could now be gazed upon directly. The pearl was enormous, large enough that the entire Isle of Fire could have been contained within it. If the sun was a giant pearl, here in the Great Sea Above, I couldn't help but wonder if, somewhere in the mythology of the ogres, there was a legend of a giant oyster.

Beneath the pearl's translucent surface, I could see the draconic spirit form of Glorious, curled into a tight ball. His snout was tucked beneath a wing, and his long tail was coiled around his entire form. He dwarfed any of the primal dragons I'd yet witnessed. Abyss had been large enough to swallow a fleet of ships; Glorious was large enough that he could have swallowed Abyss like a grain of corn.

His eyes opened as we approached.

"You're the ones I've waited for," he said, in a surprisingly gentle whisper. There was something curiously familiar about his voice as well. Then I realized it was my own voice. Glorious was speaking directly in my thoughts.

I assume Aurora received the same message. She grunted a command and Slor Tonn slid to a hovering halt. Aurora dropped to her knees and bowed on the whale's broad back. Since I was clinging to her neck, this left me staring right at the sun.

"We're sorry to disturb your slumber, O Glorious!" Aurora cried. "We recognize that we've not cleansed ourselves with the proper rituals. We ask that you –"

"There's no need for these formalities," Glorious said, shifting his face within the pearl to look upon us more directly, with eyes as large as the Commonground bay. "Do you think me ignorant of earthly plots? You've come to murder me, to release my soul to oblivion."

"No!" said Aurora. "Hush and her minions await your return to the northern reaches of the Great Sea Above. It is they who wish you harm. We've come to warn you. But... you already know of this plot?"

"The Church of the Book is not so clever as they believe," said Glorious. "They shun the use of candles and torches, since they fear that Greatshadow may gaze out of the tiniest flame. But they light their most private sanctums with glorystones. My soul fills all solar material, even these remote fragments. I'm witness to the church's every scheme."

"Then you know that the Church has produced a Writ of Judgment that can destroy you," I said.

"Yes. And I've heard their tedious debates as they convinced themselves this will not matter. They believe the sun will continue its current path through pure momentum. They shall have the chance to learn the truth, I suppose. Even without the scroll, I cannot survive an encounter with the Jagged Heart. Its hateful bitterness will poison my soul, and I will, at last, find welcome relief in oblivion."

"You welcome this fate?" Aurora asked, confused.

"For three thousand years, I've guided the sun across the skies in a never-changing path, utterly alone in my journeys. When I began my task, I was driven by pure intellectual hunger: was it possible to impose order upon a chaotic world? I believed it was, and I believed I was the only being who had the intellect and strength of will to force such a change. When I first traveled to these abstract realms, I welcomed my solitude. The material world is violent and cacophonous. I could barely hear my own thoughts. I dreamed of a better place, a domain of peace, order, and silence, where I might at last organize my thoughts and realize the true potential of my mind."

Peace, order, and silence. I wonder if Glorious knew how much his personal agenda overlapped with Purity's dream?

"When I first merged my soul with the sun, all was blissful," Glorious said. "I invented days, which gave birth to years, then to centuries. I was free at last to sequentially organize my thoughts and memories. From my vantage point above the world, I saw the changes my works had made possible. Mankind embraced time, measuring it out with sundials and hourglasses, with calendars and clocks. They sang my praises and carved my image from stone, the better to worship me."

He sounded wistful as he relayed his story, though perhaps 'sounded' isn't the correct word for a message conveyed through telepathy. Still, I was certain Glorious held the memory of this time to be bittersweet. What followed, however, was only bitter.

"My brethren dragons, alas, were slower to see the advantages of time. They were wiped out by the explosive growth of human civilization, slowly fading from history, until only the primal dragons remained. Then I watched even the primal dragons succumb, losing their intelligence and identities to the elemental forces they commanded, until only a handful of my kind endures. Alas, the survivors are the dragons who despise and resent me most. Never in all of existence has any creature ever been as alone as I am."

"But you aren't alone," I said. "If you can see through the glorystones, you're connected with the world! You must experience the lives of thousands each day."

"It is so. And, long ago, this was good. The first men to create agriculture worshipped the sun. They sang my praises and offered me sacrifices. While I no longer needed to eat, my pride fed upon their deeds. I felt... loved."

"Men still love you," I said.

"No," said Glorious. "Men now take me for granted, at best. Today, most men bemoan my great gift, time. They curse the relentless pulse of seconds, they rail against my ceaseless crawl across the vault of the heavens, and treat the years as something I steal from them rather than as a gift given freely."

"People are fickle," I said. "That's hardly a reason to want to die. Give them another thousand years and they'll be back to worshipping you again."

"You cannot judge me," said Glorious. "My loneliness increases with each year. Time has become my curse. If my loneliness is unbearable after thirty centuries, imagine the agony of another hundred, or thousand, or ten thousand. I do not possess the courage to face eternity; no being could. The cycles and patterns of life I observe once delighted me; now they bore me. There is nothing new under the sun. Thirty centuries is enough. I am done."

"What will happen when you die?" asked Aurora. "Who's right? Will the sun carry on without you guiding it? Will it meander as it once did? Or will it be extinguished?"

"What does this matter to me?" he asked. "It was never my intention to give birth to the world you know. Should I care if my choices now end it?"

"Yes!" Aurora said. "You can't condemn a world to death just because you're bored and lonely."

"I believe I can," said Glorious. "And I believe I will."

As he spoke, he uncurled his body. He was a being made of pure light, but the pearl of the sun began to rock and bob as he spread his limbs, disrupting its internal balance. His body passed though the glassy surface and he stretched his golden wings to span the horizon.

Slor Tonn wheeled unexpectedly. I clung tightly to Aurora as she struggled to keep her balance.

"What's happening?" I cried.

"That gloomy idiot has spooked my whale," Aurora shouted, as Slor Tonn fled toward the darker waters we'd come from. I glanced back, to see Glorious rising ever higher above the pearl. The waters beneath us were churning as the sun's orb bounced and twisted, moved by the dragon's struggle to free himself. I looked up, toward the distant globe of the physical world, and wondered what the sky must look like at this moment.

We were putting quite a bit of distance between us and Glorious. I shouted, "Slor Tonn can really move."

"It won't matter," Aurora shouted back. "Glorious will overtake us in the blink of an eye once he gets underway. The only thing we have going for us is that this is the first time he's been outside the sun in three thousand years. Maybe we have a minute or two while he catches his bearings."

"Then that's a minute or two for us to find Hush."

"Agreed," said Aurora. "We can stop Purity and Judge Stern. We can save Glorious whether he wants to be saved or not. Then we can talk him back into the sun... I hope."

"I'll handle the talking," I said. "I won't be much help in a fight."

"That was true in life as well."

She said this humorously, but I sensed an undercurrent of resentment that her only ally in saving the world was a legless, one-handed ghost. I sucked the bear gland nestled in my cheek and said nothing. My brain raced as I struggled to find an argument that might convince Glorious to carry on. I doubted there was anything I might say that would ease his loneliness.

But maybe I was focusing on convincing the wrong dragon. Glorious wouldn't listen to me. Would Hush?

CHAPTER TWENTY

TOO LATE

THE WAVES BELOW churned into white caps. Glorious was causing the pearl of the sun to bob and spin violently as he continued to rise, shaking his spirit free of its shell. His radiance cast Slor Tonn's shadow on the waters before us, like a long dark arrow. I cannot guess our speed, but at least several minutes passed while the waters beneath us grew ever darker. At last, Glorious was merely a glow on the horizon, and sparkling ice floes once more speckled the velvet black waters of the Great Sea Above.

The turbulent waves from the thrashing sun reached the ice floes, causing some to bob, and others to shoot into the air and hurtle towards the material world, high above. Many a night had I gazed into the dark sky and contemplated shooting stars. Had this always been their origin? Great blocks of ice breaking free from the celestial ocean to fall toward earth? It seemed so unlikely.

But I had little time to contemplate heavenly mechanics before Aurora shouted, "There!" Her arm was outstretched toward the largest iceberg I'd ever seen.

Only it wasn't an iceberg. It was Hush, walking along the surface of the ocean, which froze into thick ice sheets to support her weight. Waves crashed against the advancing ice wall, and bobbing atop these waves was a tiny boat. It stayed barely a hundred yards ahead of Hush's advance, by virtue of the furious rowing of the enslaved ice-maidens. Purity stood at the bow, her wings spread for balance. Even from this distance, I could tell by the tilt of her head she had spotted Slor Tonn. She thrust the harpoon in our direction. A pale blue beam filled the frozen air with bright sparkles as it crackled toward us. Slor Tonn banked hard to the left to avoid the attack.

"Can the harpoon hurt you?" I shouted to Aurora.

Aurora nodded. "Ordinary cold doesn't bother ogres, but the Jagged Heart isn't ordinary cold."

Slor Tonn turned back toward the boat. From our vantage point, I spotted two long bundles in the floor of the boat, one with platinum blonde hair. "I think I see Infidel."

"Good," said Aurora. "She can help even the odds once we capsize their boat."

"Infidel's lost her powers," I said. "Capsizing the boat might kill her!"

"Doing nothing means that she dies along with everyone else."

I nodded; she was right.

A second beam shot toward us. Again Slor Tonn banked to avoid it, then turned his nose straight down. Aurora said, "Hold on tight. Things are about to get rough."

"I'm ready," I said, chewing the bear gland in my cheek furiously as we plunged toward the black water.

I wasn't ready. Even with Slor Tonn taking the brunt of our impact with the waves, the cold that washed over me numbed both body and mind. In the frozen darkness, I struggled to remember where I was or even who I was. My arms went slack and I lost my grip on Aurora.

Fortunately, she had the coolness of thought to keep hold of me. We exploded from the water a moment later, with Purity's walrus-hide boat caught in Slor Tonn's mighty jaws. With a loud crunch, he bit off the front end where Purity had stood. Fear instantly wiped away my cold-induced lethargy as I thought of Infidel getting chewed by the whale's attack.

My fear was short-lived as the back half of the boat tore away and fell to the ice, sliding to a halt before Hush. Infidel was there amid the tangle of stunned ice-maidens, as well as Sorrow and Judge Stern. I could see this all plainly by the light of the Gloryhammer, which danced across the ice, free from anyone's grip.

From the corner of my vision, I saw Judge Stern rise and gaze toward the hammer. I couldn't let him get hold of it. But how could I stop him? Did I dare touch the Gloryhammer again? Before, I had been overwhelmed by the bottomless loneliness of Glorious. Now, in theory, he'd severed his connection with the sun.

"I need to get the Gloryhammer! Throw me!" I shouted. I didn't have time to weigh the pros and cons of the plan.

Aurora needed no further prompting. She grabbed me by my left elbow and flung me toward the weapon. My spinning flight, as you can imagine, was rather disorienting. I hit the ice with force enough to shatter what remained of my ribs. I was going to need a lot more bear gland to deal with my pain when all this was over. I skittered across the ice toward the hammer, my good arm outstretched, just as Judge Stern broke into a sprint for the same target.

I reached it first.

To my great relief, the overwhelming loneliness that had threatened my naked spirit earlier was gone as my fingers closed around the shaft. The surge of power Infidel had described as being filled with pure sunlight swept through me. With half my body torn away, I saw the full effect vividly. It was as if the hammer understood where the true outlines of my body should be, and filled this shell with radiant energy. I rose on legs of light. I flexed my severed left hand, now composed of fingers of dazzling luminance.

Judge Stern skittered on the ice as he tried to stop before he collided with me. He wound up with his feet out from under him, hitting the ice butt first. He waved his fist at me as he shouted, "Devil! You defile a sacred weapon! Surrender it at once!"

"Finders, keepers," I argued. I was surprised a legal scholar such as himself had been unaware of this fine point of the law.

Stern rose to his knees, then lunged with what might have been an impressive tackle at my shins if they'd been actual shins. He passed right through my limbs of light, crashing chin first onto the ice. I waited a few seconds, but he didn't get up. I was finally ready for some action, and my first opponent goes and knocks himself out. Typical.

With Purity swallowed by Slor Tonn and Judge Stern unconscious, my top priority was to speak to Hush.

Unfortunately, when I gazed at the lumbering dragon, I saw that she was about to crush the frozen bodies of Infidel and Sorrow beneath her giant claw. Conversation would have to wait. I swung my hammer toward the women, willed myself to fly, and flashed toward them as Hush's massive talon fell. I didn't know if my light hand could grab the women, so I willingly crashed into the ice, sliding into Sorrow's frosty form, using it as a cue ball in a game of body-billiards. She caromed into Infidel and they both skipped across the frozen sea. I closed my eyes as the gap between Hush's claw and the ice quickly vanished, but opened my eyes a moment later when the impact didn't come. Behind me was a thunderous sound. I'd cleared the dragon's footfall, although if I'd had physical legs I'm certain that wouldn't have been the case.

I spun around, searching for Infidel. I saw her splayed on the ice, limp, her body free of the frozen shell that had enwreathed her. My pool shot had shattered her icy cage. Was she even still alive?

As I flew toward her, she stirred, raising her hand instinctively to shield her eyes. In my panic, I'd stoked the Gloryhammer to high-noon intensity. I thrust the weapon into her grasp. My face was inches from hers as her eyes snapped open, glowing as the energy of the hammer surged through her.

"Stagger!" she exclaimed, before grabbing me by the back of my neck and pulling me to her for a powerful kiss. The kiss proved briefer than I would have liked. Perhaps she was aware of the urgency of our situation, though her haste might also be explained by the bear-piss aroma filling my mouth.

Using the power of the hammer, she spiraled up into the air. I clung to her shoulders to keep from falling. Apparently, the hammer's energy could only flow into one of us; my limbs of light were gone. She looked down and turned pale.

"Oh, Stagger," she said, sadly.

"I've been in better shape," I admitted.

"Does it hurt?" she asked.

"Yeah," I said. "But Aurora has fixed me up."

"Aurora?" She looked around, and spotted her old friend perched on Slor Tonn's back.

I took a deep breath. "We're in the Great Sea Above. Slor Tonn's eaten Purity, I've knocked out Judge Stern, but any second Glorious is going to come over the horizon intent on suicide. We have to stop Hush before she kills him and ends life as we know it."

Infidel closed her eyes and rubbed them with her free hand as we drifted higher into the sky. She shook her head and whispered, "Can't I have one freaking day when I wake up not having to prevent the imminent destruction of the world?"

"There's always tomorrow, baby," I said. "Unless, you know, there isn't. We should get to work on that."

We were now a good quarter-mile above the battlefield, not that there was much battling left going on. Sorrow had bounced back with remarkable speed and had dispatched most of the survivors from the spilled boat with a gruesome efficiency. I watched as she leapt onto an ogress who was rising to her feet. Sorrow placed her bare hand upon the ogress as she rose. Instantly dark red veins of infection spread across the ogress's skin. In seconds, her victim collapsed, coughing up blood.

Sorrow moved on to the next person rising to her feet, one of the ice-maidens, her armor cracked and missing along her left shoulder. Despite the fact that the woman had been mentally enslaved, Sorrow showed no mercy, dispatching her with the same cold efficiency.

"I wonder if she can kill Hush," said Infidel. Her voice sounded doubtful, a doubt, I suspect, both about Sorrow's offensive capacity and Infidel's own. Hush was an imposing figure as she crawled beneath us, freezing the ocean half a mile before her with each step forward. In scale, we were like fleas contemplating an attack upon a dog. No doubt we'd draw blood, but would Hush even notice?

"Fly down!" I shouted. "Get in front of her face!"

Infidel obeyed. In seconds, we were hovering before the dragon's left eye. I could see our reflection in the dark iris. I was surprised to discover that Hush had green eyes, the shade of fir boughs. Save for her pink tongue, it was the only thing about her not snowy white.

But I'd not come here to contemplate the pigments necessary to complete her portrait. Aware that time was running out, I shouted, "Hush! Please stop and listen! You don't need to kill Glorious! He's lonely! He knows he was foolish to reject you! You have a second chance at winning his heart!"

Hush didn't even pause as she marched forward. Infidel kept us flying one step ahead.

"Stop, please!" I shouted. But I couldn't tell if Hush was even focused on us. Sometimes, a gnat inches from ones face is more difficult to see than one a yard away. I don't know if she even heard us.

Slor Tonn approached us. Even the whale proved tiny in comparison to the dragon, though if we were fleas, the whale was at least a fair-sized beetle.

"She can't hear you," Aurora called out. "Her ear drums are dozens of yards across. Your voices are too tiny to register. Also, I don't know if she understands your language. I always spoke to her in my native tongue."

"But you can still talk to her?" Infidel said, her voice filled with hope.

Aurora shook her head. "I could only communicate with her via a direct spiritual connection when I held the Jagged Heart. Right now, that's in Slor Tonn's stomach."

I sighed. "I guess I'll have to go in and get it. I've made this trip before." I glanced toward the horizon. It was a pale pink. Any second, Glorious would rise above the edge of the water.

"I don't have a better plan," Aurora said, with a nervous glance at the brightening sky. "Slor Tonn, open wide!" But, rather than opening his jaws, Slor Tonn chose that moment to twitch violently. Aurora was thrown into the air as if she'd been caught by surprise astride a bucking bull. She landed on the whale's back with a thud as the beast arched his spine. A gush of dark blood sprayed from his blowhole, spattering Aurora in a psychedelic shade of purple.

"What –" escaped her lips before the whale suddenly froze stiff, coated with a thick rind of frost from jaws to tail. Without warning, the great beast dropped from the sky. Aurora tumbled from his back as he fell, and only Infidel's keen reflexes saved her as she swooped down and caught the ogress by her top knot.

"Slor Tonn!" Aurora shouted as the whale hit the ice below and shattered into a million pink and gray fragments.

Purity stood in the midst of the frozen chunks, still in her winged woman configuration, coated with ice, only seemingly much larger. In fact, there was no question: the Jagged Heart harpoon was eighteen feet long, and she quickly grew to that height, then doubled it. Her skin color changed until she had a white belly and a black back... Slor Tonn's colors.

"Wonderful," I sighed, as I adjusted my grip on Infidel's shoulders. "Looks like Menagerie's body has added whale's blood to the mix."

"Nothing can kill me in this body!" Purity shouted, eyeing us with a taunting gaze. "I can adapt to any assault! Thanks to your futile efforts, I'm more powerful than ever!"

"The only thing I hate worse than someone trying to destroy the world is a braggart," Infidel grumbled.

"Wait," said Aurora. "You're sure this is Menagerie's body?"

"At the core," said Infidel. "It's had some additions."

"As high priestess, I can summon the spirits of the dead," said Aurora. "Ordinarily, I can only call forward the shades of my own tribe. But Menagerie and I worked side by side for years. He and the rest of the Goons became my new tribe once I reached Commonground. He might respond if I called out to him."

"Do it!" said Infidel.

"There's one catch," said Aurora.

"Let me guess," I said. "You need the Jagged Heart."

"Give me ten seconds," said Infidel. Without warning, she dove toward the ground, dropping me and Aurora on the ice. With a *whoosh*, she shot toward Sorrow, who had just finished off the last ogre priestess and was turning to her father. Judge Stern was conscious once more, though his chin was coated in blood. He skittered backward on the ice as she approached.

"Away from me, you abomination!" he cried out, closing his eyes as Sorrow's hand reached for his face.

In what had to be the most surprising answer to prayer on record, Infidel stretched out her free arm and caught Sorrow by the waist at exactly that second. Sorrow screamed a very bad word as Infidel swooped her skyward.

"I need you to do that rotting trick on Purity," Infidel shouted as she swung back around.

"Ice neutralizes my powers!" Sorrow cried back.

"That won't be a problem," Infidel said as she shot toward the winged giantess.

Purity stood braced for the attack. She fired one of the thin blue rays at Infidel, but Infidel banked down at the last possible second to avoid it. Skimming along just inches above the ice, she plowed into Purity at the ankles, flipping her head over heels.

Aurora broke out in a hard run, trying to reach the shape-shifting witch before she could get back to her feet. Purity proved more resilient that we hoped, however, and in a moment she was on her knees, using the Jagged Heart as a staff to help her rise the rest of the way. As she stood, however, Infidel raced up from behind and struck a powerful blow with the Gloryhammer, directly on the back of Purity's wrist. The frozen gauntlet that coated her hand shattered, and before she could even think of reworking the ice Sorrow struck, leaping from Infidel's back to cling to Purity's log-sized forearm.

Purity screamed as red and blue veins of infection raced up her arm. Sorrow dug her fingers deeper into the putrefying flesh on the back of the witch's hand, the skin sloughing away in ragged strips, the bones visibly twisting and warping with advanced arthritis. The Jagged Heart dropped from Purity's withering fingers. Aurora was there to catch it.

Unfortunately, by now Purity had twigged to the combined sneak attack. She swung her arm with all her remaining strength, smashing Sorrow into Infidel as she prepared another hammer strike. The two women tumbled through the sky, dizzy from the impact. Sorrow crashed into the ice from a dozen feet up, while Infidel managed to halt herself in mid-air, a grimace on her face as she fought to regain her aerial footing.

Purity stared at her damaged hand. She furrowed her brow as she willed the flesh to knit itself back together. Menagerie's powers proved up to the task of reversing the damage. She capped her new fingers with a fresh coat of ice. I wondered how she had the power, since we'd robbed her of the harpoon, before seeing that she carried the Icemoon Blade in one of her lower hands, now barely the size of a dagger in her oversized grasp.

Aurora was backing up, speaking in a language I didn't understand. Though she had the harpoon in her grasp, she wasn't wielding it in any sort of defensive maneuver I could recognize. She was waving it around in the air in erratic loops, like a woman trying to swat a fly with a broom.

"Is this supposed to be menacing?" Purity growled, reaching for the harpoon.

Aurora suddenly switched from her ogre speech into the

Silver Tongue. "In your own language, old friend, I call to you," she shouted. "Menagerie, I summon your shade, that you may reclaim what has been taken from you!"

Purity snatched the harpoon away. She was now thirty feet tall. Aurora, the largest person I normally dealt with on a daily basis, looked like a toddler compared to her. Purity kicked her, sending the ogress bouncing across the ice.

"If you'll excuse me, I have a sun to slay," Purity said, turning toward Glorious as he hung above the horizon. She flapped her wings and rose toward the heavens. High above, I could see the material world floating like a blue-green grapefruit, but it was obscured by wispy tendrils of black smoke. The black smoke writhed and whirled as it descended toward us. Purity suddenly jerked her head up, gazing at the approaching smoke with a look of terror. An instant later, I could hear the sounds of wolves and lions and chimpanzees howling and roaring and screaming, above the trumpets of elephants and the shrieks of eagles. It was as if someone had rattled the cages of every zoo in the world at once.

The cloud whirled straight toward Purity. She brought the harpoon up to defend herself as the cloud took on a shape I recognized. Menagerie had been a tall man, covered with black tattoos from his scalp to his toe tips, an entire bestiary of the animals of the material world. The cloud coalesced into this tapestry of tattoos, but only the tattoos, with no underlying flesh or bone. You could see, through the gaps in his chest, the tattoos that covered his back. The tattoos looked wet, like fresh ink, and now that they were barely a hundred feet above I could see that they weren't truly black, but a deep, deep shade of red, like congealed blood.

Purity opened her mouth to scream. Before any sound came out, the tattoo swarm formed a tight vortex and spun between her lips. Her throat bulged as the torrent of blood forced itself inside her.

Purity went limp as a rag doll. The harpoon and the Ice-Moon Blade slipped from her fingers as she shrank. Her wings vanished, along with her fur and killer whale markings. In less than a second, all her animal traits had disappeared and she looked exactly like Infidel. She dropped from the sky, falling twenty feet to hit the ice with a horrible *smack*.

Any concern I felt about watching this false Infidel fall was instantly pushed away by the real Infidel swooping down and grabbing me. We flew toward Aurora, who was running to grab the Jagged Heart, which had landed tip-first in the ice and stood like an empty signpost.

Aurora's fingers closed around the harpoon. She turned to face our approach and held out her hand. "Ready to talk to Hush?" she asked.

Infidel and I placed our hands in Aurora's huge palm.

"Do it," we said, in unison.

A slow whirlwind built around us, flaking ice into snow, swirling in a gentle flurry, before building to a blizzard. The last thing I saw before the white washed away everything was Glorious, flapping his wings and flying toward us.

And then... we'd already moved beyond the material world, into the realms abstract. What lay beyond? Was reality like an onion, composed of layer upon layer upon layer?

I can only report that as the snow fell away, we found ourselves standing in a place that was neither the Great Sea Above nor the material world. We were in a vast, empty void, where the entirety of creation was the trio formed by Infidel, Aurora, and myself. Our physical bodies had vanished and we now stood revealed as beings of pure light, no longer human in shape, more like rainbows shimmering in the darkness.

Stripped of our bodies, I had no trouble recognizing Infidel or Aurora. Infidel was a nearly pure white flame, intense and focused. She had nothing that could be described as a belly, but at the core of her light a tiny white candle burned even more brightly. Our daughter? Aurora was a calmer, cooler shaft of blue. I couldn't see myself; I wondered what the others saw?

In the center of the triangle formed by our energies, the Jagged Heart hovered. The blue shaft that was Aurora trembled, and I heard her voice. "Hush," she said. "It is Aksarna, your humble servant. I've brought two guests who wish to speak with you." I was surprised that she wasn't speaking the ogre tongue. Or perhaps she was, but we were in a place where all languages were one and the same.

"You violate the sanctity of this place," the Jagged Heart answered. "You've not performed the required rites. You dishonor me."

"I beg forgiveness," said Aurora. "But time is of the essence. As we speak, the dragon of the sun approaches. Purity came to the Great Sea Above to slay Glorious. But Purity was bonded with you; if she wills that Glorious should die, it's because you wish that fate upon him."

"This is not my wish," Hush answered through the harpoon. "This is my need. Glorious must die so that I may go to my final rest. While he visits my realm, I can never know true peace. You, my priestess, know of the paradise I speak of. It is the pure silent darkness of the frozen night. It is the great calm that existed before the creation of light. It is the only hope of relief for my shattered heart. In the eternal peace of winter, I will forget all pain, all longing and loneliness."

"How about all selfishness?" Infidel asked.

"Forgive her," said Aurora. "She speaks out of fear."

"I speak out of honesty!" At these words, I swear that the shaft of white flame threw up what looked like arms in frustration. "This frigid lizard is willing to destroy the world because she's suffered a broken heart. *Boo-hoo.* Every day, people suffer loss. I watched the only man I ever loved die before my eyes. Did I think about killing myself? Did I feel like the world needed to be punished because I was alone and scared? No. I sucked up my pain, pulled on my boots, and tried to find a new path for my life. People do it every damn day. Why should this frozen crybaby feel that her suffering is any different?"

Aurora's pale column flickered, looking afraid. But the Jagged Heart floated unchanged, as the dragon spoke once more. "You cannot understand. Human lives are too short. You've no time to truly feel anything. You flash through existence like shooting stars, vanishing as swiftly as you appear. You cannot judge the pain of timeless beings."

"Then you can't judge our pain," said Infidel. "You can't understand how precious time is to us, how few hours we're given to share with those we love."

"Do not speak to me of love and sharing," Hush growled. "Your time may be brief, but while you live you're surrounded by throngs of your kindred humans. We primal dragons exist as unique beings in our own realms. There is no one to share the burden of our solitude."

"Have you tried?" I asked. "Because I heard a very similar argument from Glorious just minutes ago. He's lonely as well, lonely enough that death looks like a welcome alternative. Maybe neither of you needs to die. Maybe you need to go to one another and talk. The legends say that you loved Glorious once. When he arrives, tell him how you feel!"

"How I feel?" Hush said bitterly. "Glorious rejected my love. The shame and humiliation of that moment can never be forgotten. I shall never show such weakness again."

"Are all dragons such cowards?" Infidel asked. "Or is it just you?"

"Have a care, human," said Hush. "You stand in the antechamber of my mind. With a thought, I can erase you from existence."

"You would punish her when she's right?" I asked. "I spent ten years in the company of the woman I loved without confessing my feelings. I've no excuse for these wasted years, other than my own cowardice. I, too, was afraid of exposing myself to rejection and isolation. I dealt with my pain in pretty much the same fashion you do. You want the world to be so quiet and dark that you can go into a slumber that's like death.

HUSH

You want to just stop feeling anything. I did the same thing with booze. I'd drink until I couldn't remember my own name. I'd drink until I couldn't remember why I was drinking. Self-obliteration is the coward's path."

The flat blade of the Jagged Heart turned toward me. I swear I could see a dark green eye peer at me through the ice.

I said, "If you want to feel alive, you have to take the bad with the good. You can't feel joy unless you open your heart to sadness. You can't feel love unless you're willing to bear loneliness. When Glorious arrives, tell him how you truly feel. Confess that you love him. What do you have to lose?"

"It's too late for conversation," said Hush.

"Infidel and I are proof that it's never too late," I said.

"You don't understand. It is, indeed, too late," said Hush. "Now leave."

Suddenly we were back on the ice, standing exactly as we'd stood when the blizzard had surrounded us. Well, two of us were standing. Deprived of legs once more, I hit the ice with a loud *splat* and clawed the frosty surface to hold on as it suddenly tilted beneath me. All around us, the once solid sheet of ice had shattered into a thousand ice floes, bobbing on violent waves.

My eyes widened as I saw that Glorious had arrived while we'd been talking to Hush. He was pushed to the ice, wings down, his throat exposed, his body limp. His eyes were open, full of fear, wet with tears that ran down his golden cheeks to freeze on the ice beneath him.

Hush sat upon his chest, her jaws clamped around his throat, ready to rip through this windpipe.

"We're too late," Aurora cried, dropping to her knees, sounding beaten.

"Like hell we are." Infidel cracked her knuckles, loud enough that even Hush's green eyes shifted toward the noise.

CHAPTER TWENTY-ONE
COLDER EVERY SECOND

I BLINKED AND Infidel was gone, leaving a swirl of snow in her wake. I turned my head in time to see her punch into the side of Hush's jaw with the Gloryhammer. The thunderous blow spread in waves from the tip of the dragon's snout all the way down her serpentine neck, causing an avalanche to fall from her scales. Hush craned her head to snap at Infidel as she zoomed skyward. Infidel surprised Hush by making a mid-air U-turn and darting between the dragon's closing jaws, into the vast chasm of her mouth.

The tree-sized teeth near the back of Hush's jaws burst outward with an explosion of blinding light as Infidel hammered through them. Hush roared with pain as Infidel spiraled back into the sky.

Glorious lifted his head to see what had halted his planned suicide. His throat was bleeding, but it didn't seem to be a mortal wound. As large as Hush was, Glorious was even larger, and her initial attempt at tearing out his throat had resulted in little more than an extra-nasty hickey.

"Now that I've got your attention..." Infidel shouted down at the dragons. "Stop fighting! If you don't, I'll tear out your teeth and claws until you're too mangled to misbehave!"

"You dare threaten us?" Glorious growled, rising to all four legs. He glared at her with a look of elemental contempt.

"This isn't a threat, it's a promise," Infidel shouted. "Everyone acts like primal dragons are one step removed from gods. You're more like one step removed from spoiled teenagers, and trust me, I know about spoiled teenagers. I'm not going to sit by and watch the world get destroyed by a pair of self-important brats too childish to discuss their feelings for one another!"

"I feel only hate!" Hush screamed.

"And I deserve your hate," Glorious screamed back. "I was a fool to spurn you, too vain and arrogant to see that I might one day long for your company. I can no longer stand the suffering! End me!"

Hush's eyes widened. "You long for my company?"

"My loneliness is unbearable," Glorious whimpered. "The pain of knowing that you once offered to save me from my self-inflicted fate doubles my suffering. As I gaze down upon the world, I see the polar regions, white and dazzling like a pearly crown upon the globe, and I think of you. You were so open when you came to me, so courageous, risking your heart. My hunger to tame the sun blinded me. It was not worth the cost of your love."

"Was it not?" Hush asked, her voice calmer now. "With each passing century I've watched you as you traveled through the sky. I've hated you more with each passing year, but also envied you, and admired you. You've truly changed the world by taming the sun. If you had not rejected me, you would never have accomplished this great task. "

"But I knew it must cause you pain," said Glorious, on the verge of sobbing. "It hurts you still. My sunlight drives away frost from much of the world. I knew I was keeping you from your full potential. This is why, as I abandoned the sun, I sent it hurtling away. Even now, it slowly fades from the sky of the material world. In a month, it will be only a speck, indistinguishable from the faintest planets that travel across the night sky. Then, at last, the world will be forever dark, and you can know your final peace."

"Oh, Glorious," Hush said. "This is such a beautiful gift."

"But it's going to be an even better gift if he puts the sun back into its rightful path, right?" shouted Infidel. "That way the two of you can see each other every day. You don't have to be lonely any more!"

Hush sighed. "The annoying creature is right. If you don't rejoin the sun, you shall wither and perish. You cannot survive as a spirit untethered to matter. I... I would rather the world remain in light than lose you forever."

Glorious clenched his jaws together tightly for a moment. I couldn't read the emotions in his luminous eyes. At last, he said, "So be it. Perhaps my thirst for oblivion has proven... premature. I shall return to the sun. We will continue our conversation, come the dawn."

"I look forward to it," Hush said. Her body fell apart into a great mound of snow.

"What just happened?" Infidel asked, sounding worried as she looked down upon the collapsing white mountain beneath her.

Glorious stretched his wings. "Hush has abandoned her abstract form and returned to her true body in the material world." He gazed at Infidel and said, "Do not in any way think that your threats have altered our actions. Either of us could have crushed you with no more effort than you would put into crushing a bug."

"Yeah, whatever," said Infidel. "You just run along and jump back into the sun now."

"You speak to us with such insolence! You fail to respect our power," Glorious growled as he turned away, his eyes narrowed. Then he paused, and glanced back over his shoulder. "And for this... thank you."

"No problem." Infidel smiled as she brushed the hair back from her eyes.

"Son of a bitch," Aurora whispered, as she glanced down at me. I'd grabbed hold of her ankle to keep from sliding around on the bobbing ice. "Did Infidel just save the world?"

"Isn't she going to be a great mother?" I said.

Glorious flapped his wings and rose into the air. This created an instant blizzard as all the snow from Hush's body roared around us in hurricane winds. The air cleared as Glorious rose higher, radiant as noon. He was looking down at the ice. I followed his gaze and saw what he was looking at: a man in stark black robes standing amid the white snow, an unfurled scroll before him. Judge Stern was nearly a hundred yards away, but his deep, authoritative voice could be heard even at this distance as he shouted the verdict toward Glorious. "By the power of the Divine Author and the One True Book, the Voice of the Book has judged you, Glorious, and found you guilty of crimes against nature itself. You have trespassed upon the sun, claiming it as your own when the Divine Author gave it freely as a gift to all. The enormity of this crime is unforgivable."

"Infidel!" I shouted.

"This judgment is final and cannot be appealed," said Stern.

"Don't let him finish reading –"

Infidel started moving before I even finished my sentence. She'd barely flown a yard before Stern read, "The sentence is death, carried out by the utterance of this truthful statement."

Infidel reached Stern, flattening him with a punch that sent him skidding across the ice on his back.

It was too late. Glorious shuddered in mid-flap. The internal luminance that filled his form instantly snuffed out, leaving his spiritual form a pale, ashen gray. With a soft sigh, he fell, but never reached the ice. His body changed into a fine powder that crumbled, billowing out as a dense cloud.

I stared, mouth agape, as the dust swept toward me. What was there to say? The world had just been condemned to death.

Infidel drifted down from the sky next to Aurora. We gave each other worried looks just as the dust engulfed us. Infidel leaned over and scooped up my legless torso, holding me tightly against her side. I wrapped my arm around her and squeezed.

No one spoke a word. Perhaps we each were hoping someone else would be the first to speak, to offer some clever, last-second plan to save everything. But the minutes simply ticked by as the dust slowly settled, revealing our grimy faces one by one. We looked like miners, covered in grit.

Infidel sighed. "Maybe the Black Swan is already traveling back in time to give us another shot."

"That's not really how her powers work," said Aurora.

"So what are you saying?" asked Infidel. "That we're screwed?"

Aurora shrugged. "I'm not sure I'd use the word 'we.' I don't see how things are going to change much for me. The material world is going to freeze, but I don't know that things will change for the dead."

I thought this was a slightly selfish stance to take, but I didn't feel like picking a fight by saying so.

At this moment, there was a cough from the dust cloud behind us and we all nearly jumped out of our skins. Sorrow stumbled out of the fog, hacking up dusty spittle. She was wrapped in the coat her father had draped over her, and dragging a black walrus coat taken from one of the ogresses. In her other hand she held some oversized boots. She tossed the coat to Infidel. "Figured you'd be pretty chilled by now."

"Getting colder every second," Infidel said, softly.

"What happened?" Sorrow asked, through chattering teeth. "After Purity knocked us for a loop, I was running back to join you when the ice in front of me split open. I was trying to work my way around it when I heard a lot of shouting. Then, poof, dust everywhere. I've been jumping from floe to floe, completely lost, until I saw the light of the Gloryhammer."

"Your father succeeded in killing Glorious," I said. "Dust was all that was left."

"Oh," she said.

"To complicate matters, Glorious said he'd sent the sun away," said Infidel. "He said it would take about a month to turn into a speck in the sky. After that, permanent winter."

"I see," said Sorrow. She sat down on the ice. Her lips were completely blue. She stared out into the distance, not looking at any of us. After a moment, she sighed and shook her head. "Two minutes ago, my biggest worry was that I was going to lose my toes to frostbite."

Her toes were dark black and shiny. She started to put on the boots, which were about three times bigger than her feet, when Aurora knelt before her and said, "Now that I have the Jagged Heart once more, I can treat your frostbite."

She took Sorrow's right foot in her huge hands, rubbing them, then paused.

"Um," she said, "this isn't frostbite."

"What do you mean?" asked Sorrow.

"For some reason, your toes are covered in black scales. It's like snake skin."

Sorrow's eyes grew wide as she stared at her toes.

I asked, "Maybe Rott is somehow –"

She held up her hand, cutting me off. "I don't want to talk about it. I'll deal with it. Somehow." Then she quickly pulled on both boots and stood up. She said, "A more pressing question is, where's my father?"

"Somewhere out in the dust," said Infidel, waving in the general direction she'd left him. "I punched his lights out."

I thought this was an unfortunate choice of words.

"Do you want me to go find him?" Infidel asked.

Sorrow shook her head. "If I saw him again, I'd kill him."

"I'd be okay with that," said Infidel.

"I wouldn't," said Sorrow. "The greatest curse I could place on my father is to let him live with the full weight of his actions upon his conscience. Death would be too merciful."

Before we could further debate the appropriate fate for Judge Stern, I heard a distant cough. I spotted what looked like a naked woman stumbling towards us on an adjoining ice floe. She looked exactly like Infidel.

I asked, "Is that –"

"Purity!" Sorrow growled.

Aurora placed a beefy hand on the young witch's shoulder. "Hold on. It's not her."

The woman who looked like Infidel coughed again and rubbed soot from her eyes, as she reached the edge of her ice floe. She stared at us as if we were ghosts. Which, I guess, we were.

"Aurora?" she asked, utterly confused. "I thought you were dead!"

"Menagerie?" Aurora asked.

"Yeah," she said, frowning. "What the hell's wrong with my voice?"

The woman looked down, her eyes going wide.

"This wasn't one of my tattoos," she said, scratching her head.

"You're alive again," said Infidel. "Don't complain."

"Again?" asked Menagerie. "I was dead?"

"We're all dead," said Aurora.

"I'm pretty certain I'm alive," said Infidel.

Sorrow nodded. "My heart's beating as well."

Aurora sighed. "Fine. If you want to be picky, I suppose that only Stagger and I are truly dead. The rest of you have living bodies that came to the Great Sea Above via the Jagged Heart. I can send you back, if you'd like. Then you can freeze along with the rest the world."

"I feel like there's a lot I'm missing," said Menagerie.

Aurora began to recount our adventures, filling Menagerie in on all that had happened since he died. As Aurora spoke, Infidel sat down next to Sorrow. We had our arms wrapped around each other. She sat the Gloryhammer in front of us. It glowed like a heatless campfire, as we listened to Aurora recount the most horrible ghost story ever.

The hair on the back of my neck rose as I thought more about what I was doing. I was staring at a hammer. I was staring at a hammer that was glowing. The hammer was glowing because it had been carved out of the sun.

"I know how to save the world," I said.

"You know I married you for your brains, right?" said Infidel.

"The Gloryhammer's part of the sun," I said. "Earlier, when I touched it in the material world, I felt waves of horrible loneliness wash over me. As a spirit, I could sense the soul of Glorious inside the hammer. But when I grabbed the hammer here, I didn't feel anything. Glorious was no longer inside the sun at this point."

Sorrow's eyes opened wide. "The sun has been primed to hold a soul..."

"And now it's empty," I said. "I, on the other hand, am a spirit with barely even a phantom body to cling to any more. What if I could merge my spirit with the sun? I could guide it back to its proper path!"

"Give me a second to figure out if that's brilliant or stupid," said Infidel.

Sorrow frowned, shaking her head. "This wouldn't be something you could do for an hour or two and be done with it. Glorious had to guide the sun constantly, for three thousand years. If you could be joined with the sun, its material form would supply your spirit with the energy to endure for eons. You would have to maintain your vigilance on a scale human minds cannot grasp. Can you be trusted with such a task?"

"I can if it means that Infidel has a world to go back to where she can raise our daughter," I said. "I accept the task gladly."

"Stagger," said Infidel. "You can't!"

"Why not? What's the flaw in this plan?"

"Living inside the sun drove Glorious crazy," she said. "It's bad enough that you're dead. Now you want to be insane as well?"

"Glorious went insane because he was alone," I said. "But I'll never be alone. I'll always have you. I'll know that as I move the sun through the sky that my light is shining upon you. One day it will shine on our daughter, then her daughters, and if I have to keep rolling the sun across the sky from now until the end of time, I'll do so. How many men can say that their actions will truly be important a thousand years from now? I want to do this. I must do this. Not to leave you, but to be with you forever."

Infidel kissed me hard. When she pulled away, her eyes were glistening with tears. "You old fool. You were always too damn good at talking. Do what you have to do. No matter what, I will never, ever stop loving you."

"This is all very touching," said Sorrow. "And all completely moot. Menagerie here can occupy his new body because there's a tiny portion of his original blood within it. I was able to bind Stagger to his driftwood shell with the essence of his spiritual blood. But there's nothing here that we can use to bind him to the body of the sun. It's not just a matter of him flying inside the sun and wishing it to move. He's got to have some link, a blood-bridge between the material and spiritual worlds."

"The bone-handled knife!" I said. "Its hilt is made of dragon bone. It held my blood after I was killed. If there's still a trace left within it..."

Sorrow perked up. "That could work. Where's the knife?"

"It was in Purity's boat."

"So it could be anywhere," said Sorrow, looking around at all the carnage. "It's probably at the bottom of the sea."

"The Great Sea Above doesn't really have a bottom," said Aurora. "If something sinks, it sinks forever."

"Let's hope it didn't sink," I said.

Menagerie said, "If I had my old powers, I could change into a wolf and sniff it out. Tracing down Stagger's scent would be a breeze."

"Purity was able to shape-shift even without tattoos," said Infidel. "She was better at it that you, in fact; she could do hybrid forms."

Menagerie looked deeply offended. "Hybrid forms are decidedly *not* better shape-shifting. Animal bodies have been honed into perfect tools by natural forces. Blended forms are for amateurs. I became the whole animal because I was a true master of the craft."

"No need to get snippy," said Infidel. "In any case, when Nowowon killed you, part of your body survived as a tick.

Purity could shift into any creature from which your body had drank blood. There was me, obviously, then a hound dog, a pelican, and now a whale."

"Hmm," said Menagerie, rubbing his chin. He closed his eyes as a look of concentration passed over his feminine features. His face elongated as fur sprouted from his body. He dropped to all fours and a moment later he was in the form of a bloodhound.

"Excellent," the hound dog said gruffly. "First of all, I've never been so happy to have fur. Second, if the knife is near, I'll find it."

He loped off, sniffing the ice, leaping from floe to floe.

"There's one last problem," I said. "Let's say this works. I've got a pretty good idea of what path the sun follows through the sky. I mean, it rises in the east and sets in the west. But, up here, how do I know east from west? How do I judge if the length of a day is enough? I don't want to screw up the world with a half-ass job."

"If only we could contact my father's astrologers," said Infidel. "He's got an entire squadron of scholars whose whole job is to watch the sky. They can tell you the exact time of every eclipse for the next dozen centuries."

Sorrow tilted her head as she studied Infidel. "I'm sorry, but who, exactly, is your father?"

"Oh. I forgot, you didn't know. I'm the real Princess Innocent Brightmoon."

Sorrow chuckled, until she realized the rest of us weren't laughing. "What? Really? You're not making fun of the dwarf?"

"Nope. I'm the genuine article. Of course, I'm not really welcome company in my father's throne room any more. It's not like I can ask him to get his astrologers to help out."

"Maybe you won't need to," I said. "Glorious said he could see and hear people through the Glorystones, the same way that Greatshadow can spy on people through candles. If I were merged with the sun, maybe the astrologers could communicate with me and help guide my movements."

Sorrow sighed. "Looks like I can't let the old bastard die after all."

"What? Who?" I asked.

"My father," she said. "Infidel might not be able to ask a favor of the king, but my father can. We need to send him back to the material world with the mission to get the king's astrologers to work with you, assuming Menagerie can find the knife."

"Good plan," said Infidel, standing up. "Give me a minute."

She leapt into the air, rising a few hundred yards. She slowly turned, surveying the landscape, then darted off, vanishing behind the remnants of the dust cloud. Not thirty seconds later, she was back in view, dropping beside us with an unconscious Judge Stern draped over her shoulder.

"He was coming to when I found him. Had to give him a little tap to make him cooperative," she said as she laid his limp body before us. "He should be up and about any second."

"Let's bind his hands and feet," said Sorrow, tearing off strips from his robes. "Gag him as well." She grabbed a pocket and ripped it. A glowing ring fell out and danced across the ice. It was the glorystone ring Brother Will had worn. Had this been the unseen object he'd paused to take when his shipmates had been devoured by maggots?

Sorrow showed no sign of grabbing the ring, so I snatched it up. As she finished tying up her father, Menagerie returned, still a hound, jumping back across the cracked sea ice, the bone-handled knife held in his slobbering jaws. He dropped the blade before me.

"Sorry about the spit," he said. "It's impossible to put a bone in a dog's mouth and not get a little slobber."

"Apologies aren't necessary," I said. "Good dog."

"Don't make me bite you," Menagerie growled.

"Give me the knife and the hammer," said Sorrow. "I'll need a moment with each to attune myself to their magical resonance. If you and Infidel have any last words to say to one another, now is the time."

Infidel handed over the hammer, then picked me up, rather clumsily now that she wasn't filled with magical energy. I can't guess how heavy I was, devoid of legs and guts. She carried me about fifty yards away before setting me down. We were near a second ogress Sorrow had reduced to a skeleton. Infidel liberated her walrus-skin coat, spreading it gore side down on the ice. We lay upon it, wrapping it around us for warmth.

"I wish I had some body heat to contribute," I said.

"You're like a damn ice cube," Infidel said with a sigh. "At least I can't complain about your cold feet."

I laughed, but only briefly. "I'm sorry."

"That you're cold?"

"That your last memories of me will be as a semi-frozen, half-devoured corpse. I wish you could remember me the way I was."

"Who says I can't?"

"Gruesome memories have a way of sticking," I said.

"Baby, I've been a mercenary for all my adult life. Hardly a day goes by that I don't decapitate or disembowel someone. Any nightmares I used to have about blood and gore faded away a long time ago. My nightmares have matured considerably. What they've lost in grossness they've gained in unnerving plausibility."

"Do you have nightmares often?" I asked.

"More than I let on," she said. "As my feelings for you grew stronger over the years, I used to have nightmares about hurting you. I used to have this one nightmare where I'd kiss you and break your teeth, and wind up with blood in my mouth. And, now... well. There's a new one."

"What?"

"I've been dreaming about our baby," she said. "Wondering if she's going to be normal. She was conceived in the land of the dead. You weren't... you weren't in your real body. You were just a kind of imitation life. Will our baby really be alive? Or will she be half-alive, half-dead?"

I brushed the hair from her cheek. Ordinarily, this would have been intended to comfort her. But I couldn't help but notice that the fingers I moved her hair with were pale white and puffy. Even against the ivory tone of her delicate skin, my flesh looked dead and bloodless. The iciness of my touch couldn't have been a pleasant sensation.

"She'll be fine," I said, dropping my hand to my side.

"How can you know that?"

"First of all, when you were almost dead, I could see our baby's aura. It was bright and clean, like a little white star in your belly. Nothing corrupted by death could have shone so beautifully."

Infidel nodded, looking thoughtful.

"Second, the Black Swan said she's met our daughter. That old witch never misses an opportunity to dig her claws into you. If our daughter were some kind of monster, she would have said something."

"That's kind of a negative logic, isn't it?" Infidel asked. "Drawing a conclusion based on something that wasn't said?"

"Then here's number three," I said. "I didn't take it seriously when I was a child, but I grew up in a religion that believes that a Divine Author has written out all of our lives. I spent most of my life thinking this was bullshit, but now... Well, I didn't believe in ghosts, either. I've seen too many amazing things since I died to dismiss any possibility. Maybe there really is some guiding force out there with the job of making sure that everything works out for the good. Our lives sometimes feel like ships without a captain, at the mercy of the wind and the waves. But maybe there's someone with his hands on the wheel after all, guiding us toward our destinies. If Zetetic is right, then maybe just believing makes it true. You've had a tough life, Infidel. But I can't help thinking that you've become who you were always meant to be, and that there are even better things in store. You're going to be a mother, and you're going to be amazing."

Infidel blushed slightly. "Aw," she said, as she hugged me tightly.

"So the pep talk worked?" I asked.

"Not in the least," she sighed. "But I love you for trying. This is the Stagger I'll always remember. You're the guy who never stopped trying to make me happy. Hell, you even died and remain more of an optimist than me."

"I do these things because I love you," I said.

"And I love you," she said. "And nightmares are only nightmares. What happens in my sleep doesn't matter in the least. When I'm awake, I remember your courage. When I'm awake, I fight off all my fears just by remembering your smile."

I reached into my pocket and produced the glorystone ring. "Here's something else to remember me by."

I tried to slip it on her left hand, but it was too large for her slender fingers. We finally discovered it fit her thumb.

"It's sweet," she said. "But I liked your hair ring better. It was so much more personal."

"This is personal, too. I just stole this ring. We spent our lives together as thieves. What could be more appropriate than a stolen ring? As a bonus, if Glorious really could see the world through Glorystones, perhaps I'll be able to see you. I can be there as our daughter grows up."

Infidel kissed me. It felt as if the power of the Gloryhammer were surging through me once more as I hugged her tightly. Then something cold and wet pressed itself into the back of my neck. I opened my left eye. In my peripheral vision, I spotted furry dog legs. I broke from the kiss and turned to face Menagerie.

"Sorry to bother you," he said, his dog-breath washing over me. "Sorrow says she's ready."

CHAPTER TWENTY-TWO
STRAIGHT AND NARROW

WE FOLLOWED MENAGERIE back to Aurora and Sorrow. The air had gone eerily silent. The waves caused by the bobbing sun had died off, and the ice floes had come to rest, no longer cracking and grinding against one another. The two women's voices carried over the ice. Aurora was explaining that, from the abstract realms, the Jagged Heart could return a living being to anywhere in the material world. Stern was going to be sent back to the Silver City. Sorrow said she wanted to return to the *Freewind*.

"I'm surprised you want to go back to the boat," I said. "It wasn't in the best condition when you left it."

Sorrow shrugged. "I can't simply abandon Gale."

Judge Stern was awake now, his face turned away from us, but from the tilt of his head he seemed to be listening. I decided it was best not to ask questions that would lead to further discussion of the *Freewind*, given that Stern was part of the navy hunting the ship.

"Ready?" Sorrow asked, holding up the hammer and the knife.

"Let's do it," I said.

Infidel gave me one last kiss and placed my legless torso on the ice before Sorrow. She loomed over me as she began her improvised ritual. The binding was surprisingly simple. The dragon bone of the knife's blade served a function similar to the silver mosquito, as its porous surface formed natural cages to trap the essence of my blood required to bond my soul to matter. As for the Gloryhammer, solar matter, like all matter, proved vulnerable

315

to decay. Sorrow weakened the head of the hammer with her new command over entropy, then plunged the knife into the softened crystal. I watched with fascination as she kneaded the head of the hammer around the knife. The knife itself became malleable as clay, mixing with the crystalline matter.

I didn't feel anything happening.

I looked toward Infidel. She looked stoic, but her eyes glistened.

Tears filled my own eyes. The outlines of her body blurred.

I blinked and she was gone. Everything was gone.

I was in a world of pure white.

Only, it wasn't a world, and there wasn't an *I*. I tried to look down to see what form my spirit had taken now, but there was no down. I had no eyes, no neck, no physical sensation at all.

Was I now in the sun?

How was I supposed to move it if I couldn't even move myself?

Despair seized me. I felt even more trapped than I had in the golden cage inside the golem. In that cage, I'd at least had the hope that, if I understood myself, I might gain some magical gift. I now understood the fundamental flaw of Staggermancy. Because, stripped down to my barest essence, I had no magic. I had nothing at all.

I'd been rejected by my mother and father. The adults who raised me had not loved me. I'd become a thief and a drunkard before I even had pubic hair. I'd spent my adult life a coward, hiding my feelings from the woman I lusted after, and made my living chiefly by robbing the dead. I'd made fortunes, then squandered them on booze, in constant pursuit of oblivion. Now I'd finally caught it. Oblivion was my ultimate fate.

I'd failed the world.

I'd failed...

Infidel.

Despite my failings, Infidel had cared for me. A princess with the blood of dragons in her veins, and she'd loved me, and now carried my daughter. I never understood how a woman like her could love a loser like me.

But what if she didn't love a loser? What if she'd seen the true me, when even I couldn't?

She loved a poet, a scholar, a joker and, yes, a thief. She loved a man who'd lived his life leaping from tall cliffs and crawling headlong into dark tunnels in search of wonder. I like to say I've done it all for her.

It's a lie.

I'd lived on the edge before I ever met her, not because I pursued self-destruction, but because I loved discovering something new each day. I was besotted by the world, in all it's gritty, stinky, sweaty glory. I'd bitten into the apple of life and drunk the tart nectar. I'd loved every moment I spent on our crazy whirling planet.

Love may lead you down strange and twisting paths, but it can never lead you astray. You may follow blindly, across dangerous ground, and never quite reach your destination. But the destination never mattered anyway. Love was always the journey.

And now it was time for me to undertake a new journey, a trip that no man had ever dared before. Glorious had moved the sun with his mind, but I would move it with my heart. Understanding this, a calmness washed through me, and I fell into restful sleep.

I woke on a white sand beach, to the sound of gulls and the soft sigh of sea-foam fizzing near my feet. I raised my left hand to shield my eyes from the intense brightness that surrounded me. I sat up, squinting, unable to remember how I had arrived here.

As the warm sand shifted beneath me, I realized I was naked. I looked down at my toes and gave them a wiggle. For reasons I couldn't quite put my fingers on, I felt happy to see them. They seemed like old friends who'd been absent for some time.

How much had I drank last night? Where was I? What had happened to my pants?

I grinned. It's both a drunkard's gift and curse that his best memories are the ones he can't remember.

Looking around, I was on a long ribbon of white sand. The ocean before me was black as night, with waves topped by milky foam that reminded me of scattered stars. Behind me, the jungle was dark green, bordered with an impenetrable wall of spiky vines. Try as I might, I had no memory of how I'd come to be here.

The sky overhead was pure white; I couldn't spot the sun amid the burning haze. The light came from all directions at once, reflecting off the white sand with a ferocity that left me squinting.

Assuming I was on the Isle of Fire, most beaches with white sand lay to the west of Commonground. I rose on unsteady legs and spun to my right. I had no idea how far I needed to go to reach the Black Swan, but knew that the sooner I started walking, the sooner I would get there. I began to walk, stumbling and staggering in the soft sand.

Despite the intense brightness that surrounded me, I was grateful for the haze that rendered the sky a uniform white. If the sun had been fully exposed, my bare skin would have burnt to a crisp. The sand, while warm, wasn't burning my feet. But all it would take would be a shift in the clouds, and both of these convenient truths would vanish. Feeling renewed urgency, I stumbled on.

And kept walking.

And kept walking.

My eyes adjusted to the luminance. I had no way of measuring time, but I began to have the curious feeling that I had been meandering along this same stretch of white beach for hours. Or had it been even longer? For a brief moment, I felt I should stop and think about my situation, but when I slowed my pace a sense of dread gnawed at the back of my skull and kept me moving forward. I began to count my steps, and grew lost in the unfolding ribbon of numbers, counting, ever counting, until

I'd forgotten why I was keeping track. Only as I was reaching one hundred thousand did the size of the number strike me as peculiar. Assuming I was averaging a step a second, I'd been walking for twenty seven hours. How could that be possible? I hadn't paused to eat or drink; understandable, considering I had neither food nor beverage, but where was my hunger? Where was my thirst? Assuming I had drank gallons the night before, why had I not felt the urge to piss? If I'd been walking so long, why did the sky never darken? Where was the night? Would this day never end?

Eventually, I found footprints in the sand. My heart surged with relief at the thought that I would soon find someone who could help guide me home. Onward I staggered, picking up my pace, my feet meandering as I crossed the path of the footsteps I followed again and again. Yet despite the freshness of the trail, I never caught sight of the stranger I was pursuing. The hours wore on. At length, I came to a second set of prints. Many hours later, a third set was added. I paused to study them. My feet fit nicely within the outlines. Whoever I was following, they must have been similar to me in height; the length of my stride fairly mirrored theirs.

Much later, a fourth pair added to the growing crowd I chased. Then a fifth, and a sixth.

At about the time my internal clock advised that I should start looking for a seventh set of prints, I finally spotted a man, far in the distance. He was dressed in red robes, with black hair in a long ponytail. I began to run toward him. As I drew closer, I saw that he had a large red "D" tattooed in the center of his forehead.

Zetetic?

"Zetetic!" I cried out.

The Deceiver's eyes went wide. He stretched his hands toward me and shouted, "Stop!" Then, without pausing to breathe he cried, "Wait, don't stop, just walk!"

Confused, I halted.

Zetetic bounded across the sand and grabbed my hand, jerking me forward.

"One, two, three, four," he said, pulling me into a steady pace. He was carrying a small triangular box with slits in the side. In form, it resembled a clock, but it didn't have any numbers or hands. All it seemed to do was produce a steady, rhythmic click. Zetetic's feet fell in rhythm with each beat, and soon mine did as well as I kept pace beside him.

"What's going on?" I asked, confused. "What's that in your hand? What are you doing here? For that matter, where the hell are we?"

"I'll answer all your questions, I promise," said Zetetic, who now reached into his robes to produce a long walking stick. He began to drag the stick behind him, leaving a straight line as we journeyed. "Promise me that you'll keep walking forward, and match the pace of your stride to those of this metronome."

"Metronome?" I asked.

He handed me the box. "It's spring-operated. Slide the panel along the back to find the winding mechanism."

"Aren't these something musicians use?" I asked.

"Yes," he said. "Feel free to break into song if you wish. Anything you need to keep your pace steady. You've been staggering rather badly."

"How do you know?" I asked.

"Look at how your footprints keep crisscrossing," he said, nodding toward the sand before me.

"These are all my footprints? How? How did I make it around the island without finding Commonground?"

"You aren't on the Isle of Fire," Zetetic said. "I take it you don't remember what happened to you?"

I shook my head. "My best guess is I drank myself under a table and some punks robbed me of everything including my socks, then dumped my body on the beach. I've just been pushing myself forward until I reach home. I can't wait to tell this story to... to... oh."

Suddenly I remembered Infidel.

Suddenly I remembered everything.

"This is not a beach," I said.

"No," said Zetetic. "This is not, technically, anywhere at all. You're dealing with concepts too large for human senses to fully process, so your mind has constructed this symbolic tableau. The infinite ocean represents the void filled with stars. The green forest is the material world. The beach represents the path of the sun. As long as you travel this path, keeping the forest to your right, the sun still rises in the east and sets in the west."

"You mean... you mean I'm doing it right?" I scratched my head. Or the symbolic equivalent of my head.

"Ha!" said Zetetic. "Not even close! You're appropriately nicknamed, Stagger. The sun has been meandering in an eccentric orbit for the last week. The length of a day hasn't been the same twice since you started. This seems to have thrown the weather off, as I've heard reports of blizzards as far south as the Isle of Apes. As you can imagine, this has led to quite a bit of consternation below. Which is why I'm here."

"Why *are* you here?" I asked.

"Thanks to the information they got from Judge Stern, the king's astronomers have done a wonderful job of analyzing the problem with the sun. But they didn't possess the power to do anything to put the sun back into its correct path. For that, someone with a more specialized skill set was required. I presented myself to King Brightmoon yesterday. His kingdom is in turmoil; farmers from across the Silver Isles are at his gates, brandishing pitchforks and demanding he take action."

"You are that action," I said.

"Indeed. Through my contacts, I'd heard that Glorious had been slain and a new ghost now drove the sun. I assured the king that I possessed the ability to speak to this ghost and put him on a straight and constant path. In exchange, I've been granted a pardon and one of the king's remote island fortresses, plus all the gold, soldiers, and servants necessary to outfit it. I've always wanted a modest place of my own."

I looked at the box in my hand. "So, this is all I need to keep me on pace?"

"Almost," he said. "Once we complete an orbit, we'll find the line I'm now tracing. If you follow this line faithfully, the sun will be back on the correct path."

"And you'll stay with me as I walk?"

"This first time through. After this, I've prepped a glorystone in the Royal Observatory to serve as a channel through which you may speak and be spoken to. The chief of the Observatory, Father Luciferous, is quite eager to talk to you and learn your story."

I smiled. "I like telling stories." I looked at the stretch of sand before me. "And I like walking on the beach. But I feel like there's a lot I left unfinished in the material world."

"Every dead man I've ever spoken with felt the same way," said Zetetic.

"Fair enough. But then, I'm probably the first dead man to actually have some leverage. I'm willing to keep the sun moving through the sky at a constant pace. I'd like you to explain to the king that I feel a little gratitude is in order. I think I can concentrate on my pace a little easier if he'll do me a couple of favors."

"Are you speaking of blackmail?" Zetetic said.

"I think I might be. The king is going to get a lot of love from his subjects once word gets out that he's fixed the sun. I hope that he'll share his good fortune by issuing a few pardons. There's a family of Wanderers called the Romers. I'd like for him to leave them alone. Even more importantly, I want him to issue a full pardon for Infidel. I don't want her to have to hide from assassins while she's raising our daughter."

Zetetic's face went blank.

"What?" I asked.

"Nothing," he said. "I was... I think these are reasonable requests. I'm certain the king can accommodate you."

"I'll want proof," I said. "Glorious said he could see through the glorystones. I obviously haven't picked up that trick yet. But if there's a stone where this Luciferous guy can talk to me, I want you to promise me that you'll bring Infidel to it so I can speak to her."

Zetetic nodded. His face was completely calm and expressionless. "I'll do what I can. Of course, it might take some time to locate her."

"For you? Just tell someone you have the power to find missing people by jumping into the air and landing beside them."

He furrowed his brow.

"What's the problem?"

He shook his head. "No problem. I'm just worried we might have gotten out of step with the metronome. Let's walk in silence for a while."

"For someone called Deceiver, you're surprisingly bad at lying," I said.

Zetetic shook his head. "I'm simply concerned, is all. You must keep moving forward. You must not change your pace."

"You know something, don't you? About Infidel?"

Zetetic said, "Of course not."

I stopped moving. "I'm not taking another damn step until you tell me what's going on."

Zetetic grabbed my arm and yanked me forward.

"No!" I shouted, taking a step backward.

"Keep walking!" he cried. "Think of the chaos you cause on earth when you pause even for a moment, let alone move backwards!"

"Tell me what you know!" I shouted.

"Infidel's dead!" he screamed at me.

I fell to my knees.

Zetetic sighed, and bent down on his knees before me. He said, softly, "I'm sorry. I don't know the full story, just bits and pieces of court gossip. Judge Stern was briefly captured by

Infidel and a witch named Sorrow while they were in the Great Sea Above. Stern heard Sorrow and Infidel request to be sent to the *Freewind*, which was damaged and adrift in the artic, just north of the Isle of Grass. They wanted to help the Romers get the ship back to port."

I clenched my hands in the warm sand beneath me. I'd known Judge Stern was listening. Why hadn't I said anything?

"King Brightmoon messaged his flagship, the *Raptor*, to find the *Freewind*. The *Raptor* is capable of flight, and covered the distance to the *Freewind's* location in less than a day. One of the old, normal days, not the thirty-hour specials you've been serving up. "

"What did they find?" I asked.

Zetetic said, "I really need for you to stand up and start walking again."

"What did they find?"

Zetetic sighed. "The Storm Guard had beaten the *Raptor* to the punch with one of their hurricanes. When the *Raptor* arrived, they found timbers from the_*Freewind* scattered across the sea. The Storm Guard had crushed the ship between two icebergs. Ordinarily, the Storm Guard are eager to take prisoners to sell as slaves, but through diplomatic channels we've learned that the crew of the *Freewind* fought to the last man. Their dead and wounded went down with the ship. Presumably, Infidel and Sorrow perished with them."

I nodded. "There were no bodies?" I asked.

"Not that I'm aware of," said Zetetic. "Please get up."

I rose, brushing sand off my legs.

"Infidel's the main reason I'm doing this," I said, stepping forward.

"I understand," he said. "But she was just one person. There's a whole world that depends on you now. It's not just people at stake. Every last blade of grass on the planet needs you to keep walking. Every tree, every bird flitting between their branches, every last fish in the sea depends on you now for survival. The magnitude of your responsibility is incomprehensible."

I looked straight ahead as I walked. "I comprehend."

I matched my pace to the ticking metronome, thinking of all those blades of grass, thinking about flowers, and fields of corn, and all the farmers that worked those fields, and their cows and chickens and children. All of mankind now stared up to watch the sky, needing me to be something I'd never been: dependable, predictable, following a straight and narrow path.

And so I walked. I do it still. I'll do it until every bit of white foam on the ocean around me vanishes as the final stars burn out.

I do not fear eternity.

I have my memories. I have the promise of telling my story for generations to come.

And I have the knowledge that I'm helping Infidel. She isn't dead. Somehow, Levi convinced Gale to abandon ship. Infidel, Sorrow, the Romers... all could use the breathing space that comes from the world thinking them dead. For the time being, they'll no longer be hunted.

One day I'll learn to gaze through the glorystones, and perhaps learn the fate of those I've left behind. Already when I gaze at the luminous paper-white sky I detect all-but-invisible swirls of motion and hear distant, barely perceptible murmurs. I'm on the verge of a new sense awakening. But I don't need to see the material world to be certain that Infidel is still in it.

I know she's alive, because she's not here.

If Infidel's dead, she knows where to find me. She's had an unusual amount of practice in navigating the realms beyond life. When her soul finally departs her body, I'm certain she'll battle and bargain and blast her way across whatever abstract realms lie between us.

I can wait. I'm a patient man. The day will come when I see her on this shore. She'll smile and give me a kiss, then place her hand in mine as we walk along this beach. She can tell me what really happened when she made it back, what happened to Sorrow and Gale and even poor Bigsby. She can tell me about my daughter. I wonder what she'll name her?

It's these thoughts that give me the strength to place one foot before the other. In the end, neither of us will walk into eternity alone.

ABOUT THE AUTHOR

James Maxey lives in Hillsborough, NC with his lovely bride Cheryl and a clowder of unruly cats. He is the author of the *Bitterwood* fantasy trilogy, *Bitterwood*, *Dragonforge*, and *Dragonseed*, as well as the superhero novels *Nobody Gets the Girl* and *Burn Baby Burn*. His short fiction has appeared in dozens of anthologies and magazines such as *Asimov's* and *Orson Scott Card's Intergalactic Medicine Show*. The best of these stories appears in the collection *There is No Wheel*. For more information about James, and to follow the progress of further books chronicling the *Dragon Apocalypse*, visit dragonprophet.blogspot.com.

Now read the first chapter from
the next novel in this exciting series...

WITCHBREAKER

BOOK THREE *of the* DRAGON APOCALYPSE

JAMES MAXEY

SOLARIS

CHAPTER ONE
GRAVEDIGGERS

From the Journal of Sorrow Stern

THE BLIZZARD WAS still full force when Infidel lit out from Menagerie's safe house. I caught her as she slipped quietly out the door in early morning; she was surprised to find me awake.

I asked her to reconsider my offer. We share a common enemy. An alliance seemed obvious.

"The difference between us is that you want to fight the world," she said. "I just want to raise my daughter in peace."

"Do you want your daughter to think you were a coward?" I asked. "Don't you want to be a hero?"

"You think you're going to be remembered as hero?" she asked, looking dubious. "There's a whole army of priests telling the world that, according to their all-knowing holy book, you're the villain."

"Then I shall kill the priests and burn their book," I answered. "I refuse to allow others to be the authors of my history."

Infidel placed her hand on my shoulder. "Sorrow, you helped us save the world. You've got a good heart. Just... listen to yourself. You might be letting others define you more than you know."

We talked a few minutes more, but I knew she'd made her choice, as I've made mine.

I departed the safe house mid-morning. The blizzard had finally passed, and already the snow was melting beneath the tropical sun. I happened upon a band of pygmy carpenters, *hauling a cart loaded with good quality lumber and made a sizeable purchase. As always, if I'm to have reliable allies, I must build them myself.*

SORROW'S KNUCKLES WERE white as she gripped the sides of the dugout canoe. The Dragon's Mouth, the river that fed into the bay at Commonground, was normally a broad, placid body of water, but snowmelt had swollen the river beyond its banks. Ancient trees felled by the snow bobbed in the current, forming an ever-shifting maze.

The river pygmies she'd hired to ferry her to the Knight's Castle proved up to the task of navigating the flood, though not without visible tension. When the four canoes had first departed Commonground, the river pygmies had been chatting and laughing with one another. Now, they paddled silently, their eyes barely blinking as they studied the roiling waters, their faces hard, stoic masks.

There were eight pygmies, two in each canoe. She was their only living passenger; the rest of the canoes held her gear, plus Trunk. She'd left him inert for the moment. She didn't want to alarm the pygmies with his unusual appearance. On the other hand, the pygmies struck her as difficult to alarm. She'd allowed her hood to slip as she boarded the canoe and they hadn't even taken a second glance at her head. River pygmies dyed their bodies blue and cut fish scale scars along their shoulders and backs. Her shaved scalp studded with nails probably struck them as tame.

The terrain around the river grew more rugged and rocky. She wondered if the pygmies would be up to the task of carting her gear to her destination. She'd made her needs quite clear to the pygmy leader, Eddy (his full name, translated, was White Foam Curling Past an Eddy, which she found rather mellifluous). He'd assured her that his men were the strongest of their tribe, but the tallest of pygmies barely reached the bottom of her ribs, and she'd not packed lightly. She'd come into the jungle seeking the lost Witches' Graveyard, and was prepared for an extensive dig when she found it. The canoes were heaped with picks, shovels, wheelbarrows, ropes, tents, and enough food for a six-month expedition.

After several hours of paddling against the fierce current, their immediate destination came into view: the towering, vine-draped walls of the ruins known as the Knight's Castle. She'd lost Stagger's map in the rush to abandon the *Freewind*, but his directions were simple enough. Find the Knight's Castle and head east. Here, she'd find rows of evenly spaced depressions in the ground. Stagger had been certain the place was a graveyard, but had always assumed, since the graves weren't marked, that it had been used to bury people of little importance. No treasure hunter had ever done the hard work of digging here, because it seemed so unpromising. But she'd come seeking knowledge, not treasure, and the thought of the waiting graves filled her with an almost childlike excitement.

The pygmies guided the canoes between two enormous walls. In the flooded gap was a broad avenue, draped by shadows. Sorrow strained to see in the dim light. At the end of the avenue, steep stone steps rose from the water, leading to the top of the walls. Her canoe shuddered as it scraped over unseen stones beneath the coffee-colored river.

Eddy leapt from the tip of the canoe, his feet splashing loudly, his muscles bulging as he pulled the canoe to rest on one of the broad steps hidden just inches below the surface. Eddy wasn't a young man, but his muscles were well sculpted beneath his leathery blue hide. Sorrow was embarrassed that she'd doubted the pygmies' capacity to cart her gear. Despite their small stature, these men needed immense physical strength to survive this savage land.

Sorrow rose from her canoe as the other pygmies brought their vessels to rest on the steps. The pygmies still looked nervous, but she felt relieved to be away from the worst of the river.

She said, "Well done, Eddy. You've earned your moons today."

Eddy frowned as his men gathered around Sorrow.

"There's the matter of payment," said Eddy.

"You'll be paid when we reach the graveyard. Three moons each. We were clear on this subject."

"At the market, my brother saw you pay for provisions with a purse full of moons."

"Perhaps he did," said Sorrow. "I don't see how that matters."

"It matters because we're eight warriors," said Eddy. "You're a lone woman, far removed from any long-men who could hear your cries."

Sorrow crossed her arms. "It's bad enough that you would renege on an agreement. I can't believe you're trying to threaten me."

"No, no, no," Eddy said, laughing gently. "You misunderstand. I make no threat. I'm merely saying that, in such a hazardous landscape, you'll give us all your coins in exchange for the chance to see another morning."

He raised his left hand and brought his thumb and little finger together. At this signal, all seven of his companions drew knives from their belts.

Sorrow sighed. "I see. Fortunately for you, I abhor settling disputes with violence, and would like to avoid doing so now. Allow me to make a counter-proposal. Your men will drop their weapons. You'll unload the canoes in a neat and professional fashion. After this, we shall part ways. In exchange, none of you will die in unimaginable agony. At least, not today. "

Eddy drew his own knife. "You've a bold tongue, witch. We'll see if you're still as arrogant when I cut it from your mouth."

Sorrow stepped back as Eddy ran toward her. She snapped her fingers, then extended her hand as Eddy leapt high in the air, swinging his knife at her torso. She caught him by the arm just as a second pygmy attempted to stab her in the back of her thigh. She felt his blade tear through her pants and skitter along the hard scales beneath as she toppled backward.

Meanwhile, Trunk had heard her snapped fingers and stirred. Her last golem had been built of driftwood, but she'd had no patience for rooting around on a snow-covered beach looking for appropriate timber. Trunk's torso was a heavy cedar chest; his limbs were thick, sturdy boards. His fingers and toes were built of oak doweling. For a head, she'd used a bucket so new it had never been touched by a mop.

As expected, most of the pygmies turned toward the wooden man as he rose with a clatter. She had only to deal with Eddy, who was straddling her torso, attempting to press his knife to her throat, and the thigh-stabbing pygmy she'd fallen upon.

Dealing with Eddy was simplest. She relaxed her arm and allowed him to press his iron blade to her throat. The second it touched her flesh, she willed the knife to crumble and it did so, rusting instantly to the core and snapping as Eddy pressed down.

The pygmy she'd fallen on had managed to untangle himself from her legs, and now rose on his hands and knees directly in front of the soles of her boots. This was an unfortunate place for him. Since she'd hammered a fragment of Rott's tooth into her brain, her legs had grown a covering of overlapping serpent scales. While she wasn't happy that her legs looked like they belonged to a dragon, she was pleased that they'd become supernaturally strong. She kicked the pygmy squarely in the chest and he went flying, smacking into the vine-draped wall twenty feet away.

"Now, Eddy," she said as she grabbed the diminutive robber's face in both hands, "It's time for me to teach you a lesson in keeping promises."

She could have been merciful and killed the man. Instead, she allowed only the smallest fraction of Rott's power of entropy to surge from her bare palms. Eddy howled as his flesh sagged on his face. She pushed him away and he fell on his back, writhing in agony. He wailed as his teeth turned black, falling from their sockets. His muscles shrank, and his skin grew paper thin. He raised his hands before his face as they twisted into arthritic claws. Mercifully, he didn't have long to stare at his deformity. Thick cataracts fogged his eyes, turning them into twin white marbles.

She rose on trembling legs. When pressed into violence, she killed as efficiently and coolly as possible. She despised those who took pleasure at inflicting pain. Even so, she had to fight to keep from laughing at the man who'd threatened her with such swaggering confidence. She fought back the urge to taunt him, but not the urge to educate him.

"You called me a witch," she said, staring down at the now ancient man. "It's a term often used for women who are inadequately subservient to men. I, however, embrace the word's true meaning. I command forces you can never hope to comprehend. I'm heir to an ancient and awesome power. You should not have betrayed me."

She glanced behind her and found Trunk standing in ankle-deep water, surrounded by six headless corpses. She shook her head slowly. She'd hoped at least one survivor would bear witness to what he'd seen this day.

There was always Eddy, weeping at her feet, splayed out like a rag doll, covered in his own bodily waste. She doubted there was enough left of his mind to pass on her warning.

"What's the point in teaching lessons if there's no one around to learn?"

Then, because she was disturbed by the satisfaction she was taking from his wet, feeble sobs, she placed her boot upon his throat and pressed until his suffering ended.

She had Trunk dispose of the corpses in the river while she sorted through her supplies. They would have to cart in the gear one load at a time. Fortunately, the dug-out canoes would prove handy for storing what they left behind. Trunk turned over one canoe and placed it atop another. She used her power over wood to weave the two halves together, forming a sealed container that held most of her provisions. For now, Trunk would cart only tools and a few days' worth of meals.

She led Trunk up the stairs to the top of the wall. She shielded her eyes from the fierce noon sun as she studied the jungle, gray and withered, devastated by the cold. From her vantage point, she could see a back slope beyond the trees, evidence of a recent lava flow. If Stagger's description was correct, it looked as if the lava hadn't covered the area of the graveyard.

Two hours later, she'd barely made it a hundred yards into the jungle. The ground was mushy, and Trunk kept sinking up to his knees. Sorrow grew coated in mud herself as she worked to free him and drag their supplies forward. She lost one of her boots in the sucking mire. She pressed her lips tightly together as she stared at her now-bare foot.

She wasn't overly sentimental, but she missed her toes. During her journey to the Sea of Wine, she'd gained possession of a sliver of tooth belonging to Rott, the primal dragon of decay. It had been a gamble, nailing the sliver into her skull; without the guidance of a more experienced Weaver, she could have crippled herself. Fortunately, her many years of study had meant that she hadn't relied on blind luck alone in placing the nail. Given that she now commanded the most fearsome powers she'd yet mastered, she had no regrets about her actions.

Having no regrets didn't mean she lacked concerns. The scales coating her legs were diamond-shaped, large as her thumbnails, pitch black, and hard as iron. They'd started as small patches near her ankles, but now both legs from mid-thigh down were covered. Her feet no longer ended in toes, but instead each tapered to a banded point. If she pressed hard, she could barely feel the bones of her toes still present beneath the hard surface.

Her unusual skin condition added a sense of urgency to her quest to find the Witches' Graveyard.

The few remaining practitioners of the art of weaving placed great value in their privacy. The few she'd tracked down seldom gave Sorrow a warm welcome. Sorrow's pursuit of power had earned her more than a few enemies. Few living

Weavers wanted to make themselves a target of the forces allied against her.

Her hope of pushing her education further now lay with dead Weavers. She was certain that, if she could study the skulls of witches, she could learn a great deal by documenting how they'd placed nails into their brains. With any luck, she wasn't the first Weaver to tap the power of a primal dragon. She might yet discover the secret to using Rott's power without corrupting her body.

It was nearly sunset when she finally found the hilly slope, covered with rows of long narrow depressions, that Stagger had described. Her nostrils twitched as she hacked her way through the spiky vines that draped the area. Was she smelling fire? Or was it just a lingering odor from the volcanic eruption?

She sliced her way through a curtain of dying vines and found herself in an area relatively free of undergrowth. The canopy of trees here was particularly thick, blanketing the area in a perpetual gloom that suppressed smaller plants. She looked up the hill and saw a large granite boulder, nearly the size of a house, shaped something like a heart. It looked top-heavy, and a bit out of place, despite being girded with thick vines. She suspected it had rolled down the mountain many years ago. Next to the boulder, she saw a small makeshift tent, little more than a large blanket stretched over some branches, and near it a smoldering fire pit.

She cocked her head. She could hear voices from the other side of the boulder.

She looked toward Trunk, and motioned for him to drop his pack. She opened a bundle of tools and supplied him with an axe, then nodded for him to follow her. Armed with her machete, she crept silently up the hill. Stagger had warned her that treasure-seekers often tried their luck around the Knight's Castle. From what she knew, these were desperate men of low morals who might not behave honorably. She had no fear that they were an actual danger to her. Still, if they did look problematic, she saw no reason to waste the advantage of surprise.

She silently pressed herself against the heart-shaped boulder and listened to the voices from the other side.

"Here's another one!" said a man in a curiously high-pitched falsetto.

"Gold?" a second man asked, sounding hopeful.

"No. It's green. Maybe more glass? The light's getting bad."

"Let me see," said the second man.

Sorrow furrowed her brow. She'd heard these voices before. What were they doing out here? Then she realized why she hadn't been able to find her map when she abandoned the *Freewind*.

She marched around the boulder and saw a mound of damp earth piled high a few dozen feet away. A tall blond man was standing in a pit beside the mound, visible only from his bare shoulders up.

"Brand!" she shouted, stomping toward him.

The blond man looked up. His eyes grew wide. "Sorrow? I didn't expect to see you out here."

"I'm sure you didn't!"

He grabbed a root near the edge of the pit and started to pull himself up. He was half out of the hole when she placed her boot onto his shoulder and knocked him back in. He landed next to the second figure in the pit, a pot-bellied dwarf wearing a platinum blonde wig.

"Villain!" the dwarf shrieked, shaking his fist. "You'll pay dearly for striking the scion of King Brightmoon!"

"It's okay," said Brand, rising to his knees. "I think there's been a misunderstanding."

"You stole my map!" said Sorrow.

"Technically, I found a map in the rubble when we were hastily packing. How was I to know it was yours?"

"It was in my cabin!"

"Things got sloshed around when the ship capsized. There's no telling where it originally came from."

"You knew it wasn't yours!"

Brand nodded. "Okay, sure, that's true. But, honestly, when

I found it, I saw the word 'treasure' in large letters, underlined, and thought it was a joke. I doubt that most people who hide buried treasure do that."

"You took it seriously enough to come out into the jungle."

"Also true," said Brand. "But after Gale fired me, all the princess and I had were the clothes on our backs. We need to raise some scratch to get back to the Silver Isles. What did we have to lose?"

"The princess?" Sorrow rolled her eyes. "He still thinks he's Innocent Brightmoon? And you're still humoring him?"

"Him?" asked Bigsby. "Who's she talking about."

Brand shrugged.

"I should just fill in this hole with both of you in it," grumbled Sorrow. "The world has more than enough thieves."

"Have a care, commoner," said Bigsby, wiping a muddy strand of blonde hair from his face. "We don't care for your tone or your accusations."

"I'm not a thief," said Brand. "I'm just lucky at finding stuff."

"Like those shovels and pickaxes? You presumably didn't acquire them honestly."

"It depends on how you define *honest*. We bought them. We holed up on the *Black Swan* for a few days during the worst of the blizzard. I earned a few moons reading palms for the patrons."

"You read palms?"

"To the extent that anyone reads palms, sure," said Brand. "It's a talent I picked up traveling with the circus."

"He's very good," said Bigsby.

Sorrow clenched her fists. "You've no magical powers. I'd spot it in your aura if you did."

"I didn't say I knew magic," said Brand. "Fortune-telling is ninety percent listening to your clients, and ten percent repeating it back to them with a twist."

"So you swindle fools," said Sorrow. "All the more reason the world won't miss you if I fill in this pit."

"I didn't swindle anyone. My clients are very happy with my work. Let me do you."

"I think not," said Sorrow. "You've nothing to tell me about myself I don't already know."

"I can tell you you're not going to bury us," said Brand.

Sorrow sighed. "No, I suppose I'm not. I'll let you out if you promise to leave peacefully. If you refuse, you know what I'm capable of."

"How about this?" asked Brand. "We get out of the pit, we all eat dinner together, and tomorrow we work as a team to look for the treasure, whatever it is."

Sorrow studied Brand's face. He smiled at her, but this didn't help his cause. She hadn't much liked him when they traveled together on the *Freewind*. Brand was little more than a prostitute, a pretty young man who'd served as the sexual toy of Captain Romer, a woman old enough to be his mother. On the other hand, one reason that Gale had been so smitten with him was that Brand was a rather impressive physical specimen. Having a gravedigger with broad shoulders and a strong back could speed up her search.

"Fine," said Sorrow. "But you'll work as my employees, not my partners. I'll pay you a set fee to dig graves. What we find will be mine alone. At least you won't be digging blindly with the chance of winding up empty-handed. I'll compensate you and Bigsby a moon for each grave you excavate."

"I'm not Bigsby!" the dwarf shrieked. "Why does everyone keep calling me that? Has the whole world gone mad?"

Sorrow closed her eyes and rubbed them. The prospect of spending an extended time dealing with the dwarf was unpleasant. It wasn't too late to have Trunk dismember them with his axe. She sighed. She'd always thought of herself as a defender of those outside of the mainstream of society. An insane cross-dressing dwarf certainly fell into that category. How much did she truly believe in her own cause if, when confronted by a person who was an even more of an outcast than her, her first instinct was to bury him in an unmarked grave?

"Sorry, Innocent," she said softly. "I'm just tired. I got confused."

"You're still confused if you think you can address me in such a familiar fashion," Bigsby said huffily.

"Sorry, your highness," she said.

"The apology is accepted," said Bigsby. "But we reject your offer. Any treasure we find is rightfully ours."

"Hold on," said Brand. "We only need enough money to get passage back to the Silver Isles. We'll be rich once we're home. Why be greedy?"

"That's quite rational of you," said Sorrow. "You wouldn't be trying to trick me?"

"Nope," said Brand. He grinned. "If you can't trust royalty, who can you trust?"

"By the pure metals," Sorrow said, shaking her head. "I'm probably going to regret this."

She turned toward Trunk. "Help them out."

Brand helped Bigsby steady himself as Trunk lifted him to the surface. Brand didn't wait for Trunk to bend back again, but once more grabbed the root and scrambled out.

"If it was your map, do you have any idea of what it is we're looking for?"

"Some," said Sorrow.

"I don't suppose we're looking for very fancy knitting needles, are we?" Brand asked, holding up a slender jade shaft.

"You found one!" said Sorrow. "Where's the skull that held it?"

"There wasn't a skull," said Brand. "If these pits used to be graves, any human remains rotted away a long time ago." He pulled two more of the shafts from his pocket. "All we found were these rods of onyx and glass."

Sorrow took the glass rod, feeling both excited and disappointed. She already had a nail of glass, and saw no benefit to adding a nail of jade or onyx. "How much do you know about my abilities?"

"We know you're a witch," said Bigsby.

Sorrow nodded. "More precisely, I'm a materialist. By using these nails, I can gain mastery over objects made from the same base materials."

"How?" asked Bigsby.

"You really don't want to know."

"I do! I command you to tell me how to use these items!"

Sorrow drew back her hood, revealing her shaved scalp. "Fine. You take a hammer and nail these into your head."

"Really?" Bigsby asked. "It's that simple?"

"I wouldn't call it simple. A misplaced nail can kill a Weaver. If you're lucky enough to live, you're marked forever as a dangerous heretic who can be legally put to death on sight. All power comes with a price."

"But you could show me how to place one of the nails in my scalp?" asked Bigsby. "I could gain your powers?"

"Only women can do it. For reasons I'm not sure of, men always cripple themselves if they try."

"Why should that be a problem for me?" Bigsby asked.

"It's a problem because we're royalty, sister," said Brand. "We represent not just our people, but our religion. The Church of the Book says that witches are sinful; imagine the scandal if a princess showed up in court with a nail in her head."

"Good point," said Bigsby.

Sorrow had to admire the calm tone Brand used in addressing Bigsby. She wasn't certain he was doing the right thing by manipulating the dwarf's delusions, but he seemed good at it.

She said, "You can keep these nails. They might be of interest to collectors. The jade nail might be worth a hundred moons. What I'm looking for are nails I've never seen before. And skulls. Especially skulls." She looked around the darkening forest. There were hundreds of depressions. She shook her head. "How did you choose to dig here?"

Brand pointed down the hill. "This is pretty much the highest point among the graves, so I didn't think we'd have to deal with a lot of groundwater. The graves further down would probably fill up with water faster than we could dig."

"Probably," she said. "Still, I hate to think that our search is going to be so... random. This could take a long time."

"Do you know anything that might let us pick the best targets?" Brand asked.

Sorrow shook her head. She glanced at the smoldering fire of their pathetic campsite. She said, "Why don't the two of you get that fire going again while Trunk and I unpack? No point digging further tonight. We can eat dinner, get some sleep, then figure out the best way to tackle this in the morning."

SORROW LAY AWAKE through the night. Though she had pitched her tent twenty yards distant from the brothers, she could still hear Bigsby snoring. But, that wasn't the main reason she couldn't sleep. Partially, there was a sense of anticipation. She'd first heard about the Witches' Graveyard almost seven years ago, and it felt unreal that she'd found something she'd been searching for after all this time. The fact that three nails had been found in the first grave was a good omen. Honestly, she hadn't expected to find any nails. If these were the graves of victims of Lord Tower, the Witchbreaker, she would have guessed the nails would have been removed either before or after execution. Perhaps only valuable nails had been treated this way. Jade and onyx resembled colored glass; perhaps they'd been left in the grave by mistake.

Underlying her excitement was dread. There had been no skull, or any bones at all. What if she'd come all this way in vain? What if she spent the next year of her life digging for secrets and found none?

She was almost tempted to put Brand's fortune-telling talents to the test. Almost. He'd admitted his skills were mere trickery, but perhaps there was some value in having someone listen attentively as she spoke. She'd kept her talks with the Romer family short and professional. They'd been employees, not friends. She'd opened up a bit with Infidel, but, in the end, they'd had little to say to one another.

She found it interesting that Brand might be such a good enough listener that other people paid for the service. Perhaps it was worth spending a moon or two for a demonstration.

Still unable to sleep, she turned on her side, lowering her hand to scratch her left ankle. Her nails slid along the hard, glassy surface of the scales without managing in the least to relieve the itch. She scratched with more pressure, and succeeded only in slicing open the tip of her finger along the edge of one of the scales. She sat up in her tent and reached for her belt. She used the hard surface of the buckle to scrape her ankle vigorously.

She stopped scraping as she heard someone laugh directly behind her.

She spun around and found a pygmy standing not a yard away. How had he gotten into the tent? At least he didn't appear menacing. For starters, he was ancient, his face looking like wrinkled leather over his skull. He was so thin she could have counted his ribs. He was bald, devoid of any of scars that most pygmies sported. He was also missing the pygmy dyes that rendered river pygmies blue. He was white as cotton, save for his eyes, which were black, empty sockets in the dark tent. The skull-like quality of his face was enhanced by the way he was grinning, showing his teeth.

She reached out to grab him as she said, "How did you get in here?" He stepped backwards, and her fingers closed on empty air. He laughed softly, then sighed, shaking his head.

She lunged, this time trying to grab him with both hands. He jumped backwards. He laughed as he watched her hands flail uselessly in the space he'd stood a heartbeat earlier, but his back was now pressed against the wall of the tent. There was no more room to retreat.

"You aren't going to think this is funny when I'm through with you," she said, reaching for his throat.

He stepped backwards, fading through the tent as if it were made of fog instead of heavy oil cloth. Her hands smacked into it with a thump.

She stared at the empty wall. Had she been dreaming? Admittedly, she was exhausted, and had been drifting in and out of the antechamber of sleep. But she'd never had any difficulty mistaking dreams and reality before. She was certain her eyes hadn't tricked her.

From outside the wall, the pygmy giggled.

She scrambled to the door of the tent and rose, wearing only the cotton slip she used for sleeping. She ran around the tent and found the pale pygmy glowing in the moonlight. He was standing a few feet in front of the heart-shaped boulder. He laughed harder as he saw her, tears running down his cheeks.

"What's so funny?" she asked.

"You," the pygmy gasped, pointing at her. He spoke in the Silver Tongue, but she didn't recognize his accent. "The demons in the Forest of Torment told me I should bear witness to the return of the Destroyer." He wiped his wrinkled cheeks. "I can't believe they mistook you for a threat."

"Demons? The Forest of Torment? What the hell are you talking about?"

The pygmy shook his head. "There's no point in explaining. You're nothing but a desperate, foolish girl." He sighed. "Demons. I should have known they were trying to trick me. The dragon will devour you and return to slumber."

"The dragon?" she asked. "Are you talking about Rott? What do you mean, he'll devour me?"

"You're merely a flea; Rott is a dog. You may feast upon him only a little while before he catches you between his teeth."

"Who are you? How do you know this?"

He turned away, facing the boulder. He glanced over his shoulder and said, in a serious tone, "I've had my fill of conversation with the dead this day. At least those other souls accepted their fate." He took another step toward the boulder before looking back again. "Struggle if it amuses you. In the end, this is all there is of life. Take some comfort in the notion that your death may serve as a cautionary tale for others. Now, I must depart. I'm late for the Inquisition."

There was the sound of leaves crunching from the left side of the boulder. Brand appeared around the corner. "Who are you talking to, Sorrow?" he asked.

Sorrow glanced at him, then back to the pygmy. Only the pygmy was gone.

She ran forward and placed her hands on the rock. "Did you see him?"

"See who?"

"A pygmy. He was albino."

"They're all albino, I think," said Brand. "They just dye themselves different colors."

"Did you see him?"

"No."

"But you heard us talking?"

"I heard you talking, sure," said Brand. "But I never heard the other half of the conversation. I thought you might be sleepwalking."

She shook her head. "I think I saw a ghost."

"Really?"

"Don't sound so skeptical," she said. "You've been to the Sea of Wine. You know that souls survive death."

"I don't doubt the existence of ghosts," said Brand. "But, I've never met one. I have, on the other hand, met sleepwalkers. And crazy people."

"I'm neither."

"Just throwing out some theories." He stretched his back and yawned. "What time is it?"

"Time for us to dig," said Sorrow, heading back to her tent.

"Can't we wait until dawn?"

"You can go back to sleep if you can. I've got things to do."

"Like what?"

"For starters, I've got to move this boulder out of the way."

"What? Why?"

"Because I'm pretty sure the pygmy just walked into it."

"You think it's hollow?"

"I don't know. But, it occurs to me, if it really did roll down the mountain and come to rest here, it's probably sitting on top of more graves. Maybe no treasure hunters have ever dug here. With a house-size rock on top of them, on this high ground, maybe these graves have been protected from rain. Maybe the skeletons haven't rotted."

"That's a lot of *maybes*. And while you strike me as a person who generally gets what she wants, I highly doubt that golem of yours is strong enough to move this rock."

"I have more tricks up my sleeve than mere brute force," she said, looking back at him as she reached her tent.

"Fine," he said, scratching his head. "You can show me your tricks in daylight. Right now, I'm going back to... to..."

His voice faded off as he stared at her. She followed his gaze and realized he was staring at her feet.

"Are you... are you wearing...."

"These aren't boots," she said. "I think... I think I might be turning into a dragon. I'm hoping I can find something in one of these graves that will stop this. Perhaps you can grasp my sense of urgency."

"I see," said Brand. He nodded, then headed back toward his tent. "Let me grab my shovel."

WITCHBREAKER

BOOK THREE *of the* DRAGON APOCALYPSE

JAMES MAXEY

Coming January 2013
UK ISBN: 978-1-78108-061-0 • £7.99
US ISBN: 978-1-78108-062-7 • $8.99

ROWENA CORY DANIELLS

BESIEGED

BOOK ONE OF THE OUTCAST CHRONICLES

ISBN: (UK) 978 1 78108 010 8 (US) 978 1 78108 011 5 • £7.99/$7.99

For nearly three hundred years the mystical Wyrd have lived alongside the True-men, who barely tolerate them; but everything is about to change. King Charald is cursed with a half-blood son, Sorne, who is raised to be a weapon against the mystics. Desperate to win his father's respect, Sorne grows to use stolen power to trigger visions, setting terrible events in motion. But when he receives visions of the Wyrd in chains, he must decide where his loyalties lie.

Unaware King Charald plans their downfall, the mystics are consumed by rivalry. Although physically stronger, the men are weaker in magic than the women. Imoshen, a female mystic raised by the men, wants to end the feud. But the men resent her power, and even within her own sisterhood Imoshen's enemies believe she is addicted to the magic of men.

Convinced he can destroy the mystics, King Charald plans to lay siege to their island city. Will Imoshen win the trust of the mystic leaders and, if she does, will she believe the visions of a mere half-blood like Sorne?

> **"Rowena Cory Daniells has a splendidly devious way with plotting."**
> **– SFX on The Chronicles of King Rolen's Kin**

WWW.SOLARISBOOKS.COM

Follow us on Twitter! www.twitter.com/solarisbooks

'Ingenious, gripping, and full of pleasures on every level. Exceptional.'
- Mike Carey, NYT Bestselling author of The Unwritten

BABYLON STEEL
GAIE SEBOLD

ISBN: (UK) 978 1 907992 37 7 (US) 978 1 907992 38 4 • £7.99/$7.99

Babylon Steel, ex-sword-for-hire, ex... other things, runs The Red Lantern, the best brothel in the city. She's got elves using sex magic upstairs, S&M in the basement and a large green troll cooking breakfast in the kitchen, and she'd love you to visit, except...

She's not having a good week. The Vessels of Purity are protesting against brothels, girls are disappearing, and if she can't pay her taxes, Babylon's going to lose the Lantern. She'd given up the mercenary life, but when the mysterious Darask Fain pays her to find a missing heiress, she has to take the job. And then her past starts to catch up with her in other, more dangerous ways.

Witty and fresh, Sebold delivers the most exciting fantasy debut in years.

"Fast and fun. You'll enjoy this."
– SFX

 WWW.SOLARISBOOKS.COM

Follow us on Twitter! www.twitter.com/solarisbooks